ROSIE'S JOURNEY

When her mother remarries and emigrates with her new husband, Rosie is convinced that their separation will be temporary. However, swept away by the glamorous and decadent lifestyle in Kenya, Celia seems to forget her young daughter. Left in the care of an aunt at the family home in Devon, Rosie becomes accustomed to her mother's neglect. Eventually her mother decides the time is right for Rosie to live with her, but both Africa and the reunion with her mother prove to be mixed blessings – especially when she finds her new stepfather becoming interested in her...

ROSIE'S JOURNEY

Rosie's Journey

by

Sara Hylton

Magna Large Print Books
Long Preston, North Yorkshire,
BD23 4ND, England.

British Library Cataloguing in Publication Data.

Hylton, Sara
    Rosie's journey.

    A catalogue record of this book is
    available from the British Library

    ISBN   0-7505-1839-1

First published in Great Britain in 2001
by Judy Piatkus (Publishers) Ltd.

Copyright © 2001 by Sara Hylton

Cover illustration © Colin Backhouse by arrangement with
Piatkus Books Ltd.

The moral right of the author has been asserted

Published in Large Print 2002 by arrangement with
Piatkus Books Limited

Magna Large Print is an imprint of Library Magna Books Ltd.

Printed and bound in Great Britain by
T.J. (International) Ltd., Cornwall, PL28 8RW

To my friend Irene, for holidays and friendship, not to mention the hours at the bridge table.

Why was I so sure
that we had met before,
in some far distant place,
on some primeval shore.
Why was it I who knew your
voice, your cool sweet smile,
your eyes so blue.
How long they are, the
lonely days before you know it too.

Anon.

Book One

Book One

Chapter One

Many times over the years Rosemary Greville looked back on that warm sunny day in June, yet strangely only two things really registered: the first that her beautiful mother looked like a princess, and secondly that she was wearing her new pale blue dress.

Her mother hadn't been too happy about the blue dress, she would have preferred Rosemary in white, but in the end it had been Aunt Beatrice who said, 'Let the child please herself, Celia, the coming months are going to be traumatic enough without having an argument about the sort of colour she should be wearing for your wedding.'

Rosemary couldn't remember her father; she had been two when he was killed by a sniper's bullet when serving with his regiment in Ireland; there had always been just Rosemary and her beautiful mercurial mother. Rich, spoilt and totally lost in a cold grey world where she was expected to bring up her child without a man in her life.

Aunt Beatrice had been a rock, but Aunt Beatrice and Celia didn't get on. Beatrice was Celia's husband's eldest sister, a spinster lady, set in her ways and with rigid principles and firm views on the right and wrong of things. As the years passed she totally disapproved of Celia's lifestyle. Her string of admirers that came and went, her penchant for expensive clothes and even more expensive holidays, and her total inability to care whether Rosemary was adequately looked after by a string of nannies or home helps.

Then for a time Aunt Beatrice disappeared from their lives. Her eldest brother's wife died, leaving him with four boys to bring up, so who better than Beatrice to be asked to act as his housekeeper and surrogate mother to his boys at a house in Devonshire known as Dene Hollow. Although Celia and her daughter would have been made welcome there, they never visited, Celia on the grounds that she hardly knew Cedric and none of the boys, and perhaps more honestly, that the life she had made for herself was becoming more agreeable. She had a new man friend in the shape of Gordon Ralston.

Alan Greville, Rosemary's father had been handsome, well connected and charming. Celia had been totally in love with him since her schooldays; that he had died in such tragic circumstances Celia had had difficulty in coming to terms with. She regarded his death as inconsiderate from every point of view; to die and leave her with a young daughter was something she had never in a thousand years envisaged, and family and friends alike rallied round to cosset the distraught young woman in her hour of need.

Celia had been resilient, particularly when a group of young men seemed only too anxious to fill the void Alan Greville had left in her life.

14

More and more she came to depend on Aunt Beatrice to care for Rosemary and it was only when Beatrice informed her that time was running out and that she was leaving the area to care for her brother's children that Celia realised she would have to think seriously about her own future.

Gordon Ralston had come along at exactly the right time. He was a vet living in Kenya and home on leave for six weeks after a bout of malaria. Life in Kenya promised everything that was romantic and different to Celia Greville. Gordon was quick to tell her that she would have a wonderful social life with upper-crust people who had settled there, and Rosemary would be happy in the company of other children and numerous animals.

Rosemary was four, and immediately Aunt Beatrice offered objections related to schooling and a British way of life, which was the only life she knew anything about. Celia agreed. She had never been maternal, and she'd surely done everything that had been asked of her in bringing Rosemary up single-handed.

At four years of age Rosemary hardly understood that the one beautiful thing in her life was moving out of it, and Celia was good at consoling her with a great many presents and promises that they would be together again very soon.

She had watched her mother driving away with her new husband with bewildered anxiety. She held fast to Aunt Beatrice's hand and the tears coursed down her face, and most of the wedding guests standing around them seemed uncomfort-

15

ably aware that the day had not been entirely joyful.

Celia dabbed plaintively at her eyes and her new husband said, 'The separation won't be for long, darling, and you know Rosemary will be fine with Beatrice.'

'She'll forget me, children soon forget,' she wailed.

'Well, of course she won't. She'll be out to join us during the school holidays and you'll see how quickly the years pass; when she's older she'll come out to live with us.'

'But those four boys, Gordon. Rosemary's never been used to boys, they'll bully her and she'll be terrified.'

'Well, of course they won't bully her, I never bullied any girl in my life and I'm sure they won't, Aunt Beatrice will see to that.'

'I'm sure you were a darling boy, Gordon, but I knew a good many boys who were anything but.'

'You'll change your mind about boys, darling, if we have one of our own.'

He was so busy concentrating on the afternoon traffic that he missed the look of surprise she turned on him. They had never talked about children, she certainly didn't want any and she'd never have agreed to marry him if she'd thought children were on his mind.

He turned to smile at her and she smiled back, her pretty face guileless, its sweetness hiding the thoughts passing through her head.

Perhaps she should have married somebody older; there had been enough of them milling

16

around, but Gordon had been more dashing, more handsome and he had painted a picture of a life more exotic than any she had ever known. She found herself thinking about that film about Kenya called *White Mischief* and the glamorous degenerate lives of the people in it. She and Gordon would be models of respectability, but they could be that and still enjoy the delights that were on offer.

She sat back in her seat to think about Rosemary. Of course she loved her, she was beautiful; when she was older they'd be wonderful friends and she'd see to it that Rosemary married well. That's when their relationship would really come into its own. She wouldn't fail Rosemary then.

She was glad she'd been able to sell the house, she'd never really liked it anyway. Besides, it reminded her too much of Alan. Alan had loved the house to such an extent that he never let it rest until he'd bought it. It had been a mistake from the outset. They'd hardly got settled in before he was sent to Ireland and there had only been two very brief leaves before he was killed.

After that she'd resented the house. It was part and parcel of his death; he'd had no right to buy it and condemn her and Rosemary to a life buried in the country with little to do and no close friends.

She was missing her parents, who lived at the other side of the country, missing London and the theatres and shops and soon she would have to start thinking about a school for Rosemary.

When she voiced her fears to Aunt Beatrice she hadn't been sympathetic. What was wrong with the village school? It had a good reputation, besides, the child had lost her father, it was far too soon to be contemplating sending her away to school.

Aunt Beatrice had been very good, coming to stay with Rosemary whenever she wanted to go up to London or go to see friends, but Celia saw the red light when Cedric's wife Judith died. There were those four boys to think about and Cedric knew he could rely on his elder sister to help them out in a crisis.

Beatrice and Cedric didn't exactly get on, but blood was thicker than water and Beatrice saw her duty clear. It would mean there were fewer visits to look after Rosemary. Gordon had come along at just the right moment and Celia had had no intentions of letting him slip through her fingers.

The memory of her daughter's bewildered face tantalised her, but everybody said the young healed quickly. There would be those four boys and a whole new set of interests in her life; besides hadn't Alan always said Dene Hollow was the most beautiful place he could ever remember? Rosemary would love it.

The guests were drifting away now, smiling their farewells, telling Rosemary how pretty she looked and what a good girl she'd been, and the child had stared back at them uncertainly and clung ever tighter to Beatrice's hand.

They had to go back to the house to collect the little girl's clothes, and they walked quickly along the road towards the large grey car and the door

18

which the chauffeur was holding open for them. The large uniformed man picked Rosemary up and gently placed her on the back seat next to her aunt, and Beatrice said, 'We have to go back to my sister-in-law's house, Jeffries; it isn't far, but we need to pick up some luggage.'

She couldn't think why Celia had never liked the house. In reality it was a pretty house with large windows overlooking a landscaped garden and an apple orchard. Alan had loved the house; he always said it represented a haven of peace after spending so much time in so many trouble spots. Now she noted that the For Sale sign had been taken down and yet she was unprepared for the emptiness of the house itself.

Celia had taken pains to dispose of the furniture. The new occupants hadn't wanted any of it and she'd taken only favourite ornaments and an occasional small table and bureau which she'd arranged to have shipped out to her.

A small suitcase stood in the hall and on it, tied with string, Rosemary's favourite teddy bear. From the back of the house a plump smiling woman hurried towards them and with a little cry Rosemary ran into her outstretched arms.

Mrs Jacklin looked up into Beatrice's face and there were tears in her eyes.

'Poor lamb,' she said, 'How did she go on when her mother went away?'

'I doubt if it's registered yet, Mrs Jacklin. Is that all the luggage she has?'

'No, there's more in the living room, her toys and some more clothes. The new people are moving in next Tuesday, everything's happened so quickly.'

'Are you staying on with the new people?'

'No. I'm going to work for Dr Hayes. He's been asking me for ages but I'd promised Mrs Greville I'd stay on with her as long as she needed me. The new people seem very nice, they love the house and garden.'

'Yes, I'm sure they do.'

'Mrs Greville never settled here, not even before her husband was killed and afterwards I knew she'd leave whenever the opportunity came up. Your life's going to be changing too, Miss Greville.'

'I know, I'm taking quite a lot on.'

'Well yes, four boys and their father, and now a little girl.'

'I was looking forward to a peaceful life in my little house until I drifted gently into old age, now, like you say, it isn't going to be possible.'

'How will the boys take to Rosemary, do you think?'

'I'm not at all sure. My brother is a man who likes an orderly life so the boys have had to be reasonably well behaved. The two older boys are away at boarding school so they'll only be home for school holidays. The two younger boys might be a problem.'

'Rosemary's never been used to boys, in fact she hasn't been used to company at all. I was wondering how she'd get along when she went to school and met other children.'

'Well, we now have the job of finding a school for her. My brother's chauffeur will take the luggage, Mrs Jacklin.'

'I'd like to offer you a cup of tea but I don't even know if there's anything in the cupboards.'

'Don't worry about it, Mrs Jacklin, we'll get on our way. There's a fair drive to our destination.'

Mrs Jacklin stood at the gate to wave them off and even when the car was out of sight she still stood there, staring along the road. It would be strange not to come to the house to be greeted by Rosemary running along the path to the gate. She had loved the child, even when she viewed her mother with rather less affection.

It didn't take Rosemary long to curl up on the back seat and go to sleep. Beatrice, on the other hand, was burdened with too many problems.

As the eldest sister in a family of four, two brothers and a sister, she had for too long been the one the others turned to when they wanted help of any kind. She had only been in love once and that was in her early twenties. It had not worked out; he had been handsome, rich and more in love with himself than with Beatrice. He had left her often to pursue one hazardous adventure after another, and on his return from the last escapade she had given him his ring back and advised him to keep whatever little time he had given her to himself.

Eighteen months later he was killed in a climbing accident in the Swiss Alps, and Beatrice resigned herself to being a spinster lady, something her two brothers and her sister were eternally grateful for.

She had sympathised with and cosseted Andrea, her younger sister, through innumerable broken romances. The last one had been a more dependable romance than any that had gone before and now Andrea was living with her husband in Saudi Arabia, where he was a lecturer at the university. From her letters, which did not arrive very often, she appeared to be happy and settled.

All Andrea's two children knew about Aunt Beatrice came from the presents she sent them, the knitted garments she made for them and their mother's hopes that when they came to school in England she would provide them with a home during the holidays. The fact that she was going to keep house for her elder brother had ensured that Andrea wrote a string of letters advising her that she should do no such thing.

Beatrice had adored Alan, and done her duty nobly where his wife and young daughter were concerned. Cedric was a rather different matter.

Their temperaments were similar, except that Cedric had never given either of his sisters credit for anything. He had quarrelled constantly with Andrea, rather less so with Alan, but Beatrice he'd always regarded as uninitiated in the ways of the world for the simple reason that she'd never had a career of her own. She'd cared for both her parents until they died, looked after their home and her siblings and their families, and looked forward to the time when she could retire into the small cottage she'd bought and care for her garden and her animals.

Now she'd had to put the cottage on the market to move in with her brother and his family. His wife had been a semi-invalid for as long as

Beatrice could remember. She'd always thought that Judith was a bit of a malingerer who had been cosseted by her parents and her husband for what seemed like forever, but reluctantly she felt forced to take it all back when Judith died suddenly of a heart attack at the age of forty-two.

She was annoyed with Cedric. She felt he should have made an effort to attend Celia's wedding, but his excuse had been that he was in no mood for weddings since he'd so recently lost his wife, and in any case the two younger boys would need him at home.

He had a perfectly good daily woman who would willingly have been there to see to the two boys, but Cedric had never liked Celia and was totally unbending when it came to attending her wedding.

She wasn't sure how the boys would take to Rosemary. David was ten, a bright handsome boy who was good at sport, indeed at everything he took on, and his younger brother Noel was six, sweet-natured with a stubborn streak. When Beatrice had told them that their girl cousin would be coming to Dene Hollow they had received the news without comment, their silence merely reinforcing her belief that problems were only waiting to surface.

Gently she placed a travelling rug round the sleeping child. Rosemary was pretty, with soft golden hair and dark curling lashes brushing her delicate cheeks. She would probably grow up to be as beautiful as her mother, but not Beatrice hoped, with Celia's selfishness and needs that had always seemed paramount.

She had to make sure that Rosemary grew up to be different.

It was dark when they reached the coast, and across the bay they could see the lights from the boats moored in the harbour, and the light from the lighthouse swept across the water illuminating the steep cliffs and jagged outcrops. They were climbing the hill leading away from the village and soon they would be driving through the tall iron gates and along the drive with Dene Hollow in front of them.

There were lights in the windows and along the terrace and Beatrice felt a rush of gratitude that somebody had had the foresight to leave them on.

The chauffeur brought the car to rest below the steps leading to the front door, and then he was opening the door for them and Beatrice said, 'She's still asleep, Jeffries, perhaps we shouldn't wake her.'

At that moment, however, Rosemary opened her eyes, and holding out her hand Beatrice said, 'We've arrived, dear. Give me your hand, there are steps to climb.'

'I'll bring the cases in, Miss Greville, you carry on,' Jeffries said, smiling at the bewilderment on the little girl's face before they turned to climb the steps up to the front door.

The door was locked. Cedric was meticulous about locking doors even when visitors were expected, and somewhat tetchily Beatrice pressed hard on the doorbell, which she could hear echoing stridently behind the closed door, before she heard footsteps approaching it.

Cedric opened the door, blinking confusedly in the lights from the terrace.

'Didn't you have your door key?' he asked crossly.

'I have but I thought you'd have left the door open for us.'

'Well, of course not, you don't know who might be lurking about.'

By that time Jeffries was standing behind her with the suitcases, and Rosemary was looking round the spacious hall and wide, sweeping staircase with something akin to awe. Then she looked up at the tall slim man staring down at her before he smiled and formally held out his hand.

'So you're Rosemary,' he said with a grave smile. 'Welcome to Dene Hollow.'

'I suppose the boys are in bed,' Beatrice said.

'Yes. Mrs Humphreys left about seven and I've given Betty the evening off. I don't know why we need a girl living in, Beatrice. Mrs Humphreys is very good and she tells me she can get another woman from the village to help out. You're going to have time on your hands.'

'I have you and the two boys and now there's Rosemary. How about the other two when they come home for school holidays? I shall need some time to myself, Cedric, it's something I don't seem to have had very much of recently.'

'Well, you go off to the shops, you take walks in the garden and along the shore, what more can you want?'

'I want to read and listen to music.'

25

'You do that in the evening when the children are in bed.'

'Cedric, I have promised to act as your house-keeper for as long as you need me. I did not promise to be an unpaid servant. Besides, you could marry again.'

He looked at her with the utmost astonishment before saying adamantly, 'Beatrice, I shall never marry again. I nursed Judith through years of faints and fantasies. She left it to me to care for the boys because they wore her out, and now I'm looking forward to years of peaceful monotony with you. When the boys finally leave the nest we'll both have done our best. How long do you expect this child to be living here?'

'I don't know. She'll go to school in September, probably the local school until she's older. I have no idea when Celia will want her back in her life.'

'Knowing Celia I should think that time is far distant. She'll live it up to the best of her ability in Kenya and I should think her daughter will be the last thing she thinks about.'

'Well, I'm going to give her some hot milk and biscuits and then put her to bed. I've decided she'll go in the small bedroom overlooking the side rockery. It's the only room in the house that lends itself to a little girl.'

Cedric grunted and turned away. At the study door he said, 'I'll be in here for most of the evening, I have letters to write to the boys and Dr Allanson said he might pop round later for a game of chess. I take it you've no objections?'

'Of course not, it's your house, Cedric. I'll make coffee and sandwiches for you later.'

He smiled. 'I don't know what time the girl will get in, she's gone off to some hop in the village.'

'It's not safe for a girl to be walking along the cliff top late at night.'

'She's gone with some lad or other, she's got a good head on her shoulders.'

'Come along, Rosemary, hot milk and biscuits in the kitchen,' Beatrice said, and Rosemary looked again at the man standing at the open study door before she turned away. It was the strangest day she could ever remember, filled with people she didn't know, all of them laughing and greeting one another, embracing her, smiling down at her, before they suddenly dissolved into thin air after her mother drove away.

What was she doing in this strange house where only Aunt Beatrice was familiar, sitting opposite her at the kitchen table? It was a huge kitchen with a cool tiled floor and a colossal Welsh dresser decked out in willow pattern china. She drank her milk obediently and the biscuits were nice, but after she had finished them she said in a whisper, 'When are we going home?'

'I don't know, dear, but not for some time. You're going to be very happy here. In the morning you'll meet your two cousins and you'll be able to see the sea. It's very beautiful here, Rosemary, you'll come to love it.'

Rosemary didn't want to love it. She ached after familiar things, not the huge hall and staircase that seemed to go on for ever. Even the bedroom seemed vast and unwelcoming, but then her eyes lit up as she saw lying against the pillows her teddy bear. That at least was something from a world that seemed to have gone for ever.

After she had put Rosemary to bed Beatrice went into her bedroom to take off her wedding finery. The dress had been expensive and she would probably have no reason to wear it again. Certainly not for Cedric's bridge evenings or the occasional evening at some music concert in a nearby town.

She pushed the dress to the back of the wardrobe and her hat to the back of the topmost shelf. Then she took out a sensible tweed skirt and sweater, adequate for spending the evening on her own and serving Cedric and his guest with tea and sandwiches later.

Chapter Two

Rosemary awoke in her strange bedroom next morning to sunlight flooding the room. The curtains had been pulled back and at the end of her bed two boys stood regarding her with rapt concentration.

She sat up with a little cry, hugging Edward the teddy bear closer to her, and then the taller of the two boys smiled. He had dark wavy hair and bright blue eyes, and he had a lively alert face and he was smiling in the most friendly way. The smaller of the two had a shock of blond hair the colour of Rosemary's own, and he had a sweet angelic expression. The taller of the two said, 'I suppose you're Rosemary. I'm David and this is my brother Noel. He was born on Christmas Day, that's why he's called Noel.'

Rosemary smiled.

'My father said you were coming to live with us, that Aunt Beatrice was bringing you. Why is that?'

'My mother's gone away,' Rosemary said in little above a whisper.

'My mother died, did your mother die?'

'No. She just went away.'

'Mothers don't just go away. Where did she go to?'

'She got married. She's gone to Africa.'

The boy's eyes widened with interest. 'We're learning about Africa at school. I'll be able to tell Mr Jordan that I know somebody who's gone there.'

At that moment Aunt Beatrice came into the room and seeing the two boys there she said briskly, 'Now what are you two doing here? Go down to breakfast immediately, you're going to be late for school, David.'

'We wanted to see what she was like,' David said from the door.

'Well, you'll see more of each other later on. Now Rosemary, come along and get dressed. I'll send Betty in to help you.'

'I can dress myself.'

'I'm sure you can, but Betty will bring you down to breakfast and afterwards we'll think about what we're to do with the morning.'

'Will those two boys be here?'

29

'They're your cousins, Rosemary, and they live here. They have two older brothers who will be coming home at the end of July. David goes to school in town, Noel goes to the village school where you'll probably go in September.'

'I'm going to school?'

'Well, of course. You want to go to school don't you?'

'I suppose so.'

'Now be a good girl and start to get dressed. Betty will be here to help you and show you how to find your way about.'

The two boys sat with their father at the breakfast table and Beatrice helped herself to fruit juice and poached eggs from the side table.

'Betty's helping Rosemary,' she explained, 'she'll bring her in to breakfast when she's ready. The boys have already met her.'

'So I believe.'

'Rosie says her mother's in Africa,' David said.

'That's right, and who told you you could call her Rosie? Her name's Rosemary.'

'Why does she have to have two names?'

'She doesn't.'

'Well, we like Rosie better, the other one's too longwinded.'

'We'll see which one Rosemary prefers,' Aunt Beatrice said tartly.

'What's her mother doing in Africa?'

'She got married to a vet yesterday and his home is in Kenya.'

'Why didn't she take Rosie with her?'

'David, eat your breakfast and ask questions

later. Your Aunt Celia went off on her honeymoon. Surely you remember that Uncle Alan was killed in Ireland?'

'He was Rosie's father?'

'Yes, now hurry up or you'll miss the bus into town.'

David was on his way out of the room when Betty arrived bringing Rosemary with her, and David paused to say, 'We're going to call you Rosie, you don't mind, do you?,' then without waiting for an answer he was running across the hall and through the front door.

Aunt Beatrice showed Rosemary the array of food laid out on the side table and she selected orange juice and a boiled egg. Then she took her place next to Noel at the table.

Uncle Cedric fixed her with a brief smile. 'Did you sleep well?' he asked.

'Yes, thank you.'

'That's good then,' after which he picked up the morning newspaper and gave it his full attention.

Beatrice looked at her brother with some exasperation. Rosie was not going to have an easy ride in this household. She reflected suddenly how easily she could think of her niece as Rosie. The name suited the rosy-cheeked blonde child chatting easily to Noel, who had recovered from his early shyness. Beatrice said, 'The school bus will be here soon, Noel. Have you got all you need for school?'

He nodded, and smiling at Rosie he said, 'See you later, Rosie. I'll show you the shell pools if you like.'

31

Rosie nodded happily. Life at Dene Hollow promised to be wonderful, two boys and shell pools. Then she stole a quick glance at Uncle Cedric's absorption in his newspaper and had second thoughts.

'I suppose there's no good news in the paper?' Aunt Beatrice said.

'Is there ever?' was his reply, and then he said, 'Well, I'll get off to the office now, I have a busy day in front of me.'

'Are you picking David up from school?'

'Of course not. I won't be free at half four and in any case it's not a good idea. He should be with the other boys.'

She stood at the window, watching her brother walking to where Jeffries was holding the car door open for him. Why on earth did he need a chauffeur? He was perfectly able to drive himself, but it had been Judith who had insisted on somebody to drive her to the shops and her various meetings when her husband was at his office.

Jeffries had stayed on to drive Cedric to his club in the evening, he liked the thought of his own chauffeur and Beatrice thought it was none of her business.

Rosie was sitting at the top of the terrace steps gazing pensively across the garden. There was something in the little girl's expression that troubled her. She was gazing into the distance with a haunted bewilderment. Opening the window, Beatrice called out, 'Come along, Rosie, we're going for a walk along the seashore and then we're going into the village.'

Obediently Rosie came back to the house and watched Betty gathering the morning post together before placing it on the hall table. She looked at it forlornly and Beatrice said, 'It's too soon to find a letter from your mother, dear. One will come very soon I'm sure.'

For the rest of the morning Rosie stopped thinking about her mother, the wedding and her mother's departure. She was enchanted by the calm blue sea rolling in gently across the sand, the discovery of shell pools and thrift blooming profusely between the rocks. White gulls sailed effortlessly above their heads and their mewling cries afforded her an excitement she had never known. By the end of the morning all Rosie knew was that this was her new world; she had come to stay.

The golden days flew by and Beatrice told herself that Rosie had settled down happily. It was Cedric in one of his morose moods who said one evening when the children were in bed, 'Jeffries tells me Rosie spends a lot of time sitting out there in the morning waiting for the postman. I suppose she's hoping for a letter from her mother. Does she ever receive one?'

'I'm sure there'll be one any day and presents for her birthday.'

'And when might that be?'

'The tenth of August.'

'Good heavens, woman, she left this country in June. Does her only child have to wait two months to hear from her?'

'Cedric, she's probably very busy settling in,

neither of us know what the conditions are out there.'

'But we know Celia, don't we. My brother was a fool to marry her. Spoilt, selfish; she probably views his death as a great inconvenience and her child as an even bigger one.'

Beatrice decided silence was her best tactic. Her brother was right of course: any mother but Celia would have bombarded her daughter with letters and postcards. She was just living in hope that she would remember the child's birthday.

Noel didn't make it any easier.

'Doesn't your mother write to you from Africa?' he asked on one occasion. 'I'd want to know all about lions and tigers if my mother was out there.'

'There aren't any tigers in Africa,' his brother said knowledgeably.

'Oh yes there are,' Noel snapped. 'I've seen them in pictures. They don't have stripes, they have spots.'

'And they're leopards or cheetahs.'

'You think you know everything, don't you. I'll bet when she sends Rosie postcards there'll be tigers on them.'

Rosie wished they'd stop asking her if her mother had written to her. Perhaps her mother was dead, perhaps a lion had eaten her; they were very fierce, weren't they?

At the beginning of August the two older boys arrived home for the summer holidays. The eldest was Jerome. In Rosie's opinion he was haughty, unapproachable and uninterested in her. Jeffrey was wrapped up in his own thoughts,

34

remote and shy. They were both very good-looking.

The week after they arrived, Jerome's friend Steven Chaytor arrived to spend the rest of the holidays at Dene Hollow. Steven's parents lived in Indonesia, and apparently he was a constant visitor to Dene Hollow. Steven was nice, Rosie decided. He acknowledged her presence, smiled and talked to her. He had dark blue eyes that smiled, and dark wavy hair. He was tall and athletic and she thought he was beautiful.

Two days before Rosie's birthday, at long last a parcel arrived from Kenya and the two younger boys came close to look at what she'd received, while the rest of them looked on indulgently.

Noel helped her tear away the wrapping paper to disclose the large black doll wearing a colourful skirt, huge earrings and scarlet headscarf. The two younger boys hooted derisively. What a silly thing for anybody to receive. David picked it up and ran across to the others, waving it about by one of its arms, and Steven said firmly, 'Put it down, David, you'll break it. It isn't your doll, give it back to Rosie.'

David walked back and dropped the doll at her feet. She looked up to find the rest of them staring at her, and with a little cry she picked up the doll and fled to her bedroom.

She threw the doll to the end of her bed and sat staring at it. She wasn't into dolls. For weeks she'd played boys' games with balls and bats of one sort or another. She'd ridden Noel's first three-wheel tricycle round the gardens and shared their fishing nets. Now here was this larger than life doll staring at her with its toothy smile. She hated it. Why couldn't her mother have sent her anything but this?

When Aunt Beatrice came into her room she found Rosie stretched out on her bed in an agony of tears.

She sat down beside her and took her sobbing form into her arms. 'There's nothing to cry about, dear,' she said. 'You really mustn't take any notice of what the boys say. Remember that they are boys and boys don't play with dolls. They don't understand.'

'I didn't want a doll, Aunt Beatrice,' Rosie wailed.

'But you did want to hear from your mother. She's sent you a beautiful birthday card and a letter. She was so sure you'd love the doll, and you will grow to love it.'

'I won't ever love it, I'll hate it.'

'You only hate it because the boys didn't like it. David was being silly and so was Noel. The other boys didn't think it was silly.'

'They don't like me anyway, all except Steven, he would never laugh at me.'

'No. Steven has more sense and he's far too nice. You're here for a long time yet and you'll have to get used to being teased. Teasing is part of a boy's nature, and in time you'll give as good as you get, you'll see.'

Rosie was sitting up now, regarding Beatrice with serious contemplation.

'Leave the doll on your bed, dear, and come downstairs to finish your breakfast. We'll go into the village and you shall choose another present,

36

something from me. Besides, there are other presents downstairs that you haven't even looked at yet.'

'I wanted to see Mummy's first.'

'I know, dear. Well, come along and see what the boys have given you.'

Rosie's spirits lifted as she undid the gaily wrapped parcels while the boys looked on. There were beach balls and tennis rackets, a new fishing net which Noel had been reluctant to part with, chocolates and a new purse containing money from Uncle Cedric. He had not been instrumental in choosing the purse but had donated the money it contained. Aunt Beatrice had chosen the purse. There was also a spinning top from Betty and a small frilly apron from Mrs Humphreys.

Her spirits had risen considerably by this time, and she looked up into Steven's laughing eyes as he presented her with a beautifully illustrated book called *The Wind in the Willows*.

The rest of her birthday passed happily enough. It was only when she retired to bed that she stared doubtfully at the doll which Betty had placed on the window seat when she went to turn down the bed covers.

Her mother's letter had been sweet, telling Rosie that she was happy and that she and Gordon sent their love and hoped to see her soon. But she still didn't like the doll.

It was a warm balmy night. The older boys had gone out to stroll along the cliff top, the two younger boys were in their bedroom and Cedric sat with his head buried in a book, a whisky and soda on the small table in front of him. Beatrice sat opposite with Celia's brief letter to herself in her hands.

Celia wrote about Gordon's house, which she was in the process of changing to suit her own taste. She said she had met a group of people who were inviting them to dine and play tennis but Gordon was so busy he could seldom accept their invitations for himself.

She had found Nairobi civilised with some decent hotels and shops. She had yet to familiarise herself with Mombasa. The weather, of course, was hot and sunny. She'd been too busy to miss England; no doubt that time would come. She hoped Rosemary had settled down and would enjoy school, and she sent Cedric and his sons her best wishes. That was all.

Looking up from his book, Cedric said acidly, 'Well, what has she to say?'

Beatrice passed the letter over, and after reading it, he said, 'It's early days yet, Beatrice, either she'll get used to the flesh pots or she'll get tired of them. Either way we both know that Celia's never really settled into anything for long. What sort of man has she married?'

'I liked him. He's a professional man who enjoys his job and will do the best he can.'

'And if he puts his job before Celia then the trouble will start.'

She didn't answer even though she agreed with him. Celia had resented Alan's army career, which had kept him out of the country for long stretches of time. When she'd been able to travel abroad with him she'd enjoyed it, if the country they were living in could be called civilised and there had been a good social life to settle into. As soon as problems arose she had wanted to come home, and problems in Alan's life had never been far away.

What sort of problems would she find in Kenya? Beatrice had no doubt that they would be many and varied. When would she see Rosie? Rosie would go back to waiting for the postman, and Celia would let her down again and again.

Over the months and years letters arrived spasmodically from Kenya and the parcels when they came were filled with extravagant dolls and other toys. In Celia's thoughts her daughter was still four years old, enjoying the dolls she had liked then, never realising that the little girl was growing up.

Rosie hated the dolls and they invariably ended up at one of the church bazaars and in the hands of children whose parents couldn't afford such luxuries. Rosie didn't mind. There was always Edward Bear whom she would never cease to love, and the more realistic gifts she received from those at Dene Hollow.

Then there were the dogs, Jasper, Aunt Beatrice's pug, Jake the black labrador and Susy the Jack Russell terrier. There was also Chang, Aunt Beatrice's Siamese cat, a somewhat distant and aloof creature, but they were all far more interesting than the frilly flaxen-haired dolls she received from Kenya.

She had made friends at school: the postmaster's daughter Joyce Frobisher and the twins Vera and Freda, whose parents kept the village newsagents.

She was never around to hear Cedric's scathing remarks to Aunt Beatrice on the fact that her mother showed no interest in coming to England to see Rosie and found one excuse after another that it was inconvenient for her to go there, even during the long summer holidays.

'Do you suppose it's the husband?' he snapped. 'Maybe he doesn't like children.'

'I'm sure it isn't Gordon, he was very nice, very nice indeed to Rosie.'

The boys, too, constantly asked her about her mother in Africa. What was the use of having a parent living in Africa when you were never asked to visit?

Jerome and Jeffrey had come to terms with Rosie's presence; they neither liked nor disliked her, she was simply there. Their friend Steven was rather more receptive. He was invariably patient with her questions. Steven was never too impatient to wait for her when she dawdled during their walks across the headland, and tolerant of those times when she wanted to go fishing or sailing with them, and it was little wonder that Steven Chaytor became the idol of all her young dreams.

The two younger boys teased her about him, and Aunt Beatrice simply hoped that it was an infatuation she would grow out of when she met other boys of her own age and started to go to parties and dances.

It was one morning several years after her

arrival at Dene Hollow when she found Rosie gazing pensively across the gardens, her pretty face strangely reflective, that she asked, 'What is it, Rosie? You're miles away.'

'Shall I like going to the new school Aunt Beatrice? I'll miss Vera and Freda; their parents can't afford to send them there.'

'You'll make other friends, dear.'

'Well, there's Joyce, she's going to Chevington.'

'Of course. Besides, you'll have a new set of interests. Have you written to tell your mother that you're looking forward to it?'

'I'm not very sure that I am.'

'But you have written to her?'

'Do you think she really cares whether I write to her or not?'

'Really, Rosie, of course she cares. You must never think that she doesn't.'

'There's a girl at school, Jenny Harrison. Her parents are in India and they come home regularly to see her and she's been out there. That doesn't happen for me, and the other girls don't understand why.'

'Perhaps their circumstances are different, dear. Jenny's father is in the army and gets regular leave. Gordon is a vet and is constantly on call. I doubt if he would ever get such extensive leave of absence.'

'But my mother could come?'

'I don't know, dear. There are probably very good reasons why she can't.'

'I'll be at Chevington for years. What happens at the end – shall I come back here or shall I go to my mother in Kenya?'

'We'll have to think about that nearer the time, Rosie. You might want to think about a job, go to university if you're clever enough; it's all in the future, my dear.'

'I already know what I shall want to do. I want to come back here to Dene Hollow, I want to be with David and Noel and I don't want anything to change ever.'

'I think you'll find out, dear, that life is all change. You'll make new friends, so will your cousins. One day you'll all be married, perhaps even living a long way away from here. Time will alter many things, Rosie.'

'But you'll always be here, Aunt Beatrice.'

'No, Rosie, I won't. This is not my house and there'll come a time when none of you will really need me.'

'What will you do then?'

'I shall look for a small cottage or a little house where I can have my own things around me. Just me and my animals, somewhere for you to visit if you feel inclined, but somewhere that is truly mine and where I can please myself what I do. That will be something I haven't been able to do for a very long time and I'm looking forward to it.'

She smiled and left Rosie to digest what she had just told her.

Chapter Three

The years passed. The two older boys were at university, the two younger ones at boarding school, and Beatrice wrote to Celia to tell her that Rosemary was soon to be at Chevington and the presents she was receiving were totally inappropriate.

'I'm surprised you haven't been home,' she wrote, 'particularly as you did say Gordon would get constant leave from his duties in Africa. Your daughter is growing up and letters from you are really not enough.'

The letter she received from Celia gave her little satisfaction. Obviously she had to put Gordon first and the poor man was run off his feet; indeed, there were whole weeks when he was out roaming the countryside in search of sick animals and she hardly saw him. When he did get home she had to be there for him and it made it so much easier to bear when she knew Rosemary was being well cared for. She ended her letter by asking, 'why do you call her Rosie in some of your letters? I don't like it. I christened her Rosemary and that is what she has to be called.'

That evening after dinner Beatrice passed the letter across the dining table for her brother to read. His expression was dour.

'I don't believe a word of it,' he snapped. 'I'm sure she's surrounded by African servants, they're two a penny out there, and I doubt if she cares over much about Gordon. She was never there for Alan. There were times when he came home on leave and she was off in London visiting her parents.'

'Well, I've said my piece, there's nothing more I can do,' Beatrice said.

'What about the girl? I never hear her mention her mother. I suspect she forgets all about her until those wretched juvenile parcels arrive and then she's distressed.'

'I was so sure Celia would want to come home to visit her parents. She adored London, the shops and theatres, it was the life she loved. Surely something just as captivating must have taken its place although she makes no mention of a social life at all.'

'Well, she wouldn't, would she. Why don't you suggest going over in the school holidays and taking Rosie with you?' Cedric snapped.

'I have no wish to go to Kenya, Cedric. I never liked flying and you know I can't stand the heat.'

'Why not ask Rosie and see how she feels about it? She's old enough to travel by plane and somebody will meet her at the other end.'

'I think it would be dreadful to expect her to travel alone.'

'Why not ask her, and then ask her mother if it will be convenient for them to have her?'

Beatrice was not prepared for Rosie's answer when she put the question to her.

'Has my mother asked for me to go?' she asked.

'Well no, dear, not exactly, but I'm sure she'd be delighted to see you.'

Rosie shook her head. 'I don't want you to ask her if it's convenient for me to go, Aunt Beatrice. I want to be invited properly. She doesn't even know what I look like any more.'

'Well, of course she does. We send her photographs and she writes back to say how beautifully you are growing up.'

Rosie's smile was too cynical for her years.

'Aunt Beatrice, there are days when I can't really remember what my mother looks like. I remember her in that pale cream dress and those beautiful cream roses. I remember all the people surrounding her throwing confetti and I can still smell her perfume. She probably doesn't look like that any more, and I don't really know Gordon at all.'

When Rosie told Noel about Aunt Beatrice's suggestion, his remarks were rather more forceful.

'I wouldn't go if I were you; she still thinks you're a little girl or she wouldn't keep sending you dolls. She'll have the shock of her life when she sees you've grown up.'

'I send her photographs.'

Cedric had never been a great one for holidays away from home, so the boys came home from university and brought friends with them. Rosie got along with them very well and learned to give as good as she got. She knew how to sail a boat and ride a horse with the best of them and the liking she had always had for Steven Chaytor became a young girl's crush.

Steven couldn't fail to be aware of it, when

blushes suffused her pretty face and her eyes lit up with welcome. He was kind to her and gentle, he seldom teased her as the others did, and when he did it was in the kindest possible way, until Jerome said, 'She's fallen for you Steven, you'll have to let her down one day so if I were you I'd make it sooner rather than later.'

'What do you suggest I do, ignore the girl?' Steven asked.

'Well no, but you needn't be so nice to her. Talk about other girls you've met, let her see your interests are elsewhere.'

Steven laughed. 'My interests are nowhere at the moment.'

'That's no good, she'll think you'll come around.'

So for several school holidays Steven didn't appear at Dene Hollow and when Rosie asked where he was spending his time, Jerome said airily, 'Oh, he's friendly with some girl or other, he's probably at her place.'

He was too insensitive to know how much his words hurt her, and she was not to know that life would bring a great many hurts in a great many ways.

Rosie was happy at Chevington. She was bright and she made friends easily. When her friends were introduced to her boy cousins she became more popular still. Those warm golden summers would stay in her memory to warm colder, more melancholy times.

The presents from her mother were now of a more grown-up variety, too grown-up, and Cedric snapped, 'Does that woman ever get it

46

right? The girl's ten; what does a ten-year-old want with fripperies of the sort her mother sends her?'

When Beatrice didn't comment, he went on, 'Six years that girl has been here and all we get from Celia are excuses that her husband's too busy to take leave and she can't come without him. Either she's developed a late conscience where husbands are concerned or she's abandoned her daughter.'

'Surely not,' Beatrice murmured.

'Well, what good are photographs, unless it's to show how people have changed? In Rosie's case that she's growing up, in her mother's case that she's hardly the fashion plate she used to be.'

Indeed, Celia's early days in Kenya had been nothing like she'd hoped for. Gordon's house was situated miles from his nearest neighbour and their only contact with people were the men who worked for him and who lived in a small village together with their wives and an army of children. Two of the women worked as servants around the house; neither of them spoke much English and they seemed to spend their days giggling together and ogling the men who accompanied Gordon on his rounds.

Near to the house was the compound where Gordon kept a number of wild animals which had been injured, and it seemed to Celia that all her husband was concerned about was their injuries, the number of poachers hunting elephants and the pursuit of a black panther that was causing mayhem in the area.

When she complained bitterly that they had no social life and that she knew nobody in the area, Gordon merely said, 'They're not exactly my sort, Celia; most of them are idle, affluent and out of our league, I doubt if you'd find a friend among any of them.'

The years passed quickly. Celia's boredom increased and there were constant arguments. The honeymoon was finally over.

Gordon was not unsympathetic. He recognised that his spoilt, beautiful wife was missing the things she had grown up with; he also believed she was missing her daughter, but when he suggested they had Rosie to stay with them during the summer holidays Celia said adamantly, 'I don't want Rosemary to come here, she'd be as bored as I am. I'll have her to stay when she's older and she's less likely to remember all the rosy pictures I painted of what I supposed our life here would be like.'

'I hardly think she will remember, Celia, after all she was only four years old.'

'Nevertheless, whenever I wrote to her I told her how wonderful I was finding everything. I don't want her to accuse me of telling her lies. Besides, I don't want to interfere with her schooling, and upset her life at Dene Hollow.'

In the end Rosie was someone neither of them mentioned. On her rare visits into Nairobi Celia bought presents for Rosie, presents that were expensive and hardly suitable, Gordon thought, for a daughter who was growing up.

It was on one of those visits that Celia elected to spend the night in a hotel so that she could get her hair styled and buy some new make-up. Gordon encouraged her by saying, 'I think it's a marvellous idea, darling; you'll feel happier when you can buy a new dress and have somebody pamper you and do your hair.'

It was on that visit to the hairdresser that Celia met Ariadne Fairbrother. She was in the process of having her nails manicured when a large chauffeur-driven car drew up outside the salon and a tall, slender woman stepped out, carrying a brightly coloured parasol. When she entered the salon an army of assistants hurried towards her and she greeted them with smiling condescension. She was not strictly beautiful, but she had the air of a duchess. Her pale blue silk dress showed off her tanned shoulders and her arms, adorned by numerous gold bracelets in keeping with the diamonds flashing on her fingers.

She decided that she too would have a manicure and took the seat next to Celia, favouring her with a swift smile. Her conversation with the manicurist was all to do with the tennis club, the country club and one social event after another. Catching Celia looking at her, she asked, 'Have you just arrived in Nairobi?'

'Why no, I've been living here several years.'

'Here in the city?'

'No, we live in the country, a small place about sixteen miles from here.'

'Really. With your husband?'

'Yes, he's a veterinary surgeon.'

The woman's eyes opened wide. 'You don't meant Gordon Ralston? He's the only vet around here, I think.'

'Yes, Gordon's my husband.'

'We'd heard he'd got married. Gordon's an absolute darling but we can never get him to come out to the club. Whenever we invited him he was always far too busy, so in the end we gave it up as a bad job. My dear, you must be bored out of your skin. What a good thing I came in here today! You need taking in hand, my dear. Are you staying in Nairobi or are you returning to the country tonight?'

'I'm here until tomorrow.'

'Then we must have a nice long chat. What do I call you?'

'My name is Celia.'

'And mine is Ariadne Fairbrother. Gordon knows me quite well. In fact he met all of us in his early days in Kenya, then he simply got taken over by his work and had no time for any of us. You mustn't stagnate in the country my dear.'

'I have for far too long, I'm afraid. I began to think there was no other life.'

'Well, believe me, my dear, there is. You're young, beautiful and we want some new blood. I'm cross that Gordon's kept you under wraps.'

'Gordon hasn't much time for socialising I'm afraid, he's always so busy.'

'I know the story. Ivory-poaching and wounded animals, and darling Gordon is dedicated. He's absolutely marvellous but he should be made to see that there's another world outside his job, one that you are about to discover, my dear. Where are you staying?'

'The hotel across the street.'

'I'm at The Sheraton. My car's outside so we'll

50

drive round there and have tea around the pool. Gordon's going to be furious with me for telling you what you've been missing all these years, but I don't care. We'd heard he'd married some girl back in England but we knew absolutely nothing about you. Is it your first marriage?'

'No, I was a widow. My first husband was killed in Ireland. He was in the army.'

'Poor you. Do you have children.'

'A little girl; she's with her aunt and uncle and hopefully receiving an education.'

'Well, of course. How old is your daughter?'

'She'll be ten now.'

'Far too young to be out here and time enough to send for when she's completed her education. What is her name?'

'Rosemary, Rosemary Greville.'

'What a pretty name.'

'I thought so, but apparently her boy cousins have reduced it to Rosie.'

Ariadne laughed. 'That sounds like boys. I have a son of sixteen; fortunately he's in England with his father, ostensibly to receive an English education. His father and I were divorced when Colin was two years old.'

'Do you live here on your own then?'

Ariadne laughed. 'Why no, if I don't tell you Gordon will. I live with Johnny Fairbrother, my second husband, the man my first husband divorced me for. Gordon will tell you that he's a dissolute playboy who's never done a day's work in his life and has too much money.'

'And is he?'

'I'm afraid so. But Johnny's lucky with money,

51

always has been, that's what first endeared him to me. My first husband was very dull. He didn't like parties, he hated tennis and polo and he preferred to stay at home and play chess with his cronies. Does that ring any bells, my dear? What does Gordon do in the evenings?'

'He's usually too tired to do anything when he arrives home. We have a meal then he usually falls asleep in his chair.'

'Not at all what you expected from this neck of the woods.'

'No, I thought there'd be some sort of life. He doesn't want to go back to England. Both his parents are dead and he's not into clubs and theatres.'

'Haven't you told him you would like to go back to see your daughter?'

'Well, it's difficult. I don't want her crying to come back here with me – it would disrupt her schooling and her life with the people back there. I think Gordon understands.'

Ariadne looked at her curiously, then with a light laugh she said, 'Well, I have a wonderful life out here, I certainly don't have any cravings to return to England. You could too, my dear, think about it.'

'Gordon would have to change for me to have any sort of life.'

'That's how it was with me, Celia but I had to be adamant. If he wasn't prepared to give a little then I had to do it without him. I joined the tennis club, even when I hated the game, but I met people and had fun. Then I met Johnny and the rest simply fell into place.'

'I doubt if Gordon would take kindly to my joining the tennis club.'

'Well, of course not. Gordon probably doesn't approve of people who have too much money to indulge themselves, too much time on their hands and are too much of a crowd. The initiative will have to come from you, my dear. Anyway, telephone me when you've had a chance to talk to him. I'll introduce you to all the right people and we'll go on from there. You'll be very popular, Celia, a new young beautiful woman. The rest of us have been here a long time; a fresh face on the scene will liven things up no end.'

Celia's face was doubtful, and after a few minutes Ariadne laughed. 'You're bored but you don't want to upset him. Did he never tell you anything about his life out here?'

'Well yes, he talked about his work, his house and the servants. He said I'd have plenty of time on my hands to do whatever I wished, but since we arrived here we don't seem to have done anything.'

'Then he hasn't been strictly fair with you, has he? What you now want is some variety in your life and your marriage. When your daughter eventually does come out here let her see that you're a popular member of the community and that you're aware of all the eligible young men simply waiting to show her a good time.'

'How often do you visit Nairobi?'

'Whenever I need new clothes or a change of scenery. Whenever I need a new hair-style and a few days in a decent hotel.'

'I didn't know it was possible to get such

53

beautiful clothes in Nairobi.'

'Oh Johnny and I go off to America and Paris, occasionally to London; but he's good with money, I can have anything I want.'

'You're very fortunate.'

'I know. Anyway, darling, I must get back into the hotel to pack. I'm going back in the morning. Before I go, promise me faithfully you'll talk to Gordon and make an effort to join us. This is my telephone number and don't be put off by him. Get a taxi to take you back to your hotel and do give my love to Gordon; we'd all love to see him around.'

All over dinner and throughout the evening Celia thought about her meeting with Ariadne Fairbrother. She was not the usual type of woman she'd made friends with, but then Alan had come from a very circumspect family and indeed her own parents had always taken a keen interest in the sort of girls she took home. Nice, genteel girls whose fathers were in good professions, they lived in nice houses and attended good schools, played a little tennis and rode in gymkhanas.

Her thoughts turned to Rosemary. She sincerely hoped those boy cousins hadn't taken her over completely, calling her Rosie indeed, and no doubt introducing her to all sorts of boyish pursuits quite unseemly in a girl.

Beatrice would be too busy looking after the rest of them; she wouldn't have the time to keep a wary eye on what was happening to Rosemary, and Cedric would be happy to pass his sons on to her for attention.

She was very doubtful about Gordon's reaction to her meeting with Ariadne; whenever she'd asked him about the people they could expect to meet he'd said Kenya was hardly like England with neighbours on the doorstep, yet here was this woman with a wonderful social life and a host of friends.

She returned home the next day with every intention of telling Gordon about her new acquaintance and Ariadne's endeavours to have her join in her activities.

With this in mind she asked the servants to prepare a meal of all Gordon's favourites, and to add to the occasion she took delight in setting out the dinner table with a large centre bowl of orchids and their wedding presents of silver and cut glass.

Gordon merely looked at it all in amazement before slumping in a chair and closing his eyes. Weariness was etched on his face and his safari jacket was encrusted with dust. Celia eyed him with some distaste. Everything out there was more important than she was; some marauding black panther would take precedence over anything she suggested, but she wasn't going to let him get away with it. He had a wife, surely more important than some wild cat – if he didn't think so, why had he married her?

She let him sleep until the meal was ready and then, taking the small dinner gong from the servant's hands, she stood near him, making sure that its sound brought him out of his sleep with a new awareness.

When his startled gaze met hers she smiled

sweetly and said, 'Dinner, darling, all your favourites and I'm wearing my new dress for the occasion.'

He looked across at the candle shining on the dinner table and the array of glass and silver, then ruefully he looked down at his attire.

'Hardly suitable for such a grand occasion, Celia; what is the occasion by the way?'

'Do go and change, Gordon, and we'll talk about it over dinner.'

Chapter Four

The atmosphere was hardly congenial. Gordon had received the news of her meeting with Ariadne Fairbrother with ill-disguised annoyance, an annoyance Celia couldn't understand when she thought about Ariadne's charm and her insistence that they should visit her.

'Why don't you like her?' she demanded. 'She was very nice, beautiful, classy, the sort of woman I'd thought to be meeting here instead of a conglomeration of natives.'

'The natives are honest, good people, not the silly mercurial people Ariadne surrounds herself with.'

'I liked her.'

'Well, I'll admit she can be entertaining and charming as you've described her, but she's not a very popular person with the nicest people in the area.'

56

'Then they're probably jealous because she's captured a millionaire.'

'I don't think jealousy has anything to do with it.'

'What then? Tell me about her.'

'Nobody quite knew how she came to be here. She descended upon the area from Nairobi and worked in the stables at the Petersons' place. Margery and Alan Peterson were friends of mine. They had two children, a happy marriage and a good home life, then it all fell apart when Alan had an affair with Ariadne. Margery left, taking the children with her; she went home to England to her parents' house, I never saw her again and Alan married Ariadne. They had one son.

'In time people accepted her, because of Alan, but it didn't take Ariadne long to involve herself with Fairbrother. Nobody liked him, he was rich, brash and arrogant, and their behaviour was scandalous. Alan left her, sold up here and was given custody of their son. It was a heartrending decision for him to make; he loved it here, loved his work and his friends, Ariadne didn't care. Most of Alan's friends dropped her but she got involved with a new set, and Fairbrother, who had never been popular, didn't much care what she did.'

'But she was so nice, Gordon, perhaps she's changed. After all, everybody should be allowed a second chance, a chance to redeem themselves.'

'Ariadne won't change, Celia. She still isn't accepted by the nice people in the area, we shouldn't get involved.'

57

'So what do we do then? We never go anywhere, we never do anything. I'm so bored, Gordon. I need more than we have, life here is nothing like I thought it would be, all Ariadne suggested was a game of tennis, a drink at the tennis club and a chance to meet people.'

'The wrong people, Celia.'

'How do you know if you haven't met any of them? The people you like are probably old and stuffy, obsessed with their own importance.'

For a long moment he sat without speaking, and she knew he was thinking of other days she knew nothing about. After a while he looked up and with a gentle smile said, 'Perhaps I haven't been very fair to you, darling, I've been so obsessed with my job and I'm always so very tired when I get home. I'll telephone the Garveys and suggest that we drive over to meet them. After that I promise I'll try to make a better effort to keep you entertained, but not with the Fairbrothers or their friends.'

'Who are the Garveys?'

'He's a civil engineer, they've lived in Kenya for many years, came here from South Africa. His wife's called Mary, she's very nice; you'll like them, Celia. He's Eric, by the way.'

'How old are they?'

'Older than us, but they're both intelligent and nice company. Given them a chance, Celia.'

'When will you telephone them?'

'Tomorrow, I promise, and in August we'll go back to England. You can shop in London, buy some new clothes and see Rosemary. You'd like that, surely, darling.'

58

'I can think of nothing worse than staying with Cedric at Dene Hollow. The boys will be home, probably with a gaggle of girls, and Rosemary will probably have a group of friends she's invited too, I don't suppose she'll like having us disturb their activities.'

He stared at her in some surprise. 'She's your daughter, darling; you haven't seen her for a very long time, she'll want to be with you, she's had years of being with her friends. Suppose you write to tell them we'll be in England, then invite Rosemary to London, and one of her friends if she wants. We can show them around London, drive up to the lakes, go to see your parents and spend time with them. What's wrong with that?'

'It will unsettle Rosemary. She'll want to come back with us and you know that isn't possible. There's her education to think of.'

'Aren't you afraid that your daughter could be forgetting you, Celia?'

She stared at him in dismay. 'How can you say that, Gordon? I write to her every week, long letters. I tell her about your animals and how busy you are, when we have a social life I can tell her about that. I am her mother, of course she won't forget me. She understands perfectly why she's at Dene Hollow and we're here.'

'You'll want to see your parents, Celia?'

'Well of course, Gordon.'

'But not Rosemary?'

'Well yes, of course I want to see her, I just don't want to spirit her away from Dene Hollow. We'll stay at some hotel in the area. You haven't met Cedric, he's caustic and distant. I can't think

59

how Beatrice is getting on with him. They never did get on. Besides, there are the boys. I don't know them, four boys and I've only ever met Jerome. He was full of himself.'

Gordon decided it was not the time to elaborate on a visit to England. Celia was not in the mood and he had no doubt she would continue to place obstacles in the way of whatever he suggested.

Hopefully a visit to the Garveys would put her in a better frame of mind, and the next day he was able to report that the Garveys had received his telephone call with the utmost pleasure and they were invited to visit.

Dinner with the Garveys was a calm, civilised affair. They were a charming middle-aged couple who reminded Celia of her parents and it was hardly an evening to set the world alight. Gordon and Eric Garvey discussed politics and the state of the country; Celia talked about the life she had left behind in England and listened to Mary Garvey going on about her two sons, who were both accountants, married and living with their respective wives and families in South Africa.

'You will be missing your little girl terribly,' Mrs Garvey said sympathetically. 'You'll be able to bring her here in the school holidays; that's what most English people do.'

Celia didn't comment.

Mrs Garvey was a kind motherly woman who was content with her lot. Celia doubted if she'd ever been anything else, yet almost mischievously she asked, 'Have you many friends in the area?'

'Well of course, but we only meet up with them

60

on special occasions: Easter and Christmas, summer picnics perhaps. Distance is a problem and we're not into the smart set.'

'Why is that?' Celia asked.

'Well, dear, there have been a great many scandals, the wrong people doing the wrong things. When we first came here we enjoyed meeting up at the clubs. Eric enjoyed tennis and I played a little myself, but then new people came along and it seemed that overnight everything changed.'

'I met Ariadne Fairbrother in Nairobi. She introduced herself and I went to her hotel to take tea with her. She seemed nice enough.'

Mary Garvey smiled. 'Yes, well. We haven't seen Ariadne for some time, they live some distance away.'

'She said I should join the club, play some tennis, meet people. You don't think that's a good idea?'

'What does Gordon say about it?'

'He's not very keen. He doesn't think much of Ariadne's crowd.'

'I can understand that. Her first husband was one of his best friends. How long since you saw your daughter?' Mrs Garvey asked, changing the subject.

'Not since we came out here. I thought nothing should interfere with her schooling and she's happy at Dene Hollow.'

'With your parents?'

'No, with my first husband's sister and her eldest brother. My parents offered but mother's hopeless. She'd have spoiled her rotten and been

61

no use whatsoever with her education.'

Mrs Garvey stared at her curiously, and Celia hastened to explain. 'She was like that with me. I hated school. I only had to say so and I was moved on to something else. My father was in the diplomatic service and constantly abroad, and my mother lived for her bridge parties and various committees. Rosemary's aunt was a far better proposition to leave her with.'

Mrs Garvey asked no more questions and the rest of the evening passed pleasantly enough. Gordon enjoyed it, Celia thought most of it was a bore.

She longed to talk about the scandal that had erupted years before when the so-called Happy Valley Set held sway and when the Earl of Erroll had been murdered after driving his lover, Lady Diana Delves Broughton home from a dinner party. Her much older husband had been tried for his murder and later acquitted, but it did not stop a bestselling novel from being written and a film entitled *White Mischief* raising all sorts of speculation about the incident.

Celia had read about it avidly in the company of other girls, reading by torchlight in the darkness of their school dormitory. It was the sort of scandalous affair a group of young schoolgirls revelled in, an affair concerned with spoilt, rich immoral people in a far-off country under the African sun.

She had never forgotten it, and marriage to Gordon, she had believed, would encompass the same sort of existence. Of course she would be a highly respectable wife, but their friends would be rich, larger than life, sophisticated aristocrats, the sort of friends she would be able to talk about on her rare returns to England.

She was driving home with Gordon after dinner with the Garveys, which had not come close to her aspirations.

Covering her hand with his, Gordon said gently, 'Enjoy it, darling?'

'Yes, it was very nice.'

'They're very nice people, kind decent people, we'll visit them again and meet up with some of the others.'

'The others?'

'Well yes, friends of the Garveys, nice people. And tomorrow, why not drop a line to Beatrice and tell her when we'll be visiting? The beginning of August, I think. Rosie'll have weeks to look forward to it.'

'I'd rather you didn't call her Rosie, Gordon, it's so plebeian.'

'Well, by this time she'll be used to it, darling.'

'I'll make my feelings known, however. She was christened Rosemary, and that's what I want her to be called.'

'The boys won't like it, they'll scoff, I know what boys are like, and it could be unpleasant for her.'

'Beatrice will know how to handle them.'

'You'll write tomorrow, darling?'

'Yes, of course.'

The Garveys had watched them leave with warm smiles and words of farewell. On their return to the house, however, they stared at each other with something like uncertainty.

'Did you like her?' Eric asked bluntly.

'Well, dear, we've only been in her company one evening. She's very pretty.'

'But did you like her?'

'Did you?'

'Not really. She's a clothes-horse with very little aptitude for life here. She's a sure ringer for the Ariadne set and those other wretched people we're all trying hard to forget.'

'Surely not.'

'Well then, tell me what you did think of her, and nothing derogatory will surprise me.'

'I think we should get to know her better before we start to pull her to pieces. One evening isn't enough to decide whether we like her or we don't.'

'She has a daughter, you know. Gordon told me they were thinking of going back to England in August so that they could see her, the first time for six years, he said. Doesn't that tell you something?'

'What is it supposed to tell me, Eric?'

'Would you have left your boys for six years without seeing them?'

'Well, we were all together, weren't we? The boys went to school in South Africa, the British have always been most anxious to have their children educated in Britain.'

'She told you about Ariadne Fairbrother, didn't she?'

'I wasn't sure you'd heard; you and Gordon were talking about something else.'

'Gordon told me when we walked in the garden before dinner. Met her in Nairobi, and appar-

64

ently Ariadne was quick to invite her to spend time at the various clubs she favours. Gordon isn't keen.'

'No, I suppose not.'

'I'd like to bet she'll push it for all she's worth. A new face on the scene, a face that will fit in very well, I think.'

'Oh, Eric, you don't know that.'

'I've told you what I think. The girl's a clothes-horse and she'll not be the one to busy herself in the country if she gets a chance to spread her wings.'

Mary was thoughtful. If she took the trouble to be honest with herself she hadn't really cared for Celia; they'd had little in common and the gap in their ages hadn't helped. All the same, she really liked Gordon: he was a kind, decent man and friendship in Mary's opinion should count for something. Somewhat diffidently, she said, 'Perhaps we should arrange to meet them one evening at the new club. I've heard it's really very nice, and we shouldn't be scathing about something we know nothing about.'

She was aware of his expression, doubtful, cynically disbelieving. 'Are you serious? The last time we went there you hated it.'

'I know. They were all a lot younger than we were; perhaps we chose the wrong night. Why don't you telephone Gordon and put it to him?'

Gordon was out when Eric telephoned several days later and Celia's reaction, as he'd known it would be, was delight.

'Oh, I'm sure Gordon will take you up on it, Eric. I'll get him to fix a concrete date. He's always so terribly busy but I shall look forward to it.'

Her voice had been warm, filled with expectation, and Eric was left wondering if they'd done the right thing. One evening at the club, with younger people who were involved in all the things she'd left behind her in England, could be enough to make her more dissatisfied than he knew she already was.

'Can it be soon?' she asked Gordon enthusiastically. 'I just want to dress up for once and dance the night away, I want to feel young and beautiful again.'

'Darling, you are young and beautiful,' he said, smiling down into her eyes.

'You'd be surprised how seldom I feel it.'

'Have you written to Rosemary?'

'Yes. I've told her we'll be home for three weeks in August. We'll drive down to Dene Hollow to pick her up, then we'll spend time in the Lake District and visit her grandparents in London. If we're going to join the land of the living, Gordon, I shall need to buy some new clothes, and Nairobi doesn't have the choice of London.'

'Darling, don't get carried away. We live some distance from the club scene; we shan't be spending too much time there.'

Pouting prettily, she said, 'You've buried yourself away too long, Gordon. You didn't have a wife to take with you, and now that you have you should make the most of me.'

He smiled, and she asked anxiously, 'You will telephone the Garveys and take them up on our night at the club, Gordon?'

Beatrice looked across the breakfast table to where her brother sat frowning over his morning mail, enabling her to give full attention to the letter she had received from Celia.

They were coming to England in August; they would descend on Dene Hollow to collect Rosemary so that she could spend time with them here, there and everywhere, ending with a visit to see her grandparents. Her letter ended by apologising for the short notice but she was sure Beatrice would understand.

Looking up at Cedric's face she was aware of the frown which told her the letter he had received from one of the boys didn't exactly meet with his approval.

'Is something wrong, Cedric?' she asked him.

'Well, yes. They take everything for granted without asking if any of it's convenient. When Jerome was twenty-one last year he didn't want a party, he wanted the money instead. This year it's Jeffrey's turn and he does want a party, largely instigated by Jerome, I feel sure.'

'They want a party here?'

'That's right. They want to invite friends from the university, as well as a bevy of girls. I didn't know Jeffrey had a girl he was interested in but Jerome wants to invite Natalie Shaw. I thought he was paying her a lot of attention the last time he was home. They've been corresponding, and he's invited her to functions taking place at Oxford.'

'Didn't you like the girl when you met her?'

'She was right enough. Pretty, like all the others one sees these days. You know who her father is, of course?'

'Yes. Isn't he a town councillor? And her mother does a lot for charity in the area. Don't they live at that large house on the crossroads?'

'They do. I'm in a hurry this morning, Beatrice, but we have to talk about all this. What about Rosemary? She'll hardly fit in with a houseful of older people, and you'll be rushed off your feet with catering and other things. You'll need extra help.'

'What sort of party are they contemplating?' Beatrice asked, in spite of the fact that Cedric had risen from his seat and was half-way across the room.

'Heaven knows. At least it will be August so the weather mightn't be bad. Hopefully something we can hold outside. Like I said, Beatrice, we'll talk later.'

He paused on the threshold. 'Is there a chance that Rosemary could stay with one of her friends on the day of the party? She'll not be happy milling around with the sort of girls the boys are likely to invite, and we don't want any sulks from that quarter.'

'Why would she sulk? The two younger boys won't have girlfriends with them.'

'Don't be too sure. Anyway, like I said, we'll talk later.'

Beatrice had promised herself a holiday, some-where quiet in South Wales, or in the Highlands. Somewhere where she could do some walking and sketching, somewhere away from boys, and when hopefully Celia's mother would keep her promise to take Rosie off her hands for a few weeks. That had seemed a possibility until the wretched party idea surfaced.

She was too old to be expected to entertain a bevy of girls and young men. She wasn't going to do it. She'd suggest a marquee and caterers. More and more now people were adopting the idea and Dene Hollow lent itself to an affair of this nature. She'd tell Cedric when they had a chance to talk. In the meantime, she had to prepare Rosie for the advent of her mother and stepfather.

She was in the habit of talking to Rosie about her mother in an endeavour to keep her memory alive, because Rosie seldom mentioned her. Twice since Celia left England Rosie's grandparents had driven over from Richmond, but Beatrice had been forced to admit that their visits had hardly been eventful. Rosie had been good, too good, sitting on the edge of her chair, eating delicately from Cedric's best china and speaking only when she was spoken to. When her grandparents had left she had simply said, 'I don't know why they come. Grandma only talks about the shops and clothes and Grandpa looks bored all the time and wishing they could leave.'

'Well, of course he doesn't. If he felt like that, why would they come at all?'

'Because they feel sorry for me, because my mother doesn't come and they feel it's expected of them.'

Beatrice read Celia's letter for the third time. She would have something wonderful to tell Rosie when she got home from school that afternoon.

Chapter Five

Beatrice stood at the window, watching Rosie walking along the drive from where the school bus had deposited her near the gates. She half walked, half ran, with her school satchel slung across her shoulders, carrying her school hat in her hands, occasionally tossing it into the air and catching it before it could reach the ground.

There was a rebelliousness about her, as her feet seemed intent on finding every puddle along the road. Then, catching sight of Beatrice's figure at the window, she replaced her hat and tried to avoid the various puddles before she climbed the steps towards the terrace above.

Meeting her at the door, Beatrice said, 'Take your shoes off in the conservatory, Rosie, and put your slippers on. We'll have tea in the morning room. I have some news for you.'

Before Rosie could ask any questions, Beatrice had hurried back into the house, and Rosie stomped in an aggrieved fashion towards the conservatory.

What sort of news could she have? Nothing ever happened at Dene Hollow until the boys came home. She never for a single moment connected news with her mother.

She took off her shoes and padded into the hall, where she found her slippers in the cupboard and where she hung her coat and hat. Her hair was damp with rain and for a long moment she stood looking into the mirror. She hated her hair when it was damp, she hated the braces on her teeth. In fact there was nothing in her appearance to merit a second look from Steven Chaytor. She could hardly compare with the stunning girl Jerome had described to her, Steven's girl.

She didn't care. One day she was going to go out to Africa and marry an African chief or somebody just as grand and she wouldn't give a boy like Steven Chaytor a second thought.

Aunt Beatrice surveyed her over the teapot she was holding.

'Your hair is wet, Rosie, you'd better come over to the fire and dry it off. Are your feet wet?'

'No.'

'Why do you persist in walking through puddles? If you do that on your way to school you'll be sitting with wet feet all through class.'

Rosie helped herself to buttered scones and Beatrice reached out for Celia's letter while Rosie eyed her expectantly.

'This is from your mother, Rosie. She's coming here in August.'

Whatever sort of reaction she had expected, it certainly hadn't been a stony stare from Rosie's dark blue eyes and the apathetic shrug of her shoulders.

'Rosie, aren't you pleased? Your mother's coming home and she's coming here to take you on holiday for most of August. I thought you'd be delighted.'

'Is Gordon coming too?'

'Well, of course. You're to go on holiday with

them and then you're going to spend time at your grandmother's with them. You'll be able to go into London, to the parks and the zoo, to the museums and art galleries. If I'd been able to do those things when I was your age I'd have been absolutely delighted.'

'The boys come home in August. I enjoy the things I do with them.'

'And you've done those things for the last six years. This time you'll have your mother and Gordon. They'll come with all sorts of lovely presents for you. Think about it, dear.'

'I suppose I'll have to pretend to like the presents she'll bring me.'

'You will like them. Show some enthusiasm, Rosie.'

'She'll call me Rosemary and the boys will snigger.'

'I've been waiting all day to tell you about their visit. I was so sure you'd be delighted; now I can't understand you. We'll talk about it again when you're in a better frame of mind. Is your hair dry?'

'Just about.'

'Do you have any homework to do?'

'Some.'

'Then do get on with it, dear. Soon you're going to have to think about university and you'll really have to work there if you want to do something with your life.'

'What shall I do with my life, Aunt Beatrice? Every time I talk about it nobody seems to know. Freda wants to be a hairdresser, Vera wants to do nursing and Joyce is really very clever, she'll do well at university.'

'And you can do well too, Rosie. You seem so negative about your life.'

Rosie was well aware that she worried Aunt Beatrice but she couldn't help it. She felt more and more like a parcel left on some obscure shelf, waiting to be collected.

Beatrice felt that for the first time in her life Celia was about to do something worthwhile and at the right time. She would take Rosie off her hands instead of having the girl moping around at the boys' party. There would be older girls, the two younger boys would probably be a problem, but with Rosie it could have been dire. In league with David and Noel she could be as disruptive as they were, and then there was Steven Chaytor.

Beatrice was well aware of the crush Rosie had had on Steven since she was little more than a child, and if Steven came to the party with a girl of his own age there could well be sulks and more unreasonable behaviour to put up with.

That evening, after Rosie had retired to her bedroom to read and listen to her radio, she took the bull by the horns and tackled her brother about the catering arrangements for the party.

'You simply can't expect me to do it all, Cedric,' she said adamantly. 'How many people are we expecting? The boys will already have invited their friends, and then there will be the girls. It will be chaos in the house so you should be thinking in terms of a marquee in the garden and outside caterers.'

'Outside caterers, that's preposterous. I have a daily woman and a housemaid, and there's you.

Surely that should be enough to make refreshments for a house full of people.'

'Well of course it won't. This is to be Jeffrey's twenty-first birthday party, surely you don't want his friends saying you've skimped on it? It should be a night to remember. How much money did you give Jerome last year?'

'Enough.'

'Well, your other sons will expect the same generosity.'

'The other boys will be here partying, hadn't that occurred to you?'

'Well, yes, of course.'

'And what about the girl? She'll be here and probably wanting her friends to be here too.'

'Celia and Gordon are coming over in August and they're taking Rosie away for a few weeks, the Lakes and London. I don't think we need worry about Rosie.'

'So they're actually coming, are they? I thought it would never happen, and I won't be sure until I've seen them.'

'I received her letter this morning.'

'And what did Rosie say about?'

'Very little. There are times when I really don't understand Rosie at all. I'd have thought she'd be over the moon at the prospect of seeing her mother but she was very apathetic.'

'Of course. One learns to be apathetic about somebody who has more or less distanced herself for the past six years.'

'There've been letters and presents, Cedric. Africa is a long way away.'

'No, that won't do. I was at school with boys

74

whose parents were out of the country; they visited, the boys went out there. I hope for Rosie's sake that she finds her mother to be the same person she can only remember in the first years of her life.'

He was well aware of the doubt in his sister's eyes as they met his across the room. After a few moments, however, she picked up her pen and opened her notebook and Cedric asked, 'What have you there?'

'I've been making notes about what we shall need to do for the party. Do you suppose we'll have guests staying in the house?'

'I don't know. I think we shall have to ask the boys to tell us exactly how many people they've invited and how many of them live locally. Too many and they'll have to stay in hotels.'

'And the catering?'

'Shouldn't we wait to see who exactly is coming?'

'No. Caterers and waiters have to be booked well in advance. August is a busy month for weddings and other functions, and you'll need to do something about a marquee for the garden.'

'A marquee!'

'Either that or your house is about to be invaded and you'll not be able to get away from it.'

'I really don't know why Jeffrey couldn't have asked for money like his brother. I see Jerome behind this. He had the money, this way he gets the party too.'

Silently, Beatrice agreed with him. Jerome had always been the dominant one and Jeffrey had been content to follow in his footsteps.

'What about David and Noel?' she asked.

'Well, I certainly shan't encourage either of them to demand a party when they come of age. David is sixteen, Noel is twelve. You could suggest that Celia and her husband take Noel along with them as company for Rosie. She wouldn't be against it.'

'I rather think Celia would. It's taken her six years to get here; mention Noel and they'd be back on the next flight.'

Cedric grinned. 'Are they here for a day or so before they move off? It's not the weekend of the party, I hope.'

'No, she says the beginning of August, and the party isn't until the second weekend. Rosie was such a beautiful child; now she's at that gawky stage and those braces on her teeth don't help. Celia will come expecting to see her beautiful English Rose and she'll be sorely disappointed.'

'And she'll not be around long enough to watch her English Rose bloom, so I wouldn't worry too much about any disappointment Celia displays about Rosie's appearance.'

The last days of July were golden with sunlight, the evenings soft and balmy, the night sky clear and blazing with stars. In just a week's time the boys would be home with the guests staying in the house, while others arriving for the party had already booked into every available hotel. The villagers were agog with talk of the event, and when Beatrice shopped in the village she was bombarded with questions from the people who had seen the boys grow up.

Some of the villagers were less than pleased. The grocers who had expected to be called upon for extra provisions, the bakers for bread and confectionery, were less than pleased when they learned about the marquee and outside catering.

Rosie was beginning to look forward to her mother's visit. She talked about it to her friends, to anybody prepared to listen, but she would have preferred to be invited to the party. Aunt Beatrice explained that if she wished to attend then it would be possible, but it would hardly be her mother's cup of tea and Gordon wouldn't know any of them.

The gardens were particularly beautiful, as if the flowerbeds and colourful shrubbery were aware that they had to do the family proud, and for hours Rosie sat watching the gardeners at work, bringing them cups of tea and following them around, until Aunt Beatrice remonstrated with her that she should allow them to get on with their work.

Uncle Cedric was less enthusiastic about the party in general. He regarded it as a vast waste of money; it would have been far better to have given Jeffrey a sum of money to purchase whatever he wanted most, but Jerome had thought nothing of that idea. When he grumbled to Beatrice she merely said, 'Let the boys have their party, Cedric, if that's what they want. One day they'll all have gone and this will be something they can remember and we can remember when the house is quiet.'

'You seem very sure they'll move on,' he said

grumpily. 'They'll not be in any hurry; they know which side their bread's buttered. Are you quite sure Celia and her husband will be here and gone before the night of the party?'

'Yes, I'm sure they will. Do stop worrying about them.'

Beatrice was pleased that at last Rosie was showing more interest in her mother's arrival by spending time in her bedroom to sort out the clothes she might need to take with her.

'Do you know any girls at your old school who would be glad of the things you will no longer need?' she asked her. 'Some of the villagers don't have much money to spend on school uniforms, but we have to be careful not to appear patronising.'

'There's Molly and Edith Robins. They live in that little stone house near the bridge.'

'What makes you think they would be glad of your clothes, Rosie?'

'Well, they never had the right things for games and they always made excuses not to come to the Christmas party. Freda said it was because they didn't have the right clothes.'

'Do you know their mother?'

'Not really. She cleans house for people in the village and their father is never around. They spend a lot of time with their grandmother.'

'Perhaps it would be better if I were to ask the vicar; he would know how to approach them, or know of other people who would be glad of your clothes. They really are too good to throw out if somebody could make use of them. Are those the clothes you intend to take on holiday?'

'Yes. I wish I wasn't so tall, most of them are too short for me now.'

'We could have gone into Exeter to shop but I'm sure your mother will prefer to buy things in London, and things are so hectic at the moment, with the party and everything.'

'Will my mother come before the boys get home?'

'I do hope so, dear. We are already expecting a house full.'

She looked at Rosie doubtfully. 'Are you sorry to be missing the party, Rosie?'

'Not really. It won't be the same, will it, not with girls I don't know.'

'No. Well I'll take your old school clothes and parcel them up for whoever wants them.'

Rosie was looking at herself in the mirror, and there was such a strangely dejected air about her that Beatrice said quickly, 'Your mother will expect you to have changed, dear. You're tall and you're pretty. Stop worrying about your teeth. When the braces come off you'll be a beautiful young lady.'

'I'm not a bit like that picture in your bedroom.'

'Well no, you're six years older. You'll change a lot more before you're grown up. Think about the boys, they've changed too, all of them.'

'Will Jerome marry that girl he's invited to the party?'

'I don't know, darling, probably not. There'll be a great many girls before they decide on the right one.'

'Steven took a girl to the May Ball.'

'How do you know?'

'Jerome told me he was taking someone.'

'Well, that's what boys do. In a few years some boy is going to invite you to a May Ball and you'll have a wonderful time. Now put those clothes in a neat pile on the window seat and come down to the kitchen. We'll have afternoon tea; it might be the last peaceful moment we'll have before the world turns upside down.'

'When will my mother be arriving?'

'I really thought she'd have written but I've only had that one letter to say they were coming. She said in the first few days of August. I hope it's tomorrow or the day after. After that the marquee will be arriving, the boys and their guests will be here and it will be sheer chaos. Now I'm going downstairs. This evening I'll get the suitcases down and you can start to pack your dresses.'

Rosie scanned the clothes she had put on one side with a small frown. They were cottons in pretty pastel colours, little girl dresses, she thought irritably. She was glad she was going away, she'd have had nothing to compete with the clothes the other girls would be wearing.

The boys teased her about the braces on her teeth and she was already taller than Noel, a fact that annoyed him intensely.

Cedric voiced his opinions over the breakfast table the next morning.

'Isn't there a letter from them?' he asked shortly. 'You'd have thought that at least she'd have given you a definite time and place. In two days the boys and their friends will be here, didn't you tell her about that?'

'Yes, I told her when I replied to her letter. You know what Celia's like, she was always a terrible correspondent and I expect they've had a great deal to think about.'

'Hmm. *We've* had a great deal to think about.'

He became aware that Rosie was looking at him anxiously, and he said quickly, 'I'll be glad when all this is over, Rosie. You'll be well out of it whenever they do decide to arrive.'

'I'm sure it will be sometime today,' Beatrice said.

Later in the morning, however, she conveyed her anxieties to Mrs Humphreys.

'The marquee people are coming today, Mrs Humphreys. If my sister-in-law doesn't arrive, Rosie will be devastated.'

'That she will, she's out there on the cliff watching every car that comes along the road.'

'Oh dear, what am I to do with her if they don't turn up?'

'Oh I'm sure they will, Miss Greville. Surely they wouldn't disappoint the girl at this late stage.'

Aunt Beatrice had no such hope; her memories of Celia were hardly comforting.

Rosie sat on the cliff top with her eyes trained on the road that climbed the hill and passed the gates of Dene Hollow. Most drivers avoided the cliff road as it was very narrow with only a few passing places, so the cars were few and far between. She saw the large white van arriving bringing the marquee and she began to feel sick

81

with the tension of waiting. If they didn't come, Uncle Cedric would be furious, Aunt Beatrice would be unhappy, and the boys when they arrived would be either sarcastic or pitying.

Bored and anxious after the futility of waiting she sauntered back to the house and stood watching the marquee being erected. It was a large cream affair which she could imagine filled with party-goers dancing, drinking, enjoying themselves. She couldn't think Aunt Beatrice or Uncle Cedric would be among the revellers but that would please Jerome: he liked to be in charge.

She saw Betty walking from the house, carrying a tray on which rested an array of cups of tea, and the men erecting the marquee went forward to relieve her of her burden. Catching sight of Rosie, she called out, 'There's tea and scones in the kitchen, Miss Rosie.'

Rosie shook her head, and Betty crossed the grass to join her.

'I'm sure your folks'll be here soon they'll 'ave 'ad a long journey.'

Rosie smiled.

'Suppose they don't come today, Betty? Tomorrow everybody will be here.'

Betty nodded. 'I think your aunt's gettin' a bit anxious. Never mind, I'm sure we're all worryin' about nothin'. Aren't ye comin' for somethin' to eat, love? Yer not doin' any good waitin' out here. It won't make 'em come any sooner.'

So Rosie returned with Betty to the house, where she sat in the kitchen drinking lemonade and eating Mrs Humphreys' delicious scones.

When she took another one Mrs Humphreys said somewhat acidly, 'I doubt if the caterers will come up with anythin' better than my scones; caterers indeed.'

'Miss Greville says there'll be too many folk 'ere to expect you to cater for 'em,' Betty said.

'I've catered for Christmas when they've brought friends 'ome 'aven't I?' Mrs Humphreys said firmly.

'Well yes, but this time there'll be a lot more. My mothers says a lot o' the guests are stayin' in some of the 'otels.'

'I'm sure they are. Get out into the garden, Betty and see if the workmen 'ave finished with their cups.'

When Aunt Beatrice came bustling into the kitchen minutes later she said brightly, 'I'm going down to the village, Rosie; why don't you come with me?'

'Shouldn't I be here for when mother comes?'

'We won't be gone long, dear, and Mrs Humphreys will look after them until we get back. They'll be glad of a rest and a cup of tea. In any case, if we meet them on the road we can come back with them.'

Rosie was glad to go, anything was better than hanging around the house and garden waiting for something that might or might not happen.

Chapter Six

There was an atmosphere over the dinner table that evening. Cedric was morose, Beatrice anxious and Rosie afraid. Her mother wasn't coming, she felt sure.

To spare her feelings her aunt and uncle had not discussed their non-arrival and the only sounds invading the silence were the cries of gulls and the wind sighing through the beech leaves.

It was the distant sound of a car's engines that sent Rosie hurrying to the window in time to see a large grey car coming slowly along the drive before it turned into the square. Beatrice looked up expectantly and Rosie said, 'They're here, Aunt Beatrice!' and Uncle Cedric said, 'They would come when we're half-way through dinner.'

'Can I go to meet them?' Rosie asked, but at that moment the door opened and Betty announced, 'There's a lady and gentleman to see you, Miss Greville.'

Rosie was half-way to the door, crying, 'It's my mother, Betty!'

'It's a Mr and Mrs Clement, Miss.'

Cedric and Beatrice looked at each other in dumbfounded amazement and Rosie looked at them uncertainly, then Beatrice rose to her feet and headed for the door. 'It's your grandparents, dear, you can come with me if you like or wait here until I bring them in.'

Two elderly people stood in the centre of the hall, a tall silver-haired man wearing a dark grey lounge suit and staring around him curiously, and a woman wearing a pale grey dress and coat adorned with arctic fox and a stylish grey hat over her silver hair. She was elegant, faintly disconcerted, and meeting Beatrice's surprised gaze she came forward to embrace her swiftly.

'Were you expecting to find Celia here?' Aunt Beatrice asked.

'No, she isn't coming. She telephoned me last evening, something very important has cropped up, and it's quite impossible for them to be here just now. She made us promise faithfully that we'd come and collect Rosemary for a week or so, something about you being overwhelmed with guests here.'

'Didn't she offer an excuse, say why they couldn't come?' Beatrice asked.

'Well, you know what it's like on the telephone. She said she'd write and tell us all about it. She was really quite distraught, so something very unexpected must have arisen. I really do feel very cross with her, I have a great many obligations I can't get out of and I'm having to let people down at the last minute because of this.'

'Have you driven over from Richmond today?'

'Yes, of course, we've had to. I'm sure George is quite weary, it wasn't a very good journey thanks to road repairs and traffic.'

'You'll stay here this evening and get off in the morning then?'

'Actually we've booked in at the Esplanade, just for tonight, it was all they could offer us. We

85

didn't want to put you out. Celia said something about the party you were having here, you'd wanted Rosemary out of the way.'

'That isn't strictly true. Celia and Gordon had said they were coming, and we'd simply hoped they wouldn't clash with the party since the house will be full of guests.'

'Yes, well. We don't want to impose. Is Rosemary ready to leave with us tonight?'

'Yes, she's been packed for some days, but you must have something to eat.'

'No need, we're dining at the Esplanade.'

For the first time, her grandmother looked at Rosie and her expression showed something of surprise. 'We haven't seen you for quite some time, Rosemary. How tall you are, and really quite grown up. We'll drive back to Richmond tomorrow. You'll quite enjoy looking round London. How long have you had those braces on your teeth?'

Rosie was saved from answering by the appearance of Cedric, who stared at the new arrivals stolidly, and her grandfather was quick to explain. It was an explanation which Cedric didn't feel needed any comments from him.

The next few minutes passed as if in a dream. Rosie's case, filled with the clothes she had packed for the holiday with her mother, was brought down, and Aunt Beatrice and Uncle Cedric walked out on to the terrace to see them off. She sat at the back of her grandfather's car with tear-filled eyes as she waved to the people standing outside the doors of Dene Hollow, and as they drove at last out of the gates she had the weirdest feeling that she was leaving it for ever.

Her grandmother looked at her with some exasperation when she merely picked at her food, until Rosie explained that she had already eaten, that indeed they were half-way through their evening meal when they arrived.

'What goes on at Dene Hollow?' her grandfather asked. 'We noticed the marquee on the lawn.'

'My cousin Jeffrey is twenty-one, it's his birthday party.'

'And that merits a marquee, does it?'

'They've invited people, friends from university, girlfriends.'

'So naturally they didn't want a young girl there?'

Rosie didn't answer, and her grandmother said, 'Don't think we're not looking forward to having you with us for a couple of weeks, Rosemary, it's simply that it is all so unexpected. I believe you're going to a nice new school after the holidays.'

Rosie's heart lifted. Of course she was going back to Dene Hollow. She was going to Chevington. All her school uniforms were at Dene Hollow, everything she would need, and she hurried on to tell her grandparents what she knew of her new school. They listened quietly, then her grandmother said, 'We'd have had you to stay with us before now, Rosemary, but your mother was adamant that she wanted nothing to interfere with your education. And Beatrice has been very kind, we didn't want to cross her.'

'Everything at Dene Hollow has been wonderful. Uncle Cedric can be quite sarcastic and

87

Jerome is arrogant, but the others are wonderful, I'm very happy there.'

'That's good, then.'

There was little conversation over the evening meal; her grandparents had little to say to each other and their remarks to Rosie were concerned with her schooling, Aunt Beatrice's role in her brother's house and whether his business was thriving. On the latter subject Rosie had absolutely no knowledge to impart.

By half past eight she was taken into her bedroom, where her grandmother noted that the bedcovers had been turned down and proceeded to show her where to find everything in the bathroom and where the lights were situated.

'We need to get off home very early in the morning, Rosemary, so we shall call for you around eight-thirty and eat an early breakfast. I don't suppose you remember much about Richmond, do you?'

'No, Grandmother.'

'Well, you were only about three years old the last time your mother brought you to see us. I have a friend I play bridge with who has a granddaughter only a little older than you. I'll invite them round for tea and you and Paula can get to know one another. Her parents are abroad too, Malaysia I think, you'll have something in common.'

'I wish I had something to read.' Rosie ventured.

'Oh no, dear, you should try to get some sleep, in view of our early start. Goodnight dear, sleep well.'

There was nothing to read except the hotel brochure and the Holy Bible in the dressing-table drawer. At least some of the dark deeds in the Old Testament found a reflection in her forsaken mood.

The journey too was taken largely in silence. Grandfather concentrated on the road, Grandmother sat slumped in the front seat sleeping for most of the time while Rosie concentrated on the scenery. When at last they arrived in the tree-lined road with its large red-brick houses surrounded by green lawns, she could not remember ever having been there before. There was a large conservatory at the side of the house and the gardens were well tended. As they approached the front door it opened to reveal a large woman wearing a patterned apron, with flour-encrusted hands and a warm smile. Rosie beamed at her; at least this was somebody normal and friendly.

She stood back while they trooped into the house, then, closing the door behind her, the woman said, 'Is this the little girl then? I'd expected somebody much younger.'

'I know, Mrs Royle, so had I. I hadn't realised how quickly the years had gone since we last saw Rosemary. This is Mrs Royle, dear, she's our daily and she'll show you your bedroom and where to find the rest of the rooms.'

'Well, I've almost finished baking. After that I'll make us all a nice cup of tea and show Rosemary round the place. Did you have a nice journey?'

'Very pleasant.'

'Was there any post?' Grandfather asked.

'Yes, Mr Clement, on your desk in the study.

He left them without another word and her grandmother said, 'I'll change into something more comfortable, Mrs Royle. I'll take Rosemary up to her room, I thought the one at the side of the house.'

'Aye, it's a pretty room,' Mrs Royle said before hurrying into the kitchen.

It was a pretty room with pale chintzes and a pastel carpet: a room that overlooked the garden with its rosebeds and rockery. Rosie looked around her appreciatively and her grandmother said, 'This was your mother's room when she was very young. Later on she preferred the larger room overlooking the drive, I could never understand why.'

'Isn't she going to come at all, or has she only been delayed?'

'Don't ask me, Rosemary. I can only tell you what she told me, that something has cropped up to prevent them coming. I expect she will write to explain everything properly. It has all been very inconvenient. Your mother doesn't seem to realise that I have a life to live here, and engagements which I have had to cancel or curtail.'

'How long shall I be staying here?'

'Well, I don't exactly know, dear. It will depend when your grandfather feels like another long journey, and when neither of us has much on.'

'I can go back by train if that is more convenient.'

'Have you travelled alone by train before? It is quite a long journey, you know.'

'I know, but if you take me to the train I'm sure

somebody would meet it at the other end.'

'Well, it's an idea, Rosemary, we'll have to wait and see. Now do your unpacking and put away your clothes. I'd change, if I were you, into something more comfortable than a blouse and skirt. Have you brought summer dresses?'

'Yes.'

'Well then, why not one of those. You know how to find your way downstairs, Rosemary. We'll all be in the drawing room for tea so don't be too long.'

'When shall I be able to meet the girl you told me about?'

'Mrs Elliot's granddaughter. I'll telephone her this evening so that perhaps you can meet one morning soon.'

'Have you met her?'

'Well, of course. She's very nice, she's at school here in London but of course like you she's on holiday at the moment. Leave it with me, dear.'

'They call me Rosie at Dene Hollow; the boys think Rosemary is silly.'

'Well, of course it isn't silly, it's the name you were given and your mother won't like people changing it. It's such a pretty name, don't you like it?'

'I suppose so, it's simply that the boys preferred Rosie.'

'Do you get on with your cousins?'

'Most of the time.'

'Well, I never had much to do with young boys. I told Celia that Beatrice was an absolute brick to take you all on.'

Rosie did not enjoy her holiday in Richmond.

91

Her grandmother took her into London to look at the shops and they ate afternoon tea one afternoon in the Dorchester where she pointed out several people of note.

When she asked if they could visit the zoo her grandmother said 'Really, Rosemary, you wouldn't enjoy it, and one has to walk about a lot, I couldn't do that.'

Her grandfather spent most of the time poring over his stamp collection and disrupting the gardener, and in the middle of the first week Mrs Elliot arrived with her granddaughter Paula.

Paula was twelve, a tall gangling girl whose only interests appeared to be the pony club, tennis and the constant letters she received from her parents in Kuala Lumpur.

She had been out to see them several times and derived a certain satisfaction in being able to relate all this to a girl who hadn't seen her mother for six years. She talked constantly of the Far East, the glamour, the exotic beauty of the buildings, the scenery, but nothing of the poverty, and Rosie was left feeling very much the country bumpkin.

'Don't you want to go out to Kenya?' she asked curiously.

'Yes, of course. I will when I'm older.'

'I'd have thought you'd want to see the wildlife?'

'I do.'

Paula then proceeded to tell her about the elephants and the tigers, the pagodas glittering with gold leaf, and by the end of the first afternoon in Paula's company Rosie was left feeling that she should have some subject that might defeat Paula's showing-off.

She talked about her boy cousins and Steven Chaytor, and as Paula's association with boys was strictly limited, it did have the desired result of a change of subject.

Mrs Elliot was kind enough to take the two girls to the theatre one matinée for a Russian Ballet production of the *Nutcracker*, which Rosie adored and which Paula said she had seen twice already. On the Saturday evening Mrs Elliot and Rosie's grandmother took them to a concert at the church hall, where the local operatic society gave a selection of songs from the shows.

It was towards the end of the second week that Rosie received a letter from Aunt Beatrice, asking if she knew when she was returning to Dene Hollow. The boys' party had gone very well and everybody appeared to have enjoyed themselves. Jerome and his lady friend seemed very close, Jeffrey had a girlfriend he took to the party and the two younger boys had eaten more than was good for them. She made no mention of Steven. Uncle Cedric was going up to Scotland for two weeks to visit friends so she would be feeling rather lonely. Her letter ended by asking if they had heard from Rosie's mother. Aunt Beatrice had received no excuse for her non-arrival at all.

This last paragraph prompted Rosie's grandmother to say, 'I really do feel she owes us an explanation, she's disrupted our entire summer and we're entitled to know the reason for it. I shall telephone her this evening.'

'Waste of time,' her husband said wearily. 'It

costs a lot of money, she never telephones you and you'll get absolutely nowhere.'

'She could speak to Rosemary.'

'If she wants to speak to her daughter she should be the one telephoning you, not the other way about.'

'Beatrice wants to know when Rosemary is going home.'

'Well, why don't we ask her. When do you want to go home, child?'

'Tomorrow, soon.'

'I hate driving all that distance. I don't want to stay at the house and it's August, so most of the hotels will be filled with holidaymakers.

'Why don't I go on the train? If you tell Aunt Beatrice which train I'm on she'll meet me. Paula went all the way to Kuala Lumpur on her own.'

'Are you sure you'll be all right doing that, Rosemary?' her grandmother asked doubtfully.

'Well, of course she'll be all right,' her grandfather snapped testily. 'There's nothing better than travel to give a girl confidence, and like she says her aunt will meet the train.'

'Well, I'll telephone Beatrice and make sure it's all right. I think you'd better go down to the station and find out which train she's going to travel on, preferably one that goes straight through to Plymouth or Exeter.'

Rosie had little doubt that her grandparents would view her departure with some relief and when she told Paula she was going back to Devonshire by train the other girl said, 'Well, I went all the way to Malasyia by air and there was nothing to it. If you want to go out to Kenya it's

94

time you got used to travelling alone.'

They took her to the train on the morning of her departure and saw her seated in a carriage in the company of several older people who promised to keep an eye on her. She was handed a packet of sweets and a girl's magazine by her grandmother, and a packet of railway sandwiches by her grandfather and she dutifully received their embraces and stood at the window until they were out of sight, after which she took her seat in the carriage smiling affably at the passengers, who smiled at her.

The journey was uneventful and as the train pulled slowly into Exeter station one gentleman retrieved her small suitcase off the shelf above and another helped her down on to the platform, while his wife said, 'Come with us, dear, to the end of the platform. Are you being met?'

'Yes.'

'Then when we get outside we'll stay with you until whoever is meeting you arrives.'

'Thank you, but I'm sure I'll be fine, my aunt is always very punctual.'

They laughed and Rosie found herself wishing her grandparents hadn't been so insistent that she was unused to travelling alone.

She spotted Aunt Beatrice hurrying towards them as soon as they left the platform and she came forward smiling, greeting Rosie's companions with warm words of thanks for their kindness.

As they finished the rest of their journey in the small local train, Aunt Beatrice was eager to know how Rosie had enjoyed her time in

London, but even more anxious to know if they had had any word from her mother.

'Grandmother said she would telephone her but Grandfather didn't want her to,' she said. 'Tell me about the party, Aunt Beatrice. Were the dresses pretty, what were the girls like?'

'Well, they all seemed very nice and they looked much of a pattern. Long hair and high heels, some of them in frilly dresses, others decidedly skimpy, and the boys were thrilled with the marquee and the catering.'

'Is the marquee still there?'

'Oh no, they came the day after the party to take it away.'

'How many people stayed at the house?'

'Too many. The boys slept in the lounge and on any couch they could find, even on the garden furniture and in the conservatory. The girls had the bedrooms. Anything seemed agreeable, they all had a lovely time.'

'Did you and Uncle Cedric go to the party?'

'No. Uncle Cedric locked himself in his study and I sat in the morning room with my needle-point. It was very noisy, the music, the chatter, I went to bed early but I couldn't sleep for it. I hope I'm not around when the younger boys are twenty-one.'

'Oh Aunt Beatrice, where will you be? And if you're not around, where will I be?'

As they left the taxi Rosie looked across the garden with a bemused expression and Beatrice said, 'It's all gone love, the marquee and the balloons. They enjoyed themselves but it's nice to see the garden back to normal. Now run upstairs, dear, and put your dresses away. By the time you've finished tea will be ready. I'll come up to see if I can help you when I've had a word with Betty.'

Chapter Seven

Rosie sat on the edge of her bed looking out at the exquisite curve of the bay and the silver line of the sea, hugging Edward Bear close to her and happy for the first time in three weeks.

It did not take long to unpack her small case and put the dresses away in her wardrobe, but by the time Beatrice came up to her room she was busily filling a large carrier bag with dolls, dolls for every occasion, be they dressed in pristine organza or gingham, black dolls and white dolls, dolls with vapid pretty-pretty faces and those with exaggerated vain expressions.

Beatrice stared at them in surprise.

'Why are you putting your dolls in there, Rosie? Don't you like them around any more?'

'I never liked them at all. Did you give my school clothes to the vicar?'

'Yes, and he promised to distribute them where they would be most needed, but why the dolls?'

'Somebody will be glad of them. I know girls who never had much for Christmas, girls who never ever had dolls like these and they'll be glad of them.'

'But they were presents from your mother, dear.'

'I know, and now I want to get rid of them.'

'Rosie, I don't want you to fall out with your mother. There must be a very good reason why she hasn't arrived. No doubt we'll be hearing from her very soon. But she bought you those dolls in very good faith, she was so sure you would love them. I really don't feel you should give them all away.'

'I'm keeping Edward Bear. He was always my favourite anyway.'

'Well, put them back in the cupboard for now. We'll talk about them later.'

'I shan't change my mind, Aunt Beatrice, I don't want them any more.'

Beatrice looked at her doubtfully. Rosie's expression was inflexible, and resignedly Aunt Beatrice said, 'Very well then, we'll ask the vicar; he'll know the people he can give them to.'

Later in the afternoon, Beatrice watched Rosie walking quickly towards the cliff top, from which she took the rambling road down to the beach.

There seemed a strange loneliness about the girl as she walked with her head down, her thoughts probably miles away, and Beatrice felt a searing anger for the mother who seemed so content to leave her at Dene Hollow in an environment she had herself disliked.

A new open sports car was entering the gates. Beatrice frowned at the sight of the girl sitting beside Jerome for the simple reason that she knew his father would be displeased.

Cedric had taken his eldest son into the family

firm but Jerome had insisted on taking several weeks holiday before starting his employment, a holiday that entailed spending every minute with Natalie Shaw.

Cedric's tetchiness endorsed her opinion over the dinner table that evening. 'I know I gave him time off before he needed to make an appearance in the office but I did think he'd want to come in to see the lie of the land. The only ambition he appears to have is centred on that girl.'

'Don't you like her?' Beatrice asked.

'The girl's right enough, but he's twenty-two, he's got his way to make. There's time for girls when he's made the grade. And where's Jeffrey? Do you suppose he's with that girl he invited to his party?'

'I have no idea.'

'Well, she's not the sort of girl I thought he'd go for, pretty, ineffectual, bit of a clothes-horse, entirely the wrong sort of clothes.'

Indeed, Jeffrey's girl had been a bit of surprise to both of them.

She did not come from Natalie's circle of friends, in fact they had looked at her with ill-disguised arrogance. She'd been to the wrong school, she worked because she needed the money and she worked as a hairdresser in some obscure salon none of them used.

She had appeared at the party in a skimpy, shiny silk dress that had never been purchased in the town's most exclusive shops, but Connie didn't seem to mind. Cedric and Beatrice had made a late appearance in the marquee to watch the birthday cake being cut and drink the toast, and there they had seen Connie standing with her arms around Jeffrey in a very assertive manner.

Beatrice knew Jeffrey had had words with his father about her, since Cedric's voice had hardly been lowered to disguise the fact that he was furious.

She had heard him reprimanding Jeffrey night after night in the study, and the younger man's sulky responses.

'There's time enough for girls when you've got your degree,' Cedric had said adamantly. 'Don't think I'm paying money for you to own a car for the express purpose of taking that girl out and about,' he'd ended.

'You bought one for Jerome and he's always with Natalie,' Jeffrey had retorted.

'He's got a job, he'll be earning money. You I'll be subsidising, and the way you're going on you'll not get that degree if you're not working for it.'

Beatrice was coming to dread the time she and Cedric spent together, and on this particular evening he turned his attention to Rosie.

'No word from your mother then?' he asked her, in spite of the warning glance from his sister.

'No,' Rosie snapped.

Across the table Natalie had smiled at her. 'You didn't come to the party,' she said.

'No.'

'Why was that?'

'I was in London with my grandparents.

'How nice.'

'Rosie's parents are in Kenya,' Beatrice explained. 'Something must have happened to prevent them coming.'

Natalie smiled politely.

'Your friend Steven was at the party,' Jerome said snidely. 'He brought Moira Disley, she's the girl he took to the May Ball.'

Rosie didn't answer, and Jerome went on relentlessly. 'He didn't ask why you weren't at the party. After all, you weren't exactly very nice with him the last time he came here.'

Rosie glared at him. 'I don't care who he was with, why should you think I do?'

'Well, you always made it pretty apparent that he was flavour of the month. A little girl crush, I'm sure.'

'Stop teasing her,' Natalie said. 'You're making her cross. Steven is awfully nice, isn't he. I know a great many girls who've had crushes on Steven.'

Rosie gave all her attention to her pudding. She didn't care about Steven or the girl he took to the May Ball. She didn't care about her mother. All she wanted was to grow up quickly and feel more adequate in coping with his teasing.

To change the subject Aunt Beatrice said, 'David and Noel will be back tomorrow, Rosie. You'll have somebody to ride and sail with.'

At that moment she made up her mind that she would be there to tell the boys on their arrival not to question Rosie about her mother's non-arrival. Noel in particular would be curious. In the event, after he had bombarded her with questions, she knew she had not been far wrong.

'Her mother's a pain,' he said finally. 'All those silly dolls and she never comes here. We've got

101

friends at school whose parents live abroad. They come home and the boys go there. Why can't Rosie?'

'I've no idea, but I don't want either of you going on and on about it. She's very touchy about it, not surprisingly.'

The last two weeks before she went to Chevington were happy ones. With Noel and David she rode across the countryside or sailed with them across the bay. The sea was benign and the summer sun shone out of a cloudless sky, and by the end of August her love for Dene Hollow and its surrounding countryside had been reinforced. How could she ever think about wanting to leave it, how could she bear never to come back to it?

A parcel arrived for her from her mother two days before she was due to go to her new school. It contained a gold pen and pencil, a new dressing-gown and a cheque for fifty pounds.

Beatrice enthused about the dressing-gown and Rosie said, 'At least she hasn't sent me another doll.'

'Will you take the pen and pencil to school, Rosie? Don't you think they're really too expensive for everyday use? I would keep them until you're older. You don't want the other girls to think you're showing off.'

Rosie agreed, and picking up her mother's letter she said, 'She says they were sorry they couldn't come to England as promised but some other time perhaps. She says Gordon is awfully busy and there's so much going on there, I'll hear all about it when she gets here.'

She smiled ruefully, the sort of sad disbelieving smile that Beatrice had come to associate with Rosie's remarks about her mother.

'I hope you'll be happy at Chevington, dear,' Aunt Beatrice said. 'You'll work hard, won't you, make us all proud of you.'

'Yes, perhaps Uncle Cedric will take me into his firm like Jerome and then I can live here at Dene Hollow,' she said hopefully.

'That's too far away, dear. You'll change your mind about a whole lot of things before we need to start thinking about a job. Would you really like to work in the same profession as Jerome?'

Rosie grinned. Even with Dene Hollow as an incentive she knew she would not.

Celia had a guilty conscience about Rosie but she refused to allow it to interfere with her life. Everything was taking off. From that evening they had dined with the Garveys at the club, in her eyes everything had changed dramatically for the better.

It had all started so mundanely, the four of them arriving at the club, being made welcome by the Garveys' friends and acquaintances, sitting down to dinner and making small talk, and then suddenly Ariadne had arrived.

She had greeted Gordon enthusiastically, as if she had seen him only the day before, been charming to the Garveys, insisted on introducing Gordon and Celia to a younger crowd, the sort of people Celia associated with the sort of life she had been craving.

Rich people, owners of large estates. Gordon

was at home with them because his profession was a respected one and a great many of these same people needed him, but from across the room the Garveys and their friends had looked on with singular disenchantment.

To Celia this was living: dancing, listening to scandalous gossip, being fêted and flattered by groups of young men who were only too happy to find a fresh face, a beautiful fresh face.

She did not know when the Garveys left, but Gordon told her he had said their farewells and told the Garveys that they must visit them soon. Celia agreed, but she privately thought that would be an end to the matter.

On the way home she sank back in the car with a look of evident enjoyment.

Gordon smiled down at her. 'You've enjoyed yourself hugely, haven't you, darling?'

'Oh yes, Gordon, it's been wonderful. Why have we waited so long to meet those people?'

'You mean you actually liked them?'

'Why yes, didn't you?'

'Not particularly. They're pleasure-seekers, have too much money, and I never think they're particularly genuine.'

'Darling, that's an awful thing to say. They made us very welcome, they begged us to go there again very soon. We will, won't we?'

'I haven't made any promises. My work schedule is very demanding. This is the first time I've been to the club for years.'

'I know, Ariadne told me. Your job's all bed and work, Gordon, but it's not exactly fair to me. I loved every minute of tonight. Ariadne has asked me to play tennis but I told her I hadn't played since I left England and my tennis was rusty. But surely you can't object to my taking it up again?'

His expression was non-committal, and she was quick to say, 'You don't trust me, is that it, Gordon?'

'Of course not, darling, of course I trust you. It's just that I don't exactly trust Ariadne or her crowd.'

'That's tantamount to saying you don't trust me.'

'I really think you should make an effort to see Rosemary, darling. She must have been terribly disappointed that we didn't go home in August, and your parents too were expecting you. Your mother's last letter wasn't exactly pleasant reading.'

'My mother's never very pleasant about being put out in any way. She took Rosemary for three weeks, and that probably interfered with her bridge parties and her shopping expeditions. Aunt Beatrice hasn't complained.'

'Aunt Beatrice is the most long-suffering woman I know.'

She glared at him. 'Gordon, we've been here nearly seven years and the most excitement I've had has been a few trips into Nairobi, dinner with the Garveys, treks into the wilderness with you and tonight. Tonight was wonderful, you can keep the rest.'

'Even when it's my life and part of my job.'

'Well, I don't think I'm asking for much. A game of tennis, a few visits to the club, the chance to make friends of my own age.'

105

Gordon didn't answer; he knew that he had lost the argument. If he wanted to keep her happy he had to give her her own way. He did, however, have serious reservations about the future of their marriage.

It all started with meetings with Ariadne for tennis, then instead of driving home, tea dances and overnight stays with different people. Gordon arrived home exhausted after days tending sick animals and searching for injured wild ones. Bitterness turned to anger, then anger turned to apathy, and in the end he didn't really care whether he found her at home or away. Whenever Celia felt guilty about Gordon, Ariadne was quick to tell her it was the best way to keep husbands interested. 'You spoiled him, darling,' she said with a sly laugh, 'a little of being left alone to fend for himself and you'll see he'll be back here at the club to keep an eye on you.'

Celia didn't particularly want Gordon at the club; he would put a disapproving damper on their high spirits. Gordon was not one of them, would never be one of them.

Ariadne's husband spent most of the evenings propping up the bar, entertaining a group of men to some ribald story of sharp practices he was adept at. While they danced in the ballroom they could hear the sound of their laughter and Johnny's less than pristine English and loud guffaws.

Ariadne was happy to leave him to his own devices. She was happy to dance with the young men who laughed at her wit and flirted with her outrageously. Johnny Fairbrother was her meal ticket. He kept her in style, gave her enough money and when she got bored took her on expensive holidays.

She was tolerant of his brashness, his occasional brutality, and however often she found some young man to flirt with, be unfaithful with, he knew she'd never leave him, not unless she found somebody richer, and foolishly inclined to take his place.

Celia, on the other hand, was unimpressed by the flirtatious behaviour of the young men she danced with. She was a respectable married woman, the wife of a man who was respected by the old school and the giddy set, and she was determined to give none of them a chance to say she was being unprincipled. That was until a newcomer arrived on the scene in the person of Nigel Boyd.

He appeared in the club house one evening and stood drinking alone at the bar. He was tall and thin, very handsome in a dark saturnine sort of way, and as his eyes surveyed the room with cynical detachment they met Celia's china-blue gaze.

There was something about him that made her think of all she had read about Josslyn Victor Hay, the 22nd Earl of Erroll, who had been shot dead after driving his lover Lady Diana Delves Broughton home. All that scandal had happened when Celia was still a schoolgirl in distant England.

It had made fascinating reading to Celia and her school-friends in the dormitory of her school: the scandalous living of society people in an exotic land, tragedy and death, unfaithfulness and debauchery among Kenya's hedonistic colonial elite, rich aimless people with too much money and nothing to do.

The man standing at the bar was the living image of how she had imagined Lord Erroll to have looked, and Ariadne had already told her that her friends considered her to be a replica of Lady Diana Delves Broughton, the woman he was having an affair with and whose husband had been tried for his murder and acquitted.

With tremendous willpower she removed her gaze from his, but later in the evening he invited her to dance and for the first time in her life she fell in love, stupidly and illogically, because he was a man she knew absolutely nothing about, and yet his dark amused eyes gazing down into hers and the low-pitched charm of his voice captivated her completely.

She spent all the rest of the evening dancing with him, and people sitting and standing around the room began to speculate. Ariadne made it her business to find out all she could about the newcomer and it was later in the ladies room that she was able to pass the information on to her friend.

'He's called Nigel Boyd, the Honourable Nigel Boyd, the second son of some earl or other, some Irish peer. Not apparently the earl's favourite son; there's been some scandal.'

'What sort of scandal?'

'I'll ask Johnny, he'll know.'

'He's very charming.'

'But of course, darling. Earls' sons with bad

reputations can be guaranteed to be charming, it's their stock in trade. What's he doing here?'

'I don't know, I haven't asked him.'

'What have you been talking about?'

'He wanted to know about me.'

'And have you told him about Gordon? Have you told him about your daughter?'

'I will, given time.'

'But not too much time, darling. I'd get it in first if I were you, before other people start to tell him.'

'I told him I was married to a vet and that I'd lived here for around seven years.'

'And...'

'And nothing. I told him Gordon hated life around the clubs, that he was far too busy in his job and hated socialising. It's true, Ariadne.'

'Well, of course. And it leaves the field wide open for the Honorable Nigel to step in.'

'Really Ariadne, that isn't why I told him. He'll probably be moving on and I shan't see him again after tonight.'

'Like I said I'll ask Johnny. Are you free for tennis tomorrow?'

'I think so. What time?'

'Around eleven. You're staying over at the Gosgroves, aren't you?'

'Yes.'

'Doesn't Gordon ever mind, Celia?'

'He doesn't say he does.' She met Ariadne's eyes in the mirror. 'I never wanted it to be like this, Ariadne. I thought we'd be enjoying this sort of life together. Gordon doesn't want it, we've nothing in common any more. Anyway, you should know what it's like – you left your husband for Johnny, probably for the very same reasons that Gordon and I have grown apart.'

She looked at her friend, who was staring down at her hands, idly twisting the rings that adorned her fingers.

'Well, didn't you?' Celia demanded.

Ariadne smiled, a singularly bitter smile.

'Actually, no, Celia, I left somebody who was nice, kind, decent for somebody who was indescribably common, with money, so much money that I felt reassured that I would never have to face poverty again.'

Chapter Eight

Celia parked her car in the empty space at the end of the compound and walked between the long cages towards the house. When she first came to Kenya she had liked the house, it was large, comfortable and Gordon had given her full rein to buy new rugs and curtains. It hadn't been enough.

The cheetah eyed her with lofty disdain as she walked past his cage while the panther ignored her, his gaze fixed on the impala cavorting in the open pen. She hated the wild animals, she hated their cries; and as she neared the house two baby elephants came to the bars of their cage, thrusting their trunks forward, expecting food; but she ignored them, as she ignored everything

110

else in her husband's life.

She'd telephoned Gordon to say she was arriving early in the afternoon, but his jeep had not been in the compound and she wondered idly if he'd even remembered. Work would come first with Gordon; hadn't it always?

Ignoring the smiles of greeting from Beulah the house servant she went straight to her bedroom, flinging open the wardrobe doors and pulling out her clothes, which she strewed across the bed. She didn't want them all, not the ones she'd had for years, but there were others she'd considered adequate for the life she wanted and which had remained unworn. Now she needed them, and she was busily packing them into a large suitcase when Gordon appeared at the bedroom door.

He eyed the suitcase dispassionately without speaking and Celia, closing the lid sharply, said, 'I thought you'd forgotten I was coming today, Gordon. I've come for some of my clothes. Do you think one of the servants could take this down to my car?'

'Leave the case, Celia, it's more important that we talk.'

She looked at him nervously. 'Talk! There's nothing to talk about Gordon. I simply want some of my clothes at the flat. They're important for what I do there; they were never any use to me here.'

He looked at her levelly, and turning away, he walked down the corridor and down the stairs. When she followed him into the sitting room he was standing at the sideboard, pouring out a drink.

'What are you drinking?' he asked her.

'Nothing. I want to get away.'

'Can you remember the last time you came here, Celia?'

'Not exactly.'

'Well, I can tell you. It was the twentieth of September and it is now the third of December, I'd call that an official separation, wouldn't you?'

She didn't answer him but he knew she was nervous from the way her hands gripped the back of a chair.

'Sit down, Celia,' he said amicably. 'I would prefer to be civilised about this. Our marriage is over and I would prefer it to be legally over rather than this silly business of me here and you in Nairobi. You will never like my life and I have no liking for yours or the people in it. I think we should divorce at the earliest opportunity. I do hear something of the gossip, my dear, it's inevitable.'

'There's no need for gossip. All I do is play tennis, dance at the club, mix with people of my own age and have a little fun.'

'And Nigel Boyd?'

'I've danced with him; surely that shouldn't be the subject of spiteful gossip. He's charming, friendly, people like him.'

'A great many people dislike him, Celia.'

'You don't know him.'

'I know of him. He's been here before, on and off for years actually. His family don't want him around, there's been all sorts of scandal about him and if you're thinking something permanent will come of it you're in for a shock, Celia. It won't.'

112

'You mean you don't want it to.'

'I don't give a damn, actually. You've been too long out of my life, Celia, and I haven't liked what I've been hearing. Nigel Boyd is a playboy, if he marries at all it will be some woman with money, picked out for him by a family fed up with paying off his debts.'

'People talk about him because they're jealous without knowing anything about him. They're jealous of me. I never thought you'd take notice of malicious gossip, Gordon.'

His voice seemed suddenly tired when he answered her. 'Celia, I'm really not interested in the comings and goings of Nigel Boyd, I'm not really very interested in you any more. What about your daughter? Do you ever think about her, ever wish to see her? I do think it's your cavalier treatment of Rosemary that has changed my opinion of you.'

'How dare you question me about my daughter. You know she's been happy at Dene Hollow with Beatrice. How could I possibly disrupt her education? Her life needed to be serene and gentle, not torn between England and Africa. When she's older she'll be with me, but I shall know when the time is right.'

He shrugged his shoulders. 'Then I'm pleased, Celia, that your conscience remains so clear about Rosemary. In the meantime I'll consult my lawyer and initiate divorce proceedings at the earliest opportunity. Nobody will be surprised, neither my friends nor yours, I imagine.'

For a long moment they stared at each other, then with a brief smile he said, 'I'll get Henry to

113

take your case to your car. I have to go now. Goodbye, Celia.'

He left her without another word and from the window she saw him striding towards his jeep. He never looked back.

She felt strangely perturbed about the divorce, without knowing if this was what she wanted. It had been comfortable being married to Gordon, while she had chased the shadows with the substance behind her. Now without Gordon in her life she would be uncomfortably alone.

Single women were not what the community wanted; they were regarded as loose canons, and a single woman with a teenage daughter would hardly be welcome. At the same time it would take months before the divorce came through, and by then she would have made her own life. And there was Nigel. He was attentive, obviously besotted with her; all that spiteful gossip had probably been started by some woman who had fancied him and been spurned.

The flat she had found in Nairobi was very small, and looking round her she sensed that it was impersonal, hardly the sort of home she craved. She unpacked quickly, putting the clothes in the wardrobe and piling the shoes she had brought into a cupboard.

In the living room she poured herself a glass of gin and tonic and went out on to the small balcony to drink it. The narrow tree-lined road was quiet, the women who lived there would be at the club, the men at their different jobs. Only one woman further down the road was working in her garden, and seeing Celia on her balcony, she waved.

Celia wanted company very badly, but she hesitated to ask Julie Simpson. Julie knew everybody and everything that was going on in her neighbours' lives. Her heart sank when she saw Julie leave her garden gate and come smiling brightly up the road, calling out at Celia's garden gate, 'Are you all alone, Celia? I'll come up for a chat if you like.'

There was no help for it so she made Julie welcome on her balcony and went to pour her out a drink.

'I saw you coming in,' Julie said. 'Been to the club?'

'Actually no. I've been up country to see Gordon.'

'Really. I thought you two were separated.'

'Well, we don't exactly live in each other's pockets but we're really very fond of each other.'

'That's what I call a civilised arrangement. You weren't at the club last night. Nigel looked a bit downhearted, I thought.'

'Really. Didn't he find consolation?'

'With whom? All the women had their husbands with them, and not even Ariadne could shake him out of the doldrums.'

'She tried, of course?'

'Well, you know Ariadne.'

'I didn't miss anything else?'

'Well no. It was all rather a bore actually. We left early, Gavin had an early start this morning and he wasn't exactly in a party mood. They're starting to get things lined up at the club for Christmas; will you be here?'

115

'I expect so, but I don't really know for sure.'

'Is Gordon likely to be here?'

'I doubt it very much. The sort of things happening at Christmas at the club wouldn't interest him.'

'And he won't want you to be with him?'

'I really don't know what will be happening at Christmas, Julie.'

'Well, I'm sure you'd rather be at the club with Nigel Boyd dancing attendance than up country surrounded by wild animals. I doubt if Ariadne will be around.'

'Really, why is that?'

'She was talking about visiting America for Christmas, restocking her wardrobe. You know the things Ariadne talks about: theatres, shopping, the flesh pots.'

'Is it definite?'

'I'm not sure. You know what she's like.'

Celia smiled.

Most of Julie's gossip failed to interest her. It was trivial: clothes and small talk. Most of the women were reluctant to tell Julie very much because of her reputation for tittle-tattle, and when the conversation flagged Celia said, 'Well, I really must think about getting a meal together, either that or eating at the club. Will you be there this evening?'

'I doubt it. Gavin expected to be late back and he won't be in the mood for socialising. You really do have the best of both worlds, Celia: a husband who is content to stay in the background and a boyfriend who always seems to be there for you.'

'Another drink before you go, Julie?'

'Oh no thanks, I must be thinking about a meal too.'

Celia watched her go, smiling her farewells, and waiting until Julie reached her garden gate before waving her hand.

She wanted to go to the club. There wasn't much fun in eating her solitary meal sitting at the kitchen table, but it would do Nigel Boyd good to be missing her. So against all her better judgement she sat leafing through the latest magazines, promising herself that she would retire early and leave the club alone until the next day.

It was after eleven o'clock when the telephone rang and with a racing heart she went to answer it. Instead of Nigel however, it was Ariadne, her light airy voice amiable, unaware of Celia's disappointment that it was not Nigel.

'When did you get back?' she demanded.

'Mid afternoon.'

'And how is Gordon? Did you give him my love?'

'He's very well, Ariadne, busy as usual. We hardly had time to talk, he was dashing off.'

'Didn't he want you to stay for a while.'

'No.'

'So you didn't feel like going to the club?'

'No, I was rather tired, I thought I'd have an early night.'

'Me too, darling. I played tennis this morning and I stayed at the club chatting with all and sundry until late afternoon. I decided against going out again. Johnny's there, of course; heaven knows what time he'll be home.'

'Can we meet tomorrow, Ariadne?'

'Well, I'm not sure, Celia. I have a dentist's appointment in the morning and if I need anything doing I'll not be in the mood for the club. I do hate dentists.'

'I know. Perhaps you'd like to come round here after your appointment?'

'Like I said, it will depend on what I need doing.'

'Well, it can't be very much surely, your teeth are perfect.'

'You sound very anxious to talk to me.'

'Not really. But you do cheer me up, Ariadne. I like talking to you.'

'It sounds as though you need a confidante.'

'Not really, just someone to chat with.'

'Well, like I said, dear, it will depend on my dentist.'

'Ariadne, please come, perhaps I really do need a confidante.'

'That's what I thought. I'll be there around two.'

She had to talk to somebody about the future. A divorce, Gordon and Nigel. She'd never been able to talk to her mother; she'd always been off somewhere, her bridge parties, her golf, her shopping. Her mother had believed that when she sent her one daughter to an expensive boarding school Celia's friends would be all she needed to talk to, and her father had always been wrapped up in his own pursuits.

Alan had been in the army, more away than at home, and she had never got along with his family. Gordon had been different, sweet, in love

118

with her and wanting to make her happy; but he hadn't made her happy, he'd been too wrapped up in a punishing job that required more from him than she did. Now she was turning to Ariadne and she wasn't sure if she was the right person.

Ariadne was brittle, sophisticated and mercurial, but she was also astute, and Celia believed she would tell her the truth as she saw it.

She arrived at three o'clock with a frozen face after two fillings and feeling rather sorry for herself. When Celia offered her a drink she said feelingly, 'Perhaps later, darling, I'm all frozen up, I'd rather wait.'

They settled down on the verandah and Ariadne said, 'I really should have gone straight home but I couldn't do with Johnny sleeping his morning drinks off in the chair, then shoving me into joining him at the club this evening. I hate fillings, particularly when they leave you frozen for several hours.'

'I know, I hate them too.'

'You sounded a bit stressed last evening over the phone. Is it Gordon?'

Celia nodded.

'He wants you to go back to live in the country?'

'He wants a divorce.'

'On what grounds?'

'That I'm never there, that I'm more in tune with my life here than I ever was with him.'

'And has he mentioned Nigel Boyd?'

'He knew about Nigel. Those friends of his have lost no time in telling him about Nigel. But

119

I don't want him involved; after all, I haven't really known him all that long.'

Celia was unaware of the cynicism in Ariadne's green eyes. She thought Ariadne was her friend; little did she know that Ariadne didn't like her or women like her.

Ariadne's memories were still raw: that crumbling house in the back streets of Cardiff and the bitter wind-blown mornings when she'd trudged through the streets with her mother on the way to the houses where she cleaned and washed the steps.

That little girl had played on the kitchen floor with any toys the children who lived in the houses had left lying around. Those same children had treated her to disdainful frowns and often snatched the toys away from her and rebuked her for touching them.

They had been girls like Celia. Girls who went to good schools and accompanied their mothers to take tea with friends, always dressed immaculately, mincing daintily down the front steps without sparing her kneeling mother a glance.

Ariadne couldn't remember her father. He'd left them when she was two years old, and after that came a procession of men, none of them destined to be a father to her, and some of them not against hitting her. When she complained to her mother she merely said she'd probably asked for it, and Ariadne grew up with the resolve that one day she'd leave Cardiff, never to return.

She did what so many of her contemporaries did: she walked the streets, and she learned to use people. She made money and she saved. She was unpopular with the other girls and the pimps who fed off them, but Ariadne worked alone, and when she was eighteen she left Cardiff and went to London for richer pickings.

It was the film *White Mischief* that drew her to Kenya. This was the sort of life she wanted. Celia had thought it was her due, Ariadne thought it would be her salvation, so she counted her money, which by this time was substantial, and she flew out to Nairobi, where she looked for work, respectable work.

She was young and beautiful. She had a way with her and men were captivated with her. She found work with several different families who had horses and although she knew little about them the stable hands were only too eager to teach her all they knew, and she learned quickly.

She moved on from one stable to another, always up and up, and then eventually she was working for Alan and Margery Peterson. By this time she knew how to speak and how to act. She had learned to ride the horses she looked after and she rode with the Petersons' children. They liked her: she was fun and courageous. And then Margery's mother had had to have a serious operation and Margery went home to England to care for her. She was away six weeks, and in those six weeks Alan and Ariadne fell in love.

Ariadne thought this was what she wanted. A nice man with a nice house. Enough money and well respected. At first his friends deplored the situation and didn't make her welcome, but his wife left the area, taking the boys with her, and because they liked Alan they made themselves like his new wife.

Ariadne told herself that all the aspirations of her childhood and early teens had been realised, until she met Johnny Fairbrother. He had considerably more money and with Johnny she didn't have to pretend.

He was well aware that the veneer she had wrapped around herself was false and he didn't mind. He liked her earthiness. She didn't ask him to be a gentleman; she was happy with what she'd got.

Ariadne hadn't cared about the scandal they'd created; there'd been a lifetime of scandal and she'd surmounted it. She didn't care about the people who thought she and Johnny were trash; she had enough friends who worshipped money and Johnny had plenty of that.

What could she tell Celia that would help her to face the coming months? The sympathies of the old established families would be with Gordon; the new people would be intrigued, curious and entertained. Celia would be somebody to gossip about, a change from familiar things. Nigel Boyd was something different. As if reading her thoughts, Celia said, 'I don't want Nigel to know anything about the divorce yet. I suppose he'll learn about it sooner or later.'

'You think he'll stick around, then?' Ariadne asked with a wry smile.

Celia stared at her incredulously. 'Well, of course. He loves me. I love him. I just don't want him to feel trapped. How well do you know him, Ariadne?'

'Oh he's been around on and off for years.

When I first came here he ran with the upper-crust crowd, then he seemed to have a change of heart, became bored and moved over to the racey crowd. I was working for the Petersons when I first saw him. Later when I married Alan I got to know him rather better.'

'But you liked him?'

Ariadne shrugged her shoulders. 'I never thought about it.'

'Gordon says there's been talk about him but he didn't elaborate.'

'No, he wouldn't.'

'You like Gordon, don't you?'

'I like him like I liked Alan.'

'Alan was your husband, for heaven's sake.'

'I know, like I said I liked him.'

'Is that how you think about Johnny, you like him?'

Ariadne smiled. 'Let's talk about you and Nigel Boyd, Celia. Don't be too ready to give up the substance for the shadow until you're sure he's worth it.'

'Isn't that what you did?'

'You might describe Johnny in a great many ways, but never as a shadow. Fundamentally we're two of a kind, self-absorbed, brash and materialistic. I have to think about Nigel Boyd.'

'What do you mean?'

'Just that. I haven't made my mind up yet on what sort of man he really is. Now I must go or Johnny will be straining at the leash. I suppose they'll all be talking about Christmas and what sort of celebrations the club is going to put on.'

'This Christmas I'm looking forward to. It will

123

be the first one I've enjoyed since I came out here.'

Ariadne smiled. 'Well, I wouldn't be too sure. It hardly ever lives up to expectations.'

Chapter Nine

Ariadne found her husband slumped in a chair, staring morosely across the swimming pool, and although she greeted him cheerfully she was met with a sullen scowl.

'Where have you been all afternoon?' he grumbled. 'I've had that Boyd fella here.'

'Why, he's never been here before. I didn't think he numbered us among his close friends.'

'Nor does he, but there are rumours going around about his lady friend. He thought you'd know if they were true.'

'What sort of rumours?'

'That her marriage is in trouble and divorce is in the offing.'

'It wouldn't surprise me; after all when does she ever see Gordon these days?'

'But you don't know for sure?'

'What had he to say about it?'

'Very little. He went on about his family in Ireland, their expectations. He won't marry her, you know.'

'Why are you so sure?

'Has she any money?'

'I really don't know, perhaps not money as he

124

would expect.'

'Well, he's going home to England for Christmas.'

'England, not Ireland?'

'He said England. He has a grandmother in Dorset, apparently the old girl dotes on him and he keeps well in with her. If your friend's expecting to spend Christmas with him here she's in for a disappointment.'

'Are we going to the club?'

'You said you didn't want to go.'

'I know. I've changed my mind. The visit to the dentist wasn't traumatic, and the club will cheer me up.'

Johnny lumbered to his feet and Ariadne asked casually, 'I suppose he'll be there?'

'He didn't say. Will she be there?'

'I really don't know. She's been up country to see Gordon, I'm not sure if she's back.'

Johnny never questioned what she told him; he was never sufficiently interested and he wasn't now. He'd be content to prop up the bar for most of the evening surrounded by his particular cronies, and the comings and goings of the rest of them would hardly register.

Celia was looking forward to Christmas; that Nigel wouldn't be around would be a crushing blow.

Later at the club, Celia and Nigel were dancing together, his dark eyes looking down into hers with maddening seductiveness, and Celia was gazing up at him with the same sort of yearning. They were two people divorced from reality in a world peopled by wraiths and nonentities, and it was much later in the evening when Ariadne found them sitting alone together in a dark corner of the bar. Picking up her drink she sauntered over to join them. She would not be welcome but on this evening at least she had a good excuse to speak to them.

Nigel looked up, but without waiting for an invitation Ariadne sat across from them, and with a smile said, 'I'm sorry I was out when you called this afternoon. I had an appointment with my dentist.'

'So Johnny said. I stayed a little while, he was all alone.'

'I'm sure he was glad of your company. He tells me you won't be joining us over the Christmas period.'

'Alas no. I'm due to visit my grandmother.'

Celia was staring at him with evident surprise, and turning towards her he said with a charming smile, 'I only decided yesterday, darling, and I wasn't sure when you'd be back in Nairobi.'

'It was so urgent?' Celia murmured.

'Well, actually I do tend to spend Christmas with the old lady. She's the one member of the family who has time for me these days. She'd be very disappointed if I didn't go to stay with her as usual.'

'Does your grandmother live in London?' Ariadne asked.

'Actually no. She lives in a crumbling old pile near the coast in Dorset. She calls it picturesque, I call it antiquated, but I have to confess it does have a faded charm about it. Did you ever have a grandmother it paid you to cultivate?'

126

'Actually no. I never knew any of my grandparents, but if I'd had one with money I would probably have cultivated her. After all, why cut off one's nose to spite one's face?'

'That's what I say. Do you have grandparents, darling?'

'No.'

'But you have family in England, don't you?'

'Yes. I have parents in London and relatives in Devonshire.'

'You feel no desire to visit them?'

'Yes of course I do. I shall probably spend Christmas with them.'

Her eyes met Ariadne's defiantly. She had had no intention of spending Christmas in England until Nigel had dropped his bombshell. Now her expression was coldly determined, and Ariadne said 'I think that's a splendid idea, Celia, and your daughter will be thrilled to have you with her for Christmas.'

'You didn't tell me about your daughter, Celia,' Nigel said softly. 'I take it she's with relatives?'

'Yes, for her education.'

'And how old is your daughter?'

'She's twelve.'

'Such a disturbing age,' he murmured. 'I remember when I was twelve. I was a tearaway my family despaired of and they've gone on despairing of me. My dear old granny never has, hence my resolve to visit her.'

The evening as far as Celia was concerned was not a success. She felt furious with Nigel and only a little less so with Ariadne. At the same time she was grateful to her for bringing up

127

Nigel's visit to his grandmother. Would he have told her, and when would he have told her, she wondered.

Later in the evening she feigned a sick headache and asked Nigel to take her home.

'Is there anything I can get you?' he asked attentively, but she shook her head, saying, 'It's nothing, Nigel. The music is too loud, and it's so stuffy in there. It will be better in the morning.'

Ariadne watched them leave. Only a little later she was sitting with other people on the balcony when she recognised Nigel's car sweeping down the road on his way back from Celia's flat. Obviously Celia had parted with him on her doorstep.

For several minutes Celia sat in the darkness of her living room staring down at her hands clenched on her knees. She was hurt and angry; she was losing Gordon and Nigel was going away. Suppose he didn't come back? He'd been to Kenya before, many times. It could be months, years before he decided to come back, and he would know other women in England.

She knew what she had to do.

Her parents would probably be in bed but the telephone call wouldn't wait. If she wanted to go to England arrangements needed to be made quickly. The ringing tone on the telephone seemed to go on and on until finally her father's sleepy voice answered her. More brightly than she felt she called out, 'Father, it's me, Celia, I'm so sorry to be calling so late, darling.'

Her father's voice changed from weariness to curtness. 'Why couldn't you phone in the morning? It's very late.'

'I know, darling, but I've only just decided. I want to come home for Christmas I do hope it will be convenient for you and mother to have me.'

'I don't know. I'll get your mother, hold on.'

Her mother's voice was equally petulant.

'Why so late, Celia?' she asked.

'Mother, I want to come home for Christmas, is that convenient?'

'You and Gordon you mean?'

'No mother, just me.'

'Well, I'm not sure dear. Christmas is almost here and we've made plans for several functions. You must realise, dear, that we can't get extra tickets and such like at the last minute.'

'Well of course not, Mother, I won't interfere with anything you're doing.'

'What about Rosemary, will she be joining you here?'

'No. I'll spend a few days with you and I'll telephone Beatrice to see if it's convenient for me to go there.'

'Well, I wouldn't telephone her now.'

'No, tomorrow.'

'I can't think Beatrice and Cedric are going to be too pleased. The boys will be home, probably with girlfriends, and Rosemary too will be home. If it's not convenient then I suppose you'll have to bring her here.'

'Mother, surely they'll understand that I want to see Rosemary and you and Father. I want to see Beatrice too. I'm not bothered about the others, I hardly know them.'

'Well, dear, if you've made up your mind, when shall we expect you?'

'I'll make all the arrangements tomorrow and I'll let you know.'

'Why isn't Gordon coming? Surely he must get time off for Christmas.'

'I'll tell you all about everything when I see you, Mother. Give Daddy my love; tell him I'll see him soon.'

She didn't want to spend time at Dene Hollow but Devonshire and Dorset were close, if Nigel knew she was living conveniently close surely he would want to see her.

Beatrice's surprise was as great as Celia's parents'. She could do no other than say Celia would be welcome to stay, but she also explained that the boys would be home and Jerome and Jeffrey had girlfriends they would wish to invite.

'Darling Beatrice, I'll be able to help with preparations and it will so wonderful to see Rosemary. Has she settled down at Chevington?'

'Yes, her school reports are very good and she's made friends.'

'I'm so glad. I suppose she's changed out of all recognition.'

'She's growing up, Celia. She's tall, she still has braces on her teeth and the boys will still be calling her Rosie. You won't change that.'

Beatrice had little faith that Celia would make an appearance. She had made no mention of Gordon, and Cedric was furious.

'She evidently thinks she can just appear in our lives without a by your leave. The boys will be home, Jerome has stated that he intends to announce his engagement and that girl Jeffrey's got will be invited. Celia we can do without.'

Beatrice kept her own council but she thought about Rosie. She was happy at Chevington with her friends. She would be looking forward to spending Christmas at Dene Hollow, but would the advent of her mother after all these years be trouble free?

Rosie never mentioned her mother in her letters or when she came to the house on school breaks. Perhaps wisely, Beatrice decided that there was time enough to tell her when she arrived back at Dene Hollow for Christmas.

There had to be some reason why Celia had suddenly elected to visit, and Celia had always planned her life around herself, never to the advantage of others.

Ariadne too decided to question Celia's sudden desire to see England, her parents and her daughter, but all Celia said was that thanks to Gordon's demanding job she'd neglected Rosemary dreadfully and she had to make amends. That she had to make amends during Nigel's visit to England brought a cynical smile to Ariadne's lips.

Nigel had taken to calling at their house to see Johnny. The two men had little in common. Nigel's sophisticated charm was lost on Johnny's down-to-earth bluntness, and Ariadne rapidly became aware that it was she whom Nigel really came to see. He was wanting to know about Celia, her family in England, her background and her position with Gordon. Amused, Ariadne became equally devious.

She knew little about Celia's background except that she'd been cosseted by middle-class parents and that she was an only child. She'd married a serving officer who had lost his life in Ireland and she'd married Gordon and come out to Kenya. Celia had told her little about her one daughter, but she managed to paint a reasonably glowing picture of Celia's affluent family background to encourage Nigel to find out more.

Ariadne knew something about men like Nigel Boyd. Along the way a handful of men like him had pursued her, for her beauty and her entertainment value. For Ariadne they had been stepping stones towards respectability; for them she had been an amusing girl who was good for sex and amusement.

When Nigel Boyd married, if he married, it would be to an upper-crust girl with money. She needn't be beautiful, he needn't be in love with her or she with him, but that was the only way he could appease a family already at variance with his way of life.

Celia was in love with him; Ariadne believed him to be attracted to Celia; but it wouldn't be enough.

She was able to inform Nigel that Celia had booked her flight to London, the day and the time of her flight, and when Celia told him of her arrangements he merely said, 'What a coincidence, darling. I'm booked on the same flight. Suppose we spend a few days in London together?'

'I shall be going to my parents in Richmond,' she'd said flatly.

'Well of course, dear, and after a few days in London I'll be driving down to Dorset. How long do you propose to stay in England?'

'I'm not sure.'

'Oh well. Let us have our few days in London then I'll drive you down to Devonshire.'

'What about my parents?'

'Can't you go there on your way home? I don't suppose your mother'll mind much. I'm sure she has made her plans for Christmas.'

Celia couldn't deny the logic of his argument; indeed hadn't her mother said as much? And she wanted those few days in London with Nigel and the journey to Dene Hollow afterwards.

The outcome was that she informed her parents she would be with them after Christmas and was driving straight down to Dene Hollow to be with Rosemary.

When she told Ariadne they would be travelling to England together Ariadne had great difficulty in keeping her cynical amusement to herself.

To Celia those few days in London were an enchantment. Handsome and debonair, Nigel was the perfect escort to the theatre, the ideal dancing partner, the passionate lover, and she wished they could have stayed on in London. Why did either of them have to leave when life was so wonderful? Dene Hollow would be an anti-climax to what she had now, and Nigel would find his grandmother little substitute for what he found with her.

Nigel, on the other hand, was needing to find some money. Celia asked for the best and he was content to give it to her, but there had to be a

133

reckoning. Theatre tickets, nightclubs and the hotel itself were expensive, and he had barely enough to hire the car that was to take them to the south coast.

On their last night in London Celia presented him with a pair of gold cufflinks, beautifully engraved and obviously expensive, and he admitted with a wry smile, 'Darling, I haven't got you anything yet. It's two days off Christmas; I thought I'd surprise you when next we meet.'

'When will that be, Nigel? We've made no plans to see each other when we leave here.'

'Oh but we will, darling. I'll telephone you, Dorset's only a drive away. Besides, I'd like to meet your daughter.'

After that he insisted that she gave him instructions on how to find Dene Hollow, and Celia was left agonising over how Beatrice and the rest of them would view Nigel if and when he turned up.

She didn't worry about it for long. She loved him and she wanted him. It was entirely her affair, nothing whatsoever to do with them, and she had little doubt that Nigel would charm Rosemary and Beatrice as he charmed everybody else. Her parents too would not be proof against him. Wasn't he the sort of man her mother had always admired and hoped she'd marry?

Beatrice sat in the living room at Dene Hollow, listening to the sounds of laughter and activity emanating from the hall where Rosie and the two younger boys were decorating the Christmas tree. It was a large Norwegian spruce brought in that morning, and she had already proclaimed her view that something considerably smaller should have been chosen.

The boys thought it was perfect, and from the sounds of their laughter they were having great difficulty in reaching its topmost branches.

When she told Rosie that her mother was on the way from Kenya she had been faced with her straight blue stare and the feeling that she didn't much care either way.

Promises were made to be broken, and there had already been too many broken promises. Rosie was wishing her mother wasn't coming. After all she was a stranger now and she would interfere with the Christmas festivities she had been looking forward to for so long. Jerome would be here with his fiancée and Jeffrey with the girl his father could barely be polite to. Steven Chaytor was coming, possibly for the last time, since Steven was going to work in South Africa, and Steven was bringing a girl with him.

When Jerome had imparted this news to them she hadn't missed the devilment in his dark eyes. He still thought she had a crush on Steven, and disdaining his amusement, she had turned haughtily away and Jerome had merely dissolved into laughter.

They all seemed so grown up now, even David and Noel. Twelve was a ridiculous age to be, neither one thing nor the other, and she hated the braces on her teeth and a figure that had no shape. When she looked at the girls her cousins brought home with their pretty made-up faces and their firm young busts and rounded behinds,

135

she felt she could cry. She'd never look like them, she'd always be flat-chested and gauche.

When the rest of them learned that her mother was coming at last the response had been negligible. Only Noel, who could never keep his thoughts to himself, had said, 'About time too. I'll bet you've forgotten what she looks like.'

Rosie had not forgotten. But would her mother still look like the beautiful woman she remembered with her attire and the large becoming hat decorated with flowers?

Beatrice, for her part, tried to encourage her to look forward to her mother's visit.

'It will be wonderful for you, dear, to have your mother here for Christmas. She'll be so surprised to find four young men here instead of four young boys, and a daughter growing up so beautifully.'

Rosie had looked at her with some impatience. 'I'm not beautiful, Aunt Beatrice, I'm plain. I've got braces on my teeth, my hair's a mess and I've got no shape. My mother'll think I'm awful.'

'You're twelve years old, Rosie, and one day it's all going to change. Your hair is a lovely colour and it frames a very pretty face. The braces will go and your shape will appear. Have a little patience, dear.'

When Celia appeared two weeks before Christmas Rosie watched Beatrice greeting her on the front steps. She had stepped out of a large soft-topped tourer and a tall man had got out of the front seat and was helping her with her luggage. There was plenty of it. She could see that the woman embracing Aunt Beatrice was tall and slender. She was fashionably dressed and very elegant, and as Celia looked towards the window Rosie could see that her mother was beautiful, more beautiful than any of those silly giggling girls her cousins brought home. She had poise, an indefinable polish that perhaps only the years could bring. And then her mother was looking at her from across the room, eventually coming towards her with hands outstretched.

Celia would not believe that the young girl looking at her solemnly out of doubtful blue eyes could be the child she'd parted with after her wedding years before; this tall, gawky, solemn child with braces on her teeth and the almost stern gaze of a hostile antagonist.

'Darling, how wonderful to see you at last,' she enthused. 'And you're so grown up and tall. I always imagined you to be small and dainty.'

'I'm twelve,' Rosie said firmly. 'I expect I'll be taller yet.'

Celia smiled. 'Yes of course you will. We'll have to have long walks so that we can catch up with all we've missed.'

The tall man had followed Celia into the room, and she held out her hand to him, saying. 'This is Rosemary, Nigel. She's grown up so very tall, and the poor darling is having to wear braces on her teeth.'

Nigel stepped forward and smiled down at Rosie. His smile was attractive enough to charm her into a smile, and he said gallantly, 'I had braces on my teeth and the wretched things caused me all sorts of embarrassment. Just take a look at my teeth now: they're perfect and yours will be too.'

Indeed his teeth were perfect, and Beatrice and Celia were smiling. Rosie was not to know it then, but Nigel would always have the power to diffuse an atmosphere of uncertainty. It was a charm that could conquer a roomful of sceptics, and one she would learn to distrust.

Chapter Ten

The advent of Rosie's mother was met with a mixed reception from both the occupants and the visitors. Cedric was courteous but distant, Jerome faintly arrogant and inclined to show off, Jeffrey rather shy and uncertain. David liked her; he thought she was beautiful and interesting, while Noel merely greeted her briefly and reserved his judgment.

Natalie Shaw was unprepared for a visitor of Celia's calibre. For months she had lorded it over Jeffrey's timid girlfriend, with her superior education, her penchant for fashionable clothes and Jerome's obvious devotion. Now here was this sophisticated, travelled woman who treated Jerome's efforts to show off with total indifference.

Steven Chaytor arrived in the company of a pretty, dark-haired girl he introduced as Mary Raynor, and it didn't take Celia long to establish that Rosie was disconcerted by her visit. In Mary's company she was quiet and shy, but her eyes followed Steven with a pained awareness.

Seeing Celia watching her daughter's reaction, Jerome was quick to say, 'Poor Rosie, she's had a crush on Steven for years. She wasn't looking forward to him bringing a girl here.'

Celia smiled. 'Girls do have crushes on boys at that age, Jerome. I'm sure Natalie has one on you.'

'We happen to be engaged,' he snapped.

'Yes, of course. I hope she doesn't change her mind. Girls do that too, Jerome.'

Celia was anxiously asking herself how long she needed to remain in Devonshire. She had not heard from Nigel since he drove her down, and she was bored. Rosemary was not at all how she imagined she would be, and although she found Beatrice sweet as always she could have done without the others.

Steven Chaytor she liked. He was aware that Rosemary liked him, more than liked him and he was kind to her, but she considered Jerome to be insufferable and his fiancée little better.

She had been at Dene Hollow almost two weeks when Nigel telephoned her, his voice light and airy, the low charm of it making her heart flutter foolishly.

'Celia darling, how are you? I thought I'd let you settle in before I phoned you.'

'I'm fine, Nigel. It's nice to be with the family and Rosemary.'

'Well, of course it is. Fancy a drive out somewhere? I'm getting a bit sick of listening to Granny all day and every day.'

'That would be lovely. When?'

'How about tomorrow? I'll pick you up around eleven, we could drive along the coast. Bring Rosemary – she'd enjoy it.'

'Well I'm not sure, she seems happy enough with her cousin Noel.'

'She'll have her cousin Noel when you've gone back to Kenya.'

'Well, I'll ask her if she'd like to come, Nigel.'

'Do that, darling. See you in the morning.'

From across the room Beatrice was looking at her expectantly and she said quickly, 'It was Nigel. He wants to invite Rosemary and me out tomorrow. I don't think he's finding life with his grandmother very entertaining.'

'I'm sure Rosie would enjoy it, Celia.'

'I haven't seen her all morning, do you know where she is?'

'She was walking on the cliff with Steven the last time I saw her.'

'And where is his girlfriend?'

'She's gone into Torquay with Natalie, looking for Christmas presents, I expect.'

'Well, I'll ask her when she comes in. I'm sure it's far too cold to be walking on the cliff top today. The wind is blowing and the sea is churning up.'

Oblivious to the wind and the boiling sea, Rosie was happy strolling along the cliff top with Steven. Even when she was much younger he had always been able to come down to her level. Now she felt he treated her as a grown up.

'Jerome says you'll be going to work abroad, Steven. Does that mean you won't be coming here again?'

'Perhaps not for a very long time. I'm going to South Africa, Rosie.'

'I thought your parents lived in Malaysia?'

'They do, so when I get leave I'll have to go out there to see them. Anyway, things here will be changing too. Jerome will probably marry Natalie, and you'll be away at school. This isn't your home, Rosie; one day you'll be in Kenya with your mother.'

'That's in Africa too.'

'I know. I could visit you one day.'

'Oh yes. That would be great. Will Mary be with you?'

He looked down at her with a gentle smile. 'I've known Mary a great many years. Her parents too are in Malaysia so you might really say we grew up together. Don't you like her?'

'Oh yes, she's very nice. What does she do, for a job I mean?'

'She's working as a laboratory assistant in a large hospital.'

'In England?'

'At the moment, yes. What do you want to do when you leave school?'

'I haven't decided yet.'

'I think that one day your Aunt Beatrice is going to want her own home. She's been an absolute brick to look after all you lot. I'm sure she'll appreciate a life of her own.'

'I never thought about it like that.'

'I really think you will need to in the not too distant future.'

'But who will look after Uncle Cedric? She does so much for him and he depends on her.'

'I know, but perhaps when Jerome marries things will sort themselves out. I think we should walk back now, Rosie, it's starting to rain.'

She looked up at the storm clouds gathering over the grey sea and agreed.

Nigel called for them rather earlier than expected and Celia called out to Rosie to hurry. While she shrugged into her dark blue winter coat Noel eyed her with a sour expression.

'I don't know why you're going with them,' he said. 'You won't enjoy it.'

'Why not?'

'Well, they'll want to be off on their own and you'll feel out of it. We could have gone to see a film in Torquay.'

'Really, Noel,' Aunt Beatrice remonstrated. 'Rosie should go with her mother; after all they haven't seen all that much of each other over the years. They should be allowed to make the most of it.'

'That's what I mean,' Noel snapped.

'I suppose if I asked you could come with us,' Rosie ventured.

'Not very likely. I don't want to go with you, it's not my scene.'

As the day progressed Rosie was made to feel that it wasn't her scene either. She sat in the back seat of the car listening to their conversation. It had started to rain and she was hating the large impersonal feel of the car, with the sound of its engine and the hypnotic effect of the windscreen wipers dulling her senses.

Nigel elected to drive into the grounds of a

large hotel on the coast, saying, 'We'll have lunch here. I know this place, it has a good reputation.'

As they took their places in the restaurant he fixed Rosie with a bright smile. 'Sorry it's turned out to be such a rotten day, Rosemary; perhaps it'll improve.' Then turning to Celia he said, 'Are you enjoying your stay here, darling?'

'Well yes, are you?'

'Hardly. My grandmother hasn't much to say for herself and it was a relief to get out.'

It wasn't true. Nigel's grandmother was eighty-five years old but a very wide-awake and dominant eighty-five. She'd been quick to ask questions about his companion on the journey, who she was staying with, where exactly did the people live and how serious was it?

Nigel had told her what he thought she should know. That Celia was married to a vet, but he made no mention that divorce was in the offing.

'Are you a friend of her husband's?' she'd asked.

'Not really. They live their separate lives, he with his animals, Celia with the club crowd.'

'And which crowd are you in?'

'Darling, I'm not in any crowd. I go to the club, I have a multitude of people I know there, none of them particularly close, but I pass time there, and Celia is probably the prettiest woman on the scene.'

'So it isn't serious?'

'Granny, how can it be? You know the family, staunch Roman Catholic Irish, and even though they wouldn't be surprised at anything I do, I do have to maintain some standard of respectability,

143

whatever constitutes respectability in their eyes.'

'You lost that years ago.'

'I know, but I can't cut myself off entirely.'

'I rather think they might have cut you off, Nigel.'

'But you haven't, Grandmother. I'd like to think you still care what happens to me.'

'If you're thinking about my money, Nigel, yes. I never got on with your father. I never wanted your mother to marry him.'

Pacified, he had smiled across the table at her.

'You don't feel like advancing me a little bit of it now, do you, darling? I'm taking Celia and her daughter out in the morning and Christmas is the very devil for running away with whatever funds I'd accumulated.'

Celia was asking questions about his grandmother. Where she lived, if she knew he had invited her out; that it would be nice to meet her.

'I don't think you'd enjoy that at all, darling. She never goes anywhere; she just rattles around in that stately pile she calls home.'

'She has servants, of course.'

'Loads of them. They fetch and carry for her, cosset her in some degree of luxury and she's sleeping her life away.'

'Then you don't want me to meet her?'

'I don't want you to be bored with her, darling. I've told her about you; I doubt if she took it in.'

Lunch, as Nigel had predicted, was an excellent meal, and afterwards Nigel suggested to Rosemary that she might like to wander around the indoor pool and take a look in the hotel library. He and her mother would be waiting for her in

144

the lounge.

Watching her saunter across the room, Celia said wistfully, 'I did so want her to be pretty. She was such a beautiful little girl when last I saw her, and now she's so terribly gawky and those horrible braces don't help.'

'Isn't she supposed to be at an awkward age? That's what they used to say about my sisters. They were all golden curls and dimples, then suddenly they were tall with scraped-back hair, pimples and dental problems.'

'What are they like now?'

'Beautiful. Maeve has mahogany-coloured hair and green eyes and she's already broken a few hearts and a few marriages. Clodagh is dark and sultry. Last year she married a rich American, twice divorced, and my parents have written her off.'

'Is that what they would do to you if you married a divorced woman?'

'Well, I rather think they did that years ago.'

'For what reason?'

He laughed, his eyes filled with devilment. 'Money, my dear, and women, before I was old enough to sort the wheat from the chaff.'

She looked through the window where the gardens sloped down to the cliff top and the churning sea boiled and seethed under leaden skies, and Nigel was aware where her thoughts lay. She would be a divorced woman, from a decent but middle-class background. His family would deem her unacceptable; she didn't have enough money to compensate for the other things she was lacking.

With a smile he covered her hand with his. 'Why are we talking about my family, Celia? I don't give a toss what they think about me. I haven't seen them for years. I certainly won't allow them to manage my life now.'

She smiled tremulously.

'I've made so many mistakes, Nigel. I should never have married Alan, we were never suited, and Gordon too was a mistake. They were both nice, decent men, but we were simply not right for each other.'

'A third mistake would be catastrophic, Celia.'

'I know. I don't even know what to do about Rosemary. Will she want to be with me one day, will I want to be with her?'

'Don't you know?'

'No. When I see her at Dene Hollow with her cousins, when I saw her strolling on the cliffs with Steve Chaytor yesterday, I felt like an interloper. Those are the people she loves, the people she wants to be with.'

At that moment Nigel was seeing himself: spoilt, selfish, mercurial. Celia had always put herself and her desires before anything else in exactly the same way that he'd behaved, and as with him there had always been somebody there to pick up the pieces so that they could move on.

Celia was pinning all her future hopes on him and she might just as well hitch her future to a balloon. When he married, if he married, it would have to be for money, nor did he want somebody else's daughter to support. He loved Celia, as much as he was capable of loving anybody, but it wouldn't be enough.

They looked across the room to where Rosie stood, staring through the window, and for the first time he saw the exquisite bone structure that would shape the beauty of a face that now seemed so ordinary. Her mother wouldn't see it because she didn't want to see it, but one day, one day.

When they parted that evening, Celia felt discontented with her day. She wanted Nigel to herself, together like they'd been in Nairobi. Rosie was an intrusion, and on parting with him she said, 'I should go up to London after Christmas to be with my parents. Shall I see you there?'

'I'm not sure, darling. I play it my grandmother's way; I see her so seldom.'

'I'm in that position myself but I'd rather be with you.'

'I know, I'd rather be with you, but my grandmother is old and alone.' He did not say that it was his grandmother he would rely on for funds in the years ahead.

'You'll let me know when you intend to leave for London?' he asked.

'Yes, of course. Does that mean I shan't be seeing you here again?'

'Darling, I'm not sure. I do hope so, but I can't be sure at this moment.'

She had to be content with that. Rosie was waiting for her at the top of the steps and from the living room Noel stood watching. Why was she hanging about waiting for her mother, why didn't she come inside? He didn't like Celia, his memories were all of his cousin crying her eyes out over silly dolls and broken promises. In his boy's heart there were only two colours: black and white.

Beatrice came to stand beside him. 'Oh they're back then,' she commented. 'It looks awfully grey out there. Do go into the kitchen, dear, and ask Betty to bring tea.'

When he stood there still frowning she said gently, 'Noel, this is Rosie's mother. If it was your mother you'd feel exactly as she does.'

'I can't remember my mother very well.'

'No, well that's not surprising. You were only six when she died.'

'Well, Rosie's mother didn't die, she just left her alone for years. Now she's here and Rosie's forgotten me to be with her.'

'Of course she hasn't forgotten you. Celia will be leaving soon and Rosie will still be here.'

'Well, she'll be lucky if she expects me to wait around for her.'

Beatrice sighed. How many years would there still be to handle this disjointed family? A brother who was either tetchy or absorbed with his own thoughts and four boys who had grown up too fast. Jerome was now engaged but there were undercurrents between his fiancée and his father. Jeffrey was hardly ever in the house but elected to spend his time browsing through the town's library in the day time and most evenings at his girlfriend's house.

Connie was overwhelmed by Dene Hollow and its occupants, and Jeffrey seemed to be finding some sort of rapport with the members of her large family on the council estate on which she lived. In the evenings they went to the cinema or the dance halls in Dawlish or Torquay, and Cedric grumbled that he spent too little time studying and too much money on trivialities.

David was the cheerful one. David had never looked too deeply into anything; superficialities were enough for him. He didn't see if his younger brother was moody and sulked; he was oblivious to Jerome's pomposity and he found Connie's down-to-earth approach to life much to his liking.

Rosie's mother he could be polite to without caring about her either one way or another, and when Noel sulked and grumbled about her he merely laughed, saying, 'She's all right, Noel. What's it matter that she's never been here before? She's here now.'

One day, Beatrice told herself, I'm going to leave them to it. I'll get a little house with a small garden and move in with my dog and cat. No more thinking about school holidays and school uniforms, no more trauma about visitors and girlfriends who might or might not be suitable and no more having to listen to Cedric going on and on about business affairs, and sons who were unlikely to follow in his footsteps.

One day too Rosie would probably go out to be with her mother; although Celia had said nothing about her husband, which Beatrice found rather disturbing and she was reluctant to ask questions.

She had Christmas Day to think about. So much food to prepare, so many people to cater for and she'd get little help from Natalie, who would arrive when everything was ready or

149

Connie, who was undecided whether she wanted to be there at all. Cedric insisted that all the boys should be there with or without their girlfriends, and of course there were Steven and Mary.

Mary was a nice quiet sort of girl who had already asked if she could do anything to help, unlike Celia, who said, 'I really don't know why we make such a fuss at Christmas. We eat far too much and it's so bad for one's figure.'

On Christmas morning she elected to go to church and take Rosie with her and Cedric shut himself away in his study and asked them to inform him when the meal was ready.

Beatrice had decided that they would eat a buffet lunch and dine properly in the evening. Steven and Mary, as well as the two younger boys, fetched and carried for her, and when they arrived back from church Rosie helped, but Celia swept upstairs saying she had a sick headache and didn't want anything. She'd take a nap, that way she hoped to be better for the evening's celebrations.

Noel, catching Rosie's eye, said, 'I didn't think we'd get any help out of her. She probably wishes she hadn't come.'

It was a sentiment Celia would have agreed with. She hadn't heard from Nigel for three days and she had already decided she would go up to London before the New Year without telling him. If he rang up he would find her gone.

She supposed she would have to take Rosemary with her, but when she had mentioned it her daughter's reply had not been enthusiastic. Rosie was thinking about her grandfather's absorption

150

in his foreign stamps and her grandmother's bridge parties with a brigade of blue-rinsed ladies who had smiled and chatted before they became engrossed in their game and she was relegated to some other room to read.

The buffet meal progressed happily without Celia, Natalie or Connie, and Cedric asked, 'I suppose we can expect them this evening. What about Natalie, Jerome?'

'Oh yes, Father, she'll be here later.'

'And the other one?' his father asked pointedly, looking at Jeffrey.

'I've invited her, Father. I'll pick her up this afternoon.'

'So, what time are we dining, Beatrice?'

'I thought eight o'clock, if everybody else agrees.

Nobody disagreed so Cedric said, 'I thought I'd stroll over to see Mr Claremont; he'll be expecting me on Christmas Day. If you want any help there are enough of you. Get Celia to help. I haven't seen much evidence of help from that quarter.'

Chapter Eleven

Thanks to Rosie and the two younger boys the house looked bright and festive. The Christmas tree stood in the hall, shedding its lights into the darkest corner, while in the grates log fires had been lit; and when they trooped in the dining room just after eight o'clock they were faced with a table sparkling with glass and silver, and where a bowl containing bright red holly berries took pride of place.

As they took their places at the table Beatrice looked round her with some relief. Celia had come down to dinner after all the rest of them had gathered there, looking beautiful in dark crimson velvet, her blond hair immaculately dressed, wearing diamond earrings and a matching necklace round her throat. Beatrice reflected that her husband must be a generous man, as she had no recollection of her owning such jewellery when she was married to her brother.

Natalie sat between Cedric and Jerome. She was wearing a cornflower blue dress and was busily showing everybody the gold wristlet watch Jerome had bought her for Christmas. It was an expensive gift, and Cedric frowned. The boy didn't seem to care how much he spent on this girl; her engagement ring had cost a small fortune.

Connie was wearing a black skirt and scarlet blouse. Her hair was bleached and brittle, her pretty face had too much make-up, as usual. She viewed Natalie's watch with some envy and when Natalie asked what Jeffrey had given her she mumbled that he'd bought her a very large box of chocolates and the enamelled bracelet she was wearing. Natalie had smiled sweetly but given the bracelet a cursory glance.

Noel and Rosie were hardly on speaking terms, Noel's fault of course, and Rosie sat next to Steven with Mary on his other side. He gave his full attention to both girls and Celia, watching, wished Rosie wasn't quite so obvious in her adoration of a young man whose attentions were quite evidently elsewhere.

Celia was angry because it was Christmas Day and Nigel hadn't telephoned. Before dinner her anger had prompted her to telephone her parents in London to inform them that she would be arriving to see them before the New Year, a decision that sent her parents into some disarray. They had plans for New Year's Eve and were unsure if they could include their daughter.

'Will Rosemary be coming with you?' her mother had asked.

'I'm not sure, Mother, but don't worry, we can sort things out,' she'd replied and her parents had to be satisfied with that.

Celia decided she would speak to her daughter later in the evening. If Nigel tried to telephone her after Christmas he would be too late.

They were at the end of their meal when they heard the telephone ringing in the hall and David jumped up to answer it, returning seconds later and saying with a smile, 'It's for you Aunt Celia, a Mr Boyd.'

Unhurriedly, Celia smiled round the table and sauntered out of the room to answer it.

Nigel's voice was cajoling.

'Merry Christmas, darling. I'm sorry I haven't rung earlier but it's been a bit chaotic here, visitors to see Granny and she's not too well.'

'I'm sorry Nigel, nothing serious, I hope?'

'Well, one hopes not. Enjoyed your Christmas Day?'

'All the family are here including the girlfriends and a couple of visitors.'

'What sort of presents did you get?'

'Oh the usual. Chocolates, scarves and handkerchiefs, nothing exciting.'

'And from Rosemary? I don't suppose the kid's got much money to spend on luxuries.'

'No, she hasn't. I got a leather diary and a pen, both very nice.'

'I'll give you my present when I see you.'

'I'm not sure when that will be, Nigel. I'm going up to London before the New Year, I've already telephoned my parents.'

'Didn't it occur to you to wait until we met, darling?'

'Nigel, it is now nearly ten o'clock on Christmas Day and I hadn't heard from you. I couldn't let my parents wait any longer.'

'I'm sorry, darling. We're not having much joy with our visit to the folks, are we? I'll sort things out with Granny and get up to London as soon as I can. I have your parents' telephone number, I'll be in touch as soon as I arrive.'

'Where will you stay in London?'

'I'm not sure. I've got a pal who's a member of an officers' club; perhaps he'll fix something up for me.'

'I'll see you then, Nigel. Happy Christmas, darling.'

She put the receiver down with an absent-minded smile. She wanted to trust him, she wanted him to love her, but why were those warning bells ringing in her head? Gordon had warned her, Ariadne had warned her, and Nigel's

154

charm was such an elusive thing.

She returned to her place at the dinner table but only Noel's unfriendly eyes met hers. The rest of them were engrossed in their own affairs.

Listening to them, Cedric's expression was dour. He hoped Jerome would concentrate on his career and Jeffrey would put his back into his studies. As yet the two younger boys were not a problem. David was clever, Noel was adequate; time enough to worry about them when they got their degrees.

Rosie and Noel were ignoring each other and Steven was listening to Mary, who was beginning to resent the attention he was giving to the young girl sitting next to him.

So many undercurrents, Beatrice thought. Who would think that a family on Christmas Day could find so many things to divide them and so few things to unite them. Would there ever be a time when they could all forget their differences enough to concentrate on the good things they had in life? How long before she could start looking for her dream cottage? Nothing pretentious, but somewhere where she could make her own decisions without asking four or five other people where they were likely to be.

Natalie and Jerome were engaged, but Jerome's father would be furious if he contemplated marriage before he had properly settled in at the firm. His father was constantly telling him that accountancy had to be worked at, clients had to be satisfied with what they were getting and although they were well established in the town, behind them were a host of others waiting to step into their shoes.

Natalie, on the other hand, would not be prepared to wait too long. She was constantly informing Jerome of this friend and that who was getting married, and the implication was clear.

Beatrice liked Connie. She was inoffensive and big-hearted; she was also motherless, the eldest of a very large family with a father who spent too much time in his local and was content to let Connie shoulder the burden.

Cedric didn't approve, he thought his second son deserved somebody better, and Connie's father didn't approve because he thought she was dating a boy out of her class and one who would ditch her when something better appeared.

Then there was Rosie. Rosie was at that awkward age when she thought she was in love with Steven, she was unsure of her mother or where her future would lead her, and Celia was engrossed with Celia and only with Celia.

In the living room the three couples sat together while Noel and David disappeared. Rosie was chatting to her mother and Celia was asking, 'Do you want to come up to London with me, Rosemary? I shan't be coming back here so you will have to come back on your own.'

'I did that before, Mother, it was no problem.'

'But do you want to come?'

'I'm not sure.'

'You do realise it may be some time before we meet again?'

'Yes, Mother.'

'Then why aren't you sure?'

'Well, there's school starting early in the New

Year, and Grandma is always so busy with her bridge friends and Grandpa with his foreign stamps. I felt I was butting in with whatever they were doing.'

Celia sighed. She knew the feeling well; at the same time she didn't want Cedric and Beatrice blaming her for not taking Rosemary with her. If somebody had asked her what she wanted she could only have said that she wanted to go back to Nairobi with Nigel.

Rosie was looking at her anxiously.

'If I don't go to London with you, Mother, perhaps one day I can come out to Kenya?'

It was a sentiment that took care of the problems of the moment. 'Why yes, darling,' Celia said with a bright smile. 'Of course you can come out to Kenya, and I'll give you such a wonderful time. Shall we leave it at that? I'll go up to London, I shan't enjoy it, and I hate leaving you so soon, but they are expecting me. You and I will just look forward to the time when we can be together without having to worry about anyone else.'

Rosie too was relieved. She would go back to the joys that life at Dene Hollow afforded her. She would make friends with Noel, and there was Steven.

She looked across the room to where the three couples were sitting together chatting amiably. Jerome as usual was doing most of the talking and Natalie was gazing up at him with her customary admiration. Mary was sitting on the rug at Steven's feet, leaning against his knees, and occasionally they smiled at each other.

157

At those moments the pain was so intense Rosie could have cried out with the misery of it.

It was Connie who jumped to her feet saying, 'I think we should go now, Jeffrey, I told my dad I wouldn't be late.'

Celia caught the early morning train to London having said her farewells to her daughter and the rest of them the night before. She thought that most of them were glad that she was leaving and she herself had few regrets. Of course there was Rosemary.

They had embraced in Rosemary's bedroom and she had looked into her daughter's blue eyes and found herself regretting the obvious ordinariness of her face. All she saw were the braces on her teeth and the fine blond hair caught back from her face with a series of enamel clips.

The other girls had been pretty, even Connie, in spite of her too colourful clothes and bleached hair. She was sure that when Steven Chaytor looked at Rosemary he would feel a certain pity for a girl who thought too much of him, and would find Mary considerably more attractive.

She was glad that Nigel hadn't telephoned her again; it had caused too much speculation on the part of the others, and he had promised faithfully to get in touch as soon as he arrived in London. She had already decided she would not interfere with any activities her parents were embarked on. That would give her time to stay at home and wait for the telephone call that would surely come.

It was a grey miserable afternoon when the taxi pulled up outside her parents' front door, but she was surprised when it was immediately opened and her father rushed out on to the drive to come hurrying towards the gate, his expression apprehensive. Then her mother appeared, obviously distraught.

Her father paid the taxi-driver, and with his arms around her he shepherded Celia towards the front door, where her mother enveloped her in a tight embrace. Celia stared at them curiously; they were not usually so demonstrative. But her father was saying, 'Oh you poor girl, you must be devastated.'

Celia stared at him, and after a few shocked moments he said, 'You don't know, do you?'

'Know what, Daddy?'

He reached out to a side table and produced a newspaper, which he thrust into her hands.

The headlines leapt out at her: two Englishmen and four natives killed in an ambush in Kenya while they were apprehending ivory poachers. One of them was Gordon.

Weakly she sank down on the nearest chair and stared at her parents with wide-eyed incredulity.

'Nobody let you know?' her mother was asking in some amazement.

'Only Gordon knew where I was, Mother. Nobody else knew where I was staying in England.'

'Oh this is awful. What are you to do? You'll have to go back there.'

'Yes, I know.'

'Why didn't Gordon come with you?'

'He was too busy, Mother.'

She thought about Ariadne. Ariadne knew that

she was with her daughter but she hadn't told her where, nor did she know how far Gordon had progressed with his wish for a divorce. Nigel would have seen the newspaper by now. Would he telephone; would he come up to London?

'Well, you'd better come into the living room, darling, and I'll make a cup of tea. Are you very hungry?'

'No, Mother. I had something on the train.'

How awful to be thinking about tea and food, she thought. She went to sit near the fire and opened the newspaper. There was a full account of Gordon's prowess as a vet, his popularity in the region, the many friends who were crushed by his death, but there was no mention of his wife. His picture stared up at her from the page, the picture of a smiling, handsome young man who had been kind and caring and whom she had never deserved.

Her father was looking at her sorrowfully. 'What are you going to do, dear?' he asked.

'I've got to go back there, Daddy. I'll telephone the airline and find out how soon I can book a flight.'

'I'll ask the doctor to call round to give you some sedatives. You need a good night's sleep before you fly out there,' her mother said firmly. But Celia said quickly, 'Mother, I don't want sedatives. I want to know what I'm doing. If possible, I want to go out there tomorrow.'

Her mother looked at her sorrowfully, saying, 'I'll make the tea anyway.'

They could hear the telephone shrilling in the hall and her father said, 'It's probably some of

160

our friends; they'll have read about this.'

Seconds later, he came to tell her that the call was for her, and in spite of her anxieties her heart lifted to hear Nigel's voice saying, 'You've read the newspaper, darling?'

'Yes, Nigel. I have to go back there.'

'Of course. When will you go?'

'Hopefully tomorrow.'

'You'll go up country to the house?'

'Yes.'

'Well, I don't envy you, darling, the place will be awash with Gordon's friends. I'm not very sure how they will view your arrival, Celia.'

'No, neither am I. It has to be done, however.'

'I'll be out there when it's all over and behind you. You are staying on there, Celia?'

'For the time being.'

'What does that mean exactly?'

'Just that, Nigel. I have nowhere else to go in the immediate future. I have a flat there and I'm not sure about Gordon's place. I have a feeling that the house was owned by the government.'

'Well, that would be a good thing for you, dear, you won't have to think about disposing of it. Probably it will be needed for Gordon's replacement.'

'How callous that sounds.'

'I don't mean to be callous, darling, but I'm quoting a fact of life. Kenya can't survive without its veterinary officers. They're as necessary as bread. Besides, he has animals in the compound. You'll probably find somebody has already taken over.'

'I need somebody there with me. Gordon's

friends were never my friends; I just hope one or two of them will feel compassionate enough to help me now.'

'I'm sure they will. Aren't they the decent empire-building stock the British bred so successfully? Whatever we think about them now, they were, in Kipling's words, the best we had.'

'You sound almost envious, Nigel.'

'You know, sometimes I am envious. I'd like to have been like them, without the effort or the dedication; that's why I never could be. Anyway, darling, I'll be thinking about you in the weeks ahead. I'll see you when all this is behind you.'

'Goodbye, Nigel.'

Her parents looked at her curiously when she returned to the living room and with a wan smile, she said, 'Just somebody I knew in Kenya, who has read about Gordon in the newspaper. He wanted to commiserate with me.'

Her father nodded while her mother busied herself pouring tea.

'I do wish you'd eat something, Celia,' she said.

Celia accepted the tea and shook her head.

'How was Rosemary and the rest of them?' her father asked.

'Very well. Everything at Dene Hollow is so different now, and Rosemary is so different from how I expected.'

'How do you mean, dear?'

'Well, she's such a plain little thing. I did so want her to be a beauty. Oh, she's blond with cornflower blue eyes but her face is totally unremarkable. She doesn't take after me and she's not much like Alan either.'

'She's young, darling, she'll change. Give Rosemary a few years and she'll be different again.'

'But I never looked like that, I always knew that one day I'd be beautiful.'

'Yes dear, we were always so proud of you, your father and I.'

It was a cold, grey morning when Celia's plane few out of Heathrow, a day characteristic of England in early January when dull leaden skies held a threat of snow or sleet and when people hurried about their business bemoaning the cold.

In a few hours the plane would be flying into days filled with sunlight, but Celia's thoughts were far from sunny. How much had Gordon told his friends about the state of their marriage, and how would they welcome her in their midst for his funeral? Had any of them known that they were talking about divorce?

Ignoring her neighbours sitting out in their gardens, she hurriedly let herself into her flat to pick up her car keys, and almost immediately she was packing an overnight case to take to the country.

A pile of post lay on the floor behind the letter box, but on going through it quickly she saw there was nothing of interest, so she left it on the kitchen table. She did not know precisely what she had been looking for; a solicitor's letter, perhaps, or even one from Gordon giving her some indication of his plans; but there were only circulars and the usual invitations to sponsor some charity or other. She thought of telephoning Ariadne, then thought better of it.

163

Ariadne would in all probability be at the club and the sooner she got to the country house the sooner she would be able to think about what came next.

They were still there, the animals. The cheetah pacing about his pen; the baby elephants thrusting their trunks through the fence, hoping for some titbits or other. She half expected to see Gordon standing on the verandah waiting for her, but instead a plump, bearded man came strolling towards her, his expression curious, until Celia said hurriedly, 'I'm Mrs Ralston. I returned from England this morning.'

His face cleared, and holding out his hand, he said, 'I'm so sorry, Mrs Ralston. We've never met, I'm Roger Craddock. I'm taking over here. I just came down to take a look around. I shall be leaving presently.'

'Is there anybody in the house, Mr Craddock?'

'Only the servants. I believe people are expected later. I'm so sorry about Gordon, Mrs Ralston, he will be sorely missed.'

'You knew him well?'

'Quite well, but we both lived very busy lives, we seldom got to socialise together. I'm not in any hurry to move in here, take as long as you need to sort everything out.'

'Thank you. There's not much to sort out, is there? The house and everything in it didn't belong to us, it seems.'

'Well, there'll be personal things I'm sure. I hope some of your friends will be able to stay and help you. What a rotten state of affairs to come home to.'

'Yes it is.'

'Here, let me help you with your case. I'll let the servants know you've arrived then I'll make myself scarce.'

'I know so little about anything, Mr Craddock. When is the funeral?'

'Tomorrow. I'll be back for that, but I'm sure when your friends arrive they'll put you in the picture about everything.'

Chapter Twelve

Eric and Mary Garvey arrived in the early evening when the setting sun turned the surrounding scrubland into crimson splendour, and waiting to greet them at the top of the steps Celia could only think how beautiful it was, beautiful and wasted on her from the first moment she arrived.

They came forward with sorrowful expressions and outstretched hands, but their eyes were wary, leaving Celia wondering how much they knew about her marriage.

'It is so kind of you both to come,' Celia said with a sad smile.

'It must have been a terrible shock to you. None of us knew where to contact you, Celia, all we could do was inform the police that you were in England.'

'I was visiting my daughter for Christmas, Mary. Surely nobody would be surprised about that.'

'Well no, but none of us knew.'

'You mean Gordon didn't tell you?'

'Well, we hadn't seen him for weeks.'

'Nobody expected such a terrible thing to happen. The one person who knew where I was couldn't tell you.'

'No. Gordon's solicitor has made all the arrangements for the funeral tomorrow and Major Carruthers has done the rest. The funeral's at the English Church in Nairobi. Gordon was very well respected. It will be a very large funeral, Celia.'

'Yes, I'm sure it will.'

'Will you be returning in the morning or this evening?'

'Early in the morning. I shall come back here to sort things out later. I've met Mr Craddock; he says he's in no hurry to move in but I shan't be in his way for long.'

She sensed a hostility in Eric Garvey's attitude and Mary was trying too hard. She was wishing they hadn't come, wishing they would go, but Mary was saying, 'If you need any help here, Celia, we'll only be too glad to do what we can. We were both very fond of Gordon.'

'Yes, I know you were. He was a very sweet man.'

'I suppose his assistants will know how to look after the animals and Roger will be around to see to things. Will you be quite safe here on your own?'

'I'm hardly on my own, Mary; the servants are here and the men on the compound. I'll ask the servants to make a meal before you leave.'

'Oh no, Celia, that won't be necessary. We're calling at the Mertons on the way back to give them news about Gordon's funeral; besides you'll have a lot to do, I'm sure.'

'But you'll have a cup of tea, or something stronger?'

'No, really dear, we'll get off. We shall all be there to support you tomorrow, Celia.'

'Thank you Mary, I'm very grateful.'

She watched them leave, walking to their car in silence, and after a brief wave she returned to the house. She looked round her with grim uncertainty. It was all so impersonal: the cane furniture and damask cushions she'd insisted upon, the rush mats on the floor and the few pictures and ornaments that had been her attempt to make the room worthy of being called home. It hadn't been Gordon's fault. He'd been a bachelor too long; the job he did was too demanding and the marriage they had both envisaged hadn't been what either of them had expected.

She had married a kind, caring man who thought love was enough and he had married a spoilt, selfish girl who was crying for the moon.

As she went meticulously through the desk and the drawers in the bedroom she was amazed how little Gordon had collected in his life. There was absolutely nothing to tell her how he viewed their marriage and when he intended to end it. She supposed anything of that nature would already be with his solicitor and perhaps tomorrow she would know when she met him at Gordon's funeral.

She sat slumped in a chair, listening to the night sounds, the chattering of monkeys and the deeper more resonant roars of big cats. Once she had hated and feared them; now they represented a part of her life she needed to forget.

The large church was filled to capacity on the day of the funeral and Celia could only guess at the speculation that was going on behind her as she sat with Gordon's closest friends in the front pew. They had been courteous, extending their sympathy, even when she suspected most of them had expressed their opinions to each other.

She had seen Ariadne and her husband sitting at the other side of the church, Ariadne in expensive and fashionable black, acknowledging her briefly before giving her full attention to the leaflets of the funeral service being handed out to them. It was only later when they stood beside their cars ready to leave that Ariadne approached her.

'Will you be going back to the country tonight?' she asked her.

'No. There will be a new vet at the house. I shall be returning to my flat. When will I see you, Ariadne?'

'I'll telephone you. I'm sure you'll have a lot to see to.'

'Well, I shall need to see Gordon's solicitor. I'll speak to him about it today.'

Ariadne smiled and moved away. The mourners were leaving now after shaking her hand and muttering their condolences. Then she saw that two men were standing back from the others, and when at last she stood alone the elder of the two approached her.

'I'm sorry we meet under such sad circumstances, Mrs Ralston, I'm Horace Greenwood, your husband's solicitor. I needed to make all the arrangements for his funeral. I hope they were satisfactory.'

'Yes, indeed Mr Greenwood, I was in England with my daughter over Christmas, I'm really very grateful for your kindness.'

'Shall we walk towards the cars?'

She fell into step beside him and he said, 'This is John Appleby, my partner.'

He took Celia's outstretched hand, and Mr Greenwood said, 'You'll need to come into the office as soon as you can manage it. I like to get these things sorted as quickly as possible. When can that be?'

'Whenever you say, Mr Greenwood.'

'I'll consult my appointment book as soon as I get back to the office and I'll telephone you. Are you going back to the country?'

'No, to my flat.'

'Then I shall need your telephone number, Mrs Ralston.' She opened her handbag and took out a card, which he glanced at briefly before putting it in his pocket.

'I'll ring you later this afternoon, Mrs Ralston. Hopefully we can meet very soon.'

By this time they had reached her waiting car and she paused. The calm, urbane face of the solicitor gave nothing away, nothing to suggest he was speaking to a woman whose husband had been intent on divorcing her at the earliest opportunity.

He shook hands with her, as did his partner, then they left her to go to their car. As she drove to her flat she hoped and prayed the summons to see them would come soon; and she hated to admit, even to herself, that Gordon's financial situation had much to do with her concern.

She suddenly felt she hated the flat as much as she had hated the house in the country. She hated the clusters of people standing around in each other's gardens, and no doubt discussing her now that she'd arrived home. The flat was impersonal and functional, and there was little charm to it. Now, remembering Gordon's house, she had to admit that there had been a charm to it. She'd wanted a big house, not a vet's house, but one where she would be surrounded by the Africa scrubland and where she could invite her friends for tennis and swimming.

For the first time that day she thought about Nigel.

Would he return to Kenya or would he stay well away from her now that she was a single woman again? However much she loved him, however much she hoped he loved her, she had never been sure of him; always at the back of her mind had been the feeling that marriage had never been on his mind.

She was filled with trepidation on her way to the solicitor's, and when she arrived there was nothing in his manner to make her feel otherwise. He had been Gordon's friend; she was merely his client.

Businesslike, he shuffled the papers in front of

him. His voice was monotonous, as he set about reading the instructions on Gordon's will. At first she was too nervous to take it in, but eventually she began to realise that it was the will left by a man who treasured his wife. There was no mention of an estrangement.

Meeting the solicitor's eyes across his desk she sensed in them a vague cynicism, and in a cool voice he said, 'Do you understand, Mrs Ralston?'

'Not exactly. Are you telling me that my husband was a rich man and that he has left everything to me?'

'Indeed, it would seem so.'

'I never thought that Gordon had so much money. He never talked about it. I didn't think vets amassed fortunes.'

'Nor do they generally, Mrs Ralston, but Gordon inherited much of his money from his parents and grandparents. He was happy here with his job and his life; he never coveted the high life.'

'We never did anything or went anywhere. We could have had a better life, Mr Greenwood.'

'It depends what you call a better life, Mrs Ralston. Perhaps your ideas and Gordon's ideas were too far apart. I don't know.'

'Are there no other bequests?'

'It would appear not. The will was made soon after your marriage. He never sought to alter it. I did receive a letter asking to meet me in the New Year, but of course after what happened it wasn't possible.'

'Do you know why he wanted to meet you?'

'Alas no. I shall never know, Mrs Ralston.'

Was there accusation in his eyes? She couldn't be sure. She glanced at her watch nervously and he said, 'You will want time to consider the implications of the will, Mrs Ralston. Much of Gordon's money was invested, very well as it appears. You will probably need to take advice from us, and from his accountants. I am giving you all the relevant details so that you can look over them at your leisure.'

'Thank you, you've been very kind.'

'Just doing my job, Mrs Ralston. Do you intend to remain in Kenya?'

'I'm not sure. It's really too soon. I love Kenya and I have friends here.'

'But you have parents and a daughter in England, haven't you?'

'That's true, my daughter is at boarding school and is being well cared for by relatives. My parents live for each other. I have to make a life for myself. It isn't going to be easy.'

'Well no, but you'll survive I'm sure.'

She looked at him sharply but his expression was bland, devoid of sarcasm.

She rose to her feet and he placed the papers in front of him in a file which he handed to her.

'You have my telephone number, Mrs Ralston; just give me a ring when you decide to see me again. That is if you need any other advice, of course. You may have others who will be able to advise you.'

He walked with her to the door, where he said, 'Will you need to go to the country again? I know the new vet is already installed but you must have some personal things to collect?'

'I suppose so. I don't particularly want to go there.'

'No, I suppose not. Still, these things have to be faced haven't they, Mrs Ralston? Mr Craddock will be bringing his wife here as soon as possible; they'll need to start from scratch.'

'I didn't know he was married.'

'Oh yes. Married with two children, two boys, both of them at school in England.'

As she drove back to her flat she told herself that she was not concerned that the solicitor had been distant, businesslike, but hardly sympathetic with her loss or more congenial with the widow of a man who had been his friend.

No doubt he was fully aware of the scandal that her friendship with Nigel had aroused. Why should she care? She was rich, she didn't have to seek friendship from people she was unlikely to socialise with. Nigel would be coming back, they would be able to be open about their feelings for each other. But when would he be back?

She wished she could go to the club to be with people she knew but it was too soon after Gordon's death. They would expect her to keep to herself, mourn Gordon and forget the good life, at least until the trauma and tragedy of it had had a chance to die down.

The flat felt empty and impersonal, she was lonely, and as she sat listening to the sounds from the gardens outside she was close to tears.

She heard the sound of car engines as her neighbours drove out to the various clubs and meeting places, and more and more she felt sorry for herself. She could telephone her mother, but her mother would say she should go home at the earliest opportunity and she didn't want to go home. Rosemary would be back at school, and the mere thought of her mother's endless bridge afternoons and her father's absorption in his stamp collection filled her with gloom. She might as well be dead.

She would hardly be welcome at Dene Hollow. Cedric had made it very plain that her visit was an intrusion and what had she in common with Beatrice? She wasn't interested in trips to the shops, walks along the cliffs, sitting in the garden talking about things she had little interest in. Idly, she thought of Nigel and his grandmother. Surely he too would be straining at the leash staying with an old lady he had described as senile.

After two long days of boring inactivity the ringing of the telephone sent her heart racing and she hurried to answer it. It was Ariadne, her voice airily unconcerned as if they had spoken together only yesterday.

'You probably don't much feel like coming to the club,' she said. 'Why don't you drive over here and we can sit around the pool. I'm entertaining some of the girls.'

'I'd rather see you alone, Ariadne, I don't much feel like being with the crowd.'

'The crowd would do you good, Celia.'

'I'm not so sure about that.'

'Well, if you don't fancy it I'll keep tomorrow morning free for you. We could have lunch and then I have to go into Nairobi.'

'What time shall I come, then?'

'Oh, around ten-thirty. I'll see you then, Celia.'

When she put the receiver down she thought she'd been foolish. She should have joined the girls around the pool. After all, none of them would be expecting her to be wearing widow's weeds. They had all known about Nigel and none of them had really known Gordon.

The next morning, Ariadne greeted her with a wave from where she sat on a low sunlounger beside the pool. She was wearing a large sunhat and the ridiculous ornamental sunglasses she favoured, greeting Celia with a wide smile and indicating that she take the lounger next to her own.

'We'll talk first, then I'll get drinks,' she said. 'Johnny's gone to the club, some meeting or other. He did tell me about it but I wasn't very interested. How are you, my dear? Are you staying on here or are you going home to England?'

'I'm not going home, I'm surprised you think I might be.'

'Well, when the husband dies most of the women go home. What about your daughter?'

'She's at boarding school and I couldn't go back to my parents.'

'And I suppose you have to think about the money angle. Vets don't make fortunes, do they, and in any case hadn't Gordon asked you for a divorce?'

'We'd talked about it, yes.'

'But that's all?'

'Well yes.'

'So officially you're Gordon's widow and entitled to what he's left.'

'Like you say, vets don't amass fortunes.'

'Did you see much of Nigel in England?'

'He took Rosemary and me out for lunch one day, that's the only time I saw him.'

Ariadne's eyes opened a fraction wider. 'Really. I thought you two would have been having a marvellous time in London, with nobody looking out for you.'

'I was staying with family, Ariadne, and Nigel was staying with his grandmother.'

'Did you get to meet her?'

'No, of course not.'

'I would have thought Nigel might have been keen for you to meet her. I thought you both had something going for you, and his grandmother's been a lifeline.'

'Lifeline?'

'Well yes. Maybe they're only rumours but it was being discussed at the club over Christmas. Apparently he's the apple of her eye, she's never got along with his father and she's been the one who's kept him solvent.'

'How do they know all this? I'm sure Nigel would never discuss his grandmother with any one of them.'

'Darling, how do people get to know about anything? It's because people talk; some of it's rubbish, some of it bears a grain of truth.'

Ariadne's eyes were filled with a sly amusement. Celia knew something she wasn't telling her and Ariadne didn't know if it had to do with Gordon or Nigel. She was free now to pursue her affair with him, but for Nigel to be truly interested Celia had to have money, and there

176

was a strange complacency about her.

Johnny had told her that rumour had it that Gordon Ralston had come from a wealthy family background. His father was a pretty high-up civil servant; his mother had come from rich Yorkshire landowners.

Idly she asked, 'Did Gordon have any family in England?'

'Both his parents were dead. He never spoke about anybody else.'

'No brothers or sisters?'

'No. He was an only child.'

'Then, darling, you must look after yourself, keep that solicitor of his on his toes. You're entitled to everything he had, always assuming he hadn't begun divorce proceedings, and even then you'll have a stake in everything he's left.'

When Celia remained silent she went on. 'When I first married, his first wife really went to town on him. Of course she did have the boys, but I got to the stage when I wondered if she'd leave us with anything.'

'You didn't wonder for long, Ariadne, not after you met Johnny.'

Ariadne laughed. 'That's really quite spiteful, darling, particularly when I'm trying to advise you to look after yourself.'

'I'm sorry, Ariadne. I resent the talk here about me and Nigel; now there'll be more about Gordon's estate.'

She was looking out across the pool. She would have liked to take Ariadne into her confidence but something prevented her. She was remembering Gordon's wariness, his telling her that she should be cautious in her dealings with Ariadne. Instead she found herself saying, 'I hope Nigel will be back soon. His grandmother hasn't been well and he wasn't sure when it would be.'

'I've know him over the years; he's come and gone and nobody really knew where he went to or when he'd be returning. Perhaps you are the very special person to bring him back here.'

'Surely there have been special people before.

'There have been women in his life, you know that. I can't honestly recall anybody particularly special.'

'Do you think he'll come back?'

'How should I know? Surely you know that better than I.'

Ariadne rose from her seat and for a moment stood looking down at Celia's reflective face with a slight amused smile, then lightly she said, 'If you want my advice you'll come back to the land of the living. It would please Nigel to think that you've been living in the doldrums. The best way to hold his interest is to let him see that you're not dependent on him for amusement.'

'That's what you would do, Ariadne, I know. I'm not sure if he'd expect me to be like you.'

'Oh well, please yourself, if you don't want to take my advice don't, but I do know about men, Celia, men like Nigel Boyd.'

'He's not at all like Johnny Fairbrother.'

'I know. Nor is he as rich.'

With that cryptic remark Ariadne left her to go to the drinks trolley.

Chapter Thirteen

It was several days later on her way to Ariadne's that she saw the house standing forlorn without its usual conglomeration of gardeners and cars.

She'd always admired it and wished she had one like it. She knew that the people who lived there were elderly and took little interest in the high life of the area's more ebullient residents. She drove slowly, savouring the long white house and its stables, the extensive parkland and long curving driveway. Ariadne would know why it seemed suddenly so devoid of habitation.

Ariadne and her husband sat on the verandah, her husband immersed in the financial columns of his paper, Ariadne in a magazine. Johnny acknowledged her arrival with a curt nod, making her feel how utterly charmless he was, Ariadne with her customary bright smile.

'I'm glad you've come, Celia. I get very little conversation out of my husband,' she said.

'I thought you might like a game of tennis,' Celia replied.

'Well, anything to relieve the boredom.'

'I drove past the Moretons' house; there didn't seem much sign of life.'

'Oh, didn't you know, Celia? Algy Moreton died just before Christmas, it was very sudden. Of course you were away, and when you got back there was Gordon's funeral to think about. In any case you didn't know either of them.'

'No. But isn't his wife still there?'

'They went back to England a couple of months before Algy died. The house is up for sale.'

'I wonder if they've got a buyer for it?'

'It'll have to be somebody with plenty of money. It probably won't go in a hurry.'

Celia sat in silence but her thoughts were busy, and watching her Ariadne became suddenly suspicious. 'You're not thinking you'd like it yourself, Celia? If you can afford Malibu Lodge Gordon must have left you better off than any of us supposed.'

For the first time Johnny looked up with interest.

'I doubt if I could afford Malibu,' Celia said evenly.

'But Gordon did leave money, Celia. You've been very cagey about it.'

'I didn't want what Gordon left to become common property.'

'I thought we were friends, Celia. Evidently not as close as I'd thought.'

'I was going to tell you, Ariadne, it's just that it's all been so recent. Like I said I couldn't afford Malibu.'

'Marcia Moreton will want it off her hands as quickly as possible,' Johnny put in. 'She's looking for something in England, not too far out of London and she'll not settle for any old house. She'll want something compatible with the one she's left behind her.'

'That's what I mean, she'll want the earth for it.'

'If you're really interested I could put out a few feelers,' he replied.

'Would you, Johnny, I'd be very grateful.'

Ariadne regarded Celia with narrowed eyes and something of her old antipathy towards her surfaced. Women like Celia always fell on their feet; they never needed to plot and plan their life as she had had to do. Celia would bounce back from whatever trauma she'd encountered and nobody would think the worse of her, not like herself who had climbed up the social ladder and been castigated for it. Rustling the leaves of his newspaper together, Johnny rose to his feet, saying, 'I'm going into Nairobi. I'll be meeting up with a few fellas who might know something about Malibu. I'll keep you informed.'

After he had gone, Ariadne said softly, 'What about Nigel? Does he know you've come into money?'

'I haven't heard from him.'

'Would you go after the house on your own?'

'I might.'

'Suppose he comes back and hates the place?'

'I can't halt the rest of my life hoping that he's coming back, I have to do something with it. I hate my flat, I hate the area, it was only ever supposed to be a stop-gap until something better came up.'

'Like Nigel Boyd making his mind up.'

'I thought he loved me; he said he did. I think I had every right to suppose that one day we'd make a life together.'

Ariadne decided that she would be wise to remain silent. Nigel Boyd needed money. If he

181

thought Celia had some he could well be back, but he'd have to be sure before he committed himself. By buying Malibu Celia could convince him that she was a rich woman and he would rise to the occasion, but what of their future?

'We'll have lunch,' she said brightly, 'then we'll see about driving to the club. Is that what you want to do?'

'Of course. I never go there in the evenings now, perhaps I should start by making an appearance during the day.'

'Well, of course. Time does move on, you know.'

The club members greeted her as if she had never been away. And as they sat on the verandah watching the sun setting brilliantly in the western sky she found herself listening to the inevitable scandals, the affairs that had surfaced and died, the list of activities that were on offer. She was glad she'd gone back, but one woman more intrusive than the rest asked, 'Heard from Nigel, Celia? I thought he'd be coming back in the New Year.'

Celia smiled briefly. 'I know nothing of Nigel's plans, Elsie.'

She knew what they were all thinking. The affair was over; Nigel had moved on as he always did.

'I thought you'd be moving back to England,' another woman said.

'It's early days, I don't really know what I'm going to do yet.'

'Gracious, there'll be new people everywhere,' another said, 'what with the Moretons and now you and Gordon.'

'Gordon was never one of the crowd,' Celia said, 'and we never saw the Moretons.'

'Wouldn't you like to be near your daughter?' another asked.

'Rosemary is very happy at her school and with my first husband's family. One day, if I'm still here, she'll be able to join me.'

'You've never shown us any photographs of her. Is she very pretty?'

'Oh very, she's tall and slender, very fair. At the moment I think she's gawky and she has braces on her teeth. She'll blossom as she gets older.'

'Well, of course. I had braces on my teeth for years. When they came off it felt like being in heaven.'

She looked at the woman who had spoken and thought that she was hardly a raving beauty. She hoped Rosemary would indeed blossom into some semblance of the girl she had been.

Ariadne took little part in the general conversation. She was thinking about Celia in a not too benign fashion. Celia, who had been cosseted since the day she was born. Two decent husbands and a daughter she could afford to shelve until it suited her, and now money. It would serve her right if Nigel did marry her; they'd live in utopia as long as the money lasted, and when it was gone then Celia for the first time in her life might learn what it was like to suffer.

The woman who had battled her way from her wretched childhood to a less than euphoric existence with Johnny Fairbrother saw nothing disloyal in her antagonism towards Celia Ralston.

183

Celia wouldn't tell her how much Gordon had left, but she felt pretty sure she wouldn't be able to afford the Moreton place. Malibu was in a class of its own. The house she lived in with Johnny was flashy in comparison, but there was a timelessness about Malibu, not something that relied on flash fittings and gaudy sun loungers set around a swimming pool.

She frowned as she watched Celia's smiles on her pretty face, the elegant way she lounged in her chair, the upper-crust English accent that segregated her from the rest of them who had been exiles too long.

These were the things Ariadne had cultivated and acquired. Celia would never slip up. Suddenly Ariadne jumped to her feet, saying, 'I must go; I have things to do before Johnny comes home.'

'See you soon, Celia,' she called out.

Celia watched her walking quickly along the terrace and running lightly down the steps to where the cars were parked. All afternoon she had been very quiet, hardly entering into the conversation, and there had been a cool almost cynical detachment in her attitude for most of the afternoon.

It had been evident after her mention of Malibu. Ariadne was jealous. For years now it had been Ariadne who had been the rich woman in the company of others less fortunate. She had been the one with expensive clothes, holidays and a big house in extensive grounds and she'd revelled in it. It hadn't mattered that her husband was boorish, often uncouth and never a gentleman. It had never troubled Johnny Fairbrother but obviously it had troubled Ariadne. She had married a decent, cultured man with little money, swapping him for a man with too much money and very little else. Now Ariadne was seeing Celia as a rival.

Of course she would be foolish to even think of buying Malibu. The upkeep of the place would be tremendous and she'd need a multitude of servants. Servants were easy to get and they came cheaply, but she couldn't live in a place like Malibu on her own, she'd be afraid to.

If Nigel had thought anything about her at all he was not showing it. No letters, no telephone calls, and obviously no intention of returning to Kenya because he couldn't live without her. There were times when she told herself she hated him, his dashing good-looking appearance, his easy charm, the abandoned passion of his love-making, and she could hear his voice, smooth and low-pitched, expressing sentiments she craved for. Obviously they had meant nothing.

'You're very pensive, Celia,' Julie said. 'Is it Gordon you're missing or Nigel?'

Ignoring the question Celia said, 'I have letters to write, I should get off home.'

'I hate writing letters,' Kay Witherspoon mumbled. 'My mother gets so cross when she doesn't hear from me, but you have a daughter, don't you, Celia?'

'Yes. She'll be waiting to hear from me.'

She didn't know why she was going home, there was nothing to do when she got there. Writing to Rosemary had been an excuse to get

185

away from the gossip.

She felt strangely troubled about Ariadne. She thought of Ariadne as her special friend but there were times when she didn't understand her, when the sight of her narrowed eyes filled with a strange speculation troubled her.

Ariadne had stopped her car on the hillside overlooking Malibu and she looked down on the sprawling house surrounded by its formal gardens and stretches of scrubland. Of course Celia couldn't afford it; however much Gordon had left her it was ridiculous to think that she could live there alone and it was pretty obvious that Nigel was not in any hurry to get back.

The resentment she was feeling towards Celia was festering as she drove the short distance to her home. Suddenly she found herself finding fault with it, the too ornate design and the swimming pool she'd longed for, surrounded with its conglomeration of gaily covered loungers.

Johnny had grumbled about the pool, said it was unnecessary, even when she'd pointed out that a good many other people had them. He rarely sat anywhere near it, and he had little interest in the house. Everything in it had been her choice and she doubted if he'd even noticed until the bills came in.

The dissatisfied mood continued when she entered the house. What she had once seen as the epitome of luxury now seemed tatty and too ostentatious. She opened the wardrobe doors and looked at her clothes. They had all been expensive and there were so many of them. Now suddenly they looked too flashy. Celia Ralston

186

would never have worn them. She had considered Celia's penchant for neutral greys and beiges dull and unimaginative; now she could only think that they were classy.

She was in no brighter mood when later they sat down to dinner. She frowned at Johnny eating his meal wearing the same casual clothes he had worn all afternoon. There were food stains on the front of his shirt and he gulped his wine greedily. There was never any conversation.

'What do you think about Celia's interest in Malibu?' she asked.

'Nothing, why should I?'

'She can't possibly be serious.'

'Well, of course not, unless Gordon Ralston was better off than everybody thought he was. I didn't think vets made fortunes.'

'I happen to know that he left a considerable sum.'

'Good luck to her then. Enough to buy Malibu?'

'I don't know, but it's silly to think she could live there on her own.'

He went on with his meal, completely uninterested, and with some asperity she snapped, 'Why don't you put in an offer for it? You could afford it.'

'Are you out of your mind, woman? What do I want with a place that size? We've got this one and this is too big for us.'

'Every time I pass Malibu I stop the car just to look at it. It's beautiful. If I had a house like that I'd never ask for anything else.'

'You would, you're never satisfied.'

'That's unfair. I'm a good wife, I make a comfortable home for you. All we've got is money, we've no class.'

'If it's class you're after you should have stayed married to Alan Peterson, he had all the class you could have wanted. But he didn't have the money, did he, Ariadne.'

'I found Alan very boring.'

'You find me boring.'

'I do when you disagree with everything I say and do.'

'You're jealous of that pal of yours because she's got the sort of class you might have had if you'd stayed married to Peterson. You lost any hope of it when you married me.'

'You never try, Johnny.'

'You'd prefer that I had an upper-crust accent like Nigel Boyd and less money?'

'I didn't say that.'

'You'd have had no interest in Nigel Boyd, he didn't have enough money for you. That's what made you settle for a moron like me. Forget Malibu, Ariadne, I'm not interested.'

She bit her lip angrily. It was no use talking to Johnny. Once her sulks would have brought him round, now they had little effect. He looked at her sulky face and smiled to himself. Malibu indeed. They'd rattle in the place and she'd want one party after another just to show it off. All the same it would be interesting to see if Gordon Ralston's widow could afford it. He'd heard something about him leaving money but he hadn't taken much notice, in fact he'd doubted if she'd see any of it after her affair with Nigel

Boyd. Surely Gordon had got wind of it.

'Are we going to the club or not?' he asked.

'Not. I was there this afternoon, I don't want to go there again.'

'Well, I shall go. I want to see Harry Foxton, you please yourself.'

'Do you suppose Nigel Boyd will come back here?' Ariadne asked.

'I'm not concerned. Why should it bother you?'

'It doesn't, but it bothers Celia.'

'Well, if she's rich enough to put a bid in for Malibu it might be the incentive he's looking for.'

'That's a cynical way of looking at it.'

'Nigel Boyd and cynicism go hand in hand. He got in the habit of poppin' round most days, I never invited him but he showed up all the same. I thought you might be the attraction until he started talking about money. He had a grandmother that he was relying on for future funds, said he was the apple of her eye.'

'I doubt he'll marry Celia, she'll have to be somebody his family approve of.'

Johnny smiled grimly and left her to her own thoughts.

Several days later Celia drove through the gates of Malibu and spent all morning walking round the house and gardens. The windows were shuttered so she could only guess at the dimensions of the rooms behind them; even so she knew they would be outstanding. She had already visited the estate agents in Nairobi and found them irritatingly supercilious. That a widow, just bereaved, should be even remotely interested in an estate the size of Malibu was unconvincing.

189

She was wasting their time, and Celia had left their office with the distinct impression that they thought that Malibu was out of her reach.

That Ariadne had learned of her visit quickly became apparent.

'I take it you're still interested in moving house,' Ariadne said with a wry smile. 'I happened to see you entering the estate agents' office last week.'

'Well, I really don't like my flat, Ariadne. I have to think of something else.'

That Johnny Fairbrother played golf with Ronald Mortimer the senior partner in the business prompted Ariadne to ask her husband to make enquiries about any property Celia was interested in. It gave Johnny a certain grim satisfaction to tell her that she was enquiring about Malibu.

'How ridiculous!' Ariadne snapped. 'You're saying it's too big for us and yet she's contemplating it for herself.'

'She has parents and a daughter, perhaps she's thinking of asking them to join her.'

'Or maybe she's heard from Boyd and he's coming here.'

That talk of Malibu annoyed his wife afforded Johnny some amusement. He was under no illusions about Ariadne. He knew exactly why she'd married him and affection had nothing to do with it. She suited him. She was attractive and entertaining, she ran his house and his servants very well and she'd come into his life at exactly the right moment. He knew that if he ever lost money then she would have no hesitation in walking out, but he didn't intend to lose money, he was too astute for that, and if she so much as put a foot wrong he'd send her packing.

Sitting round Ariadne's swimming pool one day Ariadne said, 'In your position, Celia, I think you should go home to England. It's your home, after all, you have parents there, other relatives and most of all your daughter.'

'Well, you have a son in England. How long since you've seen him?' Celia parried.

'It's rather different. He's with his father, and he has been out to stay with us several times. No luck in finding alternative housing?'

'No. I've looked at one or two properties, that's all.'

'Aren't you even thinking you might go home for a few weeks' holiday?'

'No. I don't want to move back permanently and if I'm in England I might just miss anything that comes up here.'

'You could get in touch with Nigel.'

'How? I'm not sure where he is and I'm certainly not going looking for him.'

'Celia, you are right you can't build your life around Nigel Boyd, I've told you that before. He may return here, he may not. In any case he's done this before, gone away for a few years, then come back, and gone again.'

Celia didn't answer. Instead she sat looking out across the pool, her expression morose.

'No news from home then?' Ariadne asked.

'My sister-in-law tells me Rosemary is very happy at school and doing well. There's to be a wedding in the family sometime this summer.'

'You'll be going home for that, I suppose?'

'No. I hardly know the boy or his fiancée. I met them at Christmas but no, I'm not really very interested in attending his wedding.'

Ariadne kept her thoughts to herself. Celia had very little interest in anything and anybody outside herself these days.

When she spoke about her daughter, which wasn't very often, she seemed strangely disappointed. Evidently the girl was not the raving beauty she'd hoped for, not the sort of girl who would set Kenya alight, and anything less than that would be a reflection on Celia.

Chapter Fourteen

The wedding guests surged out of the house to stand in happy groups on the terrace, waiting for the bride and bridegroom to appear. It had been a day for the small seaside town to remember.

The sun shone out of a clear blue sky and the church paths had been lined with excited onlookers. Jerome had looked predictably handsome in his formal morning suit, and in company with his younger brothers and friends. His bride had been an enchanting vision in white taffeta and her three bridesmaids had fitted the bill admirably in pale peach silk.

Beatrice stood with her brother at the bottom of the steps, wishing she could escape indoors to take off her shoes. They were pinching, and

Cedric too was hoping they would disperse quickly to return to their homes.

At last Jerome and Natalie ran out of the house towards their car, a car his brothers had been adorning with balloons and a collection of trailing clanging objects which echoed noisily until Jerome ordered their instant removal.

Natalie threw her bouquet, which was caught by Brenda her younger sister; everybody cheered, and Beatrice's eyes scanned the upper terrace in search of Rosie. Eventually she found her sitting on the wall away from the other guests.

Rosie had been the youngest bridesmaid and Beatrice had been rather surprised when Natalie had asked her. Rosie was embarrassed about her teeth, she didn't look her best in pale peach and she was understandably troubled by the presence of Steven Chaytor and Mary, who now seemed to be a regular visitor to Dene Hollow.

During the few days before the wedding Rosie had spoken to Steven very rarely so that she hadn't had to converse with Mary. Beatrice felt sorry for her, sensing her despair. The girl had loved Steven too long; it had been an infatuation that should have ended years ago, but every time Steven returned, back came the old feelings.

Connie was running along the drive with the boys, her arms waving wildly, and as usual she was wearing a skirt that was too short, and the pink hat on her red hair was a disaster.

Beatrice had looked askance at the colour she'd dyed her hair; it seemed that every time she came to the house she'd changed the colour of her hair and yet there was something very likeable about

193

her. Natalie had the makings of a snob, a family who were reasonably well off, marriage to an accountant, and now the new detached house in a new complex of mock Tudor residences that had been erected on the outskirts of Totnes.

Beatrice had watched Connie's eyes grow large with envy at one of Natalie's descriptions of her new furnishings and the money they were spending on their kitchen.

Jerome had always been a role model for Jeffrey and he saw nothing wrong in their talk of the good life; that it made Connie envious and dissatisfied with her lot never occurred to him.

It had been left to David to say, 'They're always showing off about what they have and are going to have.'

Jeffrey had been quick to leap to his brother's defence, and had given little thought to Connie sitting quietly next to him.

Beatrice had tried to give her a little advice about the choice of clothes, well-meant advice which Connie couldn't take exception to, but her words had fallen on deaf ears. Connie loved flamboyant clothes and strong colours; she loved experimenting with anything new that came into the salon where she worked, and Jeffrey never found fault with it.

All his life he had lived under Jerome's shadow. Now Jerome had left the family house and Jeffrey was the eldest son living there. It wouldn't make any difference. He still refrained from having opinions of his own, because although Jerome had gone his father remained to hurl criticism at him.

David had asked permission to invite his new girlfriend to the reception and Beatrice could see them walking across the lawn with Noel.

Her name was Gloria. She was dark and pretty and she was careful not to talk out of place, but Beatrice had the impression that she was always listening and that behind that demure prettiness there was a very active mind.

Her gaze would follow Natalie as she moved around the room. She was quick to ingratiate herself with Aunt Beatrice and David's father. Connie she rarely spoke to. Noel didn't like her, David liked her too well and was obviously very proud of her.

When they reached the terrace she was quick to join Beatrice, saying, 'It has been a lovely wedding, Miss Greville; it was so kind of you to invite me.'

'I'm glad you've enjoyed yourself, my dear.'

'Natalie looked lovely, didn't she?'

'Yes indeed.'

'I'm going to look for Rosie,' Noel said. 'She didn't come down to the car.'

'She's up there at the end of the terrace,' Aunt Beatrice said.

Noel grinned. 'She's giving Steven a wide berth; it's because Mary's here.'

'Noel, be careful what you say,' Beatrice warned him.

'Well, it's true, we all know she's got a crush on Steven,' then turning to Gloria he said, 'It's gone on for years, ever since she first met him.'

'But aren't Steven and Mary engaged to be married?'

195

'Are they? I didn't know,' Noel snapped.

'Well perhaps not, I just assumed they were.'

'What are you doing tonight?' Noel asked David.

'Nothing. I'm taking Gloria home, we might go to the cinema, do you want to come?'

'No, I'll see what Rosie wants to do.'

Gloria smiled and said sweetly, 'I do hope Rosie isn't too fond of Steven, it would be so sad, wouldn't it.'

Beatrice wasn't too sure that she liked Gloria; there was something that was too nice about her, something that had yet to surface and which could conceivably cause problems for the future.

The guests were departing now and Steven and Mary had come to say their farewells. Looking up to the terrace where Rosie stood with Noel, Steven said, 'I'll say goodbye to Rosie, Aunt Beatrice. I'm off to South Africa next week so it's very much in the air if we shall meet again, at least in the foreseeable future.'

She watched him walking along the terrace, watched him take Rosie's hand and bend his head to kiss her cheek. She could only guess at the anguish in Rosie's heart.

Mary was talking about the wedding, the lovely day they had spent, the beauty of the bride and her attendants, and Aunt Beatrice said, 'Are you going to South Africa with Steven, Mary?'

Mary nodded. 'Steven is going to Cape Town to work in tropical medicine, and I'm going into the hospital to work in the laboratory. Steven and I go back a long way. Our parents are friends, they all live in Malaysia, where our fathers worked.'

The explanation had covered a great deal but had left much undisclosed. Beatrice had no means of knowing how deep their friendship went, but time would sort it out. Rosie was too young for Steven however much she idolised him, and Steven had never thought of her as anything but a child. Mary was asking, 'I suppose Rosie will join her mother in Kenya one day?'

'Well probably, but we don't really know. My sister-in-law's plans are uncertain, I'm sure.'

'It was terribly sad about her husband. I'd have thought she'd want to come home.'

Beatrice smiled but offered no comment, and Cedric said, 'I'm going inside now, Beatrice. I want to get out of this monkey suit and into something less formal.'

'You can at least wait until all the guests have gone, Cedric,' she answered him tartly.

'They'll linger on awhile, most of them are showing no signs of leaving, and you'll be here, the boys can do the honours. I'm going to change.'

He smiled at Mary who held out her hand to say goodbye. 'It's been a lovely wedding, Mr Greville,' she said, 'I suppose Jeffrey will be the next one.'

He frowned. 'Not before he's made something of himself, I hope, and hopefully not to that girl.'

Beatrice frowned and Mary looked at him in amazement. 'Oh, don't you like Connie, Mr Greville? I think she's really very nice.'

'She is nice,' Beatrice said firmly. 'He will find fault with whoever the boys bring home.'

At that moment Steven joined them, and,

sensing a moment of discord, said lightly, 'Time for us to leave now, Mary. I think we've said our farewells to everybody.'

'Perhaps you can get around to persuading some of the others to leave also,' Cedric said gruffly. 'There's nothing more for any of them to see.'

Steven laughed, accustomed to his host's mulishness, and seeing Beatrice's expression he said, 'We'll do our best to move them on.'

He shook Cedric's hand and kissed Beatrice's cheek and she said, gently, 'We'll miss you, Steven, you've been coming here for years and all that's left now is to wish you well in your chosen career in a new country.'

He smiled. 'Thank you both for everything, for long summer holidays in this beautiful house and for filling so many gaps in my life. I'll write and let you know how we fare.'

Beatrice did not miss the fact that he had said 'we', which must mean both of them.

As Beatrice changed into a comfortable blouse and skirt she thought to herself, one down, four to go. But why should there be four? Why couldn't Celia come back to England now that Gordon was dead? Surely Kenya had nothing for her any more.

The guests were drifting away now and she could see Rosie and Noel standing idly at the edge of the garden, looking out to sea. It rather looked as if David had invited Gloria to spend the evening at Dene Hollow since they were already walking towards the house. She wished she liked Gloria more; she'd never thought David

198

would be one to be so besotted with any girl but Gloria had proved to be the exception. Noel was duly scathing about it.

Jeffrey was the one who troubled her most. Cedric was so very much against his choice of girlfriend, and it was true he was neglecting his studies. Jerome had teased him unmercifully, saying he wouldn't make the grade and if he got a degree at all it wouldn't be a good one.

Jeffrey didn't seem to care. He seldom opened his books because he was out most evenings, and Beatrice had to listen constantly to her brother's tirades against him.

She met Rosie on the stairs and she thought that in some indefinable way the girl was changing. She was tall for her age and slender, but the contours of her face seemed to be changing. When she got rid of the braces on her teeth she would be the sort of beauty her mother expected.

'You're changing your dress, Rosie?' she said.

'Yes. I don't suppose I'll ever wear it again.'

'Well of course you will. What about the school party at Christmas?'

'I don't like the colour. Perhaps it will dye into something deeper.'

'Oh I don't think so, dear, it will spoil the material.'

Shrugging her shoulders Rosie disappeared into her bedroom. David and Gloria were sitting with their arms around each other in the living room and Noel was thumping out a tune on the piano. He wasn't a competent pianist and his efforts now were simply to annoy the other two.

'Has Jeffrey gone out?' Beatrice asked David.

She did not miss the look that passed between David and Noel, and more sharply than she intended she said, 'What is wrong with Jeffrey? He's been morose for days. Something's going on in that boy's head and your father's getting very impatient with him.'

'He's gone to Connie's,' Noel explained. 'He's all right.'

'Are they coming back here?'

Noel shrugged his shoulders and decided not to continue the conversation when his father entered the room.

There was an atmosphere about the house. David and Gloria went out in the early evening and Noel and Rosie elected to play table games in the study. It was then that Cedric gave full rein to his annoyance with his second son.

'I'm going to have to have words with him, Beatrice. He's no interest in his work, no wish to get back to university, all his interests seem to be with that girl and they're totally unsuitable for each other.'

'The girl's nice enough, Cedric. I know she hasn't had a very good education but she's pleasant, she'll learn as she gets older.'

'She's disruptive, they're too young, both of them.

'Perhaps when he gets back to university he'll work harder, and one or both of them could meet somebody else.'

'She won't, she's got her claws firmly fixed into Jeffrey and he's too stupid to realise it.'

'Well, I think it would be nice if we could get

today over without an argument.'

Cedric consulted his watch. 'It's half past nine, I don't suppose he'll be in much before midnight.'

'And it's too late to start arguing at that hour.'

'I want some answers,' he insisted.

Everybody had retired except Cedric, who waited for Jeffrey to arrive home.

Beatrice didn't know how long she'd been asleep but their raised voices woke her, and putting on her bedside light she saw that it was after one o'clock. Hurriedly she put on her dressing-gown and let herself out of her room in time to see Rosie leaning over the balustrade, straining to hear what was going on below.

'Go to bed, Rosie,' Beatrice said firmly. 'This has nothing to do with you.'

'But they woke me up. How can I sleep with all that going on?'

By this time the two boys had joined them and David whispered, 'Dad's in a furious rage. Jeffrey must have done something terrible.'

'Go back to bed, all of you, I'll see what's going on,' Beatrice said, hurrying along the landing and down the stairs.

Jeffrey stood on the hearthrug facing his father's chair, and Cedric's face was furiously angry, his hands clenched on the arms of his chair.

'What's going on?' Beatrice demanded. 'Your shouting has woken everybody up. Whatever it is could surely have waited until the morning.'

'Go to bed, Aunt Beatrice,' Jeffrey said shortly.

201

'This has nothing to do with you.'

'Whatever goes on in this house has something to do with me. It was made something to do with me when I was asked to live here to take care of you.'

'It's that girl,' Cedric thundered. 'She's pregnant and he says he's going to marry her.'

Beatrice sat down weakly on the edge of a chair. It was worse than anything she'd envisaged. There was nothing to do except look at her brother in horrified silence.

'He says he's no intention of returning to the university to finish his studies, he's marrying her and he's moving out of here. Where exactly he's moving to he doesn't seem to know.'

'Oh Jeffrey,' Beatrice murmured, 'you can't give up your studies, think of your future.'

'He hasn't got a future,' his father stormed. 'No profession, a girl who can't string two words together and a baby to care for. What sort of future does he have?'

'You've never liked Connie, you've never tried to like her, just because her family haven't got money and they don't live in the right sort of area. You've only come round about Natalie because her father's as well off as you are.'

'You don't have to give up everything to marry her. You can pay for the baby, always supposing he's yours, you don't have to marry the girl. Where are you going to live? Where are you going to work? You'll need to do something, I'm not prepared to keep you, and her family need everything they've got.'

'I can get a job, I'm not exactly an idiot. I can

202

get a job in a bank or an office. I can do labouring, anything. I never wanted to be an accountant or a solicitor anyway. It was you who wanted it for me, you never asked me.'

'You need some sort of training for whatever you decide to do. A shop has to be bought. Office workers need experience. What sort of experience have you had? She'll have to give up her job when the child is born.'

Wearily Jeffrey said, 'I don't want to talk anymore tonight, I've had enough. Talking isn't going to get us anywhere.'

'Nothing's going to get you anywhere; you've burned your boats and you have to face the consequences. You're a big disappointment to me, Jeffrey. I can't begin to think what your mother would have thought about you.'

'Well, she isn't here, is she, and like you say I'll face the consequences on my own.'

'I'll have a few choice words to say to that young woman, never fear. From the first moment I saw her I knew she'd be a disaster.'

'I don't want you to say anything to Connie, Father. Her father's probably said all that's necessary.'

'Not he, he'll be congratulating her that she's marrying money. She'll not be seeing much of mine, however.'

'On the contrary, Father he didn't approve of me, he'd have preferred her to marry some chap who didn't go to university, somebody from their own walk of life.'

Cedric glared at him before snapping, 'That's probably what he told you, what she told you.

203

Don't you believe it.'

'Jeffrey's right, Cedric, we can't go on talking all through the night, the problem will still be here in the morning. We should go to bed. Would either of you like a cup of tea?'

Neither of them would so Beatrice went to the door with her hand on the light switch, and after a few minutes both men walked out through the door.

As she passed the other doors she wondered how much the occupants within had heard of the row going on downstairs. It would all go on and on in the months to come; there would be no escape from it.

She deplored Jeffrey's lack of common sense, but she didn't agree with her brother about Connie: the girl was nice enough. She had a kind heart and she was honest. It wasn't her fault that she had not had the advantages money would have provided. If the truth could be told, Beatrice preferred her to Natalie and Gloria. She had just got into bed when there was a light tap on her door and Rosie came in, her face flushed, her eyes anxious.

'We all heard everything, Aunt Beatrice. Is it true that Jeffrey's going to marry Connie?'

'I'm afraid so, dear.'

'And that she's having a baby?'

'Yes, that too.'

'Uncle Cedric's furious. He really doesn't like her, does he?'

'No, he doesn't.'

'I like her, I think she's nice. What's he got against her?'

'Jeffrey's giving up university, he's disappointing his father very badly, Rosie. I hope you'll take a lesson from this and that you don't disappoint any of us.'

'I doubt if my mother'd care anyway.'

'Well of course she'd care, darling, I'd care, we'd all care.'

Rosie gave a small doubtful smile before turning away.

'Goodnight, dear, it's very late,' Beatrice said. 'Try to get off to sleep.'

Sleep was a long time coming as Beatrice lay in bed staring up at the ceiling. Her last thoughts were: two down, three to go.

Chapter Fifteen

Nigel Boyd sat back in his grandmother's drawing room to contemplate his future. It was the day of his grandmother's funeral. The old lady had died suddenly after a heart attack and he had just seen the rest of his family off the premises.

His parents had barely spoken to each other and there hadn't been a single word exchanged between Nigel and his father. His two sisters had left immediately after the funeral service and his elder brother, the heir to his father's title and estates, had been unable to be present since he was travelling in the Far East.

His grandmother's will had been read in the early afternoon and the fact that she had left all her money and her house to Nigel had earned his father's disapproval. Nigel was entirely happy with the situation. He was a rich man with a home to call his own in England.

He had no wish to live in Dorset but it would be somewhere to come back to when he grew tired of travelling and living in various places. He thought idly of Celia Ralston.

He had been vastly taken with Celia: she was all he admired in a woman, but if and when he married it had to be somebody with an income of her own, Gordon had been on the verge of divorcing Celia when he died, so probably she wouldn't have come out of her marriage comfortably off, and then there was her daughter. He wasn't really ready for a daughter of Rosie's age, indeed he doubted if Celia was ready for her either.

He decided he wouldn't linger in Dorset. He'd close up the house, keep on a few of his grandmother's servants to care for it, and he'd spend a few days in London, after which he'd decide where to head for next.

He knew where he could find most of his friends, either frequenting their clubs or gambling halls, and any one of them would be willing to put him up for a few days.

He'd been at school with Keith Saunders; they'd gone hunting together, played the casinos together, climbed mountains together, and it wasn't very difficult to find him at his officers' club in the West End.

The two men greeted each other like the old friends they were and Keith listened in amused silence while Nigel told him of his good fortune.

'So what are you going to do now, then?' he enquired. 'Where are you thinking of spending it?'

'I haven't decided, but obviously I'm off on my travels again.'

'Not going back to Kenya, then?'

'I'd like to go back but there are too many loose ends. I need some space.'

'I enjoyed myself in Kenya,' Keith said somewhat wistfully. 'I had a super time, met some great people and was reluctant to leave. However, my father was ill and the family thought I should come back here.'

'So you knew a good many people out there?'

'Oh yes. We had a very good social life.'

'Did you know the Fairbrothers at all?'

'Johnny Fairbrother, yes I knew him. Bit of a loose cannon, you know, but he was well endowed with money. How he made it I don't know, probably by dubious means.'

'Did you know his wife?'

'He wasn't married when I was there.'

'Then you never met Ariadne?'

Keith frowned, then shook his head. 'No, is that his wife?'

'Yes. Attractive. Not a girl to forget, I think.'

'Oh well, he must have married after I left.'

'Did you ever meet the vet Gordon Ralston?'

'Oh yes, I knew Gordon quite well. Nice chap, terrible shame about him getting killed out there. I believe he married?'

'Yes.'

'Well, she's come in for quite a packet. Gordon

207

was a rich man, wealthy family background and all that, although you wouldn't have known it from the way he lived; he was only interested in his job.'

'How do you know anything about his money, then?'

'Well, I was very friendly with Algy Moreton. In fact, I went to his funeral just before Christmas. You must have met them, they had a great estate out there: Malibu Lodge. They decided to come back home and put Malibu on the market. Pity he had to die before they had a chance to settle here.'

'He told you about Gordon, then?'

'Well, we were talking about old times. He told me Gordon had married, must have been after I left there. Did you meet them?'

'Yes. What else did Algy have to say about them?'

'Well, nothing. The Moretons were never ones to tittle-tattle. He did say she was an attractive woman, but then the Moretons were not members of the fast set.'

'Neither was Gordon Ralston.'

'No, but I don't know about his wife.'

'I was pretty smitten with Kenya, I might just go back there, you've whet my appetite.'

'I wouldn't mind coming with you but at the moment I'm tied up with business matters. The old man's fading in health and he's passed the buck to me. Haven't you managed to make your peace with your father, Nigel?'

'No, I doubt I ever shall.'

'But they were at your grandmother's funeral?'

'Of course. She didn't like my father and he didn't care for her. That she's left me her money didn't go down too well, I can assure you. She left nothing to my mother and she was her only daughter.'

'I know, money in families is the very devil, isn't it?'

Nigel had already made up his mind. He would go back to Kenya, but how Celia would receive him was debatable. Of course he could stress the fact that he'd been demoralised by the death of his grandmother, grovel if needs be for the months he'd neglected to get in touch with her, and be all the things she expected him to be in the immediate future.

'Did you have a property in Kenya?' Keith asked.

'Well, it wasn't much. A bit of a hunting lodge in the country, but I can look around for something a little more upmarket now.'

'So you'll be staying on there?'

'Anything can happen, Keith. I'm a free agent, I can come and go as I please.'

'Never thought of getting married?'

'I've thought about it, and nothing came of it. Perhaps I'll think about it some more.'

'You don't seem like the marrying sort to me.'

Nigel laughed. 'Oh, why is that?'

'You've been a bachelor too long; you're set in your ways, a wife would be too demanding.'

'Perhaps. It would depend on the wife. She'll have to be worth as much as my freedom, but I'll keep you informed.'

In the days that followed he took on a whole

new wardrobe, including riding apparel and what he considered to be the necessary clothes for the sort of life Celia would want, and on a warm sunny day in early September he flew out to Nairobi and the future, whatever it might be.

He hired a car in Nairobi, feeling glad that it was dark and there would be nobody around to see him arriving at his shack except the servants who came out of the house to help him with his luggage. They were a husband and wife he had left in charge of the place, and their two children stood sleepy-eyed, their dark smooth-cheeked faces showing no surprise at the new arrival.

The woman produced coffee and an indifferent meal, and the man informed him that his room would be made ready as quickly as possible. There was a pile of mail on a small table waiting for him, and leafing through it quickly he found little of importance in it. Tomorrow he'd visit the Fairbrothers. They would tell him all he needed to know about Celia: if she was still living there, if she was still alone or if some other man had entered her life. Ariadne would know all he needed to know.

All around him were the sounds and scents of Kenya and the magic was back with him, it was as though he had never been away. In his grandmother's house it had been so still, so still that the sound of a leaf tapping against the window had disturbed him.

He thought about Celia. He wanted her, he wanted her beauty and her passion through the long lonely night, but would she come back to him after months of neglect? Riches made a woman more independent, less ready to forgive and Celia had not exactly been a timid woman: she was beautiful and she'd been spoilt. In the months since they had last met she could have met half a dozen willing suitors.

Ariadne wasn't a good idea. He could picture the amusement in her narrowed eyes, the cynical smile on her generous lips, and Johnny Fairbrother was hardly the sort of man he could ask for advice.

He poured himself another drink and sat staring gloomily into space. For years he'd been the hunter, the playboy with too many conquests behind him; it hadn't mattered. Three months ago Celia wouldn't have mattered. He'd been in love with her, but love was something one got over, it didn't have to be the end of adventure. Now it was a different story. Celia was beautiful and rich, he was rich, together they could have a good life, travel, live well in some beautiful house anywhere in the world.

He reached out for the telephone and dialled Celia's number. She would probably be out, at the club; she could even have returned to England to be with her daughter, but somehow that seemed a remote possibility.

The sound of the ringing tone went on and on until he was on the verge of putting it down. Then he heard her voice, plaintive, a little aggrieved.

'Celia darling, is that you?' he said softly. 'This is Nigel.'

There was silence at the other end and he could feel his heart racing furiously, then she said, 'Nigel, do you know what time it is?'

He stared down at his watch, it was half past three in the morning and he hadn't known it.

'Darling, I'm sorry. I've only been here a short while, I had absolutely no idea of the time. I suppose you were in bed.'

'Well of course.'

'I am sorry. I'll telephone you in the morning, or better still drive round to see you.'

'What time in the morning? I have an arrangement to play tennis.'

'Can't you cancel it?'

'No.'

'Celia, I'll telephone you, I have a lot of explaining to do. A lot of things have happened since last we met, and I couldn't get back any sooner.'

'My telephone hasn't been out of order.'

'Celia, we can't discuss much on the telephone, and not at this hour. I'll ring you tomorrow morning and make an appointment to see you.'

'Yes Nigel, perhaps that would be best.'

She was angry and obviously she intended that he should know it. He wasn't much good at grovelling, he'd rarely had to do it but this was different. He could move on of course, the world was probably awash with rich widows looking for a husband, but he was in no mood to start all over again. He loved Celia, she was his sort: beautiful and passionate, and she loved him, or at least that's what he had thought.

The whisky had made him drowsy and he slept heavily. By the time he woke it was after ten o'clock and there was no reply from Celia's number. Angry with himself, he took a shower and dressed in one of his new safari suits, disdaining the breakfast his servant put in front of him, but accepting the coffee. Then he left the house and drove quickly to the club where he felt sure Celia had kept her tennis engagement.

He drove past Malibu Lodge and stared for a few moments at the For Sale notice at the gates. It was a beautiful house, the sort of house he'd always fancied owning. If Celia was amenable they could take a look at it. He parked his car and strolled unhurriedly through the gardens towards the courts in time to see Celia walking towards the club house in the company of a man. His heart sank.

They settled down on the verandah where coffee was served to them and they appeared to be chatting amiably together. Nigel went inside the club to the bar, where he was immediately hailed by two men who were merely acquaintances.

'So you're back,' the short stout man said. 'Is it likely to be permanent this time?'

Nigel merely smiled and ordered a gin and tonic.

Nodding in the direction of the verandah the other man said, 'He's fairly new on the scene, water engineer working on the new dam that's being built, seems to have taken quite a shine to your lady friend.'

'Celia's a free agent,' Nigel said coolly. 'I'll catch up with her later.'

'Oh well, he'll be off presently, he's living up country but he has become a member of the club.'

'You've confounded the team that thought you wouldn't come back,' the man Nigel remembered as Harvey said.

'Team?'

'Well yes, half the populace said you'd gone for good, the other team thought you might just come back.'

'I hadn't realised I was giving the populace so much interest.'

'Well, you know what women are like.'

He consulted his watch, and picking up his drink he went to sit in the window where he could keep an eye on Celia. They were still deep in conversation and she hadn't seen him. The man showed no signs of leaving, but one of the waiters was approaching their table along the verandah, pausing to speak to them, and then the man rose to his feet and after a brief word to Celia followed the waiter into the club.

After a few minutes he returned, calling to Celia, 'I have to go Celia, something's cropped up on the site. I'll be in touch.'

She smiled and he ran down the steps towards the car park.

Nigel unhurriedly finished his drink before walking through the glass doors on to the verandah. She looked up as he approached, her expression cool and hardly welcoming.

'I decided it wasn't a good idea to talk on the telephone, Celia, I preferred to see you here.'

He took the chair next to hers and asked what she would like to drink.

'Nothing at the moment, Nigel, we've just had coffee.'

'How did the tennis go?'

'Very well, I enjoy playing with Dennis.'

'He's new in the area.'

'Yes. He's working on the new dam.'

'Are they living in the area?'

'They?'

'Well, I didn't know if he was married or not.'

'He isn't.'

'You're very angry with me, Celia, and rightly so. I should have written to you, telephoned, but it's been chaotic, I didn't know what would happen, where I would go, things moved so slowly after my grandmother died.'

'Your grandmother died?'

'Yes. She had a massive heart attack. There had to be a funeral, the gathering of the clans, her estate to see to, and like I said the law moves very slowly. You must know that, Celia, after what happened to Gordon.'

'Actually, Nigel, my affairs were sorted out very quickly.'

'But of course. You were on the verge of divorce, Celia.'

'Gordon had not approached his solicitors with respect to that. When he died suddenly I was still his wife. I inherited his estate and whatever money he had.'

Deliberately he kept his expression relaxed. That Gordon had money had been a surprise to him and probably to everybody else. He didn't want Celia to think he knew about her good fortune.

'That would be a whole lot less worry for you, my dear,' he said calmly.

215

'Yes, it was.'

'Well, I wish I could say the same thing about my grandmother's estate. She totally ignored my mother and she'd never got along with my father. She left everything to me and you can imagine how the family felt about that. I doubt if I'll ever be welcome in their midst again. There was a lot of wrangling, her affairs were not exactly in apple pie order, but at the end of the day the old girl did me proud. I'm a rich man, with a house in Dorset and the wherewithal to tell the rest of them to go to hell.'

'What made you come back here? Didn't you want to remain in Dorset?'

'No. It will be somewhere to go back to whenever I decide to visit England, alone or with you, Celia.'

Her eyes opened wide but she didn't say anything.

'I came back to see you, Celia, to grovel if necessary, but to ask you to forgive me for all the things I hadn't done, and hopefully agree to what I hope to do.'

'And that is?'

'I came back to ask you to marry me, Celia. We'll look around for somewhere nice here, always providing you wish to remain here; if not we'll think of somewhere else, and we'll see something of the world too. I can afford it, darling.'

'We can afford it, Nigel. Gordon left me a very rich woman. I didn't deserve it but I've been looking at property with the idea of staying on here. I haven't found anything yet, but at least we

216

can think about it together.'

'So you will marry me, Celia?'

She nodded, and he reached out and took both her hands in a tight clasp. 'And I'm forgiven?' he asked.

'Oh yes, Nigel, I was so terribly hurt when you didn't write to me. I thought you'd never come back however much I wanted you to. I love you, Nigel, I always have.'

'So, where do you want us to start looking for our new home?'

'I've looked at a few houses with nice gardens but somehow none of them were exactly what I wanted. The only houses I really liked were occupied and unlikely to come on the market.'

'I see Malibu Lodge is for sale. The Moretons moved back to England and Algy died just before Christmas.'

Celia looked at him in amazement. She loved Malibu, she wanted it, but to hear Nigel mention it was making her heart race.

'It's beautiful, Nigel. I've driven up to the house and looked through the windows. I've imagined how wonderful it must be to own a place like that. But of course it's quite impossible, it's far too large and Mrs Moreton will want a fortune for it.'

'I know how much she wants for it, I knew before I left England.'

'And it's ridiculous to even think about it, Nigel.'

'Darling, we're rich, we can think about it. Tell you what, let's drive out there now and look at it together. We can look round the grounds and at the stables. Tomorrow we'll get the keys and look around the house. I can see you at Malibu, darling.'

He rose to his feet pulling her up after him, and together they hurried along the verandah and out to where Nigel's car waited.

'The car's hardly the sort you'd expect to see standing outside Malibu,' Nigel said with a smile. 'It's only a hire, I'll look around for another but there were more urgent things to see to than a car.'

Speculation was rife in the club house, where the two men had been joined by others, including several women.

'Where do you suppose they're off to?' Julie asked, her eyes watching Nigel's car receding down the drive.

Celia's thoughts were chaotic. Nigel was back in Kenya and had proposed to her. They were looking at Malibu and Ariadne would be furious. They were still friends but something had gone out of that friendship, starting from the day they had talked about Malibu. Now she wandered hand in hand with Nigel through the formal gardens which had always been lovingly tended by the Moretons' team of gardeners. The stables too were immaculate, and of course there had to be horses, beautiful thoroughbred horses. Suddenly her thoughts turned to Rosemary.

One day Rosemary would come out to Kenya, she would be older, she would have got rid of those wretched braces on her teeth and she would be beautiful. The rich beautiful Miss Greville and every eligible man in the district would want to marry her. Seeing her expression, Nigel said, 'Well, what are you thinking about, darling?'

'I was thinking about Rosemary. She is my daughter, Nigel, one day she'll have to come out here.'

'Well of course, darling, but not for some time yet. She has to finish her education and we have to enjoy ourselves, buy this place, make it to our liking, see the world. You'll have to write to them in England and tell them our plans. I don't suppose they'll want to come out here.'

'Why should they?'

'I think we should have a quiet wedding, darling. It's your third and we want to go right away, from the gossips and everybody else. You don't want a big do, do you?'

'No, I don't. Some of the women haven't been too nice to me.'

'Well then, we'll be married by special licence and get away.'

'What about Malibu?'

'Oh we'll buy Malibu. It's what we both want and I'll go into Nairobi in the morning and settle everything up. Come with me, you can do some shopping, buy some pretty dresses. We're going to have a wonderful life, darling.'

She believed him. Life was wonderful, she had Nigel and she would have Malibu. She would have the life she had always associated with Kenya, *White Mischief*, the rich and the powerful, the best of all worlds.

'We'll call and see the Fairbrothers,' Nigel said. 'We're close by. We'll tell them our news. I'm not much in favour of Fairbrother and I'm never too sure about Ariadne, but she's your friend, isn't she, darling?'

Celia smiled. She thought it very doubtful that Ariadne would continue to be her friend when she learned about Malibu.

Chapter Sixteen

Beatrice was the first one down for breakfast as always and she went immediately to the hall table where the morning's post was left. She was busy leafing through it when David came running down the stairs, asking, 'Anything for me, Aunt Beatrice?'

'I don't know; here, take a look through these.'

His face wore a disappointed look as he handed the letters back to her, but with a smile she said, 'Here's one from Gloria. You needn't look so neglected.'

His handsome face beamed with delight as he took Gloria's letter and hurried into the breakfast room to read it. At the door he called out, 'There's one here from Kenya.'

All Beatrice could think of was that it had come at last: the letter she'd been expecting for months to tell her Celia was coming back to live in England and the future of Rosemary would be her responsibility.

She opened the letter at the breakfast table where Cedric had his head stuck in his morning

220

paper. The two young men were helping themselves to breakfast from the side table.

After a few minutes Cedric looked up to find his sister staring down at the letter with an expression of acute bewilderment.

'Well,' he demanded, 'what has she to say for herself? When's she coming back?'

Their eyes met, and this time the look of incredulity on Beatrice's face made him reach out for the letter. After a few minutes he snorted angrily, 'Well, this takes the biscuit. I hope you'll write back with a few home truths.'

'What's happening now?' Noel asked. 'Nothing that woman does will surprise me.'

'She's getting married again,' his father snapped, 'and she's staying out there.' Beatrice folded the letter and laid it beside her plate. She wasn't hungry for breakfast and she'd read the letter later when she could absorb it better.

She read it later in her room, and as she read it she could picture Celia writing it, searching for the right words, her pretty face uncertain. But then Celia had never been too worried about what other people thought. Her blandishments and apologies were designed to suit herself, never other people.

'Darling Beatrice,' she began. 'I do want you to be very happy for me because of late there's been so much unhappiness in my life. Nigel Boyd has asked me to marry him and we're so very much in love. We've decided to make our home here and have bought the most wonderful country estate, called Malibu Lodge.

'It's all so exciting for us, Beatrice. We are busy

making the house feel like our own and we intend to get married very quietly here in Kenya. Just a few guests and then we hope to go off on our travels, to some places I've never been to and never expected to visit.

'Rosemary is at school now and almost an adult, so she won't be too much trouble, I'm sure. You've been absolutely wonderful, Beatrice, and one day when we really get settled in our own home and we no longer have any desire to roam the world, Rosemary will join us and you must come here too. I'll make it the best holiday you've ever spent, for as long as you like. Do wish us well, dear Beatrice, and thank you for everything.'

For a long time she sat staring out of the window, but she wasn't seeing the tossing trees and grey churning sea. She was thinking about her life.

It was later in the day when her brother said, 'I've learned something about this Nigel Boyd. He was in Dorset living with his grandmother, Lady Fitzwilliam. She died and he's got his hands on her money and her estate. The house is a great rambling affair which she hasn't spent much money on of late, but she's left him a great deal of money.

'I suppose he'll come back to it from time to time but obviously they don't seem inclined to be starting their married life in Dorset.'

'Cedric, I never seem to have had a life. I've been living in somebody else's house, and I've been looking after other people's children and I'm very tired. I want a place of my own, I want to do what I want for a change without this feeling that so many people are depending on me.'

'Well, pretty soon now I'm sure there'll be just the two of us. Noel will be at University. David's engaged and they'll be looking for a place of their own. With just the two of us you'll have all the time you want to do what you want.'

'I want my own house, Cedric. I want a small place that I can manage myself.'

'You'll never get anything more beautiful than Dene Hollow.'

'I know. But I don't want anything this size, I want a small house or cottage, a tiny garden, not too far away from the shops, just me and my animals.'

'What about Rosie?'

'I hadn't bargained on Rosie. She'll come to me for holidays of course?'

'And what about me?'

'Oh Cedric, you don't need me. You have Betty and Mrs Humphreys, and you have a chauffeur you really don't need. Why don't you ask David to move in when he gets married? Gloria loves this house; she's always going on about wishing she lived here.'

'She's a materialistic girl.'

'Well, yes she is, but it would give them a few years to save more money in case they do want a house of their own.'

'And what about Jerome and Natalie? There'd be all sorts of jealousies. Natalie likes this house.'

'I'm sure they'll all get their fair share, even Jeffrey. I can't think why you don't bury the hatchet. He's happy enough with Connie and their baby is lovely. You can't go on bearing a grudge for ever.'

'Let them stew a bit longer. I'm not ready to make them welcome yet.'

Beatrice felt angry with herself, with Celia and the world in general. For years she had been anticipating what she would do when her family were off her hands. Now Celia's bombshell had precipitated matters. It had never been her intention to raise the issue so soon.

Celia's mother telephoned her, her voice querulous.

'Who is this man she's marrying?' she demanded. 'Have you met him?'

'Briefly, one afternoon when she was here.'

'She says he's some lord's son but he isn't friendly with his family. He has a house in Dorset. I suppose they could visit pretty frequently.'

'They have also bought a property in Kenya,' Beatrice couldn't resist saying.

'Why couldn't she come home when Gordon died? Why is she so obsessed with staying on there? And there's Rosemary to consider, or hasn't she even thought about Rosemary?'

'She knows Rosie's at school here. When has Celia ever really concerned herself with Rosie?'

Her mother immediately leapt to her daughter's defence. 'Well, it has been pretty traumatic for her with Gordon's death, and she knows Rosemary has always been in good hands. She told me you never minded having her, Beatrice.'

Beatrice decided to say nothing to Celia's mother about her wish to leave Dene Hollow. After all, they had never been close and she really felt she'd done enough damage for one day.

Cedric raised the issue over the evening meal, his tone offended, his displeasure very evident.

'Your aunt's thinking of moving out into something of her own,' he said baldly.

Noel and David stared at her in surprise and Beatrice said hastily, 'I've been thinking about it for years, it's something I always intended to do when you didn't need me any more. Now you're both grown up and your father doesn't need me, he has his own interests.'

'But why now,' David asked, 'You've never said anything before.'

'It's that woman,' Noel said angrily. 'Aunt Beatrice thought she'd be coming back to England and now she's staying on there with some new husband, and she's landed with Rosie.'

'Rosie's hardly a burden,' Beatrice said gently. 'She's away most of the time and I thought you liked her here.'

'She's all right, I suppose. Why have you suddenly decided to leave us?'

'I'm not leaving tomorrow or next week either. It might take a long time to find something I really like, and I wouldn't leave without assuring myself that everything here was being taken care of. You're engaged to Gloria, David, I've suggested to your father that perhaps the two of you could make your home here until you've enough money to buy something you really want.'

David's face brightened considerably. 'I say, that's a great idea. Gloria loves this house. You wouldn't mind, would you, Dad?'

'She's little more than a child. What does she know about looking after two men and caring for a house the size of this one?'

'She could learn,' Beatrice said. 'I had to learn.'

'You were a much older and more responsible woman.'

'That's what all of you have always assumed. Good old Beatrice, she's nothing better to do with her life and she's on her own. She'll relish the company.'

'Well, you never refused,' Cedric snapped.

'I know. I had a sense of responsibility. I was the oldest and like you say I was on my own. That doesn't mean to say I was ready for a ready-made family.'

'But you cared about us surely,' David said wistfully.

'Well, of course I did, but now you're grown and don't need me. You've moved on and I must too.'

She looked at Noel staring down at his plate, his expression glum.

'There's no need to look so upset,' Beatrice chided him gently. 'You'll be leaving us soon anyway so whether I'm here or not won't exactly concern you.'

'I didn't want anything here to change,' he muttered.

'Noel, everything in life changes as we get older.'

'Well, I know that, but this is something that

didn't need to change, it's something that's been brought on because Rosie's mother's a selfish cow and doesn't care for anybody but herself.'

'She also has a life to lead, Noel, perhaps we shouldn't judge her too harshly. I just hope that she'll be happy with her new husband and that in time Rosie will find happiness with them.'

'Does Rosie know, do you think?' David asked.

'I don't know. Surely Celia will have written to her.'

'She'll probably have sent her another wretched doll to make up for it,' Noel said sharply.

'Well of course she won't have sent her a doll,' Beatrice said. 'They stopped coming years ago.'

'After you told her they were inappropriate,' Noel said.

Later that evening, when her brother had gone to see one of his cronies and the two boys were out with the boat, Beatrice realised that she had burnt her bridges and she wasn't displeased. Now she could really start to think about her future: a small cottage with her own things around her, a small garden with a vegetable plot and shops within walking distance.

A cottage with a glass porch and two bedrooms, she didn't need more, and perhaps a nice park nearby where she could walk her dog.

Cedric didn't really like animals, he was always fussing about their comings and goings and her supercilious cat had never liked Cedric.

Rosie would come to her for holidays but Rosie would miss Dene Hollow, she would miss the sea and the cliffs. But then Rosie would miss the boys: Noel would be gone and David would

227

belong to Gloria. Times were changing, and now she'd made her decision the sooner the better.

Rosie sat on the edge of her bed, staring down at her mother's letter. She was trying to remember Nigel Boyd, the man her mother was about to marry.

He had been tall and good-looking. He had been nice to her, and she was remembering sitting at the back of the car listening to their conversation and their laughter and feeling decidedly out of things.

Her mother's letter was conciliatory. 'You'll simply love Malibu Lodge, darling, there are beautiful gardens and mile upon mile of open country. The house looks like one of those pictures of plantation houses in America's deep South. The first time I saw it I fell in love with it, never thinking that one day I might be able to live in it.

'You'll remember Nigel, darling, from the day he took us out to lunch. He's so handsome and charming, and he was nice to you, Rosie, you must remember how nice he was to you.

'I'm so very happy, and I've written to your grandparents and to Aunt Beatrice to tell them. You've always been happy at Dene Hollow, Rosemary, and when you've left Chevington that is the time you'll join us here in Kenya. Nigel loves horses; that I'm sure comes from his childhood in Ireland. He's intent on buying some horses for the stables here so you'll be able to ride, and there are wonderful clubs here for tennis and swimming and other sports. You have a wonderful future to look forward to, but in the meantime Nigel and I are setting out on our travels. I'll keep you posted as to where we are and what we are seeing. Do wish me well, darling. We've elected to get married here in Kenya so that we can sort the house out before we set off on our travels. I've chosen my wedding dress, pale blue wild silk and there will only be a handful of guests. It would have been lovely if you could have been here, but we'll make up for lost time when we meet. I have invited Beatrice to spend time with us, I'm sure you will want that, darling. In the meantime I send you all my love. I'll send you photographs of the wedding later. Your most loving mother.'

How could she be enthusiastic about something in a land she didn't know concerning two people she thought of as remote? Her mother was somebody she admired, had seen seldom and wished she knew better; Nigel she hardly remembered.

She wasn't enthusiastic about joining them in Kenya. Dene Hollow had been her home for so long she couldn't visualise anything else, consequently when Aunt Beatrice wrote to say she was looking around for a small cottage it felt as if her entire world was falling to pieces.

Why was Aunt Beatrice leaving Dene Hollow? It didn't make sense. What would they do without her? How could Gloria possibly replace her? She didn't really like Gloria. Where David was concerned she was possessive; she'd resented the fact that Rosie had known David longer and known Dene Hollow better.

She hoped it would take Aunt Beatrice years to find her cottage. Two weeks later when the wedding photographs arrived she stared down at her beautiful mother gazing up enraptured into the eyes of the tall, dark-haired man smiling down at her.

She looked so beautiful in her pale blue flowing gown, her blond hair caught back from her face by a halo of white gardenias. They were standing on the lawn before an imposing house with its pillared entrance and imposing windows, and there were other people standing behind them on the lawn, women in summery dresses and men in immaculate morning suits. One woman in particular stood out from the rest because she was wearing a bright red dress and a large black hat adorned with red poppies. She was wearing sunglasses with intricately shaped frames and she had a beautiful exotic face. She was a woman who stood out from the rest of the pastel-gowned women, and there was one photograph of her standing with her mother on the steps, smiling into each other's eyes. On the back of the photograph Celia had written, 'Ariadne and me after the service'.

Rosie thought Ariadne was an unusual name to suit an unusual woman. She supposed that one day she would meet Ariadne.

Beatrice was busy consulting estate agents. Noel was working hard to achieve a degree in Civil Engineering and David was employed in the family firm where Jerome was a senior partner. Beatrice believed that, at last, she was in sight of being her own woman in her own home, but, in her innermost heart, she knew she would continue to worry about them.

She visited Jeffrey and Connie every week and thought their little boy was lovely. He was a bright child, curious about everything and with a happy disposition. Both Jeffrey and Connie were devoted parents if not very affluent ones.

Connie was doing hairdressing at her home and they had adapted the front room of their small terraced house for this purpose. She had a steady clientele, customers who had known her at the salon and now found her prices considerably less expensive. They were a loyal and happy band. The baby sat in his pram or on his high chair in one corner of the room gurgling happily; her customers plied him with sweets and chocolate and he never lacked admirers.

Jeffrey had found work running the office of a local builder. It was hardly the work his education had qualified him for but he was reasonably content. The builder thought well of him, he was conscientious and a good time-keeper, and their life was to their liking.

Beatrice seldom visited Jerome, for one thing they were away more than they were at home. Natalie had her tennis club and her golf, Jerome was an enthusiastic Rotarian and also an aspiring golfer, and all in all neither of them had much time for entertaining relatives or visiting Cedric and the rest of them.

It seemed to Beatrice that this family she had once hoped would remain close was disintegrating, and when she said as much to Cedric he said sharply, 'Well, what did you expect? As soon as the women come into it they're either jealous or resentful of each other. It'll be even worse when Gloria gets a foot in this place.'

Beatrice felt faintly unhappy about Gloria's arrival at Dene Hollow. She was prepared to give her any advice on the running of the house that she might need but Gloria was not open to advice. Gloria was going to be the lady of the manor, she would do things her way or not at all, and Mrs Humphreys was already saying times would be changing and she was prepared to look around for something else.

'Please, Mrs Humphreys, don't be in a hurry to move out. It is my brother's house, after all, and he won't let her have it all her own way.'

'Your brother'll be off with his friends and not much care as long as he's got a home to come back to and his own things around him. That little madam'll want the earth.'

Betty too was expressing her doubts. 'She's allus finding fault, Miss Greville,' she complained, 'with the way I do my hair, and with my clothes. She'll be gettin' rid of me as soon as you've gone.'

'I'm not going until I've got somewhere to go to, Betty, and I'll have a few words with Miss Gloria before I go, never fear.'

Her words did nothing to assuage the fears of Betty and Mrs Humphreys.

Meanwhile, Gloria was getting at David.

'I can't think why your father will want that enormous room at the corner of the house, we should have it. After all there are two of us.'

232

'I can't ask my father to give up his bedroom,' David said. 'He shared that room with my mother, he'll not agree to giving it up.'

'Well, we could put it to him very nicely. After all we could make it an *en suite* room with a lovely bathroom. I know there are two bathrooms but it's more personal that way and he won't want me in his bathroom if I happen to be using the wrong one.'

'We can sort all that out nearer the time, Gloria.'

'Darling, surely you can understand that I want to make changes. I want my colour schemes, my pictures, my furnishings. These things are what your mother chose.'

Gloria was entirely malleable when Beatrice spoke to her, but she was left with the feeling that everything would change when she was finally installed at Dene Hollow after their wedding. Beatrice would not be there any more, and it would be Gloria who would be the mistress of the house.

When she said as much to Cedric he merely sniffed disdainfully, 'I'm the master of the house, Beatrice and I won't let them forget it. They're here on sufferance.'

For all that Beatrice could only see a battle of wills between her brother and his new daughter-in-law.

Book Two

Book Two

Chapter Seventeen

Jeffries had received his instructions from Miss Greville. Her niece would be on the ten o'clock train from London and he must wait for her at the end of the platform. The train was on time and he looked along the platform at the stream of people who had poured out of the train.

Surely she wouldn't have missed the train; her aunt's instructions to her must surely have been as specific as they had been to himself. He had seen Rosie Greville mature, from the pretty child clutching her teddy bear on that first day he had brought her to Dene Hollow and through all the years when she'd been a tomboy one minute, in an effort to keep pace with her cousins, to that other Rosie, glum, defiant and often insecure. It was evident that she had missed the train and he contemplated several hours of kicking his heels in Exeter.

He was about to turn away when a young woman smiling broadly walked towards him and he stared back in astonishment. This was not the Rosie he knew, not this vital girl with the beaming smile and beautiful face under its halo of golden hair. She came towards him holding out her hand and he tried to disguise the dismay on his face as he reached out to take her luggage.

'I hope you haven't been waiting long, Jeffries. I think the train was on time.'

'Oh yes it was, miss. Your aunt warned me several times that I mustn't be late. You've been staying with your grandparents in London, I believe?'

She smiled. 'You looked surprised. Didn't you recognise me? After all, it's some time since you last saw me.'

'You've grown up so suddenly.'

'I've had the braces off my teeth and grandmother insisted I had my hair styled. It's such a relief to get rid of the braces; they were horrible.'

'They've done what they were supposed to do, though. You're a very pretty girl, you're going to surprise everybody.'

'Everything ready for the wedding?'

'I believe so. The reception is to be at the Esplanade, the guests appear to be taking the hotel over.'

'Will Noel be home for it?'

'He's the best man, due to arrive this afternoon.'

'And Aunt Beatrice is looking after things for the last time. Her cottage is lovely, she's very happy there.'

'Yes, I brought her here last Wednesday. She's looking very well, not nearly as much work, I suppose.'

'I'm glad she's happy. I was hoping she'd come with me to Kenya but I couldn't persuade her.'

'Of course, you're off to live with your mother very soon.'

Rosie nodded, her face reflective, so much so that Jeffries decided not to pursue the subject.

As they drove at last along the cliff top road Rosie sat forward in her seat so that she could look along the stretch of beach, at a blue sea rolling in gently towards the shore.

'You'll miss this,' he said gently.

She smiled. 'I've loved it, I'll always miss it. When first I came here I hoped it would be for ever.'

'You had some good times here, you and the boys, particularly the two younger ones. There was a lot going on in the summer holidays when they brought their friends here.'

She didn't answer. Steven came in the summer; she could see him now strolling along the cliff path with the breeze ruffling his dark hair, his smile warm on a face she had loved. Why did she remember Steven's face so vividly when she had forgotten so many others?

They were driving through the gates now and Beatrice was walking out of the French windows on to the terrace. She had evidently been watching for their arrival

Rosie left the car and ran up the steps to meet her. Suddenly she seemed so tiny, the diminutive aunt who had organised all their lives, and Beatrice looked up at Rosie and thought that her unattractive little duckling had become the most elegant of swans.

'Rosie, your teeth are beautiful. Now you have to admit the braces were good for them. And you're so tall and grown up.'

'I know, I feel like a bean pole at the side of you.'

'I can see that your grandmother has had a

hand in shaping the new you; she knows what your mother will expect.'

'I hope so. I thought I was a bit of a disappointment to her.'

'You won't be now, darling. Rosie, you're going into a whole new life and you're going to enjoy every minute of it. You'll make new friends, and in time your life here will be just a pleasant memory. Now come inside and I'll help you unpack your case.'

She stared out of the window at the scene she'd grown up with. Nothing had changed in her old bedroom but Aunt Beatrice said there had been a great many changes in the rest of the house. Gloria had had a lot of her own way.

Cedric had adamantly refused to relinquish his bedroom for the newly weds but the room that the two younger boys had shared was large, and this had now been equipped with a bathroom and new furnishings.

There was new furniture and curtains in the drawing room, not particularly to Beatrice's taste, but undoubtedly they reflected the differences in their age groups.

Rosie kept her own counsel, but she had liked the velvet drapes and cushions, the luxury of the oriental carpets. Now Gloria's choice of vibrant silks and a plain beige carpet seemed somehow cold.

'Have you heard from mother?' Rosie asked.

'Yes. I've explained that I'm not one for overseas travel, I think she understands.' Beatrice didn't offer to show Rosie her mother's letter because one aspect of it troubled her.

240

'That nice young man, Steven Chaytor, is here at the hospital and is very highly thought of. I met him at the club and he was charming. I asked him about the girl he was with at Dene Hollow and he told me he'd been with her in South Africa where she was working and I believe she's coming to the hospital here. I'm sure something will come of it, only I do hope Rosemary will have got over her obvious crush on him.'

Beatrice believed it was an unkind quirk of fate that had sent Steven to Kenya and she hoped fervently that both Steven and Rosie were now two very different people. If Steven loved Mary then he should marry her, put himself out of reach. Surely there would be other men around. But the doubts persisted.

Noel arrived in the late afternoon, greeting Rosie with enthusiasm, commenting gallantly on her changed appearance and then David was there, equally complimentary. But Cedric spared her hardly a glance, he was too engrossed with the changes to his lifestyle.

Gloria had not wanted to ask Rosie to be one of her bridesmaids, her excuse being, 'My two cousins are so pretty and Rosie is so plain with those awful braces on her teeth. Anyway, we don't really know each other very well, I'm sure she won't expect to be one of my bridesmaids,' she'd said.

She was going to have the shock of her life, Noel thought. Rosie'd be the prettiest girl at the wedding. Gloria would be pea-green with envy; Natalie too would have to look to her laurels.

Sitting with Beatrice in the church they watched the arrival of the other guests, Jerome and Natalie greeting them with effusive smiles. Natalie whispered to Jerome, 'Gosh was that really Rosie? She's quite beautiful.' Connie and Jeffrey were there with their little boy, Connie as always a shade too colourful. But her smile had lost none of its warmth, and leaning forward in their pew, she touched Rosie gently on the shoulder, 'Rosie, you look gorgeous, I wouldn't have known you.'

Rosie turned to smile at them and the little boy beamed back.

Sitting next to his sister, Cedric was not enjoying the occasion, he hated weddings, he thought they were a lot of fuss about nothing and he wasn't too happy about the outcome of this one. David was too besotted with the girl, and the more he spoilt her the more she would expect.

'Try to look a little cheerful,' his sister remonstrated.

'I don't feel cheerful.'

'It's a wedding, Cedric, not a funeral. You'll have a new girl in the family. For David's sake try to look a little welcoming.'

Gloria's mother beamed at them from across the aisle and Beatrice thought that in twenty years' time Gloria could look exactly like her. She was thin with sharp ordinary features, wearing a large green hat on her light brown hair and an expression that she had often seen on Gloria's face, cocksure and not a little vain.

Sitting in the front pew, David and Noel were

chatting amicably together, but David seemed nervous when he'd always seemed the most confident of boys.

Noel turned his head and grinned, whispering to Rosie, 'You've set the cat among the pigeons, Rosie, Natalie's not sure that she can cope with the new you.'

Rosie merely smiled and shook her head. Behind them Connie's little boy was restless and Cedric muttered, 'Weddings are no places for children; they should have found somebody to look after him.'

The music swelled, the congregation rose to its feet and the procession of Gloria on the arm of her father appeared at the top of the aisle.

David's responses showed a degree of nervousness, Gloria's were confident. She looked very pretty in a white bridal gown with a long train embroidered in palest peach, and returning to his seat, her father beamed confidently at his wife. Mistress of Dene Hollow, their youngest daughter had done very well for herself.

Later, when the guests mingled together at the Esplanade Hotel, Beatrice was aware that underneath all the gaiety and laughter there were undercurrents of resentment and envy.

Envy for Rosie from both Natalie and Gloria, who had always envied her because she was installed at Dene Hollow. They'd always thought of her as something of a nuisance. Now they envied her beauty, as they saw how much the plain, moody child had changed.

Gloria had smiled, saying, 'How nice you look, Rosie, without those horrible braces on your teeth, I expect you were delighted to get rid of them.'

'I believe you're going out to Kenya soon?' Natalie said. 'So this might be your last visit to Dene Hollow?'

'Possibly, I don't know.'

'Well, of course, if you're ever visiting in England you're very welcome to stay with us at Dene Hollow, I'm sure we'll find room for you for the odd occasion,' Gloria said.

Hearing the conversation, Noel said, 'Does that invitation extend to me also or had you forgotten that Dene Hollow is my home?'

'No of course not, Noel. We know it's your home, but it isn't Rosie's.'

'Come on,' Noel said. 'Let's get something to eat,' and putting his hand under her elbow he moved Rosie away towards the buffet table.

'That's how it's going to be,' he murmured. 'In no time at all she'll make me feel an interloper in my own home.'

'Well you mustn't let her,' Rosie said shortly.

While they helped themselves to food they were joined by Natalie and Jerome, and Natalie was quick to say, 'Everything's going to change, I'm afraid. She gives herself airs already and she's not even installed yet. I wouldn't care but Jerome's the eldest. We've made a life for ourselves, and David and Gloria have simply fallen into it.'

When Rosie didn't answer she went on, 'Have you been invited to visit if ever you come back to England?'

'Well yes.'

'That's how it's going to be for all of us. Come

244

for tea a week on Sunday. I can't think why Aunt Beatrice had to leave.'

'She wanted her own home. She's been marvellous all these years, now we're off her hands.'

Jerome joined them, nursing a plate piled high with food and saying, 'The wolves have gathered, Natalie. If you want some food I'd get over there now. So you're off to Kenya at last, Rosie.'

'Yes.'

'Looking forward to it?'

'I think so. My life is going to be very different.'

'Well, I've had a letter from Steven. He seems to be enjoying it out there.'

'I thought Steven was in South Africa.'

'He was, he's now in Kenya.'

His eyes were twinkling maliciously, and in the next breath he said, 'I hope you've got over that crush you had on him. I believe wedding bells will soon be in the offing.'

'Really. Somebody he's met out there?'

'No. Mary. She followed him out to Cape Town; now she's in Kenya. You can't say the girl isn't persistent. Feel like taking her on, Rosie?'

'You always did like to stir things, didn't you Jerome. Kenya's a big country; I might not even meet Steven.'

Across the room, Beatrice watched them talking together and her heart sank. Jerome wouldn't miss any chance to tease Rosie about Steven. Perhaps after all she should have told her that her mother had met up with him. Jerome called it teasing, she thought he was being rather spiteful.

'I'm going to have a chat with Connie,' Rosie informed Jerome. 'The little boy is lovely, I should get to know him.'

Connie was sitting at the side of the room with her young son on her knee and Rosie smiled down at them. 'You decided to call him Paul?' she said.

'Yes, I always wished they'd called me Paula. I hate Connie. I hate Constance even more.'

Rosie laughed. 'I shall have to get used to being called Rosemary. My mother hated it when they shortened it to Rosie.'

'I think Rosemary's a lovely name. I prefer it to Rosie, anyway.'

'Paul's been very good, he looks awfully sleepy now.'

'Yes. We'll be going soon. Jeffrey's gone to speak to his father then we'll be getting home. Will you ever come back here, Rosie?'

'Surely I will, but then I really don't know.'

'It'll be different. This was your home, you'll be a visitor the next time.'

'I suppose so.'

'Jeffrey comes here about once a fortnight to see his father. I don't know whether his father wants him to come but we think it's his duty. I don't come with him. I know Mr Greville doesn't really like me, but I insist that Jeffrey comes and brings our son with him. He's his grandfather, after all.'

'He ought to be very proud of him.'

Connie smiled a little sadly. 'Yes well, perhaps he doesn't like children.'

'He should, he's had four of his own.'

'I know, but Jeffrey says as a father he's always been pretty remote. I like Aunt Beatrice, she's really nice. It's been a lovely wedding, hasn't it. I thought Gloria looked lovely. I always wanted a big wedding but I didn't get one. Anyway, my father couldn't afford a big splash and we got married very quietly with only a handful of people there.'

'But you're happy, Connie?'

'Oh yes. My hairdressing business is doing really well and Jeffrey's job is right enough. It's not what he was educated for, and that I think is one reason his father is so angry. We'll move on to something better when we get a bit of money behind us.'

'I'll write to you, Connie, and if I ever come back you can be sure I'll visit you.'

'That'll be lovely, Rosie. I really don't care about the others. Here's Jeffrey now.'

Jeffrey smiled and kissed her cheek. 'Enjoyed it, Rosie?'

'Yes. It was a very nice wedding. Paul is lovely; you must be very proud of him.'

'Yes, we are. He's a well-behaved little chap, ask Connie's customers.'

He reached down and gathered Paul into his arms.

'We'll be off now, love. We'll say goodbye to Aunt Beatrice and anybody else we meet on our way out. I hope all goes well for you in Kenya, Rosie, let us know how you go on.'

'I will.'

She watched them weaving their way through the crowds with the little boy carried aloft on his father's shoulders. They were the first to leave.

From his seat outside on the balcony Cedric watched his second son and his family walking through the lines of cars to where he had parked his rather rackety old tourer. He was thinking that as usual Connie's skirts were too short, her heels a little too high, her hair under the flamboyant hat a little too blond, but at the end of the day he had to admit that Jeffrey exuded a contentment that seemed to have escaped his eldest son.

He had watched Beatrice embracing the three of them, seen the way her face lit up with smiles as the little boy put his arms around her neck. Jeffrey had disappointed him, wasted his money on his education, accepted a wife and a job that were far beneath him, and yet the boy seemed happy enough with his lot. Perhaps he'd pushed too hard, perhaps Jeffrey had never wanted what he had wanted for him.

Rosie had joined Beatrice on the steps, and Cedric's eyes narrowed as they beheld the beautiful girl in her wedding guest finery. Celia would be delighted with the transformation. His brother too would have been well pleased with his daughter.

The guests were piling out of the hotel now to stand on the balcony and the steps while they waited for the bride and groom to appear.

David and Gloria came out hand in hand, smiling broadly. She tossed her flowers in the direction of her younger sister, who caught them with a bright smile, to the cheers of the onlookers.

David's new sports car was waiting for them on the drive and they ran towards it, followed by the younger guests. Cedric hadn't bothered to ask them where they were spending their honeymoon; it was somewhere Gloria had always wanted to go, somewhere she thought of as romantic. They had said they would be back in just over two weeks.

They were leaving Beatrice to look after him but she had stated her intention of leaving before they returned home. He had only heard reports about her cottage. He would probably never visit her. After all, there had been no need for her to leave, he'd have given David some money towards a place of their own. Now he'd be saddled with this unknown girl ordering him about, ordering his son about, Jerome and Natalie would probably never come near and even Jeffrey would think twice about it.

Beatrice read her brother's expression well. He was sorry for himself, sorry and angry. His life was changing.

'I think we can make our excuses and leave now, Cedric,' Beatrice said. 'Quite a few of them are drifting away.'

He gave a short sigh of relief.

'I'll be glad to get out of this suit and put my feet up. I suppose we'd better say we're leaving to Gloria's parents.'

'Yes, of course.'

They passed Jerome and Natalie on their way inside and Natalie said with a quick smile, 'We'll call before they get back, Mr Greville. After that we shall probably wait until we're invited.'

'It is still my house,' her father-in-law said in some exasperation. 'I go where I want and invite who I want.'

Natalie smiled and Jerome said, 'Keep it up then, Dad.'

'I intend to.'

Two weeks, thought Beatrice, two weeks and I can go home. Seeing her expression Rosie said softly, 'Perhaps it won't be so bad after all.'

Oh the optimism of youth, Beatrice thought. The blind assumption that they only had to wish for a thing for their wishes to be fulfilled. In her innermost heart she believed that life at Dene Hollow would never be the same. If ever Rosie came back to it she would find it irretrievably changed.

Chapter Eighteen

Nigel brought the car to rest at the top of the hill with the house before them. The sun was setting in a blaze of glory, shedding its pink light on the pillared portico and the house's exquisite symmetry, gilding the surrounding gardens and distant hills; and Celia looked at her daughter's face while she waited for her reactions.

Rosie thought she had never seen anything so beautiful before and her expression was one of wide-eyed wonder as Nigel gently drove down the hill and up to the house.

Mother and daughter were alone together in

Rosie's bedroom overlooking the shallow lake and its flock of flamingos, and Celia was happily showing Rosie the room with its matching bathroom. Opening and closing drawers and cupboards, pointing out porcelain and pictures that she had chosen herself and which she wanted Rosie to like.

Celia had set out that morning to meet her daughter's plane with mixed feelings, anticipating the arrival of a gawky girl with few pretensions to beauty, and had been unable to believe the tall exquisite girl who had come forward to meet them. All she had ever wanted for her daughter was here. Now she could take her to meet their friends, introduce her to Kenyan society, give parties for her, find her the most eligible escorts. In no time at all Rosemary, as she wanted everybody to call her, would be the girl to be seen with, the girl who would be able to pick and choose whoever she wanted.

'Aunt Beatrice would have really loved all this,' Rosemary said wistfully. 'I wish she'd come with me.'

'Oh well, dear, she was never a great one for travelling. But we're going to give you such a wonderful time. You'll soon forget Dene Hollow; all this is far more exciting.'

'Jerome said Steven Chaytor was here. Have you met him, Mother?'

Celia frowned, puckering her forehead as if in an effort to remember.

'Isn't he that boy I met over Christmas that time? Oh yes, he's here at the hospital, with his fiancée, or is she his wife? I can't remember, dear.'

251

'But you spoke to him, Mother?'

'I think we were introduced at some party or other and he recognised me. He's a doctor here, quite well thought of, I believe. The girl is the same one he brought to Dene Hollow.'

'And they're married?'

'Does it matter, darling? He's part of your childhood. I'm opening up a whole new life for you, Rosemary, I don't want any part of your childhood to intrude into it. I remember that you liked him, more than liked him, but you were so very young and yes, he was a nice boy. I can understand why you liked him better than Jerome or the other boys. You probably won't see anything of him around here.'

'Why is that, Mother?'

'Well, he leads a very busy life. He's in the same mould as Gordon, dedicated to his profession and not one for the high life, which I hope you're going to enjoy. Now then I'm going to take you round the house so that you can see for yourself how wonderful it is. I've got one of the servant girls to look after you, her name's Tamina. She doesn't speak much English but then not many of them do.'

'Do I really need a maid, Mother?'

'Yes, you do. Rosemary, you have to start being the daughter of the house and in this part of the world we are gentry. After all, Nigel is the son of an earl even though he's completely out of touch with every member of his family.'

'But he has a house in Dorset, doesn't he?'

'Don't mention it, darling. For myself I've no wish to bury myself in Dorset. It was his grandmother's house; I'm asking him to get rid of it.'

'And will he?'

'Given time I'm sure he will. It's probably stocked with her furniture and incredibly dated.'

Celia looked at her daughter with some degree of impatience.

By the time they had finished their inspection of the house, Rosemary felt thoroughly bemused. The house was a showplace, beautiful, pristine, and every porcelain figurine, every picture and every stick of furniture screamed money. Celia was in her seventh heaven and at the end of the tour she said, 'Now, darling, you see how easy it's going to be for you to forget Dene Hollow. It can't hold a candle to this place.'

'Nigel must have an awful lot of money, Mother,' Rosemary said.

'Well, yes, he has. His grandmother left him a fortune, but then Gordon was a rich man. I wanted this house. It was beautiful, but it's more so now because everything in it reflects my taste. Nigel gave me free rein to do exactly what I pleased, and we're both happy with the finished result. We've spent the last few years travelling around, going everywhere, seeing everything. Now we've come home and we're going to enjoy this place, give exclusive parties and see that you meet all the right people.'

'What sort of people are they, Mother?'

'You know, darling, people with money, people who are going places. I've told all my friends that my daughter was coming to live with us so now they'll be expecting to meet you. We'll have parties and you'll wear your prettiest clothes for

253

the occasion. What sort of clothes do you have, dear? Beatrice never had much idea about clothes and Mother was asked to find you some dresses in London. What sort of things did you buy?'

'Well, this one. I liked it and grandmother said it would be ideal for travelling.'

'It's very nice, dear, but what did you find for the time when you won't be travelling?'

'I've got some cotton skirts and a silk dress. I really didn't know what I would need out here and grandmother didn't seem to know either.'

'And she's a different generation. She never had much idea about me, but I thought there'd be more scope in London. If nothing pleases me we'll have to go into Nairobi. It doesn't compare with either London or New York but we'll have to make the best of it.'

'I've also brought riding clothes; you said there'd be horses.'

'Oh there are, darling, beautiful pure-bred Arabs. And a swimming pool you could die for. You're going to have a marvellous life here, Rosemary; we have such a lot of time to make up for.'

While Rosemary unpacked and put her clothes away in the enormous walk-in wardrobes, she thought that this was the mother she'd believed in: enthusiastic, welcoming; not that other mother who had been too far away, her only contact the silly dolls that came at regular intervals throughout her childhood. A small tap on her door introduced Tamina's smiling face and flash of enormous white teeth.

'There's nothing for you to do, Tamina, I've finished unpacking. I'm not going to be much trouble,' Rosemary said with a smile.

Tamina shrugged her shoulders and Rosemary realised that her rapid English was lost on her. She really didn't want a maid, but even as she thought this Tamina began picking up discarded tissue paper and straightening cushions and covers that had been pulled aside. She smiled approvingly, and Tamina smiled in return. That, she thought, would probably be the extent of their involvement until they knew each other better.

In the drawing room Nigel was listening to Celia's ecstatic thoughts on how their immediate future was to be spent.

'Darling, I can't believe it,' she cried. 'I was dreading her getting off that plane, expecting a gauche, plain little girl who seldom smiled, a girl with crooked teeth and a chip on her shoulder. Instead, came this quite gorgeous girl. If I could have described to anybody how I wanted my daughter to look she would have looked just like that. She's to meet the best people, the nicest boys; the parties we're going to give for her will be famous. Why are you smiling, Nigel?'

'Yesterday you'd have given everything not to have her coming, today she's everything that's wonderful. I can see you intend to spoil her.'

'But of course, darling. I've been a dreadful mother, I've never been there. I have to make up for all that, and you'll help me, darling, won't you? I do so want you and Rosemary to be good friends.'

Nigel merely smiled, and Celia said quickly, 'You knew she'd be pretty one day, didn't you? All those times when I grumbled about her appearance you simply smiled and changed the subject. Oh I wish I hadn't told Ariadne she was a plain little thing.'

'Well now, Ariadne will see for herself that she isn't.'

'We'll never be able to shake the Fairbrothers off, Nigel, but there are nicer people we could call our friends.'

'People you think we should cultivate now that we've become landed gentry, you mean? I never played on my family name, and they all liked Gordon. What they didn't like was a new scandal rearing its ugly head.'

'It isn't a scandal now, Nigel, we're respectably married with this beautiful house. We can be a part of the crowd that don't approve of Ariadne and Johnny Fairbrother.'

'Not so long ago you regarded her as your one true friend. Neither of them care about popularity with the people you are talking about. They have money, a great deal of it, and as far as the Fairbrothers are concerned it's the only thing that matters.'

He looked at his wife's thoughtful expression and his lips twisted with a cynical smile. He understood her as well as he understood himself; they were cut from the same mould, selfish and greedy, unconcerned with loyalty or friendship that should last. The coming months would be interesting. 'Why are you smiling?' Celia snapped.

'I was simply wondering how soon you were

starting out on the metamorphosis of your daughter: new style, new clothes, new outlook. Or have you forgotten that there have been years of Aunt Beatrice fashioning the product we met this morning?'

'Beatrice hasn't done her any harm, but she was never destined to put the gloss on her. I shall do that. She'll have all Beatrice's common sense and my polish.'

'When do you propose to introduce her to Ariadne?'

'I am sure that Ariadne will be here at the earliest moment, she'll be too curious.'

Ariadne watched her husband leafing through his morning mail with cynical amusement. Johnny never received any personal mail; his only correspondence came from his stockbroker or his accountants, and her eyes went back to the pristine invitation picked out in exquisite letter-ing and gold leaf on the large embossed card. It was an invitation to attend a function at the home of Hon. Nigel and Celia Boyd to welcome home their daughter Rosemary. Only the day before she had played tennis with Celia Boyd but no mention had been made then of the forthcoming party.

'We've been invited to a party,' she informed her laconic husband.

'Party, what party?'

'At Nigel and Celia's, to welcome home her daughter.'

She handed the invitation to him across the table. He handed it back without a word.

257

'Well,' she enquired. 'Are we going?'

'I suppose you want to go to show off your finery.'

'Well, I can do that as well as the next person.'

'Bit ostentatious, isn't it? I've not heard much about the daughter before.'

'No. I've always thought she wasn't quite the girl her mother expected her to be. It might be interesting to view the finished product.'

'When is it?'

'Friday, and the invitation stipulates evening dress to be worn.'

'You know I hate dressing up in a monkey suit.'

'If you don't want to go I can make excuses for you.'

'What sort of excuses?'

'The usual ones. You have to see your lawyer; you're under the weather – in which case they'll put it down to too much whisky the night before. Surely you can make the effort for once.'

He grunted unenthusiastically. 'All right then. I'm interested to see what changes they've made to the house.'

Ariadne had already seen the house and had come away from it seething with resentment. The Celia Boyds of this world had never had to plan and fight for anything. It had always been handed on a platter for them to enjoy. Everything in their house screamed taste and money, and seeing Celia's face expressing satisfied delight that she had the home she wanted and the husband she wanted nauseated Ariadne.

Ariadne craved to be the woman other women envied and for some time she'd achieved this.

258

Now here was Celia, and she blamed herself for inviting her to be one of them when she should have been content to live in Gordon's world, a world that had been more stable than anything Ariadne's offered.

Later in the morning she surveyed her wardrobe. Something elegant, not her usual display of gaudy colours, showing too much tanned flesh. She hadn't anything she deemed suitable. She'd have to go into Nairobi but there might not be anything. She had time to fly into London. Johnny would sulk but he'd get over it. She could get round Johnny, tell him she didn't want to let him down.

Obviously the daughter that Celia had been so discontented with had changed her image or Celia wouldn't be going to all this trouble, and she remembered something Celia had said about Chaytor and her daughter's schoolgirl crush on him. She had met him only briefly one afternoon after he had been playing tennis and was going to his car. Celia had introduced them, and Ariadne had thought he was charming and extremely good-looking; then had come the many woes Celia had found to complain about regarding her daughter. She wondered idly if Chaytor had been invited to the party.

She had met him one afternoon when she visited a friend in hospital; he had smiled in acknowledgement and she had asked her friend about him.

The friend had said he was well thought of and extremely nice. He had a lady friend, some girl he had known in England and who had followed

259

him out to Africa, a girl on the staff. Ariadne had passed this information on to Celia, information which had been received with some relief.

Celia couldn't think why she had decided to invite Steven Chaytor and his fiancée to Rosemary's party unless it was to show her daughter that he was spoken for. She had made many enquiries about him and discovered that he was popular with the sort of people Gordon had liked, and she felt a certain amount of chagrin that these were the people she and Nigel should be hobnobbing with rather than the fast set she had found so entertaining.

Of course she didn't want Rosemary to marry a doctor; they didn't make fortunes. She wanted an aristocrat, somebody like Nigel, for instance. There was the Pritchard boy, he was good-looking and his mother's father was a viscount, and Martin Newley's family were rich land-owners in Yorkshire and here in Kenya, and with aristocratic backgrounds.

She wondered idly what Ariadne would wear; it was normally something entirely exotic, and there could be raised eyebrows and hushed comments. Johnny would probably arrive in that disreputable dinner jacket he'd worn for ages, reeking of cigar dust; and he'd no doubt find a useful corner where he could collect a few cronies round him and where they could swap their recent experiences on the stock market.

It was over dinner that Nigel informed her that Ariadne was in London.

'But I saw her two days ago and she didn't tell me,' Celia complained. 'Why do you suppose she's flown off to London?'

'To do some shopping, I believe,' he said dryly.

'To buy clothes,' Celia snapped. 'She'll want to outshine everybody who's coming to the party.'

'She usually does that anyway.'

'Well, I do hope it's something classy and not too brassy,' Celia said. 'I do hope all our guests are compatible. You know as well as I do that Ariadne can be controversial and Johnny can be hopeless.'

'But they're not without their entertainment value.'

'Entertainment that isn't always acceptable with certain people.'

Rosemary had already met some of her mother's friends and one or two girls of her own age. She still felt like a stranger. The girls regarded her with some trepidation and were not too forthcoming. Her mother dismissed their lack of friendliness as jealousy. 'Don't let it worry you, darling,' she said. 'They probably see you as the girl from a more affluent background and they're a little envious. You'll meet other girls, and boys. By the way I've invited Steven Chaytor and his fiancée to your party.'

'Why did you do that, Mother?'

'To show you that you want a younger boy and to make you see that he's engaged to be married and it's time you forgot about him.'

'Inviting him to my party isn't likely to help me forget him, Mother.'

'Oh, darling, don't be so tiresome. Steven Chaytor isn't for you. Now have you finally decided what to wear? I must say I was rather

261

surprised that Sylvia's had so much choice. I'm sure Ariadne could have found something quite suitable from her, she needn't have flown off to London.'

Rosemary had liked the blue wild silk, her mother had preferred the peach taffeta. In the end she had bought them both and Rosemary still preferred the blue.

Two days before the party Nigel surveyed his bank statement with something like alarm. Since they had married Celia had gone mad on the house, on their travels abroad, now on her daughter and on the party. She was spending far more than their money was earning for them, and he needed an estate manager. He had purchased a working ranch but he didn't know how to work it, and he had married a woman who thought money grew on trees. She had no idea that the money Gordon had left her was not a bottomless pit.

That was the morning Rosemary heard their voices raised in argument, witnessed her mother's angry tears and Nigel's frustration, and felt her first stirrings of doubt that her presence might have something to do with it.

Her mother was not to know that there were many times when she longed for Dene Hollow, Aunt Beatrice's logical common sense, the fun she'd had with the boys, even Uncle Cedric's tetchiness. Dene Hollow would fit into a small corner of her present home, but when she surveyed her opulent bedroom and the vast acres beyond the house she could only think of Dene Hollow with a remembered pain.

She surveyed herself in the long mirror on the night of her party and found she couldn't reconcile her appearance with that other girl, with her fine fair hair framing a face with its straight gaze out of dark blue eyes, the mouth marred by the braces on her teeth, the clear, ivory skin. Now the face gazing back at her was unbelievable in its beauty, and the blue gown emphasised the blossoming of her maturity, with the girlish gaucheness gone for ever.

From downstairs she could hear the sound of laughter. Her mother had told her she should not make her appearance until all their guests had assembled, then like Aurora in *The Sleeping Beauty* she would descend the stairs to meet them.

Apart from her mother and Nigel they would all be strangers, but there would also be Steven. He would not remember the young girl who had worshipped him in the new Rosemary. Even her name had been changed.

The door opened and Tamina's head appeared, wreathed in smiles, then holding the door open wider she beckoned. Picking up her pearl-encrusted evening bag, Rosemary stepped out into the corridor. From the top of the long shallow staircase she could see the sea of faces below and somewhat nervously she started to descend, then she saw Nigel waiting for her. She ran lightly down the rest of the steps and her mother came forward to embrace her before the sudden applause rang in her ears.

The next moments were a confused jumble of welcoming words, handshakes and embraces, and then she was standing looking up into Steven's face, and the years melted away and she was a schoolgirl again gazing into a face and into eyes that could not disguise the surprise at the transformation.

He smiled and kissed her cheek. 'How lovely to see you again, Rosie,' he said, 'or should I call you Rosemary now? You've met Mary, haven't you. Christmas at Dene Hollow, you remember.'

How could she ever forget that Christmas with her mother's presence after so many years of absence and this quietly smiling girl whom Steven had brought for the first time? In one swift moment the pain of their first meeting swept over her before reason came to her assistance and she smiled.

They belonged to the past, she was moving on; and in the next moment her mother was beside her, saying 'Come, dear, there's a young man wanting very much to meet you, Martin Newley,' and she looked up into a young smiling face before he swept her into a waltz.

Chapter Nineteen

In the years that came after Rosemary could not believe how quickly after that first introduction to her new life it all began to change. It was all a far cry from life at Dene Hollow now that she was living a life of luxury at Malibu with a mother who doted on her and a stepfather who supplied her with thoroughbred horses to ride and sufficient money to enable her to socialise with the rich young men who entertained her.

Martin Newley was good-looking, arrogant and well-heeled. He gathered around himself men and girls similarly placed, and Rosemary fitted in well with his concept of what he wanted from life.

They were the brash young crowd with their fast cars and determination to fill every moment of every day with enjoyment of one form or another, but behind that enjoyment Rosemary was increasingly aware of her mother's sulks and constant arguments with Nigel Boyd. It was usually about money.

'Why are you terribly mean all of a sudden?' Celia demanded. 'I'm spending my own money just as much as yours, and you want the sort of life we're leading. If money's so important to you why don't you get rid of that mausoleum in England? We never go there, you said you hated it there.'

'It's been in the family for generations; my grandmother would never have got rid of it,' was his constant reply.

'Your grandmother's been dead for years. Surely it's better to get rid of it than have it standing empty and going to seed.'

'There are people there who look after it.'

'And you're paying them good wages. We could be saving on that.'

'Don't tell me what to do with my property, Celia, you obviously don't understand how we value such things.'

'You mean I'm not exactly blue-blooded enough to understand.'

'If that's how you want to take it.'

'Rosemary's managed to hook the richest boy in the vicinity and nothing is going to spoil it for her. Really, Nigel, I don't know why we have to quarrel about money all the time, it's not as if we were paupers.'

'I am quite reasonably asking you to go easy. Some of our investments are a bit dicey and my stockbroker is advising caution.'

'Surely you want Rosemary to have some of the fun she missed out on, all those years she was at Dene Hollow?'

'From what I've heard of Dene Hollow I can hardly think she missed out on very much.'

'Well, of course she's not going to say very much out of loyalty to Beatrice. When I finally get what I've set out for I'll economise, Nigel.'

'You've got Malibu, you've got me. I take it the final trophy concerns your daughter.'

'I want her to have Martin Newley, and she has to have what it takes to get him.'

Rosemary had listened to their voices from the garden, where the argument floated to her through the opened windows. Then she had been aware of Nigel hurrying along the path, at the end of which he jumped into his car and drove at a great speed towards the gates. He turned right at the gates and she watched until the car was out of sight over the hill.

She guessed that he was driving to the Fairbrothers' house. Her mother joined her with a sulky face, flopping down beside her on the hammock and saying, 'I suppose you heard some of that, darling?'

'Mother, I wish you didn't quarrel all the time about money. You have everything here, what can you possibly want that you haven't already got?'

'Don't lecture me, darling. I want it for you. Has Martin said anything concrete? I know he likes you enormously; he's never away from here. I thought he'd be over this morning.'

'He's gone into Nairobi with his father, business he said.'

'Business with money attached to it. You do like him, don't you, dear?'

'Yes, Mother, we have fun, we enjoy ourselves.'

'But that isn't enough. Rosemary, how old is Martin?'

'Twenty-four.'

'Old enough to be thinking seriously about settling down.'

'But he isn't old enough, Mother. He's often silly and immature. He's fun, he's good for a laugh and he's terribly conceited. I don't think of him seriously at all.'

Her mother's horrified face suddenly made her want to laugh until she saw that she was making her mother angry.

'Really, Rosemary, here am I making every effort to give you an assured future, even quarrelling with Nigel to make doubly sure, and you are treating everything so lightly as if it doesn't matter. Don't tell me you're still cherishing thoughts of that young doctor. He's engaged to be married, Rosemary; he's evidently very much in love with her, and she followed him

267

here simply to be near him. Where is your pride?'

'You mentioned Steven, Mother, not I.'

'So he's not the reason you're so cavalier about Martin?'

'I'm not cavalier about Martin. I like him, but I'm not in love with him, and Steven has nothing to do with it.'

'I'm glad about that, at any rate. Did Nigel drive towards the club?'

'I don't know. I wasn't watching.'

'He'll probably be propping the bar up with some other disgruntled husband. I might drive up to see Ariadne, it's days since I've seen her.'

Rosemary thought she had never been more pleased to see Martin's car driving through the gates, and her mother jumped up, pulling Rosemary after her.

'Here's Martin, darling. I will drive over to see Ariadne and leave you two young people alone.'

'No, Mother, please don't go, I want you to get to know Martin; I'll rely on your judgment.' Placated for the moment, Celia went forward with a smile to greet him.

Martin could be guaranteed to make her mother laugh. His humour was audacious and he reminded Rosemary of the young Jerome before he became too pompous.

He was invited to stay for dinner, but when Nigel did not arrive home for it Celia became morose and Rosemary was glad that Martin suggested a drive to the club to meet some of their friends.

'Where does your stepfather spend his time?' Martin asked. 'He's seldom at the club these days. She was obviously put out that he wasn't home for dinner.'

'They had an argument, he's probably sulking.'

Martin grinned. 'People round here had a lot to say about them when they first got together; said it wouldn't last; said he was a playboy. They thought a lot about your mother's husband the vet.'

Rosemary stayed silent, and glancing at her, Martin said, 'Do you like Boyd?'

'He's been nice to me.'

'I'll bet he has, you're a pretty girl and he likes pretty girls.'

'That's not a very nice thing to say, Martin. He's married to my mother, he's not very likely to think of me as just any young girl.'

Uncontrite, Martin said, 'I'm only telling you what a lot of people were saying. He's been around here on and off for years.'

'How do you know? You were in England at school.'

'But I'm not too young or too old to heed the gossip!'

'Then I'd rather not hear it, Martin.'

He was silent for several minutes before asking, 'How does he get along with Ariadne Fairbrother?'

'Why do you ask?'

'Because they're something of a pair. Not a marriageable pair, you know, but a pretty smart adulterous pair. She's stirred the cauldron in more than one marriage and they'd get along.'

'She also happens to be married.'

Martin threw back his head and laughed. 'That

269

never troubled our Ariadne or Nigel.'

To Rosemary the conversation was suddenly distasteful, and as the evening progressed and they met up with Martin's usual crowd he said to her, 'Come on, Rosie, you're a spectre at the feast, you're not any fun tonight. Why don't we all go on to Paradiso? You might be in the mood for that.'

'Perhaps I should go home, I'm feeling rather tired.'

'Then we'll wake you up. Paradiso, everybody!' he shouted.

Paradiso was expensive, exclusive and very much the haunt of older people looking for good food, a quiet evening with soft music and good conversation. The mood Martin and his friends were in was designed to put an end to any hopes other people might have.

They arrived with the screech of brakes, laughter and noisy chatter, and as they breezed into the club the guests already dining there looked at them with some trepidation.

The first people Rosemary saw were Steven and Mary dining with a group of friends, and that was the signal for Rosemary to liven up. She suddenly became the centre of attraction, too loud, too flirtatious and not a little too drunk.

Martin was delighted. He thought it was for him. It wasn't, it was for Steven and the doubtful looks his party cast in their direction. She didn't care, let him look at her, let him think what he liked. She didn't need him, she was rich, beautiful, surrounded by men who admired her; let him have his quiet, gentle Mary, she'd have

Martin Newley.

By the time they left Paradiso all the others had already gone home, and by the time Martin deposited her at her front door it was well after midnight. Martin was disposed to be amorous but with a light-hearted giggle Rosemary kissed him lightly and called out to him, 'See you tomorrow Martin, not before lunchtime,' then she was running towards the house, swaying a little unsteadily as she searched in her bag for the key. Suddenly she found the door taken from her grasp, and she was staring up into Nigel's face, and the expression on his face sobered her up to such an extent that she tottered into the hall, whispering, 'I'm sorry, Nigel, I didn't mean to wake you.'

His smile was caustic.

'You didn't wake me, Rosemary, I was waiting up for you.'

'But there was no need, I had my key.'

'Oh, I felt there was a need. Young Newley hasn't the best of reputations.'

She moved to walk across the hall but he was beside her, holding her arm, and she pulled away from him. His hand tightened, and when she reached her bedroom door he opened it but he did not release her.

'What sort of an affair are you having with young Newley?' he demanded.

She stared at him in some anger. 'I'm not having an affair with him. Why do you think I am?'

'Because that's the sort of man he is. Why don't you ask him about the girls he's had and then dumped? Your mother would be horrified if the same thing happened to you.'

She looked fearfully towards her mother's bedroom door, and with a cynical smile he said, 'You know I'm right, she'd be absolutely furious if the same fate happened to you. She knows my views on the subject, so why waste your time on the likes of Martin Newley?'

'Please let go of my arm, Nigel, you're hurting me.'

He let go of her arm and lightly placed his hands on her breasts. She shrank away from him. He was smiling, and he said lightly, 'You're very young and very beautiful; you need a man in your life, not some callow boy. One day I'll prove it to you, my dear.'

She tore herself away from him and slammed the bedroom door in his face. She heard his amused laughter but she stood with her back against the door, her heart beating wildly, praying that he would not come in after her.

For hours she lay sleepless, listening to the sounds of the cicadas and the more resonant sounds of Kenya's wild life. By the time the rising sun invaded her room she was ready to get up to face the day ahead. She did not want to meet Nigel across the breakfast table or face her mother's questions on the sort of evening she had spent with Martin. She stood looking out of her window, watching the procession of estate workers trundling along the drive, men, women and children, their faces wreathed in smiles as they jested and joked together, a rag-taggle of humanity clad in bright colours, their black faces alive with that particular exuberance that sparkled in coal-black eyes and gleaming white teeth.

In only a short while she had taken Africa into her heart, its mystery and its vastness, the complexity of its people, the tempo of its music; and she had believed she would be happy. Now her hope of happiness had gone and she was afraid of what the future held.

It was early. She listened for some sound from within the house but there was only silence. Making up her mind quickly, she showered and donned her jodhpurs and riding shirt. She would take her horse out and pray that Nigel would not decide to do the same.

It was still cool as she made her way to the stables, where one of the stable hands greeted her with a wide grin and brought out her horse for saddling. He spoke little English but she had gained the hope that by and large they liked her. She was friendly with them, where her mother was superior and Nigel arrogant, and as she rode her horse along the drive and out across the veld some of the trauma of the night left her and she began to enjoy the speed of her horse and the sheer enjoyment of being young and alive.

As she rode up the hill she became aware that another horseman was enjoying the emptiness of the early morning, and as she approached him he raised his riding crop and smiled. She had not expected to encounter Steven on her morning ride and he fell easily into step beside her as they raced their horses up the gentle incline. They drew their mounts to a halt and laughed together at the sheer enjoyment of it.

It seemed to Rosemary that in those few brief moments the years had rolled away and they were riding along the sands below Dene Hollow, and the innocent joys that had been with them then had suddenly returned. Steven was the first to speak, words that were commonplace even when her foolish heart heard the clashing of cymbals, the haunting music of every unspoken desire.

'I've never seen you riding up here before, Rosie. Perhaps it was too early for you.'

She smiled. 'Yes, I'm not usually about at this time.'

'You were enjoying yourselves last night.'

'Yes, it was fun. I hope we didn't make a nuisance of ourselves.'

He smiled diffidently. 'Even the oldest of us were young once.'

'But you're not old, Steven.'

'No, but there are times when I feel old. Perhaps it's my job; suffering doesn't sit lightly on our shoulders even when we're prepared for it. Yesterday wasn't a very happy day for any of us at the hospital; there has been an outbreak of cholera in one of the villages.'

'Oh, I'm sorry. I didn't know.'

'Have you settled down well here, Rosie?'

'I'm not sure. I miss Dene Hollow and Aunt Beatrice. I miss David and Noel, the others too I suppose. Don't you miss England, Steven?'

'Yes, but then I was only ever a bird of passage. My family were in the Far East, and I was always very grateful for friends in England who made me welcome in their homes.'

'Will you stay in Africa?'

'Who can say? I've been offered posts in the Far East. Perhaps I haven't as yet put down roots.'

'Where does Mary want to live?'

For a long moment he stared at her curiously then he said, 'I really don't think she would mind. At the moment it isn't an issue but it probably will be one day.'

'She seems very nice, Steven.'

'Well, we've known each other a long time. My parents and Mary's parents were friends when we were children. Life can sometimes be inevitable.'

'Did you always feel like that, Steven, that everything was planned out for you, your job, marriage, where you'd live? I never did.'

'I always wanted to do medicine of one form or another. I never quite knew where I would settle down. I really never thought about marriage, one doesn't when one is too young. How did you feel about your life?'

'I never thought beyond Dene Hollow.'

'But you knew surely that one day you would live with your mother. You too were a bird of passage.'

'I suppose so.'

'And marriage?'

That was the moment he looked into her eyes and saw the answer clearly, and he could hear Jerome's voice, teasing, probing, 'She fancies you Steven, you're her knight in shining armour, it's time to let her down gently or otherwise.'

Oh, but surely that schoolgirl crush had flown

275

out of the window years ago, and her next words endorsed it.

'You were always so nice to me, Steven, when Jerome was always so mean. You were my very first crush. What a good thing it is that we get over such nonsense.'

He laughed. 'Yes, I'm sure you're right.'

'But you never got over Mary.'

'I never had a crush on Mary. Perhaps it was something that came later.'

'When you had more sense.'

'Maybe.'

He turned his horse and set it gently on the downhill slope. 'I had better be getting back, Rosie, another busy day ahead of us. Perhaps we'll meet up here again, either here or in one of the night spots.'

She smiled and waited on the hillside until he was out of sight.

She was still on the hillside when she saw Nigel driving his car along the road leading to the Fairbrothers' estate. Then she galloped her horse back to his stable. She could face her mother over breakfast, but it would be some time before she would feel comfortable with Nigel.

Her mother was still at the breakfast table, leafing through her post.

'I didn't hear you come in last night, dear, what time did you get home?'

'Fairly late Mother, we went to Paradiso.'

'Really. I would have thought that a little bit too staid for your young crowd. Anybody there of note?'

'I expect you would have known them all.'

'I'm making a list of guests for your birthday party, dear. Some people of my age and a good many of yours. I thought I'd like to ask Martin's parents. We don't know them very well as his mother isn't much for socialising.'

'Do I really want a birthday party, Mother?'

She was thinking about the arguments between her mother and Nigel about money. Her mother would entertain on a lavish scale, inviting people who were rich enough themselves to expect the best, and then when the cost had to be counted there would be the endless recriminations.

'What a funny thing to say, Rosemary; of course you want a birthday party, I'm very mindful of all the parties you missed and I intend to make up for them. We'll invite all those silly people who thought Gordon shouldn't have married me, let alone Nigel. They'll be pea-green with envy about the house, and that my beautiful daughter has captured Martin Newley.'

'Mother that isn't true, and his parents wouldn't like it.'

'Well, we'll see. Now do get out of those riding things, darling, and go with me into Nairobi. I want some more of those invitation cards. I was thinking that perhaps I should have asked Mother to get some for me in London but she'd only grumble about the expense in sending them out to me.'

'If my birthday's so important, Mother, it would be nice for Aunt Beatrice and my grandparents to be here.'

'You can forget that, darling. My parents would hate it here and Beatrice has never shown the

277

slightest desire to visit us.'

'Perhaps if I begged her to come she would.'

'You are not even to think about it. Now do hurry along, dear, we'll have lunch at that new restaurant and see what Sylvia's got to offer us. Did you see Nigel leaving the house?'

'Yes.'

'He didn't say where he was going? Did you notice which way he went?'

'No.'

Chapter Twenty

Celia was well pleased with everything: the flowers and the food, the gowns of the women, and the sort of people who were standing around enjoying the champagne and the sheer excellence of proceedings that were entirely appropriate for such beautiful surroundings.

Rosemary looked enchanting, quite the most beautiful girl at the party, and so thought the bevy of young men surrounding her and flattering her with their attentions. Celia's eyes strayed to where Steven Chaytor and his companion stood with a group of people near the window, and she was aware that now and again her daughter's eyes strayed in their direction.

Of course he was good-looking. He made the younger element seem flighty and too noisy, but then her eyes looked out to where Martin's father's Rolls Royce was ostentatiously parked below the terrace, guarded cautiously by its driver. She'd invited Steven in the hope that her daughter would appreciate the difference in his lifestyle compared to the Newleys' more affluent one. When Nigel joined her she said, 'Everything's going so well, darling, aren't you pleased?'

'Why do we need to kowtow to these people? Why do we suddenly need to be accepted?'

She frowned. 'Because we're every bit as respectable as they are, because we're gentry and because I want my daughter to have the best.'

'The Southerbys haven't arrived.'

'No, but they accepted the invitation. I'm sure they'll come.'

'The Fairbrothers haven't arrived, either.'

'No, I wonder why. Ariadne will never miss an occasion like this one. It's the only opportunity she'll ever have to mingle with people like this.'

'You think she cares, do you?'

'I'm sure of it. Not Johnny, he won't care, but she will. Of course she does like to make an entrance but I would have thought under these circumstances she might have behaved differently.'

'Why not give her a ring?'

'I don't think so. Ariadne's always made me feel that she was instrumental in bringing me out. Perhaps she was, but I don't have to feel dependent on her any more.'

Nigel smiled, a cynical amused smile, and sharply Celia said, 'Why don't you ask Rosemary to dance? Let everybody see that she may be your stepdaughter but you are very fond of her.'

'I might just do that,' he replied, and she

279

watched him walking across the room to where Rosemary stood with a circle of her friends.

She didn't want to dance with him, she didn't like the look in his narrowed eyes or that he held her firmly and too close.

'Relax,' he said. 'People will think you're afraid of me.'

'Perhaps I am,' she murmured.

Smoothly he said, 'Don't tell me you're seriously interested in the Newley boy. He's immature. I wouldn't advise you to throw yourself away on him.'

'My mother wouldn't agree with you.'

'Your mother is thinking about money, I can't think that would be enough for you.'

From across the room, Steven Chaytor was watching them. He had not missed Rosemary's embarrassment and the way she pulled herself away from Nigel and the tantalising smile on her partner's face. She was not enjoying dancing with Nigel Boyd. At that moment there was a stir among the guests at the arrival of John and Daphne Southerby.

'Darling, we're so sorry to be late,' Daphne gushed. 'We were a little bothered about all the lights around the Fairbrothers' house, then we heard the sirens and an ambulance swept up to the house. We waited on the road but we couldn't see anything.'

'Is the ambulance still there?' somebody asked.

'No, it's just gone down the road with the sirens blaring. Something must be terribly wrong.'

'Nigel and I have just been saying they were late but we were not unduly concerned as Ariadne does like to make an entrance. Perhaps you should telephone them, darling,' Celia said. With a brief smile Nigel said, 'I'll probably catch you later, my dear. It's a pity, I was enjoying our dance.'

He returned after a few minutes to say a servant had answered his call and that Johnny had suffered a heart attack and Ariadne had accompanied him to the hospital.

'I've never known him to be ill,' another guest said. 'He's always seemed as strong as a horse. It's probably something and nothing.'

Turning to Steven, Celia asked, 'Do you know anything about Johnny's health problems, Steven?'

Steven shook his head. 'I'm afraid not, indeed I've never met Fairbrother.'

'I thought everybody knew him,' Nigel said.

'I've heard of him, of course,' Steven said.

'Who hasn't?' John Southerby murmured, while the others smiled in agreement.

Johnny Fairbrother's problems were quickly forgotten as the guests continued to enjoy themselves. Rosemary managed to avoid Nigel for the rest of the evening and in the early hours Steven asked her to dance.

'It's been a lovely party,' he said smiling down at her. 'It was nice of your mother to invite us. Unfortunately we shall be leaving soon.'

'Has Mary enjoyed it?'

'Very much.'

She wanted to ask questions: how soon would they be getting married, where would they live, did they intend to make their home permanently

281

in Kenya, but the questions wouldn't come. She was afraid of the answers.

In her diffidence Steven recognised the old Rosie who had walked with him along the cliff top, the Rosie who had agonised about the absence of her mother, the young girl with her shy blushes and an adoration plain to see. She had troubled him then and she troubled him now. All was not right for Rosie in this glossy pampered existence her mother had planned for her.

As he drove home with Mary under a jewelled sky, she said, 'You're very quiet, Steven. Didn't you enjoy the party?'

'Yes, of course; did you?'

'Very much. I wonder how much it cost to put on a show like that?'

'I've no idea. They evidently thought they could afford it.'

'Do you think she'll marry Martin Newley?'

'I don't know. She's still very young. I can't think they really know each other very well.'

Steven wanted to change the subject. He didn't want to discuss Rosie's marriage to Martin Newley, and he felt angry with himself that it should matter. That she was some girl he'd known for too many years shouldn't count. But he was remembering her expression as she danced with Nigel Boyd: there had been that hesitancy and withdrawal as he drew her into his arms, and there had been something else, fear. That was it, she had been afraid of him.

Mary was saying, 'She's a very lucky girl to have fallen into a life like that, that beautiful house

282

and a lot of money. I hope she realises it.'

'Do you think she doesn't?'

'Well, I always thought she could be a little sulky.'

'Yes, perhaps, but there was probably a good reason for it.'

'Jerome said she'd always had a thing about you, Steven.'

'Jerome said a lot of things. He used to tease her rotten and I think there were times when Rosie felt a bit like a parcel that had been left hanging around.'

'Surely not. Aunt Beatrice was always very good with her.'

'Of course. I wonder how Fairbrother is; we'll no doubt hear all about it at the hospital in the morning.'

'I wonder if his wife's still there. I've never actually met her, I've only seen her around. She's terribly stylish, but loud, not really like Mrs Boyd.'

Steven didn't comment but he was remembering Ariadne as he had last seen her sitting with Nigel Boyd at the sporting club. A tall slender woman with long auburn hair tied back from her face with a colourful silk scarf, her green eyes flashing provocatively, her amused laughter, and then he had watched her running down to her car, long legs in white linen shorts, a sweater knotted round her shoulders, a wave of her hand in Boyd's direction before she drove swiftly away.

During the next few days speculation would be rife in the community. The Fairbrothers had been a part of that community for a good number of years and yet neither of them had been truly liked. Johnny Fairbrother had ridden roughshod over too many people and he had never cared. Ariadne too had created scandals where there should have been none, and if their world was to change few people would be around to commiserate. Ariadne would have money, but that might be all she would have.

In the hospital Ariadne stood looking down at her husband's still form in his hospital bed. He was surrounded by wires and doctors, and it seemed to Ariadne that the eyes in that still white face would never open again.

Johnny had always boasted that he'd never had a day's illness in his entire life. He drank too much, ate too much, and never seemed to care if he had enough rest, but he had seemed somehow indestructible when other men were complaining about their ailments. He had been scathing, calling them pampered egotists. When she'd told him to stop drinking he'd laughed at her. 'I might as well be dead,' he'd said contemptuously.

'Why don't you think about me for a change?' she'd said.

'I think about you all the time. While I live you're in clover. If I die you'll still be in clover.'

'That's not the point,' she'd argued. 'You'll not be behind me. I don't have real friends.'

'You'll survive,' he'd said grimly. 'You'd survive Armageddon.'

At Malibu the party was over and weary servants were clearing up after the guests had departed. Celia was well pleased with the evening's event but confessed to being worn out by the effort.

With her arm around Rosemary's waist she walked up the staircase. 'It has been wonderful, hasn't it, darling?' she asked. 'Tomorrow we must look at all your presents, there wasn't really time tonight. What did Martin get you?'

'A bracelet, silver I think.'

'How nice. Next year it could be an engagement ring. You do like him, don't you, darling?'

'Yes, Mother.' She could have added but not enough to marry him, but at three o'clock in the morning she preferred not to have an argument. At her bedroom door her mother said, 'Well, it was a wonderful party and now I'm going to bed. I doubt if I'll surface much before noon.'

She looked down into the hall where the servants were putting out the lights and called out, 'Nigel, where are you? Let the servants attend to everything,' then kissing her daughter she went to her room.

Strangely enough, Rosemary was not tired. As she slipped into her dressing-gown she went to stand on the balcony. It was a warm, humid night but there was a faint mist hiding the moonlight. She did not hear her bedroom door open until she was suddenly aware that Nigel stood beside her, and she spun round sharply with a look of alarm on her face.

She shrank back against the railings and his amused voiced taunted her by saying, 'Aren't you going to thank me for tonight, Rosemary? Such an expensive occasion deserves some sort of reward, I think?'

'I have thanked you, Nigel, Mother too.'

'Oh but not nearly enough, my dear.'

The arms he placed around her were like steel bands, and however much she struggled his lips were pressing down on hers until she felt she could hardly breathe. Then he was pulling her inside the room, his hands tearing at her dressing-gown, pushing it away from her shoulders as he manoeuvred her towards the bed. She was fighting him with all her strength.

'Keep still, you little fool,' he hissed. 'You'll thank me for tonight. It will be something to measure against all the inadequacies of boys like Newley.'

She had no strength to fight him. All she could think was that she was being raped by her stepfather and just along the corridor her mother was asleep in her bed. When it was over, for several minutes he lay on his back beside her, then without a word he kissed her lightly and left her.

There was no sleep for Rosemary that night. She lay soaking in her bath until the water went cold, then she dressed and went out of the house into the gardens. Obviously she couldn't stay at Malibu, but she couldn't tell her mother. She would never believe her.

She had to leave Kenya, go back to England and find a job. She should never have come here, but then she'd never expected such a terrible thing to happen to her. She couldn't talk about it to anybody; she couldn't stay here, but how to get away? Her mother had said she would sleep until noon but she didn't feel she could face either of them. On that morning, however, she needn't have worried because everybody between Malibu and Nairobi knew that during the night Johnny Fairbrother had died.

Celia received the news when Daphne Southerby telephoned her mid-morning.

'We knew something drastic must have happened when we drove past their house after we left the party,' she said. 'There were several cars outside and there were lights streaming everywhere. Apparently Ariadne had gone home on the advice of the doctors and they had to telephone her to say he had died.'

'So she wasn't with him when he died.'

'Apparently not. We did enjoy the party, Celia, and Rosemary looked so pretty. Is it serious between her and Martin Newley?'

'I'm not sure. Perhaps.'

She got out of bed and threw a silk wrap over her nightdress. Nigel had not come to bed. Poor darling, he was probably tired out and had gone to sleep in a chair somewhere. She left the room and ran lightly down the stairs, calling his name as she crossed the hall.

Surely he hadn't gone over to the Fairbrothers. After all, if he knew Johnny had died he wouldn't have left the house without telling her.

She was about to go upstairs when Rosemary came through the front door and Celia eyed her with some surprise. 'Good heavens, darling, where have you been? I thought you'd be in bed until noon. Have you seen Nigel?'

She was suddenly aware of Rosemary's pallor and the dark circles under her eyes. The girl looked as if she was sickening for something and she said sharply, 'What is the matter, Rosemary? You don't look well.'

'I couldn't sleep, Mother, I suppose it was all the excitement of the party. Is something wrong?'

'Yes, it's Johnny Fairbrother. He died in hospital, I was looking for Nigel to tell him.'

'I haven't seen him.'

'Oh well, I might as well get dressed and drive over to see Ariadne. If you see him tell him where I've gone, unless you'd like to come with me, dear.'

'No, Mother, I don't think so.'

She went up to her bedroom and locked the door behind her while Celia got dressed, Celia was reversing her car when Nigel tapped lightly on the window.

'Where are you going?' he asked her, and she thought that he too looked as if he hadn't slept.

He listened without interrupting her while she told him her news and where she was going. Then he said, 'I'll come with you, there might be something we can do.'

He wasn't anxious to see Ariadne at that moment, but he did not want to encounter his stepdaughter either.

Ariadne sat in Johnny's study staring down at his huge mahogany desk with an expression of disbelief on her face. This was the room where he spent most of his time, the room where he talked to his business associates, his financial advisers, his accountant; and this was only the first time she had ever set foot in it.

All Ariadne had cared about was that Johnny

had money, that the men who came to see him kept him solvent and rich; she had no desire to learn anything beyond that. Now, when she looked down at the huge businesslike desk with its array of drawers, she felt an urgent need to learn if her future was locked away behind the polished perfection of walnut.

Johnny's bunch of keys lay clenched in her hand but she was strangely reluctant to open the drawers. Surely nothing of importance would be kept here; such things would lie in the vault at the bank or in his stockbrokers' safe, and for the first time she realised that in actual fact she knew very little about the man she had been married to for many years.

Had he been married before? Was there another wife and perhaps children in the background? Had he been serious all those times when he had told her all she was interested in was his money, and now she was to be deprived of it?

Surely she'd been a good wife to him. She'd never looked at another man since she'd married him, at least not with any degree of affection, and she'd listened to his grumblings and bad humour, dressed well for him, been nice to his cronies, managed his house and servants. Johnny owed her something. Of course she hadn't wanted him dead, in a way she'd cared for him in spite of him being such an old grouch.

She played around with the keys until one of them clicked and she was able to open the drawer. She had thought to find a confusion of papers – he'd always been untidy with everything else, his appearance, his clothing – but in this drawer at least the papers were stacked evenly in cardboard folders and there were labels on them denoting which shares and syndicates they referred to.

She didn't understand a word. The other drawers were the same, filled with files containing jargon she'd never seen in her life before, but she didn't find a will. No doubt that was in the hands of his solicitor, always providing he'd had the good sense to leave one. And what about the ranch? Surely he wouldn't leave her without a roof over her head. But she was remembering his cynical asides, the expression of derision after one of her shopping sprees.

When she'd pestered him about buying Malibu he'd turned decidedly nasty, accusing her of wanting the moon, never being satisfied, and only days later he'd had his accountant round for talks. Suppose he'd made his mind up to leave his money elsewhere because he thought she'd fritter it away on some pipe dream like Malibu?

If he'd done that how everybody would laugh and sneer. They'd say she'd got her come-uppance at last and nobody would feel sorry for her. But surely Johnny wouldn't have done that? He'd been as scathing about their acquaintances as she had.

She slammed the last drawer shut and locked it. They had told her nothing. She'd get the funeral over and then she'd have to consult his solicitors to learn her fate.

There was nothing for her to do. She couldn't go out, she had to stay in and mourn for Johnny, and nobody would expect to find her sitting round the pool as if it was just another day.

Even the sunshine seemed an affront. There should be rain and high winds but then the weather had never been right for every disaster in her life.

She went to stand at the window and after several minutes was rewarded by the sight of Celia Boyd's new coupé coming through the gates. Her eyes narrowed as she watched the car coming slowly up the drive and coming to rest below the terrace. Then she saw that Celia was not alone; Nigel was with her.

In recent weeks Nigel had hardly been away from the place. He had come ostensibly to see Johnny but she'd always been aware of his dark eyes appraising her. Nigel Boyd was her sort: handsome, witty, sophisticated, but Nigel Boyd as a husband was a different matter.

Celia's smug self-satisfied face had annoyed her. She thought she had it all, but one of these days she might realise that she had nothing, at least where her husband was concerned.

She went out to meet them, having assured herself first that her face was pale, her eyes predictably tearful, her expression appropriate to the loss she had suffered.

Chapter Twenty-One

Celia was predictably emotional, proffering whatever help they could give Johnny's widow, while Nigel viewed the two women with cynical detachment. He knew that Ariadne would mourn the fact that the man who had bolstered her extravagances and her reputation had suddenly gone out of her life, but he surmised correctly that there had not been great affection for her husband.

'I'm sure he left all his affairs in good order,' he said at last, when the two women had ceased their woeful cries.

'Nigel, I don't know. I never had anything to do with Johnny's financial affairs,' Ariadne answered.

'I know, but he was very astute, I doubt if you'll have any worries on that score.'

'He was also very secretive in a great many ways. I never asked any questions.'

'Just as long as things ran smoothly.'

'You make me sound very mercenary, Nigel. It was simply that I relied on Johnny, and now that he's gone I feel helpless.'

Nigel permitted himself a small discreet smile. When had Ariadne ever been helpless? She was a survivor; she'd survive this latest catastrophe.

'When did you hear about Johnny's death?' Ariadne asked them.

'Well, we knew something was wrong when the Southerbys arrived late for the party. They said they'd seen the ambulance parked outside your house and waited until it left. Nigel telephoned and one of the servants told him what had happened. We heard this morning that he'd died.'

'They told me to come home and rest. I should have stayed to be with him.'

'They probably couldn't do anything more for him, Ariadne. Surely you won't stay on here? Won't you want to get right away?'

Ariadne's eyes grew speculative. 'I remember saying exactly the same thing to you when Gordon died but you stayed on, so why shouldn't I?'

'Well I don't know, dear, I thought it was Johnny who liked it here.'

'It's too soon to begin to think about anything like that. I should be sorry to leave this house.'

'But you were prepared to leave it for Malibu, darling,' Celia said softly.

'Oh that. I wasn't serious, and Johnny wouldn't hear of it. I love this house. Can I offer you a drink? Coffee, if you prefer it.'

'Thank you, darling, but perhaps we should be getting back,' Celia said, but Nigel was quick to say, 'We're in no hurry, Ariadne. Gin and tonic would be nice.'

He had spoken nothing but the truth when he said he was in no hurry to return to Malibu. Memories of the night before were tormenting him. He was aware that he'd committed the most stupid irrational act in his entire life when he'd raped Celia's daughter. He didn't love the girl; he

293

fancied her like he'd fancied a good many women, women who had come readily and easily and with few scruples. Not that young virginal girl who had trusted him as her mother's husband and who was still likely to be hysterically demented by what had happened.

Would she be so demented as to tell her mother, and would Celia believe her? He knew that sooner or later he had to see her, apologise and hope she would forgive him. He had to tell her that if she told her mother about it she would ruin their marriage and break her mother's heart.

Rosemary didn't owe her mother anything, she'd been a rotten mother, but blood was thicker than water. She'd obviously think twice before she destroyed the good life her mother was offering her now.

He was fed up with listening to Celia's platitudes on Ariadne's loss. The only thing Ariadne had lost was a boorish man with enough money to pander to her extravagances, and as soon as she got her hands on his money she'd be looking around for his replacement.

It was early afternoon when they eventually got away, and as they drove home Celia said, 'I can't think why we stayed so long. I can't think that Ariadne will miss Johnny all that much; they were seldom together. Even at the club he was in one corner and she was in the other.'

'It's to be hoped he's left her well provided for, if not she'll miss him sorely,' Nigel replied.

'You surely don't think he'll have left his money elsewhere?'

He shrugged his shoulders. 'Nobody really

knew Johnny Fairbrother. He was an enigma, and he had few illusions about his wife.'

'But surely he'll have left her money? What else would he do with it?'

'I don't know. Nobody really knew very much about him.'

Celia sat back in the car to reflect. Years ago she had envied Ariadne with her exotic jewellery and her wardrobe, the way she flew off to London and Paris whenever she wanted to shop. It had always seemed that their money was a bottomless pit that Ariadne could dip into whenever it suited her. Now would come the reckoning, perhaps.

'I hope Rosemary's had lunch,' she said. 'We should have telephoned her.'

When Nigel didn't answer she said, 'I'll ask the servants to make a light lunch for us. Do see if she's in her room, darling, and tell her we're back.'

It was the opportunity he was waiting for, but he knocked on her door with a racing heart. When there was no answer he opened the door gently and looked inside. The room was empty, and disconsolately he walked downstairs to be met with Celia's enquiring gaze.

'She must be out,' he said laconically.

'She's probably riding, I wish she'd left a note.'

As soon as they had eaten Nigel said he would go down to the stables and take one of the horses out. Perhaps he'd meet Rosemary somewhere on the estate.

He knew that Rosemary preferred to ride on the wild sweeping slopes they could see from the house and he made his way towards them, riding his horse briskly, covering the distance in the shortest possible time, while his eyes scanned the terrain for the sight of her. He came across her horse champing the short moorland grass and then he saw Rosemary sitting with her back against a rock. She did not see him until his shadow fell across the grass, and when she saw it was him her eyes grew wild with sudden fear.

She sprang to her feet as he leapt from his horse, but he was quicker than her as he reached out and clutched her arm.

'Rosemary, I'm not going to hurt you,' he said. 'I'm sorry and very ashamed about what happened last night. I don't know what came over me.'

She shrank away from him. 'I'm afraid of you, Nigel. It wasn't just last night, it's every time you look at me.'

'I'm sorry. I've been a fool. You're beautiful and I fancied you. Is that so very wrong, Rosemary? I'm a man looking at a lovely girl; is that so hard for you to understand?'

'You're married to my mother.'

'I know, but we're not related, are we. I'm asking you to forgive me, to try to put it behind you.'

'I can't live in the same house with you, Nigel. Every time I look at you I'll remember it. I'll always be afraid of you doing something like that again.'

'It will never happen again. I'm disgusted with myself. I swear you have nothing to fear ever again. I'm ashamed because of you, and because of Celia. It would break her heart; it would end our marriage. If I can put it behind me, can't you, Rosemary?'

'Please let go of my arm.'

He complied and she looked away towards the valley. He was aware of her profile, the gentle curve of her cheek, the gentle quivering of her lips, and at that moment he wanted to put his arms around her and hold her close. There was nothing sexual in his feeling for her at that moment, only a surprising tenderness, but he knew that any movement on his part would send her running away from him. His eyes were pleading, and taking advantage of her silence, he said urgently, 'I can't take away what happened, Rosemary, I can only emphasise my utter shame and anger with myself. I don't deserve for you to forgive me, but I am asking you very humbly to think about it. I swear that nothing like that will ever happen again, and in time, for your mother's sake, I hope you will find it in your heart to forgive me. Will you ride back to the house with me?'

She shook her head.

He mounted his horse and stood looking down at her, and at last she raised her eyes to him. His face was sad, his eyes pleading, and in a voice little above a whisper she said, 'Please go, Nigel, I'll ride back presently.'

'And you'll try to forgive me, Rosemary?'

'I'll try.'

He had to be satisfied with that. She would try because of her mother but she would never trust him. They would never truly be able to put the past behind them and he was glad that Celia was not a discerning person. As long as they could be in the same room together, speak occasionally, she would not think there was anything amiss. The secret was safe between him and Rosemary.

When they sat down to dinner that evening his expectations were realised. They talked about Johnny Fairbrother's death, the success of the birthday party and the obvious enjoyment of all concerned. If Rosemary had little appetite and contributed little to the conversation, Celia was happy to talk about the dresses worn at the party, the peculiarities of some of the guests and the fact that Martin Newley had been attentive and charming.

'Did you get to speak to Dr Chaytor?' she asked her daughter.

'Yes, Mother, they enjoyed the party,' Rosemary replied.

'Is he actually married to that girl or are they merely engaged?'

'They're not married, Mother.'

'Will he marry her, do you think?'

'Mother, I don't know.'

'Oh well, as long as you're over him, dear. The boys we idolise at twelve are most unsuitable at twenty-two. Don't you agree, darling?' she asked, appealing to Nigel.

'I have absolutely no thoughts on the subject,' he answered, his eyes resting on Rosemary's uncompromising expression.

'Well, I'm thinking of my own thoughts when I was twenty-two. It seems to me that all my crushes were silly until I met you, darling, and by that time I was in my early forties.'

Celia's chatter was annoying Rosemary, and Nigel reflected that it was hardly surprising when one of his wife's crushes had been her daughter's father.

'I think we should invite Ariadne round for dinner one evening,' he said. 'She'll be rattling in that house on her own. Besides people will expect it of us.'

'I don't see why. She was often difficult after I left Gordon.'

'There's no need for you to behave in a similar fashion, though.'

'I'll telephone her in the morning. Did she send you a birthday present, Rosemary?'

'No, Mother. She didn't come to my party, did she?'

'No, she was probably going to bring it along on the evening. We'll see if she remembers.'

Rosemary was thinking about Noel and all the disparaging remarks he'd made about her mother over the years. She'd hated him for making them, she'd wanted him to like her mother, but when they eventually met he was still sarcastic about her reasons for being at Dene Hollow. In every unfortunate remark her mother made she sensed Noel's reaction, imagined his face wreathed in a cynical smile.

Ariadne declined their dinner invitation on the grounds that she needed to be alone to think things out. She had an appointment to see Johnny's solicitor in Nairobi, and there was the funeral to think about.

It was a large funeral by any standard. He had not been popular, but people were curious and his business interests were wide and varied. Ariadne cut a tragic figure in deepest mourning, walking behind his coffin in the company of his solicitor and his accountant, looking neither to right nor left and returning to her home immediately the service was over.

One day she'd face them, one day when she was sure of her future, when she knew that Johnny had treated her fairly.

Speculation was rife and she knew what people were saying about her. She was an adventuress. She'd ruined one marriage and married Johnny because he was rich without caring the toss of a button for him. They were probably right about a lot of the things they were saying, but she had cared for him to some extent, and she'd never cheated on Johnny, largely because he wouldn't have stood for it and she had had to think about the money involved.

She was well aware that his solicitor didn't much like her. He was one of the old school, long established, knowing too much about her and despising most of it.

By the time she left his office late in the afternoon she didn't care whether he or his cronies liked her or not. Johnny had come up trumps: she had his money, she was rich.

She drove back to her house in a state of euphoria. She could spend what she wanted, go where she wanted, live where she wanted, but more importantly she could love where she wanted without having to tie herself permanently to a man simply so that she would have a roof over her head.

That afternoon she telephoned the Boyds to say she would love to have dinner with them that evening. Ariadne Fairbrother knew where her life was going, and she was not in the least concerned that the path she had set herself would bring tragedy into the lives of others.

She wore black, restrained and elegant, a foil for her dark auburn hair and pale creamy skin, green eyes tantalisingly innocent as she chatted to Rosemary about her birthday party. As she handed Rosemary a long velvet-covered box she watched while the girl opened it, exclaiming on its contents. It was a long gold chain and suspended from it was a single beautiful emerald, which gleamed and sparkled as if it had a life of its own.

The gift was expensive, guaranteed to make every other gift Rosemary had received somehow lacking in imagination, but when Rosemary thanked her, a little overwhelmed by the present, she waved a careless hand saying, 'You're young and beautiful, I have enough jewellery and you will do more justice to it than ever I could. Don't you agree, Celia?'

Celia didn't agree. She had admired the jewel for longer than she cared to admit. She had thought it ostentatious, not a little vulgar, and wished it was hers. Now Ariadne was fastening it round Rosemary's neck, where it lay against her tender young skin, glistening with a sort of wicked defiance.

Ariadne was aware of a strange tension around the dining table that night. Celia was doing most of the talking while Rosemary sat without looking once in Nigel's direction, as if he wasn't there. Nigel, when he spoke at all, confined his remarks to Ariadne about her late husband and asked if she had had thoughts on whether she would stay on in Kenya.

Celia chattered on about the party, their guests, their clothes, their presents, Rosemary's friendship with Martin Newley, and Ariadne asked with a provocative smile, 'So it's serious, is it?'

'Well, we do hope so, don't we, Nigel?' Celia said sharply.

Looking at Rosemary, Ariadne asked, 'And what does Rosemary say?'

'We're enjoying ourselves, we have a good time.'

'So I believe, too good a time according to some people.'

'What do you mean by that?' Celia demanded.

'Well, we all know what fuddy-duddies some people can be. We've all suffered at some time or another by their gibes, perhaps me more than most. I wouldn't worry about them if I were you, Rosemary.'

'But why are they talking about my daughter? She's with a young crowd and a boy who obviously admires her. What are they saying?'

Ariadne shrugged her shoulders. 'Only that they seem to be enjoying life. Don't give it another thought. You go on enjoying life, my dear, you are only young once.'

Nigel was well aware that her remarks were levelled at Celia, rather than her daughter. When he looked directly at Rosemary she averted her eyes quickly, too quickly, nor did Ariadne miss any of it.

Something had gone on between Nigel and the girl. He'd probably made a pass at her; after all, his reputation was hardly pristine where young girls were concerned. Still, in Rosemary's case he was sailing a little too close to the wind.

Celia was so terribly sure of herself, she'd never in a thousand years think she needed to keep an eye on Nigel.

Ariadne had never been one for dining in other people's homes; she always preferred a crowd. She was bored with the desultory conversation, Celia's efforts to impress her and Nigel's long silences. She wanted an excuse to leave but Celia was well launched into the latest hint of scandal to have struck the tennis club. It was something and nothing, something people with too much money and not enough to do would concern themselves with, and Nigel was evidently already bored by it. He wandered over to the piano where Rosemary was sitting staring into space. She looked up quickly, her face suffused with colour, and then abruptly she rose and walked out of the room.

Oh yes, definitely something untoward had gone on between those two. Her eyes met Nigel's and she smiled before saying, 'I really must think of going to the club. I'm out of touch with things at the moment. Johnny always said I'd bury him one day and play tennis the next. By the same token if I shut myself away in a nunnery it wouldn't bring him back.'

Nigel escorted her to her car and as she took her place behind the wheel he smiled down at her.

'You're looking very beautiful tonight, Ariadne. You've made a good start getting back to normal.'

'Well, I'm not going to wear my widow's weeds for ever.'

'What are you going to do, I wonder?'

'Nothing in a hurry. I like it here, I like the house, I'd have liked Malibu but there's no reason why I can't look around for something similar.'

He raised his eyebrows.

'You're that affluent, are you?'

'Yes, Nigel, I am. Johnny came up trumps, he's left me a very rich woman. This time I don't need to marry for security or money, I can please myself.'

'But you'll need a man in your life, Ariadne. One can be very lonely even with money.'

'I know. But this time I can pick and choose and discard when I feel like it.'

'Wouldn't it worry you that the man you chose might be marrying you for the very same reasons you married Johnny?'

'Who said anything about marriage, Nigel?'

He laughed. 'So you'd make that quite clear to him, would you?'

She looked at him with her green cynical eyes and she was aware that he desired her. It was an old desire, not born of that moment, and with a brief smile she started up the engine and drove swiftly away.

Since the first day she'd met Nigel Boyd she'd fancied him, but he'd thought her a little common. There had always been richer women until she married Johnny, then there'd been Celia. In the old days he'd searched for blue-blooded girls, then rich ones. Now she could buy Nigel with Johnny's money. All was not well between Nigel and Celia; she had begun to bore him, with her pretensions and her extravagances, and he was embarrassed by Rosemary's presence.

Knowing Nigel he'd probably tried to have an affair with the girl and she'd repulsed him. Between them they were making a very good job of pushing him in her direction.

Chapter Twenty-Two

People dining quietly at the Paradiso Club raised their eyebrows in some annoyance at the advent of Martin Newley and his boisterous crowd. They had spent their evening wandering from one club to the next, a group of amorous young men drooling over giggling young girls who went immediately to the bar, where they sat talking and laughing loudly while they waited for their drinks.

Martin sat with his arm round Rosemary's shoulders, his face against hers while he whispered inanities in her ear. Their arrival was unwelcome, a fact made evident by the disdain on the faces of the diners and several of their comments.

Steven Chaytor and Mary Raynor were dining

with a consultant and his wife who had only recently arrived in Kenya. Meeting Angela Greaves' eyes across the table, Mary said, 'Perhaps they won't stay here long. I shouldn't think there's enough going on for them around here.'

'Who are they?' Angela asked.

'Young people with too much money,' Mary replied, and meeting Steven's eyes she was aware of the doubt in them. More and more she realised that where Rosemary Greville was concerned Steven was more worried than annoyed about her behaviour.

Mary and Steven had been children together in distant Malaysia where their fathers worked for the British government. They had played together, gone on holiday together and eventually been sent to England to be educated. In England they had kept in touch, for various sporting events and University balls; visits to Mary's relatives since Steven did not have relatives in England. She had met the Greville boys at a May Ball, seen how close Steven appeared to be to them and learned that he spent most of his holidays with them at a place called Dene Hollow on the south coast of England. She had liked Jeffrey much better than she'd liked Jerome, but it had been Jerome who had told her about his young cousin's crush on Steven.

It had been Jerome who had suggested that Steven should invite her to spend Christmas at Dene Hollow. 'If my young cousin sees you have a girlfriend it might knock some sense into her head,' he'd joked.

She had made herself be specially nice to Rosemary and viewed her obsession with Steven from a singularly superior stance. The girl was a plain little thing with braces on her teeth and fine pale hair pulled back from a face of no particularly beauty. She had thought the girl's mother to be very beautiful and stylish and had felt rather sorry for her daughter, whom she seemed to regard as something of an encumbrance.

Mary felt she had nothing to fear from Rosemary Greville. She had wanted Steven for as long as she could remember, it was something her parents wanted, and Steven's. When he specialised in tropical medicine she decided it was something she wanted to do also, and with this in mind she had followed him out to South Africa, then to Kenya, to work in the laboratories. Everybody accepted that she was Steven's girl, and it was all coming right until the arrival of Rosemary Greville.

This new Rosemary was not the plain little girl she'd met in England; she had blossomed into a beauty, and with her beauty came riches and the most beautiful estate for miles. That was the problem. Rosemary had everything to live for, everything to make her happy, but she was a troubled, foolish girl who ran with the wild crowd and rapidly became one of them.

They were prancing around the dance floor now, dancing some modern movements that hardly did justice to the music the orchestra was playing, and other couples were leaving the floor to return to their tables.

Rosemary was laughing, looking up into Martin's face provocatively. Angela murmured, 'She's very beautiful. Is that her fiancé?'

'They see a lot of each other,' Mary said sharply.

'Well, they seem to be having a good time.'

'And spoiling it for everybody else. Steven, perhaps we should go now,' Mary said, raising to her feet.

Rosemary watched them leave with the utmost disquiet in her heart. They were behaving atrociously; Steven would think so. He'd favoured her with a brief smile while his companions hadn't even taken the trouble. She wanted to go home, but home was no home, it was a place where her mother and her husband were constantly at loggerheads, quarrelling all the time about money, about the estate, about everything under the sun, it seemed. And then there was Nigel.

Was Nigel in love with her? Was it that that made him so perverse with her mother? But Nigel had no right to be in love with her, she could never in a million years love him; but at the same time she felt worthless. He had violated her body and blithely asked her to forgive him. He would never touch her again, he'd said, but she would never trust him, and if he tried to touch her she'd kill him.

He spent most of his time at Ariadne Fairbrother's house and from the way Ariadne looked at her she felt sure she must know something of what had gone on. Her mother was painfully obtuse about Nigel's whereabouts. She surrounded herself with women friends who had similar taste as herself but not as much going for them. They envied her her house, her husband, her way of life and envy was something her mother delighted in.

The cool brief glance Steven had favoured her with rankled. He had little time for the crowd she ran with or for Rosemary herself. Now they had the club to themselves since most of the diners had left or were leaving. Girls were dancing on the tables, men and girls were imitating flamenco dancers, not very successfully, but their laughter encouraged the dancers to dance even more wildly.

It was almost dawn when they saw the gates of Malibu in front of them and Rosemary was reminded of that other night when Nigel had waited for her inside the hall. In sudden desperation she cried, 'Why don't we all go for a swim? I don't want to go home.'

Her suggestion was accepted by the rest of them, and then they were running across the lawns in the direction of the swimming pool.

Steven brought the car to a halt outside Mary's flat, which she shared with a colleague. Their journey had been taken largely in silence, and looking at his profile in the lights from the doorway, she was aware of his gravity and that his thoughts were miles away.

'The evening was spoilt,' Mary said sharply. 'I'm surprised that the Paradiso Club haven't banned them. They'll lose everybody else's custom if they don't ban them soon.'

309

'They're young, it was high spirits.'

'Well, we were that age once. We had some pretty hectic parties but we never spoilt it for other people.'

He didn't answer; of course Mary was right.

'Why do you always take her part?' Mary demanded. 'You don't like me saying anything about that girl's behaviour.'

'I haven't said anything for or against her, Mary.'

'That's just it, you never do. Everybody else was condemning them the other evening, particularly Martin Newley and Rosemary Greville, but you didn't say a word. What's so special about her?'

'Only that I knew her when she was a quiet, repressed little thing, and when there was a certain sadness about her. I'm finding it very hard to reconcile that girl with the girl I saw earlier this evening.'

'There's nothing repressed about her now.'

'No, and that is what worries me. People who change as much as she's changed usually have a good reason for it. Not always a happy reason.'

'Oh Steven, of course she's happy. Look at her clothes, her house, her horse, her car. She's going to be exactly like her mother and you know what everybody says about her. Surely you remember how the Greville boys disliked her.'

'I do remember, and I remember how hurt Rosie was by her neglect. I think something's gone sadly wrong in her life to change her out of all recognition. I wish I knew what it was.'

Mary was not as yet Steven's girl. They were old friends, they went back a long way and

310

people invited them to the same dinner parties. Mary had been so sure that at last Steven would come to see her as a suitable wife but there was no romance between them, only an old friendship.

She sensed his reserve; at the same time she was always available, and if everybody else thought of them as a pair, surely Steven would begin to think so too. It had been going well until the advent of Rosemary Greville. The girl gave him too much to ponder about.

All was not well at Malibu.

Celia had slept fitfully, and in her waking moments her mind was obsessed with her quarrel with Nigel the day before. It had started the day before that when she told him she had ordered new tiling for the conservatory floor.

'What's wrong with the tiling that's there now?' he'd demanded.

'Darling, it's a legacy from the Moretons. I've managed to change everything else; surely we can bring the conservatory up to date.'

'The Moretons were nice people, they had good taste.'

'But they were both getting on, Nigel. Don't you want Malibu to reflect our taste?'

'All it's doing is reflecting the money we're spending on it, and money isn't elastic.'

She had decided to let him stew about the tiling but it was over breakfast the next morning that matters became more difficult. She had watched him leafing through his morning mail, seen the angry frown on his face and the way he slammed

311

the offending letter down on the table.

'Is something wrong, darling?' she asked him.

His dark angry eyes glared across the table. 'Yes, something is wrong. You can forget about the tiling we discussed yesterday.'

'Why, what is it?'

'It's my grandmother's house in England: there's dry rot and God knows what else wrong with it. It needs a fortune spending on it unless I want it to fall down.'

'That might not be a bad idea. It seems ridiculous to me to spend money on a house we never go to, and are not very likely to go to.'

'Why do you say that? I have every intention of going there, it's part of my life. It was my legacy.'

'A legacy that costs you a great deal of money. You've never even spoken of going back there; you're just making that house an excuse not to allow me to spend money on this one.'

'It isn't an excuse, Celia, it is reality. You're a middle-class girl who doesn't understand about land or heritage. You're no worse for that, but that house means more to me than Malibu ever could.'

'Thanks for putting me in my place, but I don't see how a place in England that we never visit can mean more than the house we live in.'

'That's what I mean, Celia. You'll never understand. However, that house in England will have to have money spent on it. This one doesn't need it.'

'I've already ordered the tiling for the conservatory.'

'Then cancel it. It isn't necessary.'

312

'I won't cancel it. People will talk, they'll say we're living beyond our means, that we can't afford it. After all, nobody here is the least bit interested in that crumbling old pile in England.'

'And we don't belong here, Celia; this isn't our country, this really isn't our life, we're birds of passage and it's time we realised it.'

That had been the moment he had stormed out of the breakfast room and for the rest of the day she had seen nothing of him. She believed he had gone into Nairobi to see his solicitors but when he hadn't come home before she went to bed her fears and her anger increased.

It was light now, that first beautiful iridescent light that heralded the strident rising of the sun, and fearfully she rose from her bed and slipped her arms into the silk robe lying across a chair. Nigel had not come to their bedroom so he was probably still sulking and had slept in the dressing room or in another bedroom.

When he was not in the dressing room she looked elsewhere, and when there was no sign that he had returned to the house, her fears increased.

From outside the house she could hear laughter and the sound of voices. She couldn't think that Nigel was with the young people in the swimming pool, certainly not with Rosemary and her crowd of young friends.

She worried about Rosemary and Nigel. She sensed that her daughter didn't like him. It often happened between stepfather and stepdaughter, but Rosemary had never really known her father, she'd been too young when he died, so surely it

313

wasn't anything to do with that that made her so resentful of him. She was probably a little jealous, it couldn't be anything other than that.

After Celia had wandered through the downstairs rooms she went to the garage behind the house and there she encountered her first shock: Nigel's car was not there. Even Nigel wouldn't have been foolish enough to stay at the club, it would only have started everyone talking. And he hated the hotels in Nairobi. Where had he spent the night?

She helped herself to fruit juice and went to stand at the long window looking out towards the gates. The sun was rising now, piercingly bright, illuminating the hills and the gardens with shafts of brilliant gold, and she frowned at the sight of two young girls streaking across the lawns followed by a boy coming from the direction of the pool.

She wanted Rosemary to see as much of Martin as was possible, she was hoping they would get engaged, but she was also aware that this set of youngsters was causing people to talk. Being nice to Martin was one thing, earning a bad reputation was another. One of these days she would have to talk to Rosemary seriously and make her understand she was behaving foolishly.

She had to talk to somebody and her obvious choice was Ariadne. Ariadne would still be in bed; she rarely surfaced before ten o'clock, but surely she would see that Celia had problems. In any case she could sit in the gardens or near the pool for a while. One thing was sure, she had to get away from Malibu and Nigel's absence.

She debated telling Rosemary where she was going, but she didn't want that crowd of young people to see that she was anxious, so instead she went straight to her car and drove slowly towards the gates. There was nothing on the road so early in the morning, and if she had not been so anxious she could have enjoyed the golden beauty of the scenery and its gentle peace. Even the chattering of the monkeys was stilled; it was like some primeval dawn before time first began, and it was Nigel with his sulks and bad temper that was preventing her enjoying it. She had never thought in a million years that he would be so penny-pinching. He had always been generous, a spendthrift if you like, but recently he'd been different, their moments of rare passion unfulfilling, their anxieties too raw and abrasive.

Perhaps if they got Rosemary married off things would be different. They would have Malibu to themselves, those long silences over the dinner table between Rosemary and Nigel no longer a problem.

As she turned off the road to drive to Ariadne's house she reflected complacently that it couldn't hold a candle to Malibu. It was not surprising that Ariadne had been envious. This was a very a nice house with gardens and a pool. Once she had thought it wonderful and she'd envied Ariadne; now she had supremacy and felt warmed by it.

She left the car and sauntered towards the pool, where she sat for a while contemplating the front of the house. The curtains in Ariadne's bedroom were drawn as she knew they would be, and there

315

was no sign of life from anywhere around the house. She wouldn't tell Ariadne everything, simply that she and Nigel had had a difference of opinion about his grandmother's house in England and he'd taken exception. After all, Ariadne would be even less enthusiastic about that old house than she was. After a while they'd giggle about it, Ariadne had always been able to put matters into perspective. Complacent with her happier thoughts, she dozed off a little and it was the sound of voices that brought her suddenly awake. There were men stirring in the gardens, even though Ariadne's curtains were still drawn. She rose quickly to her feet and realised that she was being observed by the men working on the land, so without any hurry she sauntered slowly towards the house.

It was a little after nine o'clock, still too early for Ariadne, and with this in mind she took the path that skirted the house and led to the greenhouses and garages at the rear. Johnny Fairbrother had always been proud of his greenhouses; she could conveniently spend a little time wandering through them. It was at the back of the house that she encountered Nigel's car parked under the shelter of the trees.

She stared at it for several minutes in stupid amazement before anger sent her running swiftly towards the front of the house, where she hammered wildly on the door. It was opened several minutes later by a sleepy-eyed servant, but without hesitation she brushed passed him and ran beyond him into the hall.

Turning to face him she asked, 'Is my husband

here? No, I know he's here. Where is he?'

The servant stared at her without speaking, his expression blank, and without another word she ran quickly up the stairs towards Ariadne's bedroom. Her thoughts were seething. How dare Nigel come to Ariadne to regale her with his troubles? At that moment she did not even think that there could be another reason for his presence in Ariadne's house. Furiously, she flung the bedroom door open, then stood trembling, shaken to the very core of her being by the sight of Nigel and Ariadne sitting up in bed, staring at her across the room.

Neither of them spoke, and after a few minutes Celia slammed the door behind her and rushed headlong down the stairs. She heard the door opening behind her and Nigel's voice from the landing above.

'Celia, wait,' he commanded. 'Stay there.'

Celia did no such thing. Instead she rushed across the hall followed by the stares of the servants. She flung the front door open and rushed madly to where she had left her car.

Nigel watched her drive towards the gates, her foot pressed down hard on the accelerator. He heard the screech of her brakes as she swerved towards the gates, then the roaring sound of the car's engine as she sped down the road outside.

When he returned to the bedroom, Ariadne was sitting at her dressing table, and for several minutes they stared at each other in silence until she said, 'I heard you calling her to wait. Wait for what, Nigel?'

'She was upset, she was driving like a maniac. I

thought we should talk.'

'You thought she was in a mood to listen?'

'I don't know. I just didn't want her rushing off like that.'

'Talking isn't going to solve anything. She found us in bed together. Don't you think the time for talking is long gone?'

'What do you think we should do then?'

'I don't think there is very much you can do.'

'I said "we" Ariadne, not "me".'

'All right then. I'm a partner in this transgression but I'm also a free agent. Are you anxious for her to forgive you or is this the end of the road?'

'What do you mean by that?'

'Oh come on, Nigel, you know very well what I mean. Do you want out of your marriage or are you going to go crawling back, telling her our affair was a stupid mistake and she is the woman you really love?'

'I'm wondering how much you love me. I'm not very sure that you've ever loved anybody.'

She smiled. 'Do you know, darling, I never have. Unless it was me. There was a lot of things in Johnny I admired, even his bloodymindedness, but I've always thought of you as somebody like myself, selfish and greedy, completely and utterly absorbed in yourself. I don't think you've ever loved anybody either.'

'I thought I loved Celia, but she's made a very good job of killing whatever feeling I had for her.'

'Because she's made demands you hadn't expected her to make. Because she isn't quite the meek and adoring little wife you thought she'd

318

be. So don't look at me, Nigel. I'm a hundred times worse than she'd ever be. If I were you I'd follow her and make your peace with her. Let me know how you get on.'

He stared at her in angry silence before leaving her bedroom, slamming the door behind him.

Chapter Twenty-Three

They were a happy group driving in the Land Rover. Rosemary had provided them with breakfast, they had spent a happy evening driving from one night spot to the next, ending with high jinks in Malibu's swimming pool. Now they were laughing and singing as they drove to their homes and were totally unprepared for the open white sports car hurtling down the centre of the road, swerving erratically before the driver saw the Land Rover driving towards her. In sudden terror, Celia swerved, and the car rolled into a skid before turning over and over to land against the trunk of a tree, where it lay in a crumpled wreck, its bonnet pushed up against the tree, and smoke pouring out of its exhaust.

In the Land Rover there was traumatised silence, so that none of them saw from which direction Nigel Boyd's car suddenly appeared on the scene. Acting swiftly, he leapt out of his car and went to where his wife's car lay smashed like a crumpled toy, and frantically he began to tear at the door in an effort to reach his wife's still form, lying with her head smashed against the steering wheel.

Desperately he called for help, and after a few minutes three bemused young men walked unsteadily towards him.

Later, at the inquest on the death of Celia Boyd, none of those young people could remember very much. Only that the car coming towards them had skidded off the road. None of them remembered Nigel's arrival; only that suddenly he had been there and they had gone to his assistance.

Guilt and relief were uppermost in Nigel's thoughts. That his wife had discovered him at Ariadne's house was not an issue. He had discovered that she had left the house very early and had assumed that she had driven to Mrs Fairbrother's house and he had decided to join her there. Mrs Fairbrother had not been well after her husband's death and they had both spent time with her.

There had been many times when he had remonstrated with her for driving too fast. She had not thought to encounter anybody else on the road at that time. Rosemary had listened to Nigel delivering his evidence, and to Ariadne confirming that Celia had spent some time with her early that morning. Then had come a string of others who had told of Martin Newley and his friends drinking in the early morning at one club after another, but his father had defended him fiercely, saying they had breakfasted at Malibu and spent some time in the pool. His son was not intoxicated when he drove his friends home and no blame should be attached to him. There had been no witnesses to the tragedy and Celia's dangerous driving was in the end blamed for her death.

Rosemary's thoughts were chaotic. She had lost a mother she had hardly known, even though she had loved her, her beauty, her glamour and her enthusiasm for living; now she had to come to terms with the rest of her life. She could not stay in Kenya, she could not remain at Malibu.

Nigel had told her she must stay in the house and he would move out into his club for the time being. Her grandparents did not attend her mother's funeral because her grandfather was unwell. Aunt Beatrice had telephoned her many times but she was concerned with matters at Dene Hollow. Rosemary hadn't to worry about them, she had enough to worry about; in time Beatrice would tell her all about them.

To Mary's chagrin, it was Steven Chaytor who felt he should offer assistance and advice to a girl who had been a friend for many years. With this in mind he drove out to Malibu in the early evening and found in Rosemary a girl he could not reconcile with the Rosie Greville he had known.

He faced a young woman strangely composed, her beautiful face showing neither grief nor anxiety. It was only her eyes that told him something of the trauma inside. They were like blue flint as she took his outstretched hand in cool detachment.

She offered him a choice of coffee or something stronger, and he accepted the coffee, sitting facing her in the conservatory with the sound of birdsong and chattering monkeys outside. As she served the coffee he looked around him with interest, admiring the delicate fabric of the cushions and the exquisitely tiled floor, and as she joined him Rosemary said, 'It is a beautiful room, isn't it. My mother wanted to change it.'

It was the start of a conversation he hadn't expected.

'Really, why was that?'

'Oh she was always wanting to change something. She didn't like the tiles, I think she just wanted a change.'

'It's a very beautiful house but I suppose it's natural to want to stamp your own taste on the home you live in.'

'She did through the rest of the house. I was hoping she'd leave this as it is, but mother was like that, she always had to be planning something.'

'And Nigel?'

'No. They quarrelled about it. They rowed about it the day before she died.'

Steven was wishing they could change the subject; there was discomfort in the way it was going.

She pointed to a book lying open on the table between them.

'Mother loved that book,' she said with a bleak smile. 'It's about all that scandal here years ago, you know, the man who was murdered, the story of the man who was tried for his murder, and his wife who was having an affair. Mother's caused almost as much scandal, hasn't she. She'd have liked that.'

'Rosie.' He found it easier to address her in the old way, and she looked at him sharply. 'Have you had thoughts on what you're going to do now? Will you stay on in Kenya?'

'I don't know. Perhaps it's too soon.'

'And Martin Newley?'

'What about Martin Newley?'

'I thought that perhaps you were seriously interested in each other?'

'That's what my mother hoped for.'

'And you?'

'I never thought about Martin seriously. He was fun, we had some happy times. I found him immature. I'm glad they've gone away.'

'They've gone away?'

'Yes, didn't you know? The Newley's have taken themselves and Martin off to America to get over the trauma of the crash, and me too I suppose.'

'Do you mind?'

She smiled. 'No. They've gone for several months, I believe. I don't expect to he here when they come back.'

'So you are leaving Kenya, Rosie?'

'I can't stay here.'

He looked at her curiously, aware of the sudden colour flooding her cheeks.

'You mean Nigel Boyd will wish to return here as soon as possible? But surely he won't pressure you into leaving Malibu before you're ready?'

'I can't live here with him and this is his house. I have to get away as soon as possible.'

'Where will you go?'

'I don't think my mother ever expected to die

323

young. I have her jewellery, her furs, her clothes. All her money is in a joint account with Nigel, so as her husband it will go to him, as will her share in this house.'

'He has to see you solvent, Rosie; surely even Nigel Boyd will see that.'

'I don't want anything from him. Neither his money nor anything from this house. I've been educated, I'm not unintelligent, I shall get a job.'

'Here or in England?'

'Steven, I don't know. I shall need a home. Aunt Beatrice will help me.'

'So it's likely to be in England?'

'I think so.'

'You're thinking about Dene Hollow?'

'I never stop thinking about Dene Hollow. That isn't my home either. Something's going on there. Do you know what it is?'

'I hear from Jerome occasionally; he never mentions the old place, they seem to have washed their hands of it. Occasionally I hear from Jeffrey; matters are strained, I think.'

'Oh Steven, it was such a happy place once. It's the only place I can ever look back on with any degree of stability. Why does everything have to change so much?'

'Well, I think it's right to say that nothing stays the same. Never go back Rosie, not to some house and people you expect to have stayed the same. I think that way you only lay yourself open to disappointment.'

'Then what should I do?'

'A new life, new scenery, new friends.'

'I thought I had that here but nothing has been

like I thought it would be. My mother is dead. I don't want to see Martin's friends, somehow they remind me too much of things I want to forget, and living in this house is unreal, it's like a bird cage.'

'If you're so unhappy here, why not move out. I have some good friends here who would be glad for you to stay with them until you've made up your mind where you go from here.'

'I think all your friends see me as one of those noisy young people who disrupted their evenings at the Paradiso Club and elsewhere. They'll hardly give me houseroom, Steven.'

'They will, Rosie, when I tell them that that wasn't the Rosie I remember. Are you prepared to leave it with me, Rosie?'

'People will talk, they'll wonder why I'm so desperate to get away from here.'

He looked at her keenly. Again the rich red blood coloured her face, and he said gently, 'I'm wondering about that, Rosie. Why are you so anxious to leave Malibu and Nigel Boyd behind you?

She shook her head, and suddenly the treacherous tears filled her eyes and rolled unchecked down her cheeks. Concerned, Steven left his chair and went to sit beside her. He reached out and gathered her into his embrace and she clung to him, sobbing wildly.

In those first few moments Steven only remembered that this was the young girl who had run to him along the cliff top, her blond hair streaming in the wind, her eyes shining a welcome, and in the next moment he was hearing

Jerome's dry, cynical voice saying, 'She's got an almighty crush on you. Let her down lightly or there'll be the devil to pay.'

But this was not the little girl who had idolised him, this was a warm beautiful woman whose face was smooth and warm against his, whose arms were round his neck, whose body trembled in his arms.

She troubled him in ways he couldn't define. It wasn't simply the death of her mother, traumatic as that had been, it was something more than that. It was her anxiety whenever Nigel Boyd was mentioned, an underlying fear that meant that she didn't want to see him or hear his name.

When the sobs subsided he released her, and to Rosemary it felt as though she had suddenly been thrust into a cold, grey world she wanted no part of.

'Would you like me to ask the Garveys? I'm sure they'll agree that you should go to them. They were always very fond of Gordon and they knew your mother well.'

Rosie smiled, the saddest smile he had ever seen. 'The Garveys never came to see us, Steven, I don't think they thought my mother should have married again so quickly; at least that's what mother said. Mrs Garvey always looked at me so sadly, as though she expected me to behave badly, and I always complied.'

'This was your mother's home, Rosie, it isn't yours, I don't think it can ever be yours.'

'No it never can. Aunt Beatrice will be in touch, then I'll know what I must do. I just want it to be soon.'

'Well, if you're sure. I must go now, Rosie, I have a meeting in the early afternoon that I couldn't get out of.'

'Of course. How is Mary?'

He looked at her, suddenly bemused. Mary! They were considered a pair, two people destined to be together, share a home, a future wherever it might be, and until this moment he'd believed in its inevitability. Now he knew for certain that it was something he'd been prepared to drift into without really wanting it.

Mary was a nice girl, and she wanted him; she'd made that very clear by following him out to Africa. He valued her friendship, her intrinsic decency, but it wasn't love. But how could he be sure that this sudden blinding emotion he felt for Rosie was right for either of them?

Rosie would go back to England, pick up the pieces of her life, find somebody there. There were too many uncertainties. He needed to sort out his life without thinking of Rosie as being a part of it.

She walked with him to the door, where he took her hand and looked steadily into her eyes.

'You know where I am, Rosie. Don't be afraid to call me if I can help in any way.'

She smiled. 'Thank you, Steven, you're very kind.'

As he walked down the steps to his waiting car he was suddenly aware that another car was coming slowly up the drive, where it came to rest alongside his own. He waited until the driver got out of it before responding to her smile. He didn't know Ariadne Fairbrother well, only the sort of things people said about her, and he liked to make up his own mind about people. She was attractive and sophisticated, and he wasn't entirely sure that she would be good for Rosie Greville.

'You're going back to the hospital, Dr Chaytor, I hope I'm not responsible for your leaving?' she said brightly.

'Not at all,' he smiled. 'I have a meeting this afternoon.'

She waved at Rosie standing in the doorway, and with another smile walked up the steps towards her.

After kissing Rosie on both cheeks she said, 'You're looking better, darling. We do have to pick up the pieces, don't we. Nobody knows that better than I.'

'Do come into the drawing room, Mrs Fairbrother. Would you like some refreshment, tea perhaps?'

'I've never subscribed to the English fashion for tea and polite conversation, darling. Gin and tonic would be nice.'

Rosie smiled and went immediately to the drinks cabinet. Ariadne and her mother had chatted easily over their G and T's, and joining her Ariadne said, 'Your mother knew just how I liked it. Shall I help myself?'

'Yes, of course.'

'What will you have, dear?'

'Nothing, thank you, I had coffee with Steven.'

'Ah yes. He's nice, very attractive too. Streets ahead of that Newley boy. Of course the Newleys were well heeled but I can't really think that young doctor is on the bread line.'

'Steven is an old friend. I knew him in England.'

'So I believe, and that girl who followed him out here keeps very close to him.'

'She too has known him a very long time.'

'I doubt if it's going anywhere. Now, I have a message for you from Nigel.'

Rosemary's eyes opened wide and Ariadne didn't miss the sudden look of panic in their blue depths.

'I met him this morning at the sports club. I invited him to play tennis but he wasn't in the mood. I should have had more sense than ask him, he's really taken your mother's death very badly. I hadn't realised quite how sensitive he could be.'

'What is the message, Mrs Fairbrother?'

'Ariadne please, darling. Or you make me sound like some old matriarch.'

The girl was looking at her anxiously and as on so many occasions Ariadne asked herself why any mention of his name brought that sudden panic into her eyes. Of course he'd made a play for her and she was young and untried. He'd been a fool and he'd been lucky to get away with it.

'He's decided to go to England. He has a house there, he tells me. Did you know that?'

'Yes, it was his grandmother's house, on the south coast. I knew that she'd died and left it to him.'

'Really. Well, he tells me it wants some work doing on it and he feels he should go there and take a look around. He'll be gone some few weeks so there's no hurry for you to leave here. You were intending leaving Malibu, weren't you, Rosemary?'

'Of course. This is Nigel's house, it isn't mine.'

'I always assumed the house belonged to both Nigel and Celia. Didn't it?'

'Apparently not. The house belongs to Nigel.'

'But your mother's surely left you well provided for?'

'I have her jewellery and her china, her clothes and some other things. I don't suppose my mother expected to die so young...' Her voice faltered. After all, why should she be telling Ariadne anything about the state of her finances? It was really none of her business, and recognising the thoughts in Rosemary's mind, Ariadne said, 'I'm concerned for you, my dear. Please don't think I'm simply prying into matters that don't concern me.'

'When I go home to England I shall get a job. I did well at school; there'll be something.'

Ariadne nodded, then, changing the subject, she said, 'Nigel says he will have to come here in the morning to pick up his suitcase and some clothes. He's booked a flight out on Friday morning. I don't know if you want to be here when he calls.'

'Did he ask for me to be here?'

'Why no, he only told me his intentions. But surely you'll need to see him, won't you? He'll need to give you some money.'

'Money?'

'Well, of course, darling. The servants have to be paid, an estate of this size doesn't thrive on fresh air.'

'The estate isn't my responsibility.'

'I know that, dear, but you can't afford to be too proud. Pride gets you nowhere; I discovered that before I was your age.'

When Rosemary looked at her curiously, she laughed. 'You know there are some very toffee-nosed people around here who have never approved of me because I looked after number one, but then those people never had my unfortunate start in life. It was a start that conditioned me to put me first, and in the end it paid off.'

'I didn't have an unfortunate start in life, Ariadne. I was too young to lose my father and my mother came here to live. I did have an enchanted childhood, however, in a beautiful place with an aunt and cousins who cared about me. It seems I'm only just learning to struggle.'

'Which is silly when there's really no need. Make Nigel give you your mother's money; he owes you.'

Rosemary merely smiled, and after a few moments Ariadne said, 'Well, I've no doubt you'll do exactly what you want in the matter. If Nigel feels like popping round to see me before he flies out we can share a gin and tonic.'

'If I see him I'll tell him.'

She stood on the terrace until Ariadne's car left the gates.

Nigel was coming to Malibu and she didn't want to see him. She wanted to be miles away, but she had to see him. She was living in his house, waited on by his servants, riding his horses. Whatever he had done to her had to be put on one side until she knew how long she could remain in Kenya.

She hadn't been able to keep the fear from her eyes when Steven mentioned Nigel, and Ariadne too was aware that something had happened between them.

Whatever Nigel had done to her would remain locked in her heart as long as she lived. She could not talk about it to Steven, nor to Ariadne, and suddenly she found herself remembering the cool, malicious expression in Ariadne's eyes as she looked up into Nigel's face, and the way his arms had tightened round her when they danced.

They were two flirtatious people who thrived on the scandals they had created; but surely if there had been anything between them her mother would have suspected it.

Her mother had been to Ariadne's on the morning she died, and the boys and girls in the Range Rover had said she was driving her car too fast and too recklessly. Why had Nigel suddenly decided to drive out to meet her? All the doubts came back, doubts that had given her nightmares every night since her mother's death.

She was dreading meeting Nigel in the morning but it had to be done. One thing was sure, he would not find her helpless.

Chapter Twenty-Four

She sat waiting for him with her ears strained for every sound from outside the window. When she heard the sound of a car her throat felt so tight she felt that she was choking, and then she heard the sound of his footsteps along the terrace outside, the opening of the door and then again his footsteps crossing the hall and running up the stairs.

She pictured him in the bedroom opening and closing drawers, taking clothes out of the long wardrobes and flinging them on the bed, lifting out suitcases. Then she heard his voice speaking to one of the servants. It seemed a thousand years before she heard his footsteps descending the stairs and crossing the hall. Then the door was flung open and he stood in the doorway, staring at her.

After a few seconds he came into the room, turning to close the door behind him, and Rosemary felt herself tense against the arms of the chair before he walked slowly towards her.

His face was calm, but there was a wariness in his eyes as they met hers.

'I was hoping you'd be here, Rosemary, we have to talk about the future. I suppose Ariadne told you I was going to England for a few weeks. I have to see to my grandmother's house.'

'Yes.'

'It's crumbling; it needs some work doing to it. You'll stay on here for the time being, of course.'

'I'll stay on here until I hear something definite about returning to England.'

'You intend to do that, then?'

'Of course.'

'Oh well, I suppose young Newley's gone to America. Do you mind?'

'No.'

'Sensible girl, he's not been gifted with too much common sense.'

When Rosemary didn't speak he came towards her, 'I'm not sure whether you agree with those sentiments or not, Rosemary,' he said.

'I thought you wanted to talk to me about leaving here. I may leave before you return here. I need to know something about the house and the servants.'

'I'll attend to the servants and the house when I return, whenever that is. I intend to pay them several months in advance. If they spend it that's their misfortune.'

'I see.'

He moved closer towards her, and then he saw the revolver resting on the table beside her chair and his eyes narrowed.

'Was there really any need for that?' he asked sharply.

'I didn't intend to take any chances.'

'I told you I would never touch you again and I meant it.'

'The fact that you touched me at all gave me no reason to trust you. If you ever touch me again, Nigel, I will kill you. The revolver is loaded.'

334

He knew that she meant every word of it. As he took another step towards her, her hand reached out for the revolver and he smiled grimly. 'There's no need for any histrionics, Rosemary; I'm leaving.' He reached into his pocket and brought out a large envelope which he placed on a table near her chair.

'You'll find sufficient money in there to see you through the next few months, if it takes that long before you leave for England. I've left you my address in case you need to reach me.'

With that he left the room, closing the door sharply behind him.

She sat without moving until she heard the front door closing behind him and the sound of his car's engine. She went to stand at the window to watch him drive towards the gate, and then she saw that he was taking the road leading to Ariadne's house. She picked up the envelope he had left and opened it. Inside there was a wad of banknotes which she didn't bother to count, as well as his address in England. The notes would be waiting for him when he returned, she had no intention of spending any of them.

Nigel eyed Ariadne with vague resentment. There was something disturbingly too flamboyant about her, from the ridiculous sunglasses with frames like the wings of a bird and which disappeared into her hairline, to the sheath-like silk dress that emphasised her golden skin and voluptuous curves.

Celia had been more beautiful, more restrained; and in spite of his frequent jibes at her lineage she had always looked the complete lady, from her pale golden head to her narrow high-heeled shoes.

The gown Ariadne was wearing was too strident, in colours of emerald green and orange, but she could carry it off. He became suddenly aware of the cynicism in her green eyes; she knew what he was thinking.

She indicated the drinks trolley on the verandah, saying, 'Pour yourself a drink, Nigel, and bring me one.'

Her eyes followed him. He was the handsomest man in her age group. He had an air and he was well aware of it. When he returned to her chair, bringing the drinks, she said evenly, 'Did you see Rosemary?'

'Yes, I left her some money.'

'Most generous.'

'Well, I have no idea how long she intends to remain here. I don't want people saying I left her without funds.'

'Do you intend to give her some of her mother's money?'

'No. I can't afford to. Celia cost me a bomb. She was never satisfied and a lot of that money went on her daughter. She had to be properly launched in order to secure young Newley. Now that's gone by the board.'

'I don't think she cares.'

'You're right, she doesn't.'

'I called yesterday to see her, with your message, remember. Chaytor was just leaving. Celia told me Rosemary rather more than liked him.'

'Hasn't he got a girl?'

'Not so you'd notice.'

'What is that supposed to mean?'

'That the affection is rather one-sided. He likes her well enough, but he doesn't love her. If she had any sense she'd move on.'

'What makes you such a student of human nature, I wonder?'

'Experience, darling, mostly bad experience. How long are you expecting to be away, or better still, do you intend to return here?'

'I have to return here, there's the house, the house that my late wife moved heaven and earth to acquire.'

'I know. I hated her for it.'

'For wanting Malibu?'

'Yes. I wanted Johnny to buy it. He could have afforded it but he wouldn't entertain the idea.'

'Well it's there like a white elephant. Make me an offer for it and it's yours.'

'You're not serious.'

'Oh but I am. You'd love lording it at Malibu, entertaining your friends, the lady of the manor.'

'What friends?'

'Acquaintances then. People you'd like to put one over on.'

'What would I do by myself at Malibu? If some nice rich man appears on the scene it would be different. I could live at Malibu with the right sort of man.'

'I doubt if any man would be right for you, Ariadne.'

She smiled. 'Oh I don't know. I fancied you once but you didn't give me the time of day. I was that rather common girl who broke up other people's homes with indiscriminate speed. That was when you were running the gamut of a selection of bored wives. You had no right to sit in judgment on anybody.'

He smiled. 'Of course you're right, Ariadne, I hadn't.'

'Were you ever really in love with Celia?'

'I thought so.'

'And it all went sour.'

'Yes.'

'Why is Rosemary so afraid of you?'

'Afraid of me! Of course she isn't afraid of me. She shouldn't be; she's cost me plenty.'

'Oh well, it's just that I see a certain panic in her eyes when she looks at you, or when we talk about you.'

'She's probably remembering that her mother and I quarrelled constantly about everything. She's probably even feeling a bit guilty; after all her life in England never prepared her for the luxury she experienced here.'

'She told me she'd been very happy in England.'

'With a taciturn uncle and an ageing aunt. With cousins who were at loggerheads. The girl's been romancing, Ariadne.'

'Oh well, knowing your reputation I just wondered if you've been flirting with her. Her being Celia's daughter wouldn't have stopped you.'

He frowned. 'Can we change the subject, Ariadne? You're beginning to bore me.'

'You're the first man who ever said I bored him. We'll change the subject. Do you intend to sell

338

your house in England?'

He threw back his head and laughed and she stared at him in surprise.

'Ariadne, I'd sell Malibu before I'd sell that house. Celia was always on about selling it and I tried to explain to her that that house represents family and tradition. She never understood. I doubt you would either.'

'You mean I'm not upper-crust enough?'

He smiled. 'You know, dear, somehow or other I don't mind it in you. Celia strained to be upper-crust; you don't care. I'll stay in England until the work on it is finished then I'll think about coming back. By that time I would think Malibu will be standing empty and the supposition about my return will have grown. Will you be here, I wonder?'

'How can I tell? I could be anywhere, on a south sea island, in the States, anywhere on earth, or I might just be here, sitting in the sun doing nothing at all.'

He reached down, and taking her hands in his brought her upright to stand before him.

'Wherever you are I'll find you, Ariadne; on some far distant shore, or here sitting in the sun.'

'I'm flattered. I never thought to hear Nigel Boyd saying something like that to me.'

'Haven't you thought that we're two of a kind?'

'I've always thought so, and now if I don't have the breeding I have the money.'

'You think that's what I'm after?'

'The thought had crossed my mind.'

'Ariadne, I'm not a pauper and I do have Malibu, if I sell Malibu there isn't a far distant shore too far to reach you.'

'If you sell Malibu I doubt if I'd be interested.'

'So Malibu is the incentive?'

'One incentive.'

'And the other?'

'Ask me some other time. Have a good flight; give my regards to England.'

On his journey to the airport he thought about her. Life with Ariadne would never be boring, but he would never be sure of her. Johnny Fairbrother had been sure of her because he was the one with the money; now that Ariadne had it she would give so much and no more to whoever shared her life. A long time ago she might have had the capacity for loving, now she didn't need it; and he had always demanded love from the women he had fancied, without giving them much of himself.

He was not aware that Ariadne was thinking along similar lines.

From the first moment she had looked into his amused sardonic eyes she had been captivated by him, and the fact that she had married two other men had done nothing to erase that first blinding attraction.

She had watched him dallying with a great many blue-blooded girls who had appeared on the scene, knowing that she was not of his class, that he regarded her as something less than pristine. Money talked. Money had educated her to a higher level and slowly but surely they had come to occupy the same world.

Of course he would come back to Malibu; he couldn't afford to stay away and allow the house to fall into the same sort of disrepair his grandmother's house had had to suffer. But would he come back alone? And if he did, would he regard her as anything other than a member of the crowd?

She would possess the advantage he was looking for: money, and thanks to Celia's extravagances he needed money, but what would he offer in return? Ariadne was no longer looking for a man to lift her out of the sort of poverty she'd grown up with. Perhaps for the first time in his life he would confront a woman who could play him at his own game.

In England Nigel looked round his grandmother's house with dismay. A chill wind from the sea swept through the cracks in the window frames and the roof tiles. The entire house had a dejected air, from the faded carpets to the dreary windows sprayed with sea salt. His grandmother's ageing butler followed him round until eventually Nigel snapped. 'The place is a mess, Darnley; it needs a fortune spending on it.'

'I know, sir, I thought I should let you know the situation.'

'I should have come over sooner. Why didn't you inform me sooner?'

'I did write to you, sir, and tried to telephone you. Most of the time you were abroad. I spoke to Mrs Boyd. Didn't she tell you?'

'When? When did you speak to Mrs Boyd?'

'On several occasions, sir, I never heard from you. Surely Mrs Boyd told you?'

Nigel didn't speak. Celia had not told him. She

341

had hated any mention of the house in England. It was something she had wanted him to get rid of. She had never understood the affection he had had for it, with memories of his grandmother and the only period of his childhood he could look back on with some degree of warmth.

He was suddenly aware of Darnley's footsteps shuffling beside him. The old man had served his grandmother for as long as he could remember. Now he was an old man. How long would he be willing to live out his days in this crumbling pile?

The old man was looking at him anxiously, and Nigel said, 'You don't look well, Darnley. I'm not surprised, living in this draught-ridden mausoleum.'

Darnley permitted himself a small smile. 'I'm used to it, sir, but I do have a bit of bronchitis in the winter.'

'God, yes,' thought Nigel. The winter was on its way and his thoughts turned to Kenya and its sunshine, something that seemed a lifetime away.

'I'll do something about the house, Darnley. I'll raise the money somehow, even if it means getting rid of Malibu.'

'Would you want to do that, sir?'

'This is home, Darnley. Malibu was a pipedream.'

'But you were happy there, sir.'

Happy! Yes, he had been happy for those first few months; happy with a woman he had thought he loved, happy with a house they both adored. But then the rot had set in, and love hadn't been enough.

Perhaps if he got in touch with his mother. She

342

was fond of him; it had always been his father who had regarded him as of little value. That night he telephoned Ariadne.

'The house is a mess,' he informed her. 'I need to spend a fortune on it. I need to get builders in and I've no idea how long the repairs will take.'

'So you don't know when you'll be coming back here?'

'No, perhaps never.'

'What about Malibu?'

'Malibu might have to go.'

'But that's terrible. You love Malibu. How can you bear to even think of parting with it?'

'Needs must, Ariadne. This house is very precious to me in spite of its run-down state; this is where my roots are. I wasn't born in Kenya, neither of us was.'

'But you love it, as I do. Can't you raise the money some other way? What about your family?'

He laughed sarcastically. 'My family! My father despises me, not without reason, and I doubt if my mother could help me without him knowing it. My grandmother's legacy is long gone and much of Celia's money too. We frittered it away on high living, and now I have cause to regret most of it.'

'But Malibu, Nigel.'

'I know. You wanted it once, Ariadne. Would you be prepared to want it again?'

'To live in on my own. I'd rattle in that place.'

'Oh, I don't know. You could throw parties and dazzle all those people you once called snobs.'

'Isn't that how much of your money went?

343

Lavish parties for people you couldn't give a fig about?'

'You're right. You're right about a great many things. What a pity that I didn't see all that years ago.'

'You wouldn't have, Nigel, not when I was a girl on the make and you were a young aristocrat with every socialite for miles chasing after you.'

He laughed. 'It's amazing how the mistakes of our youth have a nasty habit of catching up with us. I'll come over to see what can be done about parting with Malibu. I'll be in touch, Ariadne.'

When she laid the receiver down she sank down on to the nearest chair, with her thoughts utterly bemused.

She wanted Malibu, she wanted Nigel Boyd, but did she want to pay the price? With some of her money he could repair his grandmother's house, keep Malibu; but to a woman who had always been the taker, suddenly becoming the giver needed a great deal of thinking about.

Nigel had always loved beautiful women and gained himself a bad reputation because of it. She found herself thinking about Rosemary Greville's haunted expression whenever she'd been in the same room with him. Something had happened between them, but she couldn't ask Rosemary, and she couldn't ask Nigel.

The following morning she drove her car to Malibu to inform Rosemary that Nigel would be coming back and Rosemary's expression only served to confirm her suspicions.

'Did he say when he was coming back?' Rosemary asked.

'Not in so many words, but he may have to part with Malibu. The house in England needs a great deal of money spending on it.'

'Does that mean that he is going to live in England?'

'I'm not sure.'

She could follow Rosemary's thoughts. England was not big enough for the two of them and Rosemary desperately wanted to return there. But neither did she want to be here when he returned to Malibu.

'Have you heard from your folks in England?' Ariadne asked her.

'My grandfather is not well but grandma tells me I can go there until something else crops up. My aunt is at Dene Hollow for some reason or other. I would like to go to her.'

'Well, why can't you?'

'She's going to tell me all about it in a letter. I'm sure she'll be able to tell me something concrete.'

'You've made up your mind to go back there, Rosemary?'

'Yes, of course. I need to get a job. I have some money in the bank that came from my father. I can go to secretarial college and get some training. Surely I can get a job of some sort when I qualify.'

'Yes, I'm sure you can.'

While Rosemary served them with coffee, Ariadne reflected that she herself had never thought in terms of the sort of work Rosemary was talking about. In her case it had been work where she could meet men, rich men. Softly, she asked, 'Why don't you have a chat with Dr Chaytor? I'm sure he'll be only too happy to help in any way he can.'

'Steven has been very kind. He was always nice to me when I was growing up and he came to stay with my cousins. But I'm not his responsibility, now. He has his fiancé. I don't want Mary thinking I'm latching on to him.'

'Would she think that about an old friend?'

'I don't know, perhaps.'

Dryly, Ariadne said, 'I'm not really very sure that she is his fiancé; a good friend perhaps, but I doubt there's anything else.'

Rosemary decided not to pursue the topic. Everything to do with the past had to be put behind her; it was the future that mattered now.

Chapter Twenty-Five

They came to the front of the house and stood in an orderly line to say their farewells. Their dark faces were unduly solemn, for they had liked the English girl with her bright smiles and kindly manner.

She stroked the long satiny neck of her horse and tears came into her eyes at the thought that she would never see him again.

'You'll take good care of him, won't you, Simeon?' she said, smiling at the tall African who stood holding the horse's reins.

The man smiled and nodded, then Rosemary

346

turned away to say goodbye to the others. She embraced Tamina, who allowed the tears to roll unchecked down her cheeks. So few of them spoke any English, but their sadness at her leaving was evident in their expressions.

Most of her luggage had been sent on earlier, but the remaining two cases had already been placed in the taxi. Now, with another smile and a wave of her hand, they were driving towards the gates. The taxi-driver turned round. 'You wish to go to airport now, Miss?'

'I wish to call at the hospital first. I shan't keep you waiting long.'

In her handbag was a letter she had written to Steven. It was a letter of farewell in case he was not available to say it in person. She had seen him only once since he had called at Malibu and that had been when they had ridden their horses on the hills above the house.

She had sensed a certain constraint in his attitude and she had put it down to that rare moment of intimacy when he had tried to comfort her by putting his arms around her and holding her close. She had lived that brief moment over many times. Now, she thought, it was evident that Steven wished to forget it.

She was standing hesitantly in the main hall of the hospital when she saw Mary walking with another girl along the corridor, and she hurried forward to meet her. Mary paused while the other girl walked on, and Rosemary asked nervously, 'Is it possible to see Steven, Mary? I'm leaving this morning.'

'He's at a meeting just now,' Mary answered.

347

'Can I ask him to telephone you?'

'My flight leaves early this afternoon, but I'd be obliged if you'd give him this letter. It's simply to say goodbye.'

'Aren't you coming back here?'

'No. I'm going home to England.'

'To Dene Hollow?'

'To London to stay with my grandparents. I'm not sure where exactly I go from there.'

Mary took the letter and slipped it into her pocket. Then, holding out her hand, she said, 'I'll say goodbye then, Rosemary, I hope you'll be happy in England. It was so awful about your mother, perhaps going home is really the answer.'

Rosemary smiled. 'Yes, I think so. Goodbye, Mary.'

Mary watched her crossing the hall and running lightly down the stone steps to where her taxi waited for her. She felt suddenly wretched.

She had told Rosemary a lie. Steven was not at a meeting; he was working alone in the laboratory and she could quite easily have asked him to come out to speak to an old friend. It had been her jealousy and insecurity that had prompted the lie and as she walked across the hall she fingered the letter in her pocket and knew that she would not give it to him.

In many ways she felt justified in her action. She loved Steven. She'd known him longer than Rosemary, probably known him better because she was a mature woman, not some little girl with a crush. She'd followed him out here feeling sure their future lay together, and now she was terribly unsure.

There were too many times when Steven sat wrapped in his inner thoughts. He seemed happier when they were in the company of others, and now it had become too much of a crowd and not enough of him. He was wary when they were together that she would expect some commitment and obviously he had none to give her.

It was ridiculous that he should suddenly have found out that Rosemary Greville meant something to him, but obviously something had happened to make him so strangely distant.

Her friend was waiting for her in her office, eyeing her expression with anticipation.

'Wasn't that the Greville girl?' she asked.

'Yes.'

'What did she want?'

'She wanted to speak to Steven; she's leaving this afternoon for England.'

'Is she coming back?'

'I don't think so.'

'Well, if you ask me that's a good thing. You and Steven can get back together again. It's not really been going so well has it, Mary?'

'You noticed then?'

'Well of course we all did.'

'What made you think it had anything to do with her?'

'Well, I've seen them riding once or twice and you did say they were old friends.'

'Old friends is all they were,' Mary said. 'Rosemary was only a schoolgirl.'

'She's not a schoolgirl now, Mary.'

'No, but she is on her way home.'

'Will you tell him she was here?'

'Oh course.'

'Didn't she want to see him?'

'There wasn't time; she was in a hurry.'

'Oh well, then perhaps we are reading more into it than there was.'

'I'm sure we are. Can't we talk about something else?'

Something where there was no guilt, something that didn't involve an affinity that she had thought meant nothing and which had suddenly surfaced to mean everything.

Alighting from her taxi at Nairobi airport, Rosemary could hardly believe her eyes at the sight of Nigel Boyd leaving the airport followed by a man pushing his luggage, which seemed to involve several large cardboard boxes.

She felt faint with the relief of knowing she had left Malibu and was leaving Kenya. At least she had no more cause to worry that she might meet him again; he was out of her life.

She watched his taxi driving away before she entered the terminal building. Now, she need not feel afraid that she would meet him in England.

Nigel drove straight to Malibu. It was too bad if the girl was still there but he needed to take his luggage and the things from his grandmother's house to Malibu, where they could be stored properly.

'Get some servants to help with my luggage,' he instructed the servant who opened the door to him, 'and tell him to be very careful with the boxes, their contents are expensive.'

The man nodded. He understood English very

well. As Nigel strode towards the staircase, he turned to ask, 'Is Miss Greville at home?'

'No sir. She left this morning.'

'Left?'

'Yes sir, she go home to England.'

Changing his mind, Nigel retraced his steps to the drawing room. The beautiful room was strangely devoid of recent habitation. There were no flowers, no magazines left lying about, but his eyes fell on an envelope propped up against an ornament on the mantelpiece.

He opened it quickly, staring at the thick bundle of banknotes that fell down on the rug at his feet. The letter was brief. It informed him that she was flying home to England, that she had returned all her keys to Thomas the butler and she was returning the money he had left for her; she had not needed it. It was simply signed Rosemary Greville, and his lips twisted with sudden contrition and the memory of something he desperately wanted to forget.

In a very short space of time he had unpacked, showered and changed his clothing and was on his way to see Ariadne. For good or ill, matters had to be settled quickly. He had never been a man to put off something until tomorrow that needed to be attended to today.

He frowned at the sight of several cars parked along the drive, which told him that Ariadne was entertaining guests, and around the pool a party was in progress. Women were sitting and standing around in colourful swimwear, large hats and sunglasses, while others were in the pool, splashing about and laughing joyfully. Ariadne sat in her favourite chair, her dog beside her on his satin cushion, and as Nigel strolled from his car to join them he was the object of a dozen pairs of eyes. Ariadne waved a languid hand and as he joined them he was aware of the speculation that surrounded him, in spite of their bright smiles and words of welcome.

'I didn't expect you home so soon, Nigel,' Ariadne said. 'I thought you'd be stuck in little old England for months. Did you mange to get everything sorted?'

'More or less.'

'And you're here to stay?'

'For the moment.'

'I suppose that means you'll soon be getting itchy feet and moving out again.'

'It depends on a great many things.'

'Do you know that Rosemary's gone?'

'Yes, she left me a note.'

'Really? A fond farewell note?'

'Something like that.'

'Well, do help yourself to a drink, darling, and bring up a chair. Do you mind all these girls around you? It's my party to celebrate six months of freedom.'

'You think that's something to celebrate, do you?'

'Well, you know me. I couldn't think of anything else to celebrate, it's not my birthday, wedding anniversaries are out and there's no new wedding in the offing. I couldn't think of anything else.'

The girls showed no signs of departing. They were enjoying Ariadne's excellent buffet and endless supply of drinks. The sun was shining, the water was cool and they were having fun. Nigel's frustration soon became apparent and Ariadne eyed him with some amusement.

'You're bored, Nigel. Why don't you go home and I'll telephone you later?'

He scowled. 'If I'd thought the telephone would have solved anything I wouldn't be here. I need to talk to you urgently, Ariadne.'

She raised her eyebrows maddeningly, then with a cynical smile, said, 'I'm very honoured, Nigel, but you do see, don't you, darling, that I can't get rid of my guests simply because you've breezed in. After all, if you'd let me know you were coming home so soon I'd have been here waiting for anything you had to tell me.'

'I'm being predictably selfish, Ariadne. I'll get back to Malibu and like you say we'll talk on the telephone.'

He rose to his feet, his eyes sweeping across the lawns and the crowd of women around the pool.

'They won't be in any hurry to go home,' he said somewhat sourly. 'You've been overly generous. They'll not leave until they've exhausted every moment and every morsel.'

She laughed.

'Like I said, darling, I'll telephone you.'

'I might go to the club. I shan't enjoy eating alone, I need company.'

'In that case why not come up here tomorrow morning and we can talk then.'

With a shrug of his shoulders and a brief wave of his hand in the direction of her guests he strode off to his car.

Ariadne too was getting bored with the chatter, the hashed-over scandals, and she knew Nigel's visit would set in motion more scandal to be talked over when the guests had left the party. When she walked to the pool one woman said slyly, 'Nigel gone then? He didn't have much to say for himself.'

'Well, it is a bit overpowering to be confronted with a bevy of half naked women when you've just more or less stepped off a plane.'

The women laughed. 'I don't suppose naked women have ever bothered him before. Is he home for good?'

'I didn't ask him.'

'Rosemary has just missed seeing him. Hasn't she flown home to England today?'

'Yes.'

'She didn't even say goodbye to Dr Chaytor.'

'How do you know?'

'Oh, I saw Mrs Garvey at the flower show, she said Steven had seemed rather concerned about her.'

'I do hope that you don't mind if I wind the party up now, girls. I've got one of my sick headaches. I don't suppose sitting in the sun all afternoon has done much for it.'

'But you were wearing your hat, darling. I didn't know you were subject to sick headaches.'

'Well I am. It's a form of migraine. I intend to go indoors when you've left. If I go to bed with the shutters drawn perhaps I'll be able to sleep for a while.'

'Well, of course we'll go. I'll gather up the others. Do tell me if you're no better in the morning, Ariadne, and I'll call round to see if there's anything I can do.'

Ariadne smiled. 'That's very sweet of you, Paula. They usually last about a day and then I'm over it.'

What ages it seemed to take for them to gather up their belongings and say their farewells. When they offered to help clear the buffet away she said sharply, 'The servants will do all that, girls. Thank you so much for coming, we'll be in touch.'

When Nigel received her telephone call several minutes later he smiled with satisfaction. Evidently he was more important than her gaggle of girlfriends.

He suggested dinner at the Paradiso and her first thought was that he evidently didn't mind them being seen together so soon after his wife's fatal accident.

She wore her new French navy dress with her three-strand pearl necklace and the approval in Nigel's eyes was evident. The people dining there were too refined, too genteel to show any surprise at their arrival together, and Nigel laid on all his considerable charm for her benefit. It was only later, when he looked into Steven Chaytor's eyes across the room, that he felt vaguely discomforted by the hostility he surprised in his cool straight gaze.

He felt sure that Rosemary would never tell a living soul of what had happened between them. At the same time, could she have hidden her pent-up anger and hatred from somebody as astute as Chaytor, a man who had known her since she was little more than a child?

Ariadne had seen the look that had passed between them and it only served to confirm what in her heart she had known. Nigel had made a play for Rosemary, but how far it had gone she had no idea.

Mary too was concerned. It was not going well between them. Steven was withdrawn; slowly but surely he was making it obvious that they were friends, and there was nothing more to it than that. She had hoped that with Rosemary back in England their life together would resume its familiar pattern, but they didn't have a life together. She had heard it said, read about it many times, that there was nothing so dead as a dead love.

After they had finished their meal Ariadne said, 'Are we staying on here, Nigel?'

'Is that what you want to do?'

'I really don't mind, it's up to you.'

'We'll drive back to Malibu then. I have a great deal to tell you.'

She had expected as much, but the drive back to Malibu was taken largely in silence. Occasionally she glanced at his face but she could not read its expression in the darkness. His eyes were trained on the road ahead and she had the distinct feeling that she was momentarily forgotten.

At the house he served drinks and she waited patiently, aware that even Nigel was finding it difficult to talk about things that were evidently causing him concern. At last, impatient with the small talk, she said, 'Tell me about your grandmother's house, Nigel; you were very worried about it. Is it all sorted out now?'

He frowned, and with a big sigh said, 'Far from it. The house is in a mess; like I said it needs a great deal of money spending on it, money I haven't got.'

'Then what will you do, sell it?'

'My dear girl, who'd want to buy it as it stands at present? The roof is leaking, the windows need replacing, the floorboards are rotten in places, even the stonework wants something done to it.'

'Then what are you going to do?'

'It has to be repaired, of course. Celia never understood and I don't expect you to understand either, but that house means something to me. It really is a very beautiful old English manor house. It dates back to the sixteenth century, the gardens can be beautiful; but it needs money, lots of it. To find that money I have to part with Malibu.'

'That's definite then?'

'Absolutely.'

'You're putting Malibu on the market?'

'My dear, there is no alternative. My real roots are in England, or Ireland, where I originally came from. I can expect no help from the family; I've got to do it on my own. This is a beautiful place, surely there must be somebody with enough money to buy it, somebody who wants to settle in this part of the world. Have you heard any talk while I've been in England?'

'Oh yes, there's been talk, but it was all speculation. There's nobody I know with the sort of money you'll want for Malibu.'

'Nobody, Ariadne?'

'Are you asking me if I want to buy it, Nigel?'

'You wanted it once.'

'I know, that was when I had Johnny and he wouldn't hear of it. I have the money to buy it, but I'm not a fool. I've stopped wanting to impress people with my money. If I bought Malibu I'd be the subject of every snide remark from miles around. Besides, what would I do in a place this size on my own? I hope you hadn't pinned your hopes on me, Nigel.'

'Not exactly. I hoped that together we could perhaps come to some understanding.'

'Understanding?'

'It's taken a long time to realise it, but you're the only woman I care the toss of a button about. Even when I never really knew it, I admired you, your guts, your style; even when everybody else was scathing about how you'd acquired it.'

'Don't tell me you're in love with me, Nigel; all you love about me is my money.'

'I knew you'd see it like that, it's the only way you can see it, but it isn't strictly true. I admire you as a woman; together we could be a force to be reckoned with.'

'Are you asking me to marry you?'

'You made it very plain you wouldn't marry anybody.'

'And I meant it.'

'What's marriage anyway? A piece of paper with our names on it. Together we could have the good life, this place, the house in England when we feel like it, travel, this beautiful sunny land, and underneath all that we do understand each other and the mutual attraction is there.'

She sat with a half smile on her face, a smile

358

that belied the rush of thoughts buzzing about in her head. This place and Nigel Boyd, two things she had always wanted, but was he asking her to buy him?

His expression was appealing but she was thinking about the years when she had stood on the sidelines watching him flirting with so many monied girls, ending with his marriage to Celia. She had felt sick with anger over that, to have Malibu and Nigel Boyd, so that Johnny's brash vulgarity had irritated her until she felt she couldn't stand another day of it.

'Nigel, I have to think about it,' she said stolidly. 'It's so soon for both of us.'

'I'd rather know sooner than later if you're not interested in sharing my life, Ariadne.'

'You're rushing me.'

'Not really. I know what I want. I want you and I want to share this house with you. If you don't want it you only have to say so.'

'At least let me sleep on it.

But Ariadne didn't sleep. She paced about her bedroom and long before the first golden shafts of dawn crept across the lawns she knew where her future lay. Not perhaps in marriage, that was something for the future, but she couldn't allow him to get out of her life. Her life in Kenya would be empty if he left it, the same old crowd and scandals, the influx of new people, younger women, and the years would only bring their problems of loneliness and fear.

She knew that later that morning she would tell Nigel that their future, whatever it might be, would lie together.

Chapter Twenty-Six

Rosie had been with her grandparents seven months. She had reverted to the name of her childhood but two things were worrying her. Aunt Beatrice was at Dene Hollow caring for her brother who was not too well, and had advised her to delay her visit until matters changed.

Steven had not replied to her farewell note and this surprised her very much. She thought that at least he might have wished her well for the future.

Her grandfather was petulant after his illness; her grandmother involved with so many problems either real or imaginary. The new gardener, her bridge afternoons, the fact that some of her old friends could no longer attend because they were either ill or too old.

Her grandfather bemoaned the fact that his doctor had advised him to give up his car, the pristine immaculate Daimler he had always adored.

'I don't want anybody else to have it,' he said almost tearfully, 'but if you'll look after it, Rosie, you can have it.'

Rosie demurred on the grounds that it was far too large for her, and that it ate petrol. In the end, with the help of her grandmother, who wanted the large car out of the garage, he capitulated and allowed it to be sold and Rosie was able to buy a smaller one.

She had enrolled at a secretarial college where she'd got a first-class diploma and was now scanning the local paper and employment centres for work. Her grandmother was not happy with the situation.

'I don't want you looking for a flat, Rosie, you must stay on here. Both your grandfather and I are getting too old to manage the house, the garden and the shopping on our own. If you get a job near here you can live with us and help us when necessary. Besides, if you move into a flat you could be getting involved with all sorts of undesirable people.'

'Granny, you know I'll help whenever I can, but I do have to go where my job takes me.'

The matter of a job was shelved, however, when several days later she received a letter from Aunt Beatrice inviting her down to Devonshire. The letter told her very little of the state of things at Dene Hollow. Aunt Beatrice had always been guaranteed to write long newsy letters that told her everything she needed to know about her cousins and her Uncle Cedric, but this letter was bland and hardly encouraging.

When she showed it to her grandmother, she said, 'Why is she there? I thought she had her own cottage. She was desperate to get somewhere on her own.'

'Perhaps it's Uncle Cedric. He never wanted her to move anyway.'

'Well, he won't want a housekeeper now. Hasn't he got a daughter-in-law and son to look after him?'

Rosie nodded. 'Oh well, I'll soon know what's going on. I've written back to say I'll go down there at the weekend.'

'What about the two jobs you were thinking about?'

'Well, I haven't applied. Perhaps I'll wait until I get back.'

So on Saturday morning Rosie drove from her grandparent's house to the Devonshire coast. She was excited to be going back to Dene Hollow, to the long beautiful sweep of the bay and the fishing boats in the harbour, to the meandering cliff walks and the white house nestling against its backdrop of hills.

She wanted to find it unchanged but she knew in her heart it was too much to expect. The boys were scattered, their wives were part of the picture, but it couldn't all have changed. David and Jeffrey were still there, Aunt Beatrice was there and everything from the past would all come rushing back to her when she was in familiar surroundings.

It was as though Kenya and her years there had never existed. There were many times when she thought about her mother, graceful and lovely, queening it at Malibu, but she never thought about Nigel; over the last few months she had successfully been able to blot him out of her existence. But she thought about Steven, and if he and Mary would marry. She could have loved Kenya, but there had been too many problems stacked against her. Occasionally she thought about Martin Newley and the young crowd that he surrounded himself with. They had been fun, but nothing more than that.

She drove slowly towards the house, relishing every moment of the garden, but the garden had changed. The shrubbery was vastly overgrown and a flagged patio had been laid out with tables and chairs. There were rose beds in the long sweep of lawns, and the old conservatory which had so complemented the rest of the house had been replaced by a more modern version. Instead of mahogany there was now white stucco and modern windows.

She sat back in her seat to contemplate the changes, but was disturbed by the sharp slamming of a door and the sight of a woman rushing headlong along the terrace and down the steps to an open two-seater waiting below.

The car set off with a roar from its exhaust pipe, then careered down the drive at great speed, and in that speed Rosie recognised anger, the sort of anger she had witnessed from her mother after one of her interminable arguments about money.

It was evidently not the most opportune day to be visiting, and she looked up at the facade of the house hoping for a welcoming figure at one of the windows. She was disappointed, and after locking the car and picking up her suitcase she walked towards the front door. She was unprepared for the maid in frilly apron and fluted cap, looking at her enquiringly, but then of course Uncle Cedric's servants would have long gone.

'Is Mrs Greville in, or Miss Greville?' she enquired with a smile.

'Mrs Greville has just gone out. I think Miss Greville might be in her room. Who shall I say is calling?'

'Miss Rosie Greville, her niece.'

There was a gleam of surprise in the girl's eyes. Rosemary Greville was evidently somebody she had never heard of.

She opened the door wider, saying, 'Please come in,' then eyeing the suitcase, 'Are you expected, miss?'

'Well, I rather think my aunt might be expecting me.'

'I'll tell her you're here.'

Rosie watched her running up the stairs, then she heard the opening of a door and the sound of voices.

She did not have long to wait. In only minutes Aunt Beatrice was hurrying down the stairs, holding out her arms and enveloping Rosie in a warm embrace.

'Oh Rosie,' she breathed. 'I'm so glad to see you. I expect you'll have the room at the end of the first corridor but Sally will look after your suitcase until we're sure.'

For the first time she looked into her aunt's eyes and saw that they were very troubled. When she was about to speak, Beatrice shook her head and said, 'Sally, do you think we could have tea in the morning room? Are you hungry, dear?'

'No, not at all, I stopped for lunch on the way.'

'Then we'll just have tea and biscuits. Come along, dear, there's so much to tell you.'

The morning room afforded her another surprise. Gone was the oriental carpet with its soft pastel colours and exquisite texture to be replaced by a more strident Axminster and new chairs in limed oak instead of the warm walnut she had loved.

Seeing her surprise, Aunt Beatrice said, 'The rest of the house has changed too, Rosie. All the walnut, English oak and mahogany has gone; now we have this stuff, teak and bamboo. There's also a preponderance of marble in the drawing room.'

'And the bedrooms?'

'All changed. Gloria has gone into Exeter; the master bedroom is being changed now.'

'But how about Uncle Cedric, doesn't he mind?'

'He doesn't have a say in the matter. He's gone into Willow Bank.'

'Willow Bank?'

'It's a home for the elderly and for people who are not in the best of health.'

'But Uncle Cedric isn't old, at least not really old.'

'No, he's sixty-five in September, and most of the people at Willow Bank are considerably older. He went in there because he wasn't well, presumably for the short term, but now that he's well enough to come home Gloria says she's not prepared to have an invalid on her hands. She's not well enough herself to cope.'

'Isn't she very well?'

'She's a bag of nerves, mostly self-inflicted. She's obsessed with making changes, bringing this house into some faithful copy of every house she sees in those glossy magazines she spends a fortune on. I try to tell her this isn't that kind of property, but it's no use.'

'But is she able to do that? The house belongs to Uncle Cedric.'

'I'm not even sure about that any more. I rather think he signed it over to David, thinking they would be in a position to care for it more.'

'Surely David wouldn't take advantage of that?'

'My dear girl, David has changed out of all recognition. He doesn't listen to me, he didn't listen to his father. Gloria is the only one he listens to, and if he didn't he'd be subjected to all sorts of tears and tantrums. She's very good at that.'

'I don't recognise David in all that.'

'Nor I. Of the four boys I always thought David would be the most intelligent. Jerome was pompous, even as a child, and Jeffrey too easily hurt. Noel, as you know, was inclined to be prickly, but David was always the one to pour oil on troubled waters, always reasonable, always generously kind. Now that kindness is being taken advantage of by his wife.'

'But they're happy, surely?'

'Perhaps it's easy to be happy when one person is getting all her own way. I always understood that marriage was a partnership, not a takeover.'

'Oh Aunt Beatrice, I've been so looking forward to coming back here. Now nothing is the same and I'm not even sure I'll be very welcome.'

Without reassuring her, Beatrice said, 'Look around you, dear, and see how everything has changed, the house, life as you knew it, everything. All those beautiful ornaments and china,

366

some of them that once belonged to my parents, all the Wedgwood, the Crown Derby, the jade that my father brought from China, all gone.'

'But what has she done with it?'

'She said they were dust collectors. Most of them were given to her mother or her sisters, entirely without my consent or Cedric's.'

Rosie was remembering all the beautiful things she had loved as a child; how she had stroked them after being warned of their value and told that she should be careful. Now they had all gone and in their place were modern showy ornaments without either charm or real value.

'Did Gloria say anything about my coming here?'

'She won't have forgotten, but it's very difficult to get through to her.'

'Do Jerome and Natalie visit, and what about Jeffrey?'

'Jerome and David meet at the office; they are both in the family business, but neither Jerome nor his wife come here. Natalie and Gloria have never got along and Jeffrey only ever came to see his father on Sunday mornings. He brought the boy with him.'

'Connie never came?'

'Never.'

'That is so awful, surely Uncle Cedric was fond of the little boy.'

'Yes, but when Gloria was around it was don't touch that, don't run around the house, it was all very difficult.'

'Are they still in the same house?'

'Oh no, dear, they've moved into a nice house

in the next village, a house with a nice large garden, and Connie has opened a new hair-dressing salon in the village. It is very highly thought of. Jeffrey has a decent job too, they've really fallen on their feet.'

'I'm so glad.'

'How long are you staying here, Aunt Beatrice?'

'Until I've assured myself that Cedric is settled in Willow Bank. I shall never come back here, Rosie, at least not unless things change.'

Over the evening meal Rosie thought she was sitting with strangers. David had greeted her with an absent-minded smile, and looking up into his familiar face she found it strangely unfamiliar. His hair was peppered with grey and there was a distant, careworn expression on his face that was totally remote from the smiling face of the boy she remembered.

Gloria was thin and restless. There was a highly-strung nervousness about the way she twisted and turned the napkin on her knee, and the sudden darting of her dark eyes around the table, questions that were sharply asked, answers that were ignored. Rosie thought she would never again be so relieved to reach the end of a meal.

'See anything of Steven Chaytor in Kenya?' David asked.

'Yes. He came to my birthday party and I saw him around the place.'

'With Mary, I suppose?'

'Yes.'

'She was quick to follow him out there,' Gloria said acidly. 'He hasn't been in any hurry to marry her. Will he, do you suppose?'

'I have no idea.'

'I suppose you'll be going round to see Jeffrey and his wife?'

'I'm sure I shall.'

'She's opened a new salon in the village. I don't go there myself but I hear it's not too bad.'

'Then I'll probably go there myself.'

It had been the wrong thing to say. 'Really, how long are you intending staying then?'

'Not very long, I'm sure, but I do hope to catch up with a few people whilst I'm here.'

'What do you think about the house? I've made some changes. I'm sure you'll agree they've brightened the place up and modernised it.'

Rosie smiled politely.

'Not that you'll get Aunt Beatrice to agree with me, of course,' Gloria added.

The inquisition went on relentlessly over coffee.

'It was quite awful about your mother,' Gloria said. 'I suppose you've got her things?'

'Her things?'

'Why yes. Didn't she live in a most wonderful house? Surely you've got some of that as well as her jewellery and her other belongings. Why did you come back to England?'

'When my mother died Kenya was not my home. The house belonged to my mother's husband, not to me.'

'But she left you well provided for, surely?'

'I have her jewellery, and some of her possessions she thought highly of.'

'But what about her money?'

Seeing Rosie's discomfort, Aunt Beatrice said

sharply, 'I don't suppose Rosie wants to talk about her mother. It is very painful and very recent.'

'I didn't ask about her mother, only about her entitlement!'

'Which is nobody's business but Rosie's.'

Gloria scowled. 'Well, in my family we all know exactly what we're going to get when the parents have gone. In Rosie's case there was nobody else for it. I don't think my question was unreasonable.'

Aunt Beatrice bit her lip nervously and picked up a magazine from the table in front of her and proceeded to open it.

'How are Jerome and Natalie?' Rosie asked.

'We never see them here. David sees his brother at the office but we never socialise,' Gloria answered.

'And Noel?'

'Noel's in Indonesia. We get the usual Christmas card and nothing more.'

Across the room, Rosie looked into David's eyes and surprised a sudden stark misery in them. David didn't want this; he wanted it to be like the old days, but those days, it would seem, had gone for ever.

Later, in her room, Rosie stood looking through the window at a pale young moon illuminating the waves rolling inland towards the shore, scenery she loved and had looked forward desperately to seeing again. Now everything was alien to her, the house and the people in it.

All those years she had thought of Dene Hollow as home, the only real home she had ever

370

known, so that even when her mother had proudly introduced her to Malibu, this was the place she had yearned after, the place dearest to her heart.

Her eyes smarted with unshed tears and she was about to turn away when a soft tap on her bedroom door sent her hurrying across the room. Aunt Beatrice stood there, and the pain in her eyes was all too apparent.

'Can I talk to you for a few minutes, dear?' she asked plaintively.

'Yes, of course. Aren't you cold? You should have put something warmer on.'

'Gloria doesn't like the central heating on before October, even on a chilly night. I've been sitting in my chair just thinking, I didn't even bother to get undressed. Rosie, I'm so sorry your first night here has been so controversial.'

Rosie pulled a chair forward for her aunt to sit in while she sat on the edge of her bed, and Beatrice looked around her.

'You should have been in your old room. I wanted to do that but Gloria said it was now a guest room with twin beds and this would do very well.'

'She's probably quite right.'

'I've made up my mind, Rosie. I'm going to see Cedric tomorrow. I'll have a word with the matron and explain the position, but in the end dear David and his wife will have the last word. David is his son. I'm only his sister.'

'He has other sons, Aunt Beatrice.'

'Cedric couldn't go to Jeffrey's and Jerome wouldn't want him, or rather Natalie wouldn't

371

want him. Perhaps staying in Willow Bank is the best answer to the problem. My cottage is very small, just big enough for me and my animals. I do have a guest bedroom, but it wouldn't do for Cedric. He came to see me when I first moved in there. He said you couldn't swing a cat around in it; he felt claustrophobic.'

Rosie laughed. 'I can hear him saying that.'

'It didn't matter. I was never intending him to live with me.'

'So, after you've seen Uncle Cedric, what will you do?'

'Go home, Rosie. Go home never to return.'

'Can I come home with you, at least for a few days?'

'You can stay as long as you like, and in these next few days you can call to see the other two boys. You liked Connie, didn't you?'

'Yes. Oh I know she wasn't exactly Uncle Cedric's idea of a wife for one of his precious sons but she was honest and very kind. She's proved herself to have been the best wife of the lot.'

'I know. She's a girl kind enough to offer his father a home, but that wouldn't do. The other two girls would accuse her of looking after the main chance. That's something both of them have been doing for a long time.'

'Natalie too?'

'Well yes. Oh not the house, but their expensive cars and expensive holidays. Their house is as grand as this one and Cedric's contributed plenty towards its upkeep.'

'Didn't he help Jeffrey?'

'Jeffrey wouldn't take anything even if it was offered. He said he'd do it on his own, and he has.'

'And Noel?'

'Noel doesn't know what's been going on. He washed his hands of the place years ago.'

'Why don't I go downstairs and make coffee? We can drink it here, and carry on with our conversation.'

'No dear, I think I shall go to bed now. I simply wanted to tell you what I'd decided. We'll talk again tomorrow, sleep well.'

But sleep was a long way away. Rosie lay tossing and turning in her narrow bed listening to the sound of the waves and the wind in the trees. Their plaintive sounds seemed to echo the darkest shadows in her life, clouding over all the happiness she had thought would be hers when she returned to Dene Hollow.

When she fell asleep at last it was not of the present that she dreamed. She was a girl again, running along the cliff path towards the sea, and in the distance a boy raised his hand in greeting. He turned away and although she ran as fast as her legs could carry her, it was not fast enough. Steven Chaytor was as far away then as he was now. It seemed to Rosie on waking that time and distance separated them as irrevocably now as they ever had.

Chapter Twenty-Seven

Rosie and her aunt breakfasted alone. David had gone out early and Beatrice said Gloria seldom surfaced much before ten-thirty, and today was Sunday.

Beatrice was visiting Cedric so Rosie decided she would visit Jeffrey and Jerome.

'I should telephone to make an appointment if you want to visit Jerome and his wife this morning,' Beatrice advised. 'I always do. Natalie likes to be informed before anybody descends on her unannounced.'

So Rosie telephoned and was told she would be very welcome to call in the afternoon by Natalie, who asked no questions either about her wellbeing or anything else.

'Do I need to telephone Jeffrey?' she asked.

'Oh no dear, they'll be home and very pleased to see you.'

They received her with warmth and affection but when she asked about their son, Connie was quick to explain that on Sunday he went to his grandfather's.

'My father spoils him rotten; after all he's had to be two grandfathers to him. Jeffrey's father wasn't interested in him and Dad's tried to make up for all he was missing.'

'Perhaps I'll see him before I leave,' Rosie said.

'Oh yes, you must come again, anytime you

like. This is a picture of him taken at his school.'

She handed over the picture of a charming boy with a bright smile, and his face reminded her so much of David's face as a boy. Open and friendly.

'I like your house, Connie. Aunt Beatrice said it was nice.'

'Oh yes it is. We like it here, it's just the right size and just the right distance out of town. My salon is doing very well, did Aunt Beatrice tell you?'

'Yes, she did, and Jeffrey too is settled?'

'Yes. The best thing about it is that we've done it on our own without any help from anybody. I know I'm not like the other two, educated and fashionable, but I have made Jeffrey a good wife and I'm a good mother to my son.'

'I'm sure you are, Connie. I'm so pleased for you.'

'What do you think of Dene Hollow now?'

'I didn't recognise it as the house I knew. You never go there?'

'No. I never went to see Jeffrey's father because I knew he didn't want me for his son, and Gloria never invites us. Jeffrey won't go there now his father's in a home.'

'And Jerome?'

'Natalie calls sometimes. She doesn't invite us back, she only comes here to go on and on about Gloria. They hate each other, those two.'

They sat in the kitchen where Connie was baking scones, then they sat at the kitchen table to drink coffee and sample the scones, which were delicious.

'I'm not the cook my mother was,' Connie said

with a grin. 'My father's always saying that, but I do try. You'll not be sitting in the kitchen this afternoon, you'll be in the parlour with dainty cakes and fancy napkins.'

Rosie laughed. 'You don't change, Connie. Everything else has changed, and I'm glad you've stayed the same.'

Jeffrey came to sit at the table with them, helping himself to scones and strawberry jam.

'So you're going to see Jerome this afternoon,' he said with a smile. 'I hope you eat lunch with us first.'

'Thank you, Jeffrey, I'd like that.'

'We don't see much of them. Jerome's still the same and you'll find Natalie very obsessed with her poodles and her committees. She blinds Connie with science whenever she calls here.'

'I can imagine.'

'Tell us about your mother, Rosie. We read about it in the paper. It must have been a nightmare for you.'

'Yes, it was. One minute she was there, warm and beautiful, the next moment she was dead.'

'It said in the paper that the house was beautiful,' Connie said softly.

'Yes, it was. The most beautiful place I've ever seen, surrounded by wonderful scenery, but it was never home.'

'Not like Dene Hollow?'

'No. Not like the Dene Hollow I remember.'

Jeffrey smiled sadly. 'It's changed out of all recognition. I hated going there, seeing my father pushed on one side with everything he'd worked for, loved, gone.'

'I know.'

'Did you get along with your stepfather?'

'We saw very little of each other.'

Under the table her hands clenched tightly together. How long would she remember, suffer, hate him? The trauma of it hung round her neck like a stone, making her feel soiled and unworthy.

'It said in the paper that he was in Dorset, something to do with his grandmother's house?' Jeffrey said.

'Yes.'

'If he knows you're here he might want to see you,' Jeffrey added.

'He's back in Kenya. I shall never see him again.'

Two pairs of eyes looked at her curiously, suddenly aware that mention of Nigel Boyd was unwelcome, and Rosie to change the subject quickly said, 'Aunt Beatrice has gone to see your father. I rather think she's anxious to get back to her cottage.'

'I'm sure she is, and it would seem my father's to stay where he is.'

'Do you mind very much, Jeffrey?'

'Yes I mind, even though we've not been too close. David's the one I don't understand.'

She read the pain in his eyes and it was her pain. The memory of a boy who had always been kind, a gentle boy who had always been quick to see the best in people and pour oil on the often sarcastic comments of his younger brother.

Jeffrey shook his head slowly. 'I can't reconcile my brother with the sort of man he is now. Never in a million years could I have thought that he might be taken over by a woman less intelligent than himself, a woman who is greedy and self-seeking.'

'Let's not talk about them,' Connie said quickly. 'It always depresses us to talk about them, you know that. Let's talk about Rosie and Kenya. Did you see Steven Chaytor there?'

'Yes. He came to my birthday party. I left him a note simply to say goodbye. He was busy at the hospital so I didn't get to see him.'

'Jerome hears from him from time to time,' Jeffrey said. 'I wonder if he'll marry Mary.'

Rosie looked at him curiously. 'Surely he will. I thought that was the idea in her going out there.'

'It might have been Mary's idea, I'm not too sure about Steven. He hasn't mentioned marriage to Jerome. He used to tease you about Steven, didn't he, Rosie? It made you so cross.'

'Jerome could always make me cross.'

Jeffrey laughed. 'He had that effect on me sometimes. He was always the older brother, always the one who knew everything and knew better.'

Connie produced an excellent lunch and Rosie reflected that the one daughter-in-law that Cedric should have valued had been left out in the cold. In some strange way, perhaps he deserved what was happening to him now, but she knew that nice, honest Connie would be the last person to agree with her.

They stood at the front gate waving their hands as she drove along the road, and she felt sure the rest of the day would not be nearly as companionable.

Indeed, the ceremony of afternoon tea in Natalie's pristine drawing room was a far cry from the lunch she had eaten with Jeffrey and Connie in their small dining room, where the budgie sang in his cage and a large mongrel dog sat hopefully at their feet.

Natalie's blond shingled hair had lost none of its allure and her make-up as always was perfect. She was wearing an expensive tweed skirt and cashmere twin set, and tea consisted of dainty sandwiches, small scones with strawberry jam and cream, and with them a large cream sandwich cake, all set out on her best Royal Doulton.

'Did you say you were going to see Jeffrey and Connie this morning?' she asked.

'Yes, they invited me for lunch.'

'How nice.'

'Yes it was. Paul was with his grandfather so I didn't get to see him. I saw his photograph. He looks a charming boy.'

'Yes, I suppose he is. I've never been one to drool over children. It's fortunate Jerome feels that way too.'

'So you're not contemplating a family?'

'Gracious no. I'm too busy with my committees, and I doubt if Jerome would be a good father. He's not at his best with children.'

'I'm glad that you call to see them, Natalie.'

'Oh well, I call when I have the time. She doesn't change much, although her salon is very popular. She keeps her prices pretty low, probably that's why.'

'You don't think that it's probably because it's good?'

Natalie laughed. 'It could well be. Was that very spiteful? What's it like up at Dene Hollow?'

'Well, I only arrived yesterday. I doubt if I'll be staying long.'

'And Aunt Beatrice?'

'She's getting anxious to go home.'

'We never go there, you know, not now that Cedric's father's not there. The last time we called to see him we were appalled, all those beautiful ornaments gone to be replaced by modern stuff of little value. She's passed them on to members of her family without even asking Jerome or Jeffrey if they wanted anything.'

'Did Jerome say anything?'

'Well yes. There was a terrible row. He accused her of getting rid of his inheritance, said he'd a good mind to take her to court over the whole wretched business. David sat there and never said a word.'

'Yes, that's probably the worst of it.'

'She's parted with things that belonged to Jerome's mother and his grandmother, things that Beatrice should have had. It seemed to me that she simply wanted to obliterate every single memory that Beatrice and the boys had, you too, Rosie.'

'Well, nothing at Dene Hollow belonged to me.'

'But you were entitled to be asked. After all, you lived there for years, and you are a relative. She simply took over, and now the old man is in a home for the elderly and he's not old enough for that, and not ill enough.'

'Where else could he have gone if she didn't

380

want him at Dene Hollow?'

'Well, he wouldn't have gone to Beatrice, and why should he go anywhere when Dene Hollow was his home? Jerome is furious about her. We'll never set foot in the place again as long as she's there.'

Rosie didn't speak. The whole situation was depressing, and after a few moments Natalie said, 'It was awful about your mother. What happened exactly?'

'She crashed her car, driving too fast. I know she often did that.'

'Was she driving alone?'

'Yes, it was very early in the morning. She'd driven up to see a neighbour. She skidded into a tree and then into the ditch to avoid a Land Rover.'

'Oh yes, it said that in the paper. Some young people driving home from a party.'

Rosie decided not to enlighten her further.

'What was her husband like?'

'Good-looking.'

'Did you like him?'

'I never really got to know him.'

'But you were there some time Rosie.'

'I know, but I met people of my own age. Life was pretty fast out there.'

At the sound of a door opening, Natalie said, 'Here's Jerome, he said he'd be home a little earlier. We're out to a magistrates' dinner this evening. I find them terribly boring but we have to be there, of course.'

Rosie's first impression was that Jerome had put on weight. Weight and prosperity, however, sat easily on his shoulders, and he greeted her with a smile, his eyes filled with their usual sly amusement.

'Well, I have to say you're still looking very attractive, Rosie. Steven Chaytor said he'd met you in one of his letters; he thought you'd blossomed into a very beautiful girl. Pity it's too many years too late, Rosie, what do you say?'

'Too late for what, Jerome?'

He laughed. 'Well, for you and Steven, of course. Has Mary been able to pin him down yet?'

'I'm sure she will.'

'Don't be too sure. He's had enough time to make up his mind and he doesn't appear to be in any hurry. What do you think about the set-up at Dene Hollow?'

'Not very much.'

'No, it's dreadful, and Dad's in a home.'

'I know, that seems to be the worst thing of all. Can't you do anything Jerome?'

'Not much I can do. We could offer to have him here, but I doubt if he'd come; and really why should we when they've had the house and probably most of his money?'

'You'll visit him at Willow Bank, though?'

'I suppose so. I've hated seeing him these last few months; he's simply sat in his chair not speaking, staring down at his knees, his mind miles away. If we'd got up to leave I doubt if he'd have noticed.'

'Does Noel know what has been happening?'

'Well, I've never really been close to Noel; he and David were mates. I shouldn't think David's kept him in the picture.'

'He'll find great changes when he does come home. I think perhaps he should be told what is happening.'

'You tell him, Rosie, you and he were always good pals.'

Rosie knew that she would not tell Noel anything; none of this wretched business should come from her.

Jerome was helping himself to sandwiches while Natalie poured tea, afterwards saying, 'Rosie's had lunch at Jeffrey's house.'

'I suppose you had the usual, roast beef and veg, Connie hasn't a lot of imagination where food's concerned.'

'It was very nice. I enjoyed it and it was kind of them to ask me.'

'She's not a bad lass, better than the other one. The one up at Dene Hollow hasn't a good word to say for her, probably hasn't a good word to say for us either.'

His words were borne out forcefully that evening, when Gloria said, 'What had Connie and Natalie to say for themselves?'

'We chatted, they made me very welcome.'

'I hate Jeffrey's house, I don't like the village. I told them so.'

Rosie looked at her, 'You told them?'

'Yes of course, nobody can accuse me of saying I liked a thing when I didn't. Wouldn't you have said something?'

'Actually no. I was brought up on the adage that if you can't say something nice about something or somebody don't say anything at all.'

'Well, of course. You were a produce of this upper-crust establishment; I was an onlooker from the sidelines. But this is my house now and I can say what I like.'

She did not know how much David loved Gloria. He had loved her once; now, with her spite and her malice, how much of that early feeling was left? She was his wife, he would never betray her, but love was something else. Could a man really go on loving a woman who was capable of hurting his family and demoralising his life?

'How was Uncle Cedric, Aunt Beatrice?' she asked, in an attempt to change the subject.

'He looked rather better today, dear. He's found a gentleman there who plays chess and the vicar had been to see him.'

'That's good, then.'

'Yes. I'm thinking of going home on Tuesday, Rosie. Will you be ready to come with me?'

'Well of course. I'm dying to see your cottage.'

'So am I.'

'Is somebody looking after your animals?'

'Yes, my next door neighbour. She's very nice, and she loves them.'

For a long time she had yearned after Dene Hollow, and longed to come back here, never dreaming that after only two days she would be anxious to leave.

'I came by train,' Aunt Beatrice was saying. 'I don't have very much luggage, but will you have room for it all in your car, dear?'

'Yes, of course. Are we getting away early?'

'After breakfast, I thought.'

Rosie smiled. 'And what are we doing to-morrow?'

'Well, I'm going to say my farewells to the two boys and their wives. If you come with me to Jeffrey's you can see Paul when he gets home from school.'

Rosie spent the morning walking along the shore, pausing to pick up familiar shells in the shallow pools left by the tide. In her ears was the murmur of the surf; she could smell the salt-laden air, see the shining clumps of seaweed on the rocks, feel the wind that swept across the sand. She could feel the taste of salt spray as it mingled with the tears that coursed slowly down her cheeks, and memories as elusive as some forgotten life trailed noiselessly by her side.

She had thought that over the years she would come back to Dene Hollow again and again. Relive the scenes of her childhood, meet again the people she had known here; but it had been Steven who had said 'Never go back, Rosie, never even try to recapture people and moments that have gone for ever.' Steven, who had been kind and wise and lost to her, Steven who had not even taken the trouble to answer her letter to wish her well.

She had to forget Dene Hollow and Steven Chaytor. She had to forget Nigel Boyd and what he had done to her; but memories were not something that she could hurl over the cliffs like discarded toys. Memories were real, punishing things that she could only expect to fade slowly with the passing years.

She went with Connie to meet Paul at the

385

school gates, a boy who reminded her so much of the young David, fresh-faced and clear-eyed, running ahead of them along the lane, his sturdy feet dancing joyfully across the cobbles in the square; and in her memory she could see David and Noel walking up the drive at Dene Hollow, their school satchels slung across their shoulders, laughing together, teasing her with their banter.

Those two boys belonged to the memories of another life, happier days, blessed with values that mattered.

'When are we likely to see either of you again?' Jeffrey asked evenly.

'I really don't know,' she answered him. 'I have to find a job, do something with my life; but we'll keep in touch, birthday cards and Christmas cards, we'll speak on the telephone. I'll never forget any of you.'

Only David arrived home from the office in time to see them depart, shaking their hands solemnly, his smile grave, his attitude singularly remote, and they drove in silence for many miles.

It was only when they had left the coastal road behind them that Beatrice said softly, 'Well, that's that. How much more will it have changed if we ever need to return there?'

Chapter Twenty-Eight

Ariadne was well aware that all around her was speculation and curiosity, but nobody knew for sure that she and Nigel Boyd were an item.

That she spent most of her time at Malibu was evident. She was never at home when people called, never there to answer the telephone, but at the bottom of it nobody could quite see that she was Nigel's type. Not Ariadne with her imperfect past and the years she had spent with Johnny Fairbrother.

Then, of course, when they couldn't think of why they were together, they thought it must be her money, Johnny's money; and Nigel had never made any secret of the fact that Celia had been too extravagant.

Ariadne was making no changes to Malibu, she liked it as it was, and although she spent most of her time there she played a game of uncertainty until in exasperation Nigel said, 'People are talking about us now. They can't say anything more if you move in here.'

'I'm not concerned with what people say. If ever I move in here it'll be because I want it, when the time's ripe.'

'And when will that be, do you suppose?'

'When I'm sure it's me you want and not just my money.'

'You've been generous, Ariadne, you've paid for

387

the alterations to the house in England. I'll repay it eventually, and the rest of your money is in your name. You can keep it that way.'

'Is there any reason why we can't just stay as we are?'

'Living in two establishments, do you mean? You'd have even more money if you put your house on the market.'

'This is your house, Nigel. At least with Johnny it was home.'

'You said you wouldn't marry me; that was your decision.'

'I know. Perhaps I don't really know what I do want.'

'I thought you had what you wanted, Ariadne: me, Malibu and Johnny's money. Now ask yourself what I want.'

'Perhaps it's time you told me.'

'I want stability. I want to stop looking for something new, wandering on and then wandering back. I want a woman who has stopped searching for the moon and can be happy with what she's got. I want all the things I threw away so lightly and not very long ago.'

'And do you think you might have stopped looking?'

'Yes. I rather think I might have found it all.'

'How long have you known me, Nigel?'

'A few years. I never really knew you at all before then.'

'How much has knowing me to do with Johnny's money, my money?'

'If you're always going to think like that, Ariadne, is there really any point in going on?'

She was thoughtful, sipping her wine, her eyes wandering around the room where other diners were trying not to look at them, even though she knew they would be the main topic of conversation after they had left.

Her eyes caught the gaze of Steven Chaytor, and it was something in his expression that made her say, 'Don't you have the feeling that Dr Chaytor harbours distinctly hostile feelings for you, Nigel? I wonder why.'

'I hardly know him.'

'But Rosemary knew him very well, If something went on between you and your step-daughter perhaps she told him.'

'Don't be silly, Ariadne, she was Celia's daughter. If she told him I'd flirted with her she was lying.'

'Flirted?'

'Well, you know I like pretty girls and Rosemary was very pretty. I might have teased her a little; there was nothing more. Surely the time hasn't come when a man can be accused of admiring a beautiful woman.'

'Why don't you ask him?'

'Ask him what, for heaven's sake? Why he doesn't like me, what I've done to arouse his hostility?'

Steven's companion was looking at them and with a cynical smile Nigel raised his glass in their direction.

The girl smiled but Steven Chaytor averted his gaze and went on with his meal.

'I think I want to leave now, Nigel. I don't know why we came here; we'll be the topic of

389

conversation as soon as we've left,' Ariadne snapped.

'You mean they'll have nothing better to talk about. Don't you want anything else?'

'No, I want to leave.'

'Very well.'

He beckoned the waiter over to settle the bill and Ariadne gathered her wrap and evening bag. Nigel inclined his head in the direction of a group of people dining at a nearby table but Ariadne looked neither to right nor left as she stalked across the room.

There were one or two raised eyebrows but few comments, which might have surprised Ariadne, but the people who dined at Paradiso were not the crowd she'd mingled with over the years. Many of them had known Nigel for many years but had hardly been numbered among his intimate friends.

'You don't like him, do you?' Mary said softly.

'Not particularly,' Steven replied.

'Why, he's always been perfectly charming.'

'Too charming.'

'Oh Steven, is it because of something Rosemary said? If he quarrelled with her mother it was natural she should take her mother's part.'

'What makes you think it has anything to do with Rosemary?'

She blushed with annoyance that she should have mentioned the girl's name.

'Well, it's just that you've felt this way about him since she left.'

The waiter came to fill up their glasses and Steven said, 'Do you want anything else, Mary? I don't want to be late, I have an early call in the morning.'

The drive was taken mainly in silence. It seemed Steven had a great deal on his mind, but when he turned to look at her he smiled gently and her spirits lifted. Outside the flat she shared with her friend he said, 'Are you on early call, Mary?'

'No. Aren't you coming in for coffee?'

He consulted his watch, and hastily she said, 'I wanted to ask you about holidays, Steven. We can surely talk over a cup of coffee.'

'Very well, but like I said I don't want to be late.'

He was restless. While she made the coffee she could hear him walking round the living room, taking books out of the bookcase, rustling the newspapers. When she carried the tray into the room he turned and sat down in front of the window.

'I've had a letter from my parents this morning, Steven, they would like us to visit them in Kuala Lumpur. Can't we go there? Your parents would be so glad to see you.'

For what seemed an eternity he sat staring down at his hands resting lightly on his knees; then, as if he had suddenly arrived at a decision he had been searching for weeks he said, 'Why don't you go, Mary? You have holidays coming up; don't bank on me.'

'But Steven, I do bank on you. Our parents are delighted that we're together, they'd be thrilled if we both went out to see them.'

For a long time he remained silent, searching

for words, and in her heart she knew he was going to hurt her. They were not together, they had never been together, at least not in the accepted sense.

When he looked up his eyes were tender, his voice filled with a great regret.

'Mary, I'm really very fond of you, we go back a long way, since childhood, but it isn't enough to make me want to marry you, and it isn't enough for you to build your life on.'

She sank down weakly on the nearest chair and at that moment she hated him. Steven had never asked her to follow him out to Africa; she'd done it all on her own in the hope that it would start with them being two old friends together and end with them falling in love. Her parents had wanted it, Steven's parents had hoped for it, and now here he was saying it had all been a great mistake.

Angrily, she said, 'I thought all these years would come to mean something, Steven. Apparently I've been wasting my time and yours.'

'None of it has been wasted, Mary. We've had nice times together. I never said I loved you, I never hinted that there might be more. Now it's time for us both to move on. There'll be somebody else for you, Mary, somebody you haven't met yet.'

'And for you?'

'Who knows?'

The silence was uncomfortable, and after a few minutes he said, 'When are you thinking you might go to see your parents?'

'I don't know. Soon.'

'They'll be pleased to have you home.'

'What shall I tell them about us?'

'There was never anything to tell, Mary. Give them my regards, tell them we'll always be very good friends. It's nothing but the truth, Mary.'

She was glad for him to go. When her friend arrived she found Mary stretched out on the sofa in a flood of tears.

It took some time for Mary to console herself and tell the other girl what had happened, and fortunately she could not see the other girl's expression. She had known that Mary was reading too much into her friendship with Steven Chaytor; their friendship had been close, warm even, but entirely passionless. It had all been too one-sided: Mary had wanted Steven, Steven had never wanted Mary.

'You'll get over him,' Mary's friend said encouragingly.

Mary shook her head. At that moment she believed she would never get over him. Why had he done this to her? Where was he going? Who was he going to? And her thoughts fled to Rosemary Greville.

Stephen took Mary to the airport for her flight home to Kuala Lumpur. But her attitude was distant. She knew in her heart that she was not being scrupulously fair. In her eyes they had been a couple, in Steven's they had been old friends. They had never been lovers even if she had hoped it would come to that.

None of their friends in Kenya were surprised since none of them had really thought they were going anywhere; at the same time none of them had associated Steven with Rosemary Greville. She'd been Newley's girlfriend, one of the rich pleasure-seeking group most of the older residents looked upon as too loud, too unconventional and too spoilt.

Steven and Mary were soon overlooked in the wake of Nigel Boyd's obsession with Ariadne Fairbrother. Of course he was marrying her for her money, everybody said so; why else would a member of an aristocratic family even think of marrying a woman whose origins were obscure and who had caused so many scandals in the life of the community?

They were married very early in the morning in the grounds of Malibu by the minister of an unfashionable chapel, witnessed only by a handful of their servants and two of Johnny Fairbrother's more disreputable friends.

Almost immediately they set off on a flight to Cape Town and onward to Singapore. By the time they returned to Kenya their marriage would be a nine days' wonder.

In England Rosie had little difficulty in finding a secretarial position in a large pharmaceutical firm within driving distance of her grandparents' house. Weekends she spent visiting Aunt Beatrice, where she occupied most of her time in walking across the downs with the dog. She felt she was living in limbo.

Aunt Beatrice worried all the time about her brother, constantly saying, 'He's not sick enough to be a permanent resident in that home. It's terrible that he isn't allowed to spend the rest of his days in his own home.'

'But isn't that up to David?' Rosie asked.

'David won't do anything to cross that wife of his.'

They were unprepared, several days later, for an insistent knocking on the front door. Rosie was enjoying the first week of a two-week holiday and they had spent the day shopping in Cheltenham. They had driven through the beautiful Cotswold villages Aunt Beatrice loved, and for the first time in several weeks the problems of their distressing family situation had been laid aside. Now the sudden banging on the door brought Aunt Beatrice out of her bedroom with anxiety written large on her pale face.

'It's Cedric,' she gasped. 'Something must be wrong at Dene Hollow.'

'I'll go,' Rosie cried. 'Do be careful, Aunt Beatrice, when you go downstairs. I'll put the light on in the hall.'

The banging increased and a man's voice called out, 'Hello, is anybody at home?'

Rosie pulled back the bolts that her aunt had insisted on having installed on the outside door, to reveal a young man standing in the porch, shaking the raindrops from his hat, before eyeing her with a smile and saying, 'What an age it took, were you in bed?'

'Of course, it's after two in the morning.'

She stared at him in some annoyance but he grinned at her unabashed, then with a little cry she ran into his arms. It was Noel.

In the next moment he had swung Aunt Beatrice off her feet and she was saying, 'Why didn't you let us know you were coming?'

'There wasn't time.'

'Well, come into the living room. Rosie will make coffee. Take off that dripping macintosh and hang it in the porch. When did you arrive back in England?'

'Yesterday morning around this time.'

'And you came straight here?'

'No. I went home to Dene Hollow.'

Both Rosie and her aunt stared at him without speaking and Noel said, 'I know, it isn't home any more, is it. It's a pitiful shadow of what it was. We had one blazing row and David told me to get out, get out, indeed, of my home!'

'It's David's home now, Noel. He purchased it from your father for himself and Gloria, your father must have allowed it.'

'On the understanding that he would continue to live there, and I've no doubt he repaid them by his generosity.'

'Well, Jeffrey and Jerome were married with homes of their own, and you were abroad. Nobody knew if you'd be coming back, not even for a visit. He was living with David and they were looking after him.'

'Looking after him! They've been damned quick to put him in a home. And have you seen what they've done to the house? All that beautiful furniture gone, those ornaments that were my father's joy, replaced with new stuff that has little value.'

'I know, but it was their home, Gloria was allowed to please herself.'

'But why?' His voice was filled with exasperation. 'Has David been brainwashed or something? Couldn't he see what she was doing to the house, to my father and to him?'

'Apparently not.'

'And what about Jerome? Couldn't he have done something? Why didn't they all gang up against her, stop her in her tracks?'

Rosie handed him a cup of coffee, and looking up at her he said, 'And what about you, are you living here with Aunt Beatrice?'

'No, just spending a few days' holiday. I live with my grandparents in London for the time being. I have a job in London.'

'I heard from Jeffrey about your mother; that was terrible. But she always lived her life in the fast lane didn't she Rosie?'

'Yes, I suppose she did.'

'What are we going to do about my father, Aunt Beatrice? I've got a month's leave, can't we sort something out?'

'But what, Noel? He's not unhappy at Willow Bank. Obviously he couldn't go back to live with David and Gloria. He's never approved of Connie, and Jerome and Natalie are hardly likely to want him with them. They go here, there and everywhere; they're not likely to take kindly to anything that interferes with their social life.'

He sat drinking his coffee, his face wearing a worried frown, and Rosie thought that of her four cousins he was the one who had changed the least. His face still wore that handsome, confident air which could once again surface when the doubt was erased from it. Seeing Rosie looking at him, he smiled, 'It's a devil of a mess isn't it, Rosie? Who would have thought when we

397

were kids growing up at Dene Hollow that one night we'd be sitting here talking about so many terrible changes.'

She smiled, and he said, 'Any man in the offing, Rosie?'

'No.'

'Didn't you meet anybody in Kenya?'

'Nobody important.'

'I would have thought your mother would look around for the richest man in the dark continent. Didn't she come up with anybody?'

'Nobody important.'

'See anything of Steven Chaytor in Nairobi? Wasn't he working at one of the hospitals there after he left Cape Town?'

'Yes, I saw Steven several times, and Mary.'

'Mary?'

'Yes, Mary Raynor. He brought her to Dene Hollow one Christmas.'

'Oh yes, I remember. That was Jerome making mischief: he told Steven to invite a girl because you were getting too fond of him.'

'Well, it seems to have lasted. Perhaps Jerome did him a good turn.'

'They were kids together out in the Far East, he'd known her for years, their parents were friends. Do you think it was serious?'

'I have no idea. Is there somebody for you, Noel?'

'Nobody special. I have a few lady friends. Good job there was nobody special, she wouldn't have been welcome at Dene Hollow.'

'I've only two bedrooms,' Aunt Beatrice said practically. 'I'm afraid you'll have to sleep on the settee tonight, Noel, I hope you don't mind.'

'Of course not, I came unannounced. I'll book in at the hotel in the morning.'

'You intend staying in the area, then?'

'Aunt Beatrice, we've got to put our heads together and think about my father. We can't leave him in that home, we can't let Gloria destroy Dene Hollow, we can't allow her to go on taking from the family.'

'She's David's wife, Noel.'

He looked at her helplessly, then after a few minutes he said, 'You know what's going to happen, don't you? One of these days David's going to wake up and see her for what she really is. Then he'll leave her and he'll leave her in Dene Hollow that she has absolutely no right to.'

'David won't leave her, Noel. He'll go on closing his eyes and his mind to everything because he loves her.'

'You can kill love, Aunt Beatrice; love can't survive against every terrible thing one person can do to it.'

'Noel, David has condoned what she's done to Dene Hollow and to your father.'

'He's been brainwashed.'

'Perhaps.'

'But David's changed, he doesn't look happy, in fact he looks bloody miserable.'

'I'm tired, Noel, we'll talk tomorrow. Rosie, there are some blankets in the chest on the landing and some spare pillows in the wardrobe in my bedroom. You'll be comfortable here for one night, Noel.'

'Don't worry Aunt Beatrice. If you'd seen some

of the places I've had to sleep in you'd think this was paradise.'

Together Rosie and Noel made his bed on the settee and Aunt Beatrice went up to her room. After she had gone, Noel said, 'What do you really think about things, Rosie? I think I might have said too much for Aunt Beatrice.'

'Not really. She's very concerned for Uncle Cedric, for David too. For years she's been looking forward to living in her own cottage and now her family is still living her life for her. It seems she'll never get away from us.'

'I hope your mother left you well provided for, Rosie? Or did that new husband take most of it?'

She had forgotten how quickly his mind could move from one topic to the next.

'I got everything I needed, Noel.'

'How did you get along with him?'

'We didn't see much of each other.'

'Not very well, I take it.'

She smiled. 'It's much too late to talk about my life in Kenya, Noel. We'll meet again at breakfast. It would be nice if you made it.'

He grinned. 'I'm glad you're here, Rosie, you make it more like old times.'

Chapter Twenty-Nine

Mary Raynor's letter to Steven arrived just as he was leaving his house for the hospital, so he slipped it into his pocket and promptly forgot about it until several days later.

He expected it to be filled with reproach and a certain bitterness; he was, however, unprepared for the other letter she enclosed with it. Mary's letter was cool; she had arrived safely in Kuala Lumpur, her parents were both well, she hoped to meet up with Steven's parents during the next few days, and she hoped he was well.

He opened the accompanying letter and turned to the signature, Rosie. The full implication hit him immediately. Mary had been nursing this letter since the day of Rosie's departure and she had evidently read it.

It was a friendly letter. Rosie was leaving Keyna to return home to England, where she expected to be living with her grandparents for the foreseeable future. She hoped to visit Dene Hollow, but she had no idea what was happening there. She thanked him for his friendship and his many kindnesses over the years and she wished Mary and himself every happiness for the future.

There had been no reason for Mary to withhold the letter, but she had evidently done so out of her own insecurity. Throughout the day both letters bothered him: the unwritten accusation in Mary's, the unspoken anxieties in Rosie's.

He remembered the last time they had met and the panic in her eyes whenever Nigel Boyd's name had crept into their conversation. There had been desperation in her need to leave Kenya before he arrived back. And she was going back to the trauma Jerome had spelt out in his last letter.

Jerome was not a good correspondent, but when he did get down to putting pen to paper his description of present upheavals were more than adequate. Steven's thoughts went back to other years when life had been good for them at Dene Hollow. In this tropical land of hot sunshine and exotic scenery his mind had often strayed to England with its mist-laden mornings and gentle rain that lay across the hills and valleys like a benediction. Now he was remembering it all too vividly.

He stood staring through the window, but he was not seeing the palms swaying in the light breeze or the distant purple hills; he was seeing the sea cascading over the rocks below the gardens, the steep cliff walk and a young girl coming forward to meet him, her eyes shining brightly in her delicate face. That little girl had worn braces on her teeth, and her fair hair had been pulled back from her face and tied with a silken ribbon. A thin gangling little girl with short gingham skirts and ankle socks, and with little promise of the beauty that had enchanted her mother's world.

For days and then weeks he couldn't escape from the restlesssness her letter had aroused in him. There was no hidden meaning in that letter, but the memories of the joy he had always been aware of in her eyes whenever they met refused to go away.

He was remembering Jerome's cynical expression and even more cynical views. 'She fancies you rotten, Steven, let her down gently, let her see you with somebody else.'

He hadn't meant to use Mary. He liked her, she was a friend, but Mary had wanted to be more than a friend and he felt in some strange way he had betrayed them both. He couldn't do anything about Mary, but he had to try with Rosie.

In his next leave he would go home to England; and he smiled wryly when he realised he had thought of England as home.

In England, Noel was spending most of his time at his aunt's cottage, trying to persuade her to go with him to Dene Hollow to talk to his brother.

Aunt Beatrice was adamant that it no longer had anything to do with her.

'So you're going to abandon my father and let that woman have all her own way,' he accused her. 'You're my father's sister; don't you care any more?'

'Of course I care, but Dene Hollow is your brother's house and Gloria is his wife. There's nothing any of us can do.'

'Well, I'm not going to leave it like that. Dene Hollow became theirs so that my father could live with them; it was his home. I think he was very foolish to sign it over to David when he had three other sons, but he probably did it on the understanding that he would continue to live there.'

Aunt Beatrice didn't answer. Noel had merely confirmed her own understanding of the situation.

'What do you think, Rosie?' he asked.

'It all happened after I'd left to live with my mother.'

'But surely you understand how it was meant to be?'

'I don't see that anybody can do anything about it now.'

'Well, they're not getting away with it. I'm going back there, what about you, Rosie?'

'They'll say it's none of my business Noel.'

'So I'm on my own?'

'You have two brothers. Ask Jerome and Jeffrey to help you, although I think you'll be flogging a dead horse. I'm sure your father has left you adequately provided for moneywise. He's probably given David Dene Hollow in place of more money.'

'Money doesn't make up for the loss of that house and all that was in it. We should have been asked if we wanted Mother's stuff, and Grandmother's.'

'You were miles away, Noel.'

'I know, but none of us was asked, were we?'

At the end of the week, Noel decided he would return to Devonshire and Beatrice asked, 'Where will you stay, not at Dene Hollow, surely?'

'I'll stay at some hotel or other.'

'Not with your brothers?'

'I'm not over-fond of Natalie and Connie's got enough on with her salon and the boy. No, I'll stay at the hotel; I can mooch around on my own. I'll try talking to David; oh, not about the house, simply about father going back to live with them.'

'David will have to talk to Gloria, Noel, she does have a say in this.'

'She's had too much of a say. You know I never liked her. I never thought she was right for David. Did you like her?'

'Well, I didn't know her very well.'

'Always so ingratiating, simpering, too bloody nice. Surely you noticed.'

'I didn't think anything of it. I supposed that most young girls would try to be considered acceptable.'

Noel couldn't see it. Noel had always had fixed ideas about everything. David had been the one who tended to take people at face value. It had always been Noel, who had gibed at Rosie's mother.

They saw him depart on Friday morning, and Aunt Beatrice shook her head sadly. 'It won't do any good, Rosie. I'd rather he didn't interfere.'

'Can't you understand him wanting to interfere, Aunt Beatrice? I can.'

'But of course, dear, I just don't think it will do any good, that's all.'

Noel drove to the hotel on the cliffs, a ten-minute walk to Dene Hollow. After he had eaten lunch he decided to walk along the shore and climb up the steep path towards the house, that way he was hardly likely to encounter anybody who might know him. At the top of the cliff he stood looking at the house that from the outside seemed largely unchanged, apart from the new conservatory, which could barely be glimpsed from where he stood. Those gardens had been his playground, the shrubbery his adventurous initiation into the woods behind the house, which had been a boy's jungle.

A chill wind swept across the lawns and a thin spiral of smoke rose from two chimneys. Gritting his teeth, he started to walk towards the house.

The maid with the frilly apron answered the door, looking at him inquiringly, and brusquely, Noel asked, 'Is my brother in?'

'Mr Greville?'

'That's right.'

'Come in, sir. Who shall I say is calling?'

'I came the other day. I'm still the same person, Mr Greville's brother.'

'Wait in here, please. I'll see if Mr Greville is in.'

Noel scowled. Trust Gloria to saddle herself with a parlourmaid. Of course David was in. The girl didn't need to protect him from callers, unless the bailiffs needed to be called in.

He looked around the hall with jaundiced resentment. The picture of his grandfather that had stood at the head of the first flight of steps had gone and in its place hung a large embroidered fan of Spanish origin.

Noel scowled. He had always been a little afraid of his grandfather's portrait. It had been expertly painted but the eyes in the picture had followed him wherever he went, and when he'd been naughty they seemed to mirror the utmost disapproval. Jeffrey had experienced the same sort of fear.

The long monk's bench where the boys had once kept their tennis shoes had been replaced by a modern glass-fronted cabinet which Noel thought had no place in a hall and should have been in the dining room.

He was stopped short in his meanderings by the sound of footsteps coming towards him along the passage, and David stood looking at him across the hall. It was impossible to read his expression but it was hardly welcoming. Noel said, 'We have to talk, David, but not in here, surely.'

David opened the morning room door and went inside, expecting Noel to follow him.

Inside the room he motioned to a chair and took the one opposite.

He waited. Noel had said they needed to talk so it was evidently up to Noel to start the conversation.

Noel had been so sure of what he wanted to say. Now, with his brother's uncompromising face the words wouldn't come, and after a long silence all he could find to say was, 'Why, David?'

'Why what?'

'Why is my father in a home? Why has the house been changed to such an extent that I don't recognise it any more?'

'We should surely be able to do what we want with our own home.'

'But not with things that should have been divided between us. All the ornaments, most of them very valuable, the pictures, some of the furniture. I was miles away, but didn't you think

407

to consult Jerome? You're with him every day at the office.'

'Why would Jerome want any of it? He has a house filled with the sort of stuff his wife likes. And why give it to Connie? She wouldn't begin to know the value of it anyway.'

'But Jeffrey knew the value of it.'

'Jeffrey listens to his wife, they wouldn't have wanted any of it.'

'And you've evidently listened to yours.'

'Meaning?'

'Did you just hand it to her on a plate to do what she wanted with it? Did you consult Father?'

'He wasn't well, he never noticed anything, he never noticed the changes.'

'I'm sure he did. My father isn't senile, he was simply ill. And what about Aunt Beatrice and Rosie?'

'Aunt Beatrice has opted to live in a small cottage just about big enough to swing a cat round, and Rosie went off to her mother in Kenya apparently to live the life of Riley with a mother who had married into the aristocracy.'

'Even so, some of the things in this house belonged to our grandmother, Rosie's grandmother. What happened to them?'

David shrugged his shoulders, and after a few moments said, 'I suppose she sold some of them, some she gave away.'

'Did you never ask?'

'Gloria's my wife, I gave her a free hand.'

'With other people's property?'

'With my father's property, and he signed the

house and everything in it over to us.'

'So that he could continue to live here.'

'Gloria wasn't well; she couldn't cope when he became ill.'

'So you allowed her to hand over our property to members of her family and put our father in a home. Well done, David.'

'I don't see why I should listen to you pontificating on any of this. You went away, you hardly ever corresponded and none of us knew if or when you'd come back here. This is our home, it's how we like it, and none of it is your concern.'

'My father is my concern and should be yours.'

'He's very happy in Willow Bank. It's costing a small fortune to keep him there. If you're thinking about his money there'll be very little of it left.'

'I'm not concerned about his money, I don't need it and I don't want it. I should think most of it's gone on the alterations here, and they're pretty dire in anybody's book. If the rest goes on his stay in Willow Bank I'm glad your silly wife's not going to get her greedy little hands on that.'

The two brothers looked at each other with undisguised anger. At that moment the door was flung open and Gloria stood looking at them. She was aware of the tension in the room, and Noel rose to his feet and walked towards her.

'I'm just leaving,' he said. 'I've said all I wanted to say to David.'

He stared down at her, trying to reconcile the pretty girl who had been quick to flatter where it had most mattered, attentive to his father, anxious to consult him always on the most trivial matters, copying Natalie's clothes, even her table manners; polite but distant with Connie and exhibiting a strange, underlying jealousy towards Rosie. Now this slender, thin-faced woman seemed a bag of nerves.

'You're welcome to stay for a meal, if you wish,' she snapped, in a voice that was hardly welcoming.

'No thank you, I'm staying at the hotel.'

'The hotel?'

'Yes, I need to see my father as often as possible while I'm here.'

'Natalie didn't offer to have you?'

'I'm quite happy at the hotel.'

'Did Grangers telephone about the curtains, David?'

'No.'

'You haven't been out, have you? You said you'd stay in case they telephoned.'

'I haven't been out.'

'I'm so cross about them, they promised faithfully, their prices have risen sky-high and they can't even bother to telephone.'

Across the room Noel looked into his brother's eyes and found them strangely disturbing.

It was a little later that he drove his rented car into the grounds of Willow Bank, and as he passed the window he could see his father sitting in his deep armchair, asleep near the window.

A young nurse greeted him with a smile, saying, 'Your father's in the lounge, Mr Greville. Would you like a cup of tea?'

'Thank you, that would be very nice.'

He pulled up a chair next to his father and

410

gently laid his hand on the other man's arm. 'Hello, Dad,' he said. 'Just having forty winks?'

His father opened his eyes and stared at him, then with a small smile he said, 'So you're still here. I thought you were going to see Beatrice.'

'I went over the weekend. Rosie was with her.'

'What about the cottage? I found it poky. Why she ever wanted to move away from Dene Hollow to live there I can't imagine.'

'It's big enough for Aunt Beatrice, Dad. Besides, how could she have stayed on at Dene Hollow after David and his wife lived there?'

His father's eyes shifted. It was not a topic he wished to enlarge upon.

'What's happening with Rosie? Is she going back to Kenya?'

'No. She has a job in London, she's living with her grandparents.'

'Did she tell you anything about what happened out there?'

'No. I should think the subject is pretty painful for her.'

'I suppose so. Nothing that happened to Celia surprised me; she was catastrophe waiting to happen.'

'Why do you say that, Dad?'

'Well, she lived her life like that, in the fast lane. Men. Each one a bit more glamorous than the last one, richer. Always in the fast lane. You never liked her, Noel.'

'No, I never did, but I never thought you'd noticed.'

'You'd be surprised how much I noticed even when I never said very much.'

411

'Are you happy here, Dad?'

'It's right enough.'

Noel looked around the room to where several old ladies were fast asleep and those that weren't sat staring into space, and angrily he said.

'You're not ready for this, Dad.'

'I've no complaints, son. The food is good, I have a very nice room overlooking the garden and I've got old Mr Charlton to play chess with. It could be worse.'

'What has Jerome had to say about it, or Jeffrey?'

'Why should they say anything at all? Jeffrey came at the weekend, brought the boy, nice boy he is.'

'Yes, I'd say Jeffrey's the happiest of the lot, a decent job, a child and a nice wife.'

'There's nothing wrong with Jerome's marriage.'

'No, perhaps not, but Natalie's too restless for me, she needs a lot of living up to.'

He'd noticed that his father had not mentioned David or Gloria, and refusing to let him get away with it, he said, 'I called to see David this morning. His wife's changed.'

'Changed. How do you mean?'

'Well, she was a girl with a lot to say, fussy. I don't like what they've done to the house.'

'She wanted it to be more like Jerome's.'

'It's not in the least like Jerome's. Natalie's taste isn't Gloria's.'

'I'd like another cup of tea, Noel. Ask in the kitchen, they'll bring another one in here.'

It was palpably obvious his father didn't want

to discuss either David or his wife, and when Noel returned to the lounge his father's first words were, 'How long are you staying in that hotel, then? How long is your leave?'

'About a month.'

'That's a long time.'

'Not really, Dad. I haven't taken much leave since I went there.'

'Things might have been very different if you hadn't gone out there so quickly, Noel.'

'What do you mean, Father?'

'Well, I'd always hoped you'd go into the family firm with the other two. That way Beatrice might have stayed on at Dene Hollow and we'd still be there.'

'You can't say that for sure, Dad. I could have got married to a girl every bit as mercenary as the other two and then where would we be?'

'Perhaps it's just as well we can't see into the future, Noel. If we could we'd do things differently. But I do have happy times to look back on.'

'There were times, Dad, when I never really knew if you were happy or not; you were always a bit taciturn.'

'It was nice when you all came home from school to be there, and that nice boy Jerome and Jeffrey brought home. His parents lived in the Far East. Steven, his name was.'

'Yes, Steven Chaytor. Rosie met up with him in Kenya.'

'Her eyes used to light up whenever he came into a room. She liked that boy too much, too soon.'

Noel stared at his father curiously. Had any of

them ever really known him, the man who was now showing so much compassion for Rosie concerning her first love.

Chapter Thirty

Jerome seldom listened to his wife's conversation over the breakfast table since it was largely concerned with what her friends were doing, the tennis club, the golf club and any new expensive shop that had recently opened in the near vicinity.

An occasional 'that's nice Natalie', or 'fancy that' and she was satisfied she had his attention. This morning he sat staring down at a letter he had received from Steven Chaytor. They had corresponded spasmodically over the years, but now here was Steven saying he expected to be in England for several weeks at the end of September and would like to meet up with him again.

Seeing Jerome's absorption in his letter when he should have been answering her question, Natalie said, 'You're not listening, Jerome.'

'No, this is a letter from Steven Chaytor. He's coming back to England in September.'

'To stay?'

'Well, he says for a few weeks. He'd like to meet up with us again. We should invite him to stay, Natalie. It would be nice to see Steven again, tell him what's been happening at Dene Hollow.'

'Will he be coming on his own?'

'I assume so. He doesn't mention anybody else.'

'But there was Mary. Wasn't she in Kenya with him?'

'She was certainly in Kenya, whether she was with him or not, I'm not sure.'

'I don't mind Steven staying with us, but I don't particularly want a woman guest. I have so much to do, and I'd feel I had to entertain her all the time and take her everywhere. Can't you find out if she's coming with him?'

'I suppose so. Steven hasn't said anything about staying with us. He'd stay at the hotel if we tell him it isn't convenient.'

'It is convenient, Jerome, for Steven and only Steven.'

'Oh well, I'll write back and suggest it. He'll tell us if he's travelling alone.'

'Will Noel still be here?'

'I've no idea. He's got extended leave, but how far that stretches I don't know.'

'Steven will be appalled at how things have changed; it will be nothing like the old days. He won't want to see Dene Hollow looking the way it does now.'

'Nevertheless, I'll tell David he's coming. It's up to them if they invite him to visit.' He grinned. 'We could invite Rosie, see if that old crush is still there.'

'Oh Jerome, she's a woman now, she was a schoolgirl then.'

'I know, and that plain gawky little girl is long gone. Our Rosie's a beauty, even Steven would have to admit that.'

'Surely he met the new Rosie in Kenya? She'll be no surprise to him.'

'Perhaps not, but it might make life interesting. We'll push the boat out. Have a big family party.'

'And where will you expect them to stay for this party? Not at Dene Hollow because Gloria will never ask them, and I hope you're not expecting to have them all here.'

'Well, it's not all that many. Father, who will come from Willow Bank, Aunt Beatrice, Rosie and Steven.'

'What about Noel?'

'Well, he's at the hotel, so whether he's here or not is no problem.'

'I really don't see why we should splash out money for a party when those two at Dene Hollow don't even invite us for a cup of tea.'

'All right then, forget the party. We have to do something to entertain Steven. I simply thought for the sake of old times it was a good idea.'

'We can take Steven out to dinner at the golf club. Probably Aunt Beatrice and Rosie won't come and Noel could have gone back. There might only be the three of us.'

'You're probably right.

Natalie watched him fold Steven's letter and replace it in its envelope. When had Jerome ever had an idea he enthused about and was prepared to forget? He'd think something up and probably tell her about it when it was too late to think of alternatives.

The same thought was passing through Jerome's mind. Quietly, he said, 'Isn't our wedding anniversary in September, darling?'

'No, nor is it my birthday or yours.'

'I've forgotten when Rosie's birthday comes round, and Noel's is in December?'

'Why are birthdays suddenly so important? We're not celebrating any birthdays. In any case Steven may only be here for a few days. I'm sure there are plenty of things for him to do in England without spending too long in Devon.'

'Yes, of course, I'm sure you're right, dear.'

Natalie looked at him sharply. 'I know you, Jerome Greville. Whenever you get a bee in your bonnet you have to do something about it. I notice you didn't mention Jeffrey and his wife.'

'Only because they live here, they wouldn't expect to stay anywhere except in their own home.'

'It would take me all my time to be civil to Gloria.'

'Yes well, let's forget about it, shall we? See you around five-thirty. Are you going out?'

'I'm having lunch with my mother.'

'That's nice, give her my regards.'

As he drove to the office his idea of a family get-together was still uppermost on his mind, so half-way through the morning he invited himself into his brother's office for coffee. David was alone, and he looked up with evident surprise. He couldn't remember the last time Jerome had entered his office for conversation.

Jerome took the chair opposite his desk. 'I've had a letter from Steven Chaytor this morning. He's coming over to England in September for a few weeks.'

417

David stared back but made no comment.

'We had some good times at Dene Hollow in the old days. I thought it might be a good idea to have a get-together.'

'A get-together?'

'Yes. It would cheer Father up and Steven could meet us all again.'

'Us?'

'The family. We are still a family, I hope. Noel's over here, Aunt Beatrice and Rosie would come, then there's Jeffrey and Connie, you and Gloria and Natalie and I.'

'And where would you be proposing to hold this get-together?'

'Well, not at Dene Hollow, that's for sure. Steven will come back like Noel and Rosie came back, thinking to find everything the same. It isn't, is it, David?'

'No. How could it be?'

'Oh, it could be. If we'd taken over Dene Hollow it would still be exactly as it had always been. A get-together at Dene Hollow would have been like something out of the past, unchanged and unchanging. So I'm thinking in terms of some hotel or the golf club. We'd have to talk about it.'

'And all this is for Steven's benefit?'

'Well, obviously he doesn't know anything about it. I just thought he might appreciate it, that's all.'

'Well, you were always a great one for organising parties, Jerome. Marquees on the lawn, endless guests, most of them unknown to the rest of us.'

'They went down very well, though. Don't tell me you didn't enjoy them.'

'I did then. I'm a different person now.'

Jerome rose to his feet. 'Yes, you are David, more changed, I think, than any of us. If you don't like the idea you only have to say so. Or would you like to mention it to Gloria first?'

'She's not much into parties these days.'

'No, that's what I thought. But she was at one time, wasn't she? I remember that she lapped those parties up at Dene Hollow, she'd have been mortified not to have been invited.'

'I'm not really very interested in a family party, count us out. Steven is welcome to visit us if he feels like it.'

'How could he refuse such a warm invitation?'

David shrugged his shoulders in a take it or leave it manner, and Jerome said, 'So you're not prepared to discuss it further.'

'No.'

With that terse reply there was nothing for it but to leave his office.

Jerome was not done with the idea yet and in the late afternoon he visited his father at Willow Bank, only to find that the idea didn't much interest his father either.

'Family get-togethers belong in the past, Jerome.' he said firmly. 'They were a part of Dene Hollow when we were a family. Your mother loved them when you were children, Aunt Beatrice tolerated them. They weren't always occasions to look back on with pleasure.'

'Why do you say that?'

'Because often there were undercurrents,

419

particularly when you grew older.'

'What sort of undercurrents? I wasn't aware of them.'

'Then you were not as astute as I gave you credit for.'

'Well, I know you didn't take kindly to Connie, and Rosie's mother wasn't exactly a welcomed guest, but we can discount that one visit she made. And Connie's made Jeffrey a decent wife in spite of your objections.'

'Why this sudden urge for a get-together?'

'Well Steven Chaytor's coming back to England for a few weeks, he'd like to spend a little time with us.'

'To stay with you?'

'Well, obviously, he won't be invited to stay at Dene Hollow.'

'Well, he was your friend, not David's.'

'You're still covering for him, Father.'

'I don't know what you mean.'

'Never mind. So I can count you out even if Aunt Beatrice and Rosie come, even if Noel's still here?'

'Steven is very welcome to visit me here.'

'That's what David said.'

'So you've approached him, have you?'

'Yes. I got the same response I got from you.'

His father nodded, and exasperated, Jerome said, 'Right then, Father, we'll go ahead without you. I'll bring Steven to see you one day and I'll try not to bore you with anything Natalie and I plan for his entertainment whilst he's here.'

At that moment a maid came into the room pushing a tea trolley, and Jerome said, 'I'll get off now, Father. It's almost six o'clock, and I told Natalie I'd be home around five-thirty.'

Natalie was not in the best of humour.

'You're late,' she accused him. 'You know it's that meeting at the golf club. You'll have to have sandwiches and a cold sweet; I've got to go in a few minutes.'

'You women have more meetings than all the men put together.'

'I know we're second-class citizens but we do most to raise money for the club. Where have you been till this time?'

'I called to see Father.'

She raised her eyebrows. 'Why, for heaven's sake? I thought you preferred to go at the weekend, golf permitting.'

His two previous encounters had not prepared him to be pleasant with Natalie.

Sharply, he said, 'I want to see him about dinner with us when Steven's here. I thought my previous idea was a very good one. He doesn't think so, and neither does David.'

She stared at him in amazement. 'So you're still thinking about it, Jerome. I knew you would, every time you get a bee in your bonnet like this one there's no forgetting it. I knew David wouldn't be interested, and I'm not surprised your father isn't either.'

'No well, we can manage without them, we don't need them.'

Natalie left the house, slamming the front door behind her, and he sat at the table listening to the sound of her car's engine dying away along the road. She was furious, but she'd get over it. He wasn't going to be put off; like everything else he'd ever wanted it would all come right in the end.

That evening he telephoned Aunt Beatrice.

He decided to lead up to it gently after explaining that Steven would be staying with them.

'How nice for you, Jerome. You were very good friends; do please remember me to him.'

'I want to do rather more than that, Aunt Beatrice. I want you to come over to meet him. Steven's expressed a wish to meet up with all of you again.'

'Well, I don't know, dear. I don't drive long distances any more. I only ever drive around the village to go to the shops.'

'We wouldn't be asking you to drive, Aunt Beatrice. Rosie would bring you.'

'But Rosie has a job, Jerome. In all probability she'll have used up her holidays by September.'

'Then she can take unpaid leave. I'd subsidise her for that.'

'Jerome, I can't speak for Rosie. Is Steven coming alone or is he bringing that girl with him?'

'Which girl?'

'You know very well which girl: the one he brought that Christmas to Dene Hollow.'

'Oh that one. Mary Raynor. They were old friends, nothing more.'

'Are you sure?'

'Well, he doesn't mention she's coming with him and he would have done, I'm sure.'

'Rosie told me she often saw him with Mary in Kenya.'

'So she has talked about him, then?'

'Oh Jerome, you're mischief making again. Rosie was very fond of Steven, it's over. She's grown up and he's probably spoken for. I don't really think your idea of a family party to welcome Steven is a good one; we're not a united family any more.'

Jerome's next call was to Jeffrey, a far more promising proposition than any of the others.

Jeffrey was surprised at the invitation but said he would very much like to see Steven again.

'So you think it's not a bad idea, then?'

'Not really, but we have the boy to think about. He'd be the only child there.'

It was something Jerome hadn't really thought about, but he said, 'Couldn't you leave him with Connie's father? You needn't be late home and the kid wouldn't enjoy a party at the golf club with a lot of older people.'

'So it's to be at the golf club.'

'Well, we can hardly hold it at Dene Hollow.'

'No, I suppose not. Would David be there?'

'No, he isn't interested.'

'And Father?'

'No, he isn't interested either.'

'Some time in September, did you say?'

'Yes, I'll give you all the details later. Mention it to Connie.'

'Oh, I will.'

'The salon's booming, and she has a lot of assistants.'

'How do you know?'

'Well, she's poached several of them from Natalie's hairdresser; word gets around.'

423

Jeffrey laughed, thinking it was like Jerome not to miss a trick.

It was only a little while later that Jerome heard the sound of a car's engine outside the house, and looking at his watch he saw that it was only a little after nine. Surely it was too soon for Natalie's meeting to have finished. The meeting was a girly night that usually went on some hours.

He got up and went to the door in time to see Noel climbing out of his rented car, and Noel thought that Jerome's smile was unexpectedly welcoming.

After he had poured drinks out for them he passed Steven's letter over for him to read.

Noel passed it back, saying, 'Where will he stay? Here, I suppose.'

'Well of course, where else is there?'

'He doesn't say how long he expects to be here.'

'No. We have to make him welcome, make him feel he's never been away. How about a get-together for old times' sake? Jeffrey's in favour and I've approached Aunt Beatrice. She'll think about it. And there's you. I hope you'll still be here. Dad and David are not interested.'

'So you've asked them?'

'Yes. Their attitude didn't surprise me.'

'And Rosie?'

'I haven't mentioned it to Rosie, but I hope she'll come and drive Aunt Beatrice over.'

'And Mary Raynor?'

'What do you know about Mary Raynor?'

'I know that she was constantly with him in Kenya.'

'He's coming here alone.'

'But he'll go back to her?'

'How should I know?'

'Oh well, I suppose Rosie's over him by this time. I'm not sure I'll still be here. I got extended leave but it isn't elastic.'

'But a few more days surely couldn't he asking too much.'

'You're flogging a dead horse here, Jerome. Nothing's going to change. Father will stay in Willow Bank and Dene Hollow as we knew it has long gone.'

'We need this party, Noel. Let David see that with him or without him we're still a family. It might just bring him to his senses.'

'It's a pipe-dream, Jerome. David is not the David we knew, he's Gloria's David and it's Gloria's house. I doubt if I'll ever come back to England again, when I've finally washed its soil from my shoes, that's it.'

Jerome watched his youngest brother leave with a feeling of finality in his heart. Why should he bother? Natalie was right. Why not simply entertain Steven for as long as he wanted to stay with them then let the matter drop?

When Natalie returned home soon after eleven she found him slumped in his chair, wearing a depressed look on his face. The evening had been convivial and much of her good humour had been restored.

'Do you want coffee?' she asked him.

'No thanks.'

'Has anybody called?'

'Yes, Noel.'

'Really. So you were able to put your idea of a party to him?'

'Yes, if he's still here, he's for it.'

'Is he the only one?'

'There's Jeffrey.'

'And?'

'I've had enough of it for one evening.' Then, seeing his wife's amused expression, he said, 'Leave it with me, they'll come round. I thought the get-together would enable us all to sort things out.'

Jerome had never been one to let the events of the day interfere with his sleep. After a few tosses and turns he lapsed into deep slumber, not aware that the day's events were causing several other people hours of restlessness.

Connie had never been at her happiest at Dene Hollow parties, always aware that she could not compete with her two sisters-in-law, and aware of her father-in-law's disapproval. Jeffrey was only too well aware of her insecurity.

Noel didn't see how it could be a family party with so many people missing, and Aunt Beatrice was worried about Rosie.

Rosie talked about Steven Chaytor and it was there in her eyes, in her voice, an infatuation that refused to go away.

Rosie would settle down in England, enjoy her new environment, make new friends. It was unfair to drag her back into a past that had gone for ever.

Let Steven Chaytor come and go. She would tell Rosie nothing of his visit. But she had not reckoned with Jerome.

Chapter Thirty-One

Natalie regarded her husband with a jaundiced eye. He was like a dog with a bone whenever he got an idea into his head. He also annoyed her because she thought he was being secretive about it where she was concerned.

'How can it possibly be a family party without your father and David and his wife?' she asked him.

'They've been invited. It's their own fault if they're not coming.'

'Why can't we simply have Steven staying with us and forget about the rest? If he wants to visit them whilst he's here that would be up to him.'

'Not a good idea. Beatrice and Rosie are too far away. Visiting Father in that home will be worrying enough and not seeing David at all will hardly make him feel it's like old times.'

'I want to know exactly who will be staying here. I shall be the one doing most of the work, anyway.'

'Steven will be here, the others can stay at the hotel with Noel.'

'We can't possibly ask your aunt to do that.'

'You can leave Aunt Beatrice to me.'

Aunt Beatrice proved herself to be his second obstacle.

'Really, Jerome I don't think I should go. Your father isn't going, and I'll be the oldest one there.

427

I've so much to do here at the cottage and there are the animals to think of.'

'It's only for a weekend, Aunt Beatrice, surely somebody would look after them for two nights.'

'No, it's an imposition. And what about Natalie? I'm sure she won't want a houseful of people.'

'There won't be a houseful, just Steven, you and Rosie.'

'Rosie's in London, it's a very long drive into Devonshire.'

'She'll cope.'

'Then it's up to you to ask her.'

'I'll happily pay for the two of you to stay at the hotel.'

'The money has nothing to do with it, Jerome. If things were like they used to be with all of us being together then I'd think about it, but without your father and David I don't think it's a good idea.'

'I intend to ask Rosie. Surely she'll want to see Steven again.'

'You made mischief between those two in the old days, Jerome. You embarrassed Rosie terribly and possibly Steven too. Rosie's grown up, she won't want to be reminded of those days.'

'Well, I'm going to telephone her. She's at her grandfather's; I've got her number.'

Of her four cousins Jerome had been the one she'd known least, even when she'd often been the butt of his amusement. Hearing his voice, her first reaction was one of surprise. He sounded very confident.

'Rosie, I'm asking you to keep a few days free

sometime in September. I'm organising a little party here for old times' sake. I hope you'll come.'

'What sort of party?'

'Dinner at the golf club, a farewell party for Noel if you like and a chance to meet up with Steven Chaytor again.'

'Steven? Will he be there?'

'Yes, he's staying with us. He wants to meet up with everybody again.'

'Everybody?'

'Well, everybody who's interested.'

'And they are?'

'Me and Natalie. Noel, Jeffrey and his wife, You, hopefully.'

'But not David or your father? Not Aunt Beatrice?'

'I've asked her but she's concerned about her animals, and my father doesn't want to come. He'll be pleased to see Steven at the home.'

'Was David invited, Jerome?'

'Of course. It's up to him whether he comes or he doesn't.'

'I met up with Steven and Mary in Kenya not very long ago.'

'I know. I doubt if Mary will be coming; he hasn't mentioned her.'

'Can I think about it, Jerome?'

'Rosie, Steven's hoping to see you, all of us, surely you can make up your mind now. After all, it's only for a couple of days.'

'And you'll probably be at your most sarcastic and embarrass both of us by talking about my ridiculous crush on Steven and his need to show me he wasn't interested.'

'Rosie, you were a little girl and he was a young man. Now you're a very beautiful woman. Who knows?'

'I'll only come if you promise to behave and not make us both feel that we've been dragged together in the hope of better things.'

'I promise on my honour, Rosie. I'll be as good as gold. Steven is staying with us. You can too, we'll be pleased to have you.'

'No, Jerome, I'll stay at the same hotel as Noel.'

He laughed. 'Just as you like, my dear, I'll mail you with full details nearer the time.'

When he replaced the receiver he rubbed his hands with glee. It was going to be fine, just a nice number and a good meal at the club. When David saw what was happening he could change his mind. He just hoped that he'd been right in his supposition that Steven wasn't bringing Mary Raynor.

Rosie wasn't sure it was a good idea, the opening of old wounds, childish hurts that had faded slowly over the years; and seeing Steven again would surely bring back to her all the trauma of those all too few years in Kenya. Nigel Boyd and her mother, Mary and Steven together, and Martin Newley and his crowd of party-goers. She wouldn't be alone with Steven; there would be little opportunity for them to discuss their time in Kenya. Steven had been aware of her feelings of anguish when Nigel's name had been mentioned.

In September Jerome met Steven at the airport and Natalie came out of the house to meet them.

She had always considered Steven Chaytor to be one of the most handsome boys she had met, and now he seemed doubly so, with maturity sitting easily on his shoulders.

'What made you decide to come to England on your own?' Jerome asked. 'We thought you and Mary Raynor were an item.'

'Why should you think that?'

'Well, Rosie said she'd met up with you both in Kenya, and it seemed to us that you and Mary were always together.'

'Mary and I went back a long way. We found ourselves in the same place at the same time, that's all.'

Jerome would have pursued the subject had it not been for Natalie's warning glance.

Over dinner that first night Steven learned of the many changes that had occurred in the lives of his old friends, and his expression registered his sadness and disappointment. As a boy he had regarded Dene Hollow as another home, somewhere to go to with joy and the promise of friendship. The boys had been his friends, Rosie had been a little sister, Cedric and Beatrice had taken the place of his parents, however briefly. Now those same boys were strangely divided, Cedric and Beatrice were out of their lives and Rosie was somebody he had yet to discover.

Jerome was determined to bring the talk around to Rosie, however much Natalie tried to change the subject. At last it was Steven who said, 'Do you see much of Rosie?'

'She's living in London with her grandparents and she's got a job there,' Jerome answered him,

431

but he was looking into Steven's eyes and was rewarded by the disappointment he saw in them.

'She's coming here for the dinner party so you'll see her this weekend,' he relented.

'She's staying here?'

'Actually no, she's staying at the hotel with Noel. There'll just be seven of us; David and his wife declined.'

'I'm sorry. It's as bad as that then?'

'I'm afraid so. I have to see a very important client in the morning, but that shouldn't be any problem. You know the area, you can go out on a voyage of rediscovery, and in the afternoon if you like we could call to see Father.'

'Yes, of course. Is he happy in the home?'

'He doesn't say much. I suppose he's making the best of it.'

'And Beatrice?'

'She's shelved the lot of us. She's got a poky little cottage for herself and her animals. It's in the main street of a very small village with a pub at one end and a church at the other. She thinks it's wonderful. Can't say I blame her.'

'She was an absolute gem to put up with us all. She won't be happy about the situation now.'

'Gracious no. She was invited to come here but she made one excuse after another. I think being here causes too much anguish.'

'I can understand that.'

'What happened about Rosie's mother? We all read about it in the paper, even the local rag got their hands on it. Strangely enough, my father wasn't surprised. He said Celia'd always lived her life in the fast lane, moving on and upwards, then

432

crashing to earth. I must say she was a corker to look at, but then so is Rosie.'

'There was an inquest. She was driving too fast, too erratically. The people in the Land Rover didn't see her, and she ended up in the ditch. She had no chance.'

'But where was she driving to?'

'They said she was driving back to her house from her neighbour's house. Her husband was on the scene very quickly. They brought in a verdict of accidental death.'

'Well, it was evident Rosie didn't want to stay out there, nor does she want to talk about it. What was the husband like?'

'I hardly knew him.'

'And Rosie doesn't want to talk about him.'

Steven looked at him sharply. 'You're tried to talk to her about him?'

'Well you know, making conversation, that's all.'

Rosie had found Noel decidedly silent over breakfast, only speaking when she spoke to him, so that at last in desperation she said, 'It's not exactly going to be a welcoming party if you're going to behave like this all day.'

He stared at her, then with a little smile said, 'I'm sorry, Rosie, I'm a rotten companion. You'd have done better to stay with Jerome. At least Natalie can be relied upon to have something to talk about, even of it's only the latest fashions, and money.'

'You're as caustic as you ever were.'

'I know. Why are we having this get-together Rosie? It's not as though we're a united family

433

any more.'

'Can't we forget about a get-together and simply make it an occasion to see Steven?'

'Oh well, I can see that aspect of it will delight you. It's the rest of it that worries me.'

'Well, I'm going for a walk along the cliff. Do you want to come with me?'

'No, I have letters to write. I'll see you later.'

Rosie knew every inch of the cliff paths that meandered between clumps of autumn bracken and thrift. Below her, the cliffs dropped steeply away to where rock-strewn coves were lashed by the incoming tide. Further out the sands gleamed golden in the bright sunlight, and now that the children had gone back to school they were deserted.

From the cliff top she could look back on Dene Hollow glowing with Virginia creeper, and somehow it seemed that at any moment she would see the boys running across the lawns, hear their voices, warm to their laughter. Then the moment was gone as she saw a gardener trundling his wheelbarrow along the path and a small slender woman hurrying out of the house to speak to him. The woman was gesticulating towards the shrubbery, while the gardener rested his wheelbarrow and appeared somewhat nonplussed by what she was saying. At last she turned to walk back to the house, turning to stare across the gardens in Rosie's direction before she entered it.

Gloria found her husband leafing through his morning mail, and she said sharply, 'There was a woman standing on the cliff path looking at the house. I thought it was Rosie but I couldn't be sure.'

When David didn't answer her she went over to the window and gazed through it. 'There she is,' she cried. 'Come and look.'

Obediently David got up from his chair and went to stand at the window. 'I don't know, she's too far away,' he said.

'Well, isn't this the weekend they're dining at the club? Jerome told you Steven Chaytor would be here.'

'I haven't seen much of Jerome this week.'

'But I'm right about the meeting?'

'Perhaps, I'm not sure.'

'You know what the talk will be. Your father in Willow Bank, the house, your family's precious ornaments. We're going to give them something else to talk about. I'm fed up with the shrubbery.'

David looked at her sharply. 'What is wrong with the shrubbery?'

'I hate it. I want a rose garden there with neat ordered paths and a fountain.

'There was a rose garden at the front of the house which you said you didn't like? Why make a new one?'

'I'd prefer it where the shrubbery is. I've never liked the shrubbery.'

The shrubbery had been their adventure playground: a place to hide in, a boy's joy with its colourful shrubs and winding paths, and memories of other days came flooding back to him. He looked into her sharp little face with its narrowed speculative eyes and not for the first time a feeling of tormented anger filled his heart.

Wearily he said, 'Gloria, aren't you a little tired of stamping out every single memory of my life in this house? You wanted to be a part of it, now you want to destroy it.'

'Because I'm swallowed up by it.'

'How? How are you swallowed up by it?'

'My background was no better than Connie's but she never learned. I did. I copied Natalie and your Aunt Beatrice. I watched Rosie and her mother and I got what they had. Now I can get rid of these things and put the things I like around me. Oh, I know they're not exactly your taste. Jerome's only been here once or twice since we married but I can tell from his expression, and his wife's. Well, this is how it's going to be. Let them have their get-together, I don't want any part of it. I've got Dene Hollow and my parents have all those things I didn't want and which they thought so much about.'

With a long hard look in his direction she left the room, closing the door sharply behind her.

It was Jerome's get-together that had got to her, but it had got to David in a different way, a far more subtle way.

Rosie continued her walk along the cliff top to where she knew of a sheltered nook half-way up the cliff path. The tide was coming in so it would be risky to walk down to the beach, but as she clambered down the few steps to the rustic seat set against the cliff she saw the solitary figure of a man strolling across the beach in the direction of the path.

She knew him instantly. How many times had she looked for Steven in this exact place? How she had waited for his face to light up with a smile, run forward to clutch his hand. But then she had been a child and now she could only wait with a fast beating heart to see if his smile would be still as welcoming, his eyes as kind.

He was half-way up the path when he saw her waiting for him, and as always his face lit up with a smile and this time he did not take her hand, he put his arms around her and held her close.

When they sat together at last he still held her hand and he said gently, 'I'm so glad you came, Rosie, I wasn't sure.'

'I thought you would have answered my letter, Steven. When you didn't, I realised that I should put you behind me for ever.'

'I only got your letter when Mary went off to see her parents in the Far East. For some reason she didn't give it to me immediately.'

'I wonder why?'

'Perhaps she saw things more clearly than I did, Rosie.'

When she didn't speak he went on. 'Perhaps if you hadn't gone out to Kenya, Rosie, Mary and I might have drifted into something more permanent. We went back a long way, I was very fond of her. In retrospect that was all there ever was: fondness, empathy, never love.'

'She must have disliked me very much not to give you my letter.'

'No, Rosie. She simply hoped I would forget you. She'll find somebody who will love her, which I never could.'

'You know that everything here has changed horribly, don't you, Steven?'

'Yes, Jerome and Natalie have put me in the picture. I'm very sorry. I was looking forward to finding things much the same, but I remember I did once caution you on coming back here. What did I say to you that morning?'

'I remember, Steven. Never go back and expect to find people and places unchanged. But I had to come back, Steven, there was nowhere else for me to go. I had to get away from Malibu.'

'And unhappy memories, among other things.'

She looked at him sharply. 'Yes, Steven, there were other things that I never want to speak about to anybody, not even to you.'

'Then we won't speak of them. Don't you want to know anything at all about Malibu?'

'I know that Nigel Boyd has gone back there. I saw him at the airport boarding a plane for Nairobi.'

'He is living at Malibu with Ariadne Fairbrother. I believe they are married.'

When she didn't immediately respond, he looked at her curiously, and after a few moments she said, 'It doesn't surprise me, Steven. I knew there were undercurrents, I sensed them around the time of my mother's death. There was more to that than the stuff that came out.'

'You think they were having an affair?'

'I suspected it.'

'Do you think your mother suspected it?'

'I don't know. They quarrelled all the time about money and other things but she idolised him, adored him. She would never in a thousand years have believed anything bad about him.'

'So if you'd discovered anything you couldn't

438

have told her?'

She shook her head and he knew she would say nothing more. Whatever Nigel Boyd had done to Rosie would remain locked in her heart for ever.

'I'll walk back to the hotel with you, Rosie. I'd like to see Noel,' he said, pulling her to her feet.

'Well, he wasn't in a very good mood this morning, but he'll be delighted to see you.'

'He's upset about his father and David?'

'Yes, very. He and David were such very good friends, and now they don't see each other. They don't even correspond when Noel is abroad. When he goes back there it will be as if he had no family here to come back to.'

They walked slowly back along the cliff top and it was only when they could look across the lawns to where Dene Hollow stood with its backdrop of purple hills that Steven said, 'It looks much the same even though I know it isn't. I feel I should call to see them, but the advice I gave to you is uppermost in my mind. Never go back, never lay yourself open to hurts and old memories that have gone for ever.'

'Perhaps we can shelve them for one night, Steven, make our family party something good to remember even if it will be rather depleted.'

'Yes, I think we owe it to the past to try to do that.'

'Here's Noel coming to meet us, and he does look rather happier than he did this morning.'

The two men shook hands warmly and Rosie walked between them towards their hotel.

She knew that she and Steven needed to talk about the future. She loved him as much as she had always loved him, but this time with a maturity the young Rosie had never contemplated. But there was still a great deal to be resolved if they were to have a future together.

Stephen's work was in Kenya and she could never go back there, not to that life with people who had known her mother, knew Nigel Boyd and Ariadne. She could never look at Nigel Boyd without remembering that terrible night when he had taken away her innocence and every dream of love she thought she had ever known.

Chapter Thirty-Two

Jerome was in his element. This party he'd dreamed up was going to be a great success in spite of the fact that four people were missing. The golf club had a good reputation for catering and they dined in the newly decorated dining room at a large table in the window, from where they could look out across the bay and the sun setting in golden splendour.

The ladies had dressed for the occasion in long evening dresses, and after leaving their wraps in the cloakroom Connie whispered to Rosie, 'Do I look all right? I'm not sure about the colour but Jeffrey chose it.' The dress was a dark green silk jersey which fell to her feet in heavy folds. Rosie said she had never seen her looking so elegant. Indeed her hair, which had sported a great many colours, was now a dark auburn and the frizziness had gone to be replaced by a smooth flattering style.

Natalie looked at her in some surprise before saying, 'I like your dress, Connie, and your hair. I'd keep it that colour, if I were you.'

Natalie had a penchant for beige; she thought it a good neutral colour that was always right for everything. Connie whispered to Rosie, 'I never know whether what she's wearing is new or not. Her clothes are always the same colour.'

Rosie was wearing blue, and Steven immediately recognised it as a gown she had worn at the Paradiso, about which Mary had murmured, 'She's very beautiful, but who wouldn't be in a gown that must have cost the earth?'

Jerome set out to be the perfect host. The meal was excellent and he was determined to steer the conversation away from the people who had stayed away.

'I always loved parties,' he said with a broad smile, 'any sort of party. I was a great one at planning for them.'

'I remember you didn't have one when you were twenty-one,' Jeffrey commented drily.

Jerome laughed. 'You're right. I had the sports car instead.'

'You caught up on the party when it was my turn,' Jeffrey added, and Jerome chuckled complacently. 'I did, didn't I, and everybody had a wonderful time.'

Turning to Connie, he said, 'You're looking very elegant this evening, Connie. I've already complimented my wife, and now it's Rosie's turn. You never cease to amaze me, Rosie. Where has

441

that glum, tetchy little girl gone?'

Rosie smiled. 'You made me tetchy, Jerome. I never quite knew how to take you.'

'What do you think about our Rosie now, Steven?'

Steven smiled at her across the table, 'I think we should forget about the old Rosie. This Rosie is very beautiful.'

'You were very gallant with the old Rosie.'

'Yes. How long are you staying here, Noel?'

'Another week, then I have to get back.'

'How long before your next leave?'

'I don't know. But I shall spend it travelling around. I doubt if I shall come back to England.'

'How about you, Steven? Are you staying on in Kenya?'

Rosie looked up into Steven's eyes, desperately aware that her entire future rested on his answer.

'I've been thinking of moving on for some time. In less than four months I have to decide.'

'Where would you go?' Jerome asked.

'I have a choice. Back to South Africa, I really liked it there. Or to the Far East, it doesn't really matter to me.'

Softly, Rosie asked, 'Don't you have a preference, Steven?'

'Not really. I could see more of my parents if I accepted the post in Singapore, but I found South Africa good too.'

'So which will it be?' Jerome asked.

'I don't know. It will depend.'

His answer did not satisfy Jerome, who chortled, 'It can only depend on some woman giving you the all clear. Now who is she, Steven?

442

You can't just leave us in thin air.'

Across the table Steven looked long and deeply into Rosie's eyes, and reassured by her expression, he said softly, 'What do you think, Rosie, Cape Town or Singapore?'

Everybody round the table was looking at him expectantly, and then Jerome said, 'Rosie, after all these years, you've finally made it.' Jerome embraced Rosie warmly, then shook Steven's hand while the rest of them smiled and offered their congratulations.

Later, the rest of them went to sit in the cocktail lounge so that Steven and Rosie could saunter out on to the balcony. The night was soft and balmy and a thin crescent moon had risen, casting its silvery light on the incoming tide.

'What would I have done if you'd said, Steven, I don't know what you're talking about?'

She laughed. 'I did know, though. Oh Steven, I've loved you such a long time, but if you'd said you were going back to Kenya I couldn't have gone with you.'

'I know. You have few happy memories of Kenya, Rosie.'

'I couldn't have asked you to move away; it had to come from you, Steven.'

She looked up at his grave face etched in moonlight and at that moment there was an expression on it she was unable to read.

Rosie and he would be married, they would go side by side from now on. But ahead of him yet lay the breaking of Mary Raynor's heart and all the hurt and disappointment he would bring to his mother and father. He would have to do that alone, when he returned to Kenya. Mary knew he didn't love her, and now he had to tell her that he intended to marry Rosie.

Looking down at her, Steven asked, 'What do you suppose Aunt Beatrice will say?'

'She'll be happy for us. She knew I always loved you. She'd hoped I was over it.'

He laughed. 'I'll go with you to see her. I need to have her blessing.'

She shivered in the chill little wind that crept across the headland, and drawing her close, he said, 'You're cold, Rosie. We should think of joining the others.'

Natalie was doing most of the talking, concerned with her golf handicap, her various charities, which kept her very busy, and her recent elevation to the Bench.

Connie was listening to her wide-eyed and somewhat enviously. Jumping to his feet, Noel greeted the two new arrivals with enthusiasm.

'Well,' he asked. 'Have you two decided when the wedding's to be? I doubt if I'll be here for it.'

'Oh, Noel, you should be, it's months off yet, after Steven leaves Kenya. Who's going to give me away?' Rosie queried.

'I am,' cried Jerome, 'I'm the eldest after all, and Steven was my best friend through school and university.'

The girls talked about dresses, bridesmaids and honeymoons, the men of more mundane things, and Jerome asked, 'Where is the wedding likely to be? Rosie lives with her grandparents in London, Aunt Beatrice lives in the Cotswolds and we're here in Devon. Of course Dene Hollow will be out of it.'

Later, as they left the club house Rosie felt relieved that her wedding to Steven had occupied most of the conversation, steering it away from the subject of a divided family and traumas that might never be resolved.

As they walked slowly down the path towards the cars Rosie looked out across the bay. She could hear laughter and conversation, but as she looked upwards she was suddenly aware that the night sky was illuminated by wafts of crimson clouds, and sparks were flying upwards into the night.

She heard Noel cry out behind her, then they were all running towards the cliff top. Noel said, 'It must be the hotel, something out there's on fire.'

They stood in a group staring out across the bay. Then Rosie cried, 'Oh no, it isn't the hotel, it's Dene Hollow.'

They stared at each other in dumbfounded silence until Jerome said, 'Come on, get into the cars, we're driving out there.'

It was late, the narrow cliff road was deserted, but as they drew nearer to the glow they could all see that it was indeed Dene Hollow, and as they drove through the gates they could see crowds of villagers and firefighters dealing with the blaze, which had taken a firm hold on the building.

They left the two cars and ran across the lawns, but they could see now that the house was well alight. The firemen told them to stand well back.

'Is anybody in there?' Steven asked.

'I don't think so. The servants are out, Mr

445

Greville's over there.'

They looked to where David stood at the edge of the shrubbery, staring up at the house. Beside him on a lead stood Ranger his golden retriever, his beautiful coat darkened with soot. There was no sign of Gloria.

Rosie was the first to reach his side, taking hold of his arm and saying, 'David, where is Gloria? Is she in the house?'

For several seconds he stared at her blankly, then he said in a flat, lifeless voice that brought the tears into her eyes, 'She's gone with her father. There's nobody in the house.'

'How did the fire start?' Jerome asked sharply.

David merely shrugged his shoulders and offered no reply.

'They'll never save any of that,' Noel said. 'The house is done for.'

David smiled. 'Yes, I'm afraid so,' he answered.

Rosie was looking at the house. Dene Hollow had gone.

They stared at the burning house with mixed feelings. Jerome's thoughts were bitter: he was glad it was gone. Now David and Gloria had lost it, for all their scheming. Dene Hollow had repaid them for putting his father into a home and emptying it of everything that belonged to them, for tearing the family apart.

Connie had had no love for it, had never been welcomed there and if it had gone, so much the better. She and Jeffrey had a whole new life, and Jeffrey would forget his time at Dene Hollow.

Rosie, on the other hand, stared at it with anguished eyes. Steven stood with his arms

446

around her and all they could both think about was warmth and memories that were good and sweet, days filled with laughter and the warmth of companionship.

In the years to come she and Steven would talk about Dene Hollow and they would remember only the good things, never the petty hatreds and jealousies that had torn them apart. They would always associate it with their love, which had been born here and which had outlived so many traumas.

None of them asked themselves how the night's events would be resolved. Noel said, 'There's nothing any of us can do here. I'll drive you over to Gloria's parents' house if you like, David.'

David shook his head. 'No, I'll stay at the hotel. There'll be a room, I'm sure, at this time of the year.'

Nobody at that moment thought it strange, and Jerome said, 'I suppose we'll need to meet in the morning. There are a lot of questions to be asked.'

Sharply, David said, 'There are no questions that concern any of you. The house was mine, it has burned down, nothing is left. No doubt the police will ask questions of me and only me.'

'What about Father?' Jerome snapped.

'If my father doesn't already know I will inform him tomorrow.'

'Shall I see you in the morning?' Steven asked gently, and Rosie said, 'I'll drive over, Steven.'

'There's no need, I'll hire a car from the local garage, we need to be by ourselves.'

They drove to the hotel in silence and on arrival

447

David went immediately to the reception desk to ask for a room. The staff were sympathetic; it seemed that everybody within the area had witnessed the fire. Turning to Noel and Rosie, he said, 'I'm going to bed now, I'm really very tired. I'll see you in the morning.'

'Fancy a drink?' Noel asked after his brother had left them, and she went with him into the cocktail lounge.

'I don't get it,' Noel said. 'She's with her parents, he's here, you'd think that at a time like this they'd be together.'

'It's no use our speculating, Noel, he'll probably tell us what happened in the morning.'

'God, what a mess. I never thought I'd see my brother looking like this. He's like a zombie.'

'Well, of course he is, it's been a terrible night for him.'

Noel was silent for some time before saying, 'I'm going back to the Far East as soon as possible. I wish I'd never come. It's served no good purpose and now the sooner I leave the better.'

'It hasn't all been wasted, surely. You've seen your father and Aunt Beatrice, and we were enjoying our party until this happened. In time you'll probably forget the bad and remember only the good.'

Noel grinned. 'And the good for you is Steven, Rosie. I'm glad for you. I always liked him and you always loved him. Now you're together and if one good thing's come out of tonight this is it.'

At his house Jerome sat slumped in his chair, a large whisky and soda on the small table beside him, and an uncomfortable silence all around him.

'Questions are going to be asked, a whole damned lot of them. How did the house come to burn down? What started it? Where was she?'

'Well, I'm going to bed,' Natalie said. 'It's no good your going on and on about it. It's happened, and like your brother said, it was his house. It had nothing to do with you.'

Jerome glared at his wife across the room. 'Well, of course it has something to do with all of us. It was our family home, we grew up there. You don't care, Connie doesn't care, but Jeffrey'll be upset, I'm upset. I don't know what my father's going to say.'

'Well, like I said, I'm going to bed. If you sit up all night thinking about it it's not going to do any good. Goodnight, Steven; see you at breakfast.'

After she had gone, Steven looked across at his friend's angry face and thought silence was the best policy. He thought about Rosie. She would be devastated by the night's events and he wished he was with her. He wanted the next few months to pass quickly so that they could be together. It really didn't matter where except that it couldn't be Kenya for either of them.

His thoughts went back across the years and his thoughts were all of a young girl waiting for him on the cliff path, her fair hair tied back from her child's face, which had no particular allure with its pale smudge of brows and lashes, and the disfiguring braces on her teeth. He found himself remembering the girl he had seen at the Paradiso, incredibly beautiful, laughing and flirting,

449

filling every minute with enjoyment, which he knew had only covered hurts and anguish that nobody in that room had had any conception of. He knew now that he had been the only person there who had known the real Rosie, the troubled, lonely girl beneath the brittle veneer of sophistication, and he knew that for the rest of his life he would be helping her to forget the demons that had chased her for so long.

Jerome finished his whisky and got to his feet.

'I suppose we might as well go to bed, there's nothing to stay up for. Tomorrow will perhaps bring some answers to my questions.'

Natalie was sitting up in bed, looking at a magazine.

'Well,' she demanded. 'Have you decided to forget Dene Hollow for the time being?'

'I don't want to talk about it any more tonight.'

'Perhaps we can get some sleep then.'

'You can sleep, I doubt if I shall,' he said sharply.

In his hotel bedroom, David sat staring through the window.

The glow from the burning house had left the sky and only occasionally clouds of acrid smoke drifted across the hotel garden, and he could smell burning wood and other smells borne on the night wind.

Gloria had gone to bed early on the pretence of a sick headache, but he had stayed up in the morning room to do some work. It had grown chilly and he had added coal to the fire.

Conversation had been spasmodic all evening. Gloria kept on and on about the family get-together at the golf club. She hadn't wanted to be there, but she was incensed that it was taking place. Her parting words before retiring for the night were, 'They're all envious of us, David, that we've got the house, that they can't get their greedy hands on anything. Let them have their party. I hope it's a disaster.'

For a long time he'd sat staring into the fire, until the embers had burnt low and he was remembering other days, days that had been warm with friendship and laughter, and he was thinking that now all those people had gone out of his life and only Gloria was left.

Every week, every month, something changed, and now he could hardly recognise the past in the things she had made in the present. Now his beloved shrubbery was going and some sense of deep anger stirred within him. She'd wanted him, she'd wanted Dene Hollow, why did everything have to change, why had she destroyed the past as well as the present?

He'd added more coal to the fire, and then he'd retired for the night.

Gloria had been fast asleep, but for what seemed hours he'd lain with his eyes wide open, staring at the crescent moon through the window, listening to the wind whistling through the branches of the trees. He'd smelt the smoke before he heard the crackling, then he'd suddenly been wide awake. The room was filled with smoke and his eyes were smarting with the smell and feel of it. He shook Gloria awake, seeing the terror on her face before he dragged her to the door.

He could hear and see the flames, and after pulling her away, he went to the window and realised it was their only avenue of escape. She was screaming, her eyes wide with terror.

The gardens below them were filling up with people who had seen the blaze, and from the distance they could hear the approaching sound of bells as the fire engines arrived. All the time she was screaming, until he had to shake her, saying, 'Stop it, Gloria, you'll be rescued. We couldn't have gone downstairs.'

They took Gloria first and then they came back for him. By this time her parents had arrived, and without looking at him once she went with her father, driving through the avenue of onlookers and staring straight ahead.

He remembered piling coal on to the dying fire, remembered that he hadn't once looked at it before leaving the room. It had all been his fault, and a strange feeling of relief engulfed him with the realisation that he didn't care.

What did it matter that the shrubbery was going, that every precious thing within the house had long gone? With the burning of Dene Hollow the slate was wiped clean.

He could not think what would happen if Gloria did not come back to him. Somehow it wasn't very important. It was more important that bridges needed to be built, perhaps not tomorrow, but one day, and if Gloria didn't want to cross those bridges with him then he would have to cross them on his own.

The rising sun was already touching the incoming tide, gilding the sailing boats anchored in the bay, tinting the red cliffs with shades of scarlet and tragic crimson, and he got up from his chair and went to stand on the small balcony overlooking the harbour.

He had meant it when he'd told Jerome none of the night's events had anything to do with him, but he'd been wrong. He couldn't shut out the past any more than he could erase the last few hours.

Gloria was his wife and they had to talk sooner or later, but he had to make her see that with the going of Dene Hollow something else had to take its place.

The early morning sunlight filled his room, and with its coming he wanted to think that the shadows it was chasing away were the shadows that had hovered for so long in his life.

Chapter Thirty-Three

Steven rode his horse on the hills above Malibu for the last time. Below him stretched the vast house surrounded by its parkland, and he pulled his horse up so that he could look down on it.

He would miss Kenya and the friends he had made there. Over the last few months he had been acutely aware of their unease at the ending of his association with Mary Raynor and his resolve to marry Rosemary Greville. He knew that the Rosemary they remembered was a girl with brittle laughter, who flirted with those young men she surrounded herself with. The girl who had lived her life in the fast lane, with the fast crowd, and they did not know that this was not the real Rosie and he saw no reason to explain.

It was several months since Mary had returned from the Far East but he had seen her only briefly at the hospital. He wanted to think that they were still friends but news of his forthcoming marriage in England had no doubt upset her.

He could not linger long on the hillside, but he had felt a pressing need to be alone in the stillness of the early morning. The rest of the day would be spent saying his farewells to colleagues and friends before he collected his belongings and headed for the airport. With this in mind he wheeled his horse in sharply and galloped down the hillside.

He had almost reached the road when another rider appeared in front of him and Nigel Boyd pulled up his horse shortly, his expression wary. Steven would have preferred to ride on but there was no way he could have done so without appearing discourteous.

'I hear you're leaving us,' Nigel said evenly.

'Yes. In the morning.'

'Fed up with Kenya, then?'

'I'm ready for a change.'

'I heard you're getting married, to my stepdaughter of all people.'

'Yes.'

'You will allow me to wish you well, I hope?'

'Thank you. Now if you will excuse me I have a

great deal of work to sort out on my last day.'

'You'll remember me and Ariadne to her, wish her all the best from us?'

'Yes, thank you, I'll do that.'

He galloped swiftly away. One day she might tell him, but he was sure something had occurred between Rosie and Nigel Boyd to upset her profoundly whenever his name was mentioned.

As he walked to his office door he was aware that a girl was standing outside it, staring uncertainly at it, and then turning nervously to face him. He said gently, 'Mary, I'm so glad you came. I was hoping to see you before I left.'

She smiled hesitantly, and he said, 'Come into my office, we can chat over a coffee. I want to know about your visit home.'

Mary had always talked of Malaysia as home, Steven had never quite understood why. Even though he'd spent years there, even though his parents lived there, he had never thought of it as home. Home had always been a cool, green land far removed from the exotic country of his adoption.

She followed him into his room, and while Steven poured coffee from the thermos jug she watched him silently, aware of the dull ache in her heart and the sickening feeling that perhaps she should not have come.

He took the seat opposite, saying, 'Now tell me about your visit to Kuala Lumpur and your parents, and if you saw anything of mine.'

'They came over for dinner twice, Steven. They both look very well. I know they'll be glad you're going out to the Far East to work.'

455

'Yes well, this offer came from Singapore, not too far away from them. Your parents are well, too, Mary?'

'Yes. Dad's talking about retirement. I thought he never would.'

'And will they stay out there?'

'I don't know. I can't think that he'll retire, he's talked about it before.'

She looked over to the table near the window on which stood a wooden model of an African elephant, beautifully carved in some quite exotic wood, and rising to her feet, she went over to look at it.

'Your wedding present from the staff?' she said.

'Yes. It was something I wanted. I had a choice, a giraffe, a zebra or an elephant, and that was my choice.'

'Yes, it would have been mine.'

So many questions hung between them, and neither of them was anxious to be the first to ask them. It was Mary at last who said, 'When are you getting married, Steven?'

'The beginning of December. It has to be then, the new job starts in January.'

'I see. Will it be in Devonshire?'

'No. I'm afraid Dene Hollow is no more. It was burnt down some little while ago.'

She stared at him in astonishment. 'Burnt down! But how? What happened? It was such a beautiful place.'

'Yes. I don't know the full story. Perhaps somebody will be able to tell me when I see them again. It was very traumatic at the time.'

'So where will you marry, then?'

456

'Rosie is living with her grandparents in London, so it could be there or somewhere else. I shan't really know until I arrive in England.'

'Will it be a big wedding with all the trimmings?'

'I don't think so. But then again, I know very little about the arrangements just now.'

'But you're happy, Steven?

'Yes, Mary. It seems to me that what has happened to us was something inevitable, something that had to be. I want something like it to happen for you one day, Mary. Don't settle for anything less.'

'I'm sorry about the letter, Steven. I should have given it to you that day but I held on to it. Am I forgiven?'

'It took quite a lot of courage for you to send it to me. I'm not sure we shall ever meet again, Mary, but I shall think of you often and wish you well.'

He embraced her and for several minutes she clung to him. She still loved him, she wanted the embrace to go on and on but he released her, smiling down at her with a sweet smile that she believed she would remember for the rest of her life.

As she walked back along the corridor she could feel the sting of tears in her eyes, and when she met one of her colleagues the other girl sensed her misery. Taking hold of Mary's arm, she said, 'Come in here, Mary. It's Steven, isn't it?'

Mary nodded, allowing the other girl to drag her into an empty room, where she sat miserably and sobbed into her hands.

'Honestly, Mary, you'll get over him,' her friend told her. 'There'll be somebody else once he's away from here. I can tell you he won't be the only love in your life.'

Mary dabbed at her eyes and didn't answer.

'It's his choice of a wife you object to, isn't it? You don't like her.'

'It's not that, Denise, but she had everything: money, that beautiful house, a bevy of friends and a mother who adored her and spoilt her rotten. I'm not the only one who's surprised he's going to marry Rosemary Greville.'

'Are you really so sure she had everything? She had a mother who died in a terrible road accident, she had a stepfather who was quick to marry Mrs Fairbrother, and she was quick to leave the good life behind to return to England. That crowd she ran with didn't stay around and they were involved in her mother's accident.'

'So you're on her side?'

'I'm not on anybody's side, I'm simply stating facts. Mary, you've got to get over Steven Chaytor and rejoin the land of the living. Do what she did, party every night and run with the jet set.'

'I don't know anybody in the jet set.'

'Then we'll find somebody. Look, Mary, I have to go now, I'm due at a meeting and I'm already late. Put some make-up on and don't let anybody else see that you're mooning about the place thinking about Steven. He's gone and he's not coming back.'

Mary had known that Denise Clarke could be

guaranteed to be forthright about her misery about Steven. Denise had run the gamut of a string of young doctors without falling in love with any of them. She was brittle and worldly but Denise had been better for her than any of her more sympathetic friends.

In the ladies room she made up her face, and looking at her reflection in the mirror she said, 'Pull yourself together, Mary. You're not bad-looking, you've got possibilities.' Then, with a cynical smile, she went back to her work.

Later in the day Steven had said his farewells to colleagues and friends. Their good wishes were tinged with doubt and certain feelings of dismay that he was really going out of their lives to marry the daughter of Celia Boyd, but then none of them were there when two days later Steven swept Rosie into his arms at Heathrow Airport.

They spent two ecstatic days together in London and Rosie enlightened him on the wedding day arrangements. Her grandfather was recovering from a stroke and had stated his intention of keeping well away from the festivities. Her grandmother said she would not be able to leave him, and although they wished the couple every happiness, Rosie for one was not surprised that they had both elected to stay away.

They would be married in the village church near Aunt Beatrice's cottage in the Cotswolds, and Jerome would give her away.

'Don't you mind that your grandparents are not able to be there?' Steven asked her.

'Not really. Granny is so much like mother; other things have always come first. She doesn't really need to stay with Grandfather, he has a nurse who cares for him very well, but Granny didn't like to think she would need to entertain guests if we were being married from their house, and it suits both of them for Aunt Beatrice to do the honours.

'The people coming up from Devonshire have booked into the only hotel in the village. It has a good reputation; they'll be very comfortable there, and really, Steven, I'm very glad to be getting married from Aunt Beatrice's house. She's the one who looked after me as a child; she practically brought me up.'

'Who exactly is coming from Devonshire?'

'Jerome and Natalie. Jeffrey, Connie and the boy. Not Uncle Cedric, and Noel is unable to get leave so soon after last time.'

'How about David and Gloria?'

'They are no longer together. After the fire they split up. David is living in a small house near Jeffrey. He's been invited; I don't know if he'll come.'

'So it's going to be a very quiet affair?'

She nodded. 'Your parents won't be here either, Steven.'

'No, but we're going out to stay with them before I start the new job. You'll like them, Rosie, and they'll adore you, I just know it.'

Her smile was rather sad. 'I hope they will when they've forgotten their disappointment about Mary. Did you see her to say goodbye?'

'Of course. They gave me a good send-off.'

He decided to say nothing about his meeting with Nigel Boyd and she made no mention of either Nigel or Ariadne.

As she looked up into his eyes she could hardly believe that Steven was hers really hers, after all the long years. It had always seemed to her that he had come to her out of a past known to both of them, something she had always known but he had yet to discover, and as Steven looked down at her face shining with love for him he was like a wanderer returned after long years, who hesitates for an instant upon the threshold, not yet daring to realise that they belonged together.

Three days before their wedding Steven called for Rosie and Aunt Beatrice to take them to dinner at the village hotel, where the rest of the family were waiting for them. As Rosie took her place in the car beside him she said, 'I do wish everybody could have been here, don't you, Steven?'

Steven merely smiled, and sitting behind them, Aunt Beatrice agreed with her.

The manager of the hotel met them with a welcoming smile, escorting them to the first floor and the room kept exclusively for private functions.

Jerome was the first to greet them, revelling in this self-appointed role as host for the evening, and with him stood Natalie, obviously enjoying an evening where she could wear her most exclusive dinner gown and the jewellery she favoured.

Once Connie would have been totally eclipsed by her more fashionable sister-in-law; tonight, however, she was looking very attractive in a new jade-green gown that complemented her auburn hair, which did so much more for her than the blond curls she had once favoured. Jeffrey was smiling, bringing his son forward with fatherly pride.

There was evidently good reason for Jerome's gratification when from across the room Rosie found Noel and David waiting to greet them.

The evening was a happy one, and from her seat at the head of the table Aunt Beatrice felt a contentment she had not known for some considerable time. They were a family again. Dene Hollow had gone, but people were more important than bricks and mortar, and she felt a comforting satisfaction that she had done her best.

In the months since Rosie had returned to England Beatrice had sensed in her an anxiety. She told herself that it was her mother's death that had caused it, but in her innermost heart she thought that there were other reasons, but she'd been wise enough not to ask questions. Tonight, however, Rosie's face was alive with warmth and enjoyment, and Beatrice allowed herself to feel a new contentment concerning her future.

She had watched Rosie's attachment for Steven dominate her childhood and wished fervently that she could forget him; but now when she saw them together it seemed that their love for each other was something as inevitable as tomorrow.

They would soon be leaving to start a new life together in a far distant land, but in her heart she knew they would always come back. England was home; didn't they always come back?

The publishers hope that this book has given you enjoyable reading. Large Print Books are especially designed to be as easy to see and hold as possible. If you wish a complete list of our books please ask at your local library or write directly to:

Magna Large Print Books
Magna House, Long Preston,
Skipton, North Yorkshire.
BD23 4ND

This Large Print Book for the partially sighted, who cannot read normal print, is published under the auspices of

THE ULVERSCROFT FOUNDATION